STARING AT THE CEILING

A novel by Steven Crane

FOREWORD

What can I say? "We spent a lot of time staring at the ceiling" would be an acceptable answer to the question, "How did you spend your late adolescence in the early 1990s in a medium-sized college town in South Carolina?"

This book's protagonist, Andy Maxwell, is a lot like a lot of us back in our 20s; he finds himself ensnared in his bad habits, his daydreaming, and his putting off adulthood for as long as humanly possible. We've all done it, maybe more than most of us reading this book, and those of us who remember the parts of the house on Cypress Street where much of the action of *Staring at the Ceiling* takes place.

I knew Steve in those days and saw much of Andy in him.

"Saw" because Steve is pretty far from Andy these days. Lots of folks who came in through that front door, off that front porch, have put in the work to change into a better person, and to do so intentionally. And it's that time, we were always meant to be together, we were always meant to encourage each other. That's what I learned from those days. You can lean on your friends, especially if those friends are not like most people in your little college town.

Columbia, SC. Our capital city college town. So many people and bands came in and out of that house.

Members would bring a guitar, then the drums, and amps. Before you knew it, we had a party with like four bands. I can still see the drumhead that said 'Margo sells Cargo' bouncing with the clash and crash of the kick drum. People would slide in through the window, to kip on the couch in the middle of the night.

We knew them, of course. They'd be in Five Points, or at Rockafella's (herein referred to as "The Cactus Club"). In the morning, instead of giving them the boot, Steve would fire up the Nintendo Entertainment System. *Brett Hull Hockey. Rock & Roll Racing. Mortal Kombat.* "Refreshments."

I lived in that house on Cypress Street with six others. My room was wedged between Steve's and another roommate. We were all stuck somewhere in between adulthood and adolescence. Even now, so many of these memories make us who we are today.

It's a miracle that many of us are still here to tell the tale. There were hard truths learned over the years. People die, people get sober, people find themselves or find God, or find a relationship with God, and that's what this book is about.

Throughout all the bad behavior in this book, there is a golden horizon to all things inside the story. The do-it-yourself ethos of getting a few bands together for a book release party, to stop just existing and express yourself, even if that expression is you deciding to swing several pairs of shoes up a tree. Make a bunch of art with your friends and enjoy it together.

I'm surprised the "Apple Pie Shooters" episode doesn't appear in *Starting at the Ceiling*. The basics to an Apple Pie Shooter are simple: Get a beat-ass-old recliner and lean it all the way back, have someone lie down and open their mouth. On either side of this future unfortunate soul are two people, one pouring vodka into the soul's mouth and the other pouring apple juice. Others oversee the whipped cream and cinnamon. Once full, said soul swishes the concoction around, swallows the whole thing (which tastes "exactly like apple pie, amiright?)", before being violently "helped" (i.e., "catapulted") up. Said soul then tries walking in a straight line toward the rest of their night. Good luck.

To me, what really works about *Staring at the Ceiling* is watching someone gain a purpose in their life. That's what's missing from Andy's life, and without spoiling anything too much, he finds that purpose.

Steve also found *his* purpose, did so years ago, and reading this book is an enduring reminder of that eternal possibility.

And what a book it is. Ten years later, this new draft is leaner, meaner, and unabashedly unafraid to show all sides of our struggle. Thousands of words were cut, and what remains is a more distilled, more direct, more heartfelt story we can all get behind. It's not all ugly, most of it is well-intentioned, and a whole lot of it is beautiful and strange, just like we are, and always will be, moving forward while staring at the ceiling.

Adam Strong
Portland, OR
6/8/2025

1

Graduations are supposed to be fun, and if he could think about it properly, Andy Maxwell had plenty to celebrate. But, as his parents backed out of the short gravel driveway and left him standing in the front yard of his home on Cornwall Street, Andy couldn't help but think he was probably the least satisfied person he knew.

"Are they gone?" Jeff asked.

"Yeah. Just now. And look."

Andy dug a fist into the pocket of his green corduroy pants. What emerged was thick and equally green. He took the stack of bills and began peeling off twenties and fifties.

"Holy shit!" said Jeff. He'd only ever seen that much cash on the other side of a television screen, and it usually meant that something illegal had either just happened or was about to. "That must be..."

"One thousand, six hundred and seventy-four dollars." Andy interrupted his roommate before lighting the cigarette he'd been dying to smoke since his parents showed up at their house this morning. "But it doesn't even matter. Every dime of this is already spent, and I still owe more. This little windfall is nice, but it ain't enough to keep me from having to move back home."

"You'll figure something out," Jeff reassured. He wanted them both to believe it. Still, his optimism grew thinner and less justified with each passing week of his roommate's unemployment.

"Figure what out?" Andy countered. "What the hell I'm doing? What I'm *supposed* to do?"

Jeff knew better than to light his friend's short fuse. Andy hardly ever needed an excuse to explode.

"I mean, look around," he continued, his voice rising as fast as his indignant arms. "What's the point? There are assholes driving truck bombs under the World Trade Center... and our own government is burning armed zealots to death in Waco. What are *any* of us doing here?"

There was no good answer to that question. The best Jeff could do was offer practical redirection.

"Well, right now, what we're doing is taking you to the bank, so you can put that shit away before something stupid happens."

"Can't," said Andy. "Bank's closed on Saturday."

"So then, what?"

"Get in," Andy ordered, heading for his car. "I have a better idea."

2

"You're just gonna give all this shit away? For free? I oughta kick your ass on principle," Jeff said as they began to unload a massive alcoholic arsenal from the back of Andy's brand-new forest green SUV.

The graduation present from his parents was lavish by any standard–a fact that was at least partially lost on its young, unaccomplished owner. None of his friends drove anything even remotely as nice or new.

"Technically, everyone who sent me graduation money is giving this stuff away. But, if this works out, it'll be worth every penny."

"Whatever, man. But do you really want to celebrate your graduation in jail?"

"For what? I'm not sure anything about this will be illegal. It's not really a crime; it's more of an urban beautification project. Anyway, quit worrying and help me ice all this shit down."

Jeff went to the back of the house in search of two large coolers. Andy dropped into an overstuffed brown armchair and puffed on a cigarette.

"But, why shoes? What's the big deal about shoes?" Jeff asked, returning through the kitchen.

"Nothing really. It's random," Andy replied. "Shoes are universal, you know? Just one of a million things nobody thinks about, until they see them in a place or way they don't belong. It's when things pop up that aren't supposed to be there that people get nervous and start asking a bunch of questions."

"So, this is a political thing, then?"

"Fuck politics, man. It's just shoes. If it weren't shoes, it'd be something else, but this time it's shoes. It's whatever you want it to be. It's universal, like I said."

"And you think people will just give you the shoes straight off their feet?"

"Are you kidding me? Half the people we know would sell their grandmothers for a night of free beer. Don't worry, they'll come, and there will be shoes. But not if we don't get off our asses and get the word out. Oh, and we need a band. We can't have a party without a band."

3

"**F**or free? Are they crazy?" Ellen was confused.

"Yeah, it's all free. Well, almost free anyway," Traci answered across the bar at The Green Room. Ellen had tended there for over a year, the last five months full-time, since her parents' finances took an unscripted plunge. Given the choice, she would have gladly continued school. But when her college fund ran dry halfway through her undergraduate studies, she pragmatically folded her tent and moved to the next best option.

"What do you mean, almost?" Ellen pressed, tugging and rolling a strand of her long brown hair impulsively around her index finger. The twirling was a nervous habit she developed as a child. It had lain dormant for many years, but she was keenly, uncomfortably aware of its recent return.

"Get this. They want shoes. Don't ask me why, but that's what they said. Everybody who brings them a pair of shoes drinks for free."

"Sweet Jesus, I can't wait to see this one," Ellen said as she snubbed a Marlboro in the ashtray. "I gotta get back to work, Trace. But do me a favor. Get over there early and make sure nobody fucks up my stuff. And tell Jeff to close my door. With all the freaks we know, anything could happen."

4

Five hours (and not enough tip money) later, Ellen fell behind the wheel of her piece-of-crap, two-tone brown '82 Chevrolet Chevette. She lovingly referred to him as 'Chet,' partly for its phonetic similarity to 'shit' when said just the right way. She took a deep breath and lit a Marlboro Red for the four-block commute home. Taking the last left onto Cornwall Street, her suspicions were confirmed. The first and most disturbing thing she saw was the gaudy, bright yellow school bus parked outside their equally hideous mint green house.

Oh, God. It's Graham, she thought, looking for a safe place to put Chet down for the night.

Graham Lafley was only twenty-three years old, but he'd already lived through more than most folks twice his age. His mother succumbed to cancer when he was twelve. And then, just two years ago, the hand of fate punched Graham square in the face again. On a routine business trip from Atlanta to London, his father was among 108 souls lost on a plane that inexplicably fell out of the sky and into the Atlantic. It was one of those things people say 'never' happens. Except, sometimes they do.

Through no desire or doing of his own, Graham had become instantly independent—no parents, no siblings, no real family. On the one hand, he had no support; on the other, no responsibilities. And, due to a substantial inheritance, he was now also relatively wealthy.

Not long before leaving Bradford, Graham acquired a beat-up, decommissioned short bus that had previously served the "special" kids of Preston County's public schools. It was a highly impractical vehicle, but Graham had little care for practicality.

There was plenty of amusement, but no real surprise, the first time Graham came rolling back through Bradford behind the wheel of the rolling freak show. He'd kept the first two rows of benches and added seat belts. But he gutted the rest, outfitting it with a killer stereo, bean bag chairs, a small refrigerator, and a fold-down futon bed. For over a month, he'd used it as a mobile home, driving wherever the wind and whim took him. But once he put a double-wide trailer down on 30 acres of land outside Asheville, the bus resumed its station as a full-on party wagon. It might not have come literally full circle, but on plenty of occasions, the bus was still charged with transporting "challenged" youths. After all, the Cornwall Street kids were "special" in their own way, although most of their damage was self-inflicted.

* * *

As Ellen approached, the wail of angsty guitars poured from their under-insulated four-bedroom dive. The dilapidated rental was more than eighty years old, and the sonic battle was one the walls could never win.

A small group huddled together on the front porch, engulfing a hideous, smoke-stained orange couch that had once belonged to Jeff's grandmother. The group acknowledged her and casually continued passing a joint. Ellen was instantly grateful for the small handful of ephedrine tablets that came with Traci's preemptive visit to The Green Room. It would be a long night, and a little speed would go a long way.

Blasts of sound and smoke greeted her as she entered the house. Five feet from the front door, the bassist of a local rock group was feverishly pounding out the low end, oblivious to her arrival. A drum kit lay where there once was another couch. A thin man with no shirt and a greyish-white crew cut beat the toms like a rented mule.

Ellen closed the door and fought upstream through the sea of sweat and smoke, heading straight for her bedroom in case it was on fire, or someone was riding in circles around her bed on a Harley-Davidson. Jeff and Traci intercepted her before she even got close.

"Wow, not bad," Ellen shouted. "Who are all these people?"

"Andy can be a dick, but at least he's a loyal dick who knows how to throw a party."

"So, where *is* our happy little graduate?"

"He's over there, with Graham," Jeff said.

The boys sat on a metal desk in the corner, sharing a joint and looking at each other like long-lost brothers.

"El! Jesus, it's about time!" Andy said, handing her the contraband as she approached.

"Actually, I'm early, you stoner. This is great, but we're not going to be talking to cops tonight, are we?"

"Probably not," he replied, shrugging.

"Why, Miss Ellen, so nice to see you again," Graham drawled with intentionally exaggerated formality, extending his hand to hers.

"Hey Graham, how's it going? Did you get bored out there in the big, weird world and have to come home to us again?"

"Something like that. It is good to be back, though," he said, flashing a grin and sliding into the crowd.

They all knew the drill. Graham would disappear for months and then pop up unexpectedly and with great fanfare. Ellen parked herself next to Andy on top of the desk. They both took long swigs and exchanged the joint several times before sharing words.

"So, how was work?" he asked as if the answer would ever change. Surrounded by scores of their degenerate friends, and plenty of strangers, with a live band wailing in the background, the question took on an almost comedic casualness – the kind of stock inquisition an old married couple had been trading for years.

"Same old shit," she said. "You know how it is. People got problems, people go drinking, people get drunk. They forget the problems they came in with or trade 'em in for new ones. As long as they keep tipping, fuck 'em. It's all good."

"Alright then," Andy said. "You wanna see something crazy?"
He stood and walked away, knowing she'd be right behind him.

5

The smallest of the four bedrooms at Cornwall separated Andy's room in the back of the house from Ellen's and served two primary functions. It contained most of the home's electronic equipment, sort of a pauper's multimedia palace. As Cornwall's most central, discreet, and comfortably furnished room, The Den's other purpose followed naturally enough. It was the home's de facto epicenter of debauchery.

Posters celebrating heavyweights like Hendrix, Kubrick, and Dali adorned the walls. The incandescent bulbs overhead worked just fine, but were usually left off in favor of the black-light lamp in one corner. Opposite this sat a mini refrigerator, the contents of which were restricted to beverages of an alcoholic nature. The room's single window was covered by a large black tapestry adorned with smiling psychedelic moon and sun faces.

Jeff and Graham made their way through the house. Bellows of laughter guided them straight to The Den.

"You're full of shit!"

"No, no. I'm serious as hell, man."

The accuser was still a mystery, but the defense came from none other than Eddie French. There was no context to help Jeff and Graham. Much of what Eddie said was dubious. Sometimes, it was intentional, a devious ruse to keep people guessing. Most of the time, you just weren't sure.

"I'm not shittin' you, man, it's real," he persisted.

"What's real, Eddie?" Graham asked through the smoke.

"Holy shit! Graham?" Eddie said, trying but failing to stand and greet his old friend. Graham thrust a hand toward Eddie, who settled back on the couch and shook it.

"Been too long, man," said Eddie. "You still got the Magic Bus?"

"She's right outside. Now what kind of bullshit are you feeding these people?"

"That would be perfect! We could pack that fucker up and leave tonight!" Eddie forgot he had been asked a question.

"What the hell are you talking about, Eddie?" Jeff pleaded.

Eddie looked up through a veil of short, curly black locks, pushed the silver-framed glasses up the bridge of his nose, and rose to the occasion with a devilish grin and a single word.

"Stull."

"Jesus! Stull again, Eddie?"

Graham had watched this scene play out more than once and already knew the ending.

"What's Stull?" asked a girl with short blond hair and wide, interested eyes.

Graham and Jeff exchanged glances, trying to decide who would field the question. Eddie was a master at whipping a crowd into a frenzy and leaving someone else to defuse the bomb. The first few times, it was funny. But this particular rabbit hole could test one's patience. Andy, who often had the same effect on people for different reasons, loved Eddie and found him endlessly amusing.

"Stull," Graham began, keeping a careful watch on the young girl's face to see how the story played, "is this ridiculous little bullshit town in the middle of nowhere, Kansas. Eddie's got this warped idea that it's a magical place."

"No. For real. It's true," Eddie replied, intent on finishing what he'd started. "See, there are trans-dimensional gates, portals really, between our world and alternate realities. It's all based on forces of the natural world… you know, electromagnetic fields, the moon, shit like that. Anyway, there are seven of these gates on the planet, one at the exact geographic center of each continent. Stull, Kansas, is the exact center of North America and therefore, a portal."

"You know that's just the continental U.S., right?" Jeff corrected him. "The epicenter of North America is actually in a field somewhere in Rugby, South Dakota. I looked that shit up after the last time you tried to sell this adventure, Eddie."

The group sat silently through the bonus geography lesson as Eddie considered a response to the challenge.

"Whatever, fucker. It's Stull. The portal's in Stull." The fact there were roughly 350 miles between the two destinations seemed inconsequential to him.

"So, you're sayin' we load up the bus and drive thousands of miles to some desolate Midwestern ghost town in search of an alternate dimension?" Graham asked. He was pleased with exactly how ridiculous the words sounded as they rolled out of his mouth.

"I've got an alternate reality for you, Eddie," Jeff joked as he went to The Den's closet. He paused dramatically before opening it and bringing forth the three-foot, double-chambered hookah bong the residents of Cornwall Street reserved only for special occasions. Tonight was already remarkable, but things were headed to another level, and the heavy artillery seemed only appropriate.

6

"So, whatcha got?" asked Ellen as they neared the back of the house.

"I think you might like this one. Sit on the bed and close your eyes."

She finished pulling her long brown hair into a tight bun atop her head, sat down, and waited to be amazed. Andy went to the corner of the bedroom and grabbed a large black trash bag. Ellen's eyes were still closed as the shoes began spilling around her.

"I've always thought you were crazy, Andy. And don't get me wrong; I love that. But this is weird, even for you."

"Thanks. I try."

He emptied just one of five such bags but made sure she noticed the others stockpiled along the wall. Andy lowered himself onto the overstuffed ottoman across from her and began to massage his kneecaps.

"You okay?" she asked, lighting a smoke.

"Yeah, just old and tired," he tried to joke.

Born with a muscular defect that left his lower extremities severely underdeveloped, Andy's legs resembled those of a chicken—matchstick-thin calves struggling to support comparatively massive thighs. After a childhood featuring more surgeries than birthdays, and thanks to modern medicine, he could walk, albeit with a noticeable limp. Two decades of unbalanced pressure on his legs, coupled with chronic arthritis, regularly left his knees and back throbbing after only minor exertion.

"How many are there?" she asked, rifling through the footwear with genuine interest.

"At last count, we had fifty-seven pairs."

"You know my next question."

"What would a twenty-two-year-old straight man want with one-tenth of Imelda Marcos' closet?"

"Do you think she misses these?" Ellen asked, holding a fabulous pair of neon pink Reebok high tops.

"There's no accounting for style," he said, fetching a smoke from the carved rosewood box on his desk.

"So, what's with the shoe fetish?"

Andy only half-heard the question, distracted by the master plan swirling in his head. He often struggled to maintain a single path of thought, getting lost in countless tangents until something caught his focus.

At this moment, that something was a burgundy leather wingtip colliding with his chest at a modest speed. Ellen sat studying him from across the room. In her left hand was the other wingtip; in her right, a slow-burning Dunhill.

"You were saying?" she prompted.

"Not yet. We need Jeff and Graham. Oh yeah, and Eddie too. I only want to go through this once. I'll get the boys; you get the beers. Meet me back here in five minutes."

7

Five minutes passed quickly, and so did the next thirty or so it took to round up the necessary personnel for Andy's mission. This wouldn't be their first late-night expedition, but it was the strangest yet.

An odd pattern formed soon after they'd moved into the house on Cornwall Street. Like moths to a light, their friends and associates flocked, drawn by the glow of constant chicanery. All three of its residents were sociable people, but Andy had more of an agenda. He preferred to think of hosting as having a home-field advantage. For Andy, it was all about control, his truest addiction.

Initially, he got enough of a fix just by being in his own predictable environment. Sometimes, he'd press, wrangling control of the music or the distribution of party favors. Slowly but surely, though, like all addictions, his need for control grew.

And that's when the "missions" began. They were typically simple outings for which the spontaneity was reward enough – fun for the sake of fun. But that's not to say there weren't times when the group would return with something of value.

Cornwall Street had become home to several such treasures. They'd acquired a parking meter from which the kingly sum of $41.75 had been rescued. A few random road signs haphazardly decorated the house. And then there was the picnic table. This was unique because no Cornwall residents had been involved in its procurement. To his surprise, Jeff discovered the table placed neatly in a shaded corner of the home's small back garden, one Saturday morning. In the months since, several of their friends claimed involvement. Still, none of the residents knew for sure how it got there.

Most of these adventures were spontaneous, lacking focus or even purpose. Tonight was different. Tonight, Andy had a plan.

8

The five friends settled in an arc, not quite encircling the bounty of black trash bags. While rounding up the gang, Andy noticed the house was nearly empty. Just about everyone who could walk or stumble away had already done so.

Each held a can of Milwaukee's Best beer, though Graham and Ellen's were still unopened. Like locusts, the partygoers had descended and decimated the generous supply of free booze. Andy had thoughtfully stashed a 12-pack of the Beast in his closet, just in case the well ran dry. The beer was nasty and warm, but no one complained about free alcohol, and never at 2:00 on a Sunday morning.

Eddie rubbed his glasses with the sleeve of his dirty T-shirt and said with a delirious grin, "So what's with the pow-wow, Andy?"

"It's time for a little fun, Eddie. We're going out tonight."

With this, Andy began to relieve the bags of their cargo. In total, sixty-one pairs of shoes tumbled to the floor between them. A remarkable crop they were. Among the regular white Nike tennis shoes, sandals, and multi-colored Converse All-Stars you might expect, there were some real prize winners. A mismatched pair of ten-hole Doc Martens (one blue, one red); several pairs of heels, each varying widely in height, color, and seriousness; a lovely pair of sequined ballet slippers; a pair of U.S. Marine issue combat boots, which, according to a reliable source, had been worn in the Desert Storm invasion; and many other oddities lie before them. Andy had hoped to find a pair of bunny slippers among the haul for maximum comedic effect. Instead, he would have to settle for a pair of purple and green high-top canvas sneakers that bore a rather ominous rendering of The Incredible Hulk down each side.

The group sat silently, contemplating. Sure, they were fucked up and confused, and it was very late, or early, depending on your view.

But mostly, they decided that when confronted with a man who randomly presents you with sixty pairs of shoes, it was wise to let him speak first.

Andy paused, giving his friends a minute to take it all in. He cleared his throat and reached again for the rosewood box. He pulled out a Dunhill, lit it, and passed the box to Graham on his left.

"Have a smoke," he offered. The box made its way around the arc, and each took a cigarette, except Ellen, who already had a lit Marlboro Red. Even Eddie, who smoked about as often as an electric train, bellied up.

"What we have here, gentlemen, is a shit load of shoes."

It was commonly understood, and not unappreciated by her, that Ellen was not considered an actual female by either of her roommates. Jeff and Andy would both admit she was pretty, but in truth, she spent so much time toggling between the roles of sister and mother in their little family that any physical attraction was impossible. For better or worse, she was 'one of the boys,' at least as far as Andy and Jeff were concerned.

"I wanna make something," Andy continued, "or at least confuse the hell out of a bunch of people."

"Well done on that second part." Eddie teased.

"I want to build a shoe tree," Andy declared as if it made perfect sense.

"A what?" Graham asked, looking up from the desk upon which he'd just finished rolling another joint.

"A shoe tree," Andy repeated. "I want to see what these sixty-one pairs of shoes look like hanging from a tree in the middle of this crappy little town."

"But why?" Eddie needed to know.

"Because I want to watch people try to figure out why somebody would put them there. Besides, it'll look cool."

"Hey, these are mine!" Jeff had been rummaging through the haul and sorting the shoes into like piles.

He held aloft a pair of dirty, old black Vans and said again, "These are fucking mine! I let Paul borrow these about a month ago and haven't seen 'em since. That son-of-a-bitch traded me my own shoes back for a night of free beer. Bastard!" he added for good measure, reclaiming his pilfered footwear.

Jeff quit ranting long enough to take the joint as it reached him. He pulled deeply, letting the smoke fill his lungs and brain. Andy seized the moment to elaborate.

"I've got the perfect tree picked out, too. You know where the Gryphon Theater is; right next to that big-ass Baptist church?"

They all nodded, trying to picture the target or perhaps what it might look like when they finished.

"It's got hundreds of branches, and it's tall as fuck. It's perfect." Andy had no idea what type of tree it was; he just knew it looked right.

"So now wait a minute," Eddie implored, with glazed eyes. "My little road trip to Stull is '*crazy as hell*,' but running around and throwing like a hundred shoes in a tree in front of a Baptist church in the middle of the night is perfectly sane?"

"Next door," Andy insisted.

"Fuck your neighbors, man! This is nuts!" Eddie shouted.

"The tree is *next door* to the church, Eddie, not in front of it."

"Jesus. There's gonna be a bunch of wigged-out Baptists walking down Decatur Street tomorrow." Graham offered.

"Exactly." Andy beamed as they began to see his glorious vision. He had grabbed a legal pad off the desk, sketched a crude map, and placed it in the middle of the floor.

"There's a wall here, between the theater and the church, surrounding the cemetery. If two of us stand here, on the far side of the..."

"Wait. So now we're in a cemetery?" Ellen said, a bit uneasy.

"No," Andy corrected, frustrated at his cohorts' lack of focus. "No one's *in* the cemetery. But the wall will help shield us from view if anyone is around."

Andy kept moving, referring again to his sketch. "We'll need two throwers, a lookout on the street, and two more on the far side of the tree catching the errant shoes."

"Not bad," Graham commended, snubbing the burnt roach in the ashtray. "Been watching reruns of *The A-Team* again?"

"Well, they do keep threatening to cut off our cable. Gotta get it while I can."

Andy began re-bagging the ammunition. There were now exactly sixty pairs of shoes. He liked the round number even better. They briefly discussed the map and jockeyed for stations. Ellen and Eddie agreed that two lookouts would be safer. Andy and Jeff would send the shoes skyward, and Graham would sweep behind them, retrieving the misses.

The shoes were placed 15 pairs in a bag, two bags apiece for Andy and Jeff. Andy figured it would take fifteen minutes to get all sixty pairs hung. But, being a shoe tree virgin, the estimate was understandably rough.

"And what about the police?" Ellen wondered.

"What about them?"

"Well, let's suppose, there we are, just hanging out in front of Bradford Baptist at 3:00 on a Sunday morning, and the cops wander by. What then?"

"Tell them you couldn't wait six more hours to talk with God," Graham joked.

"Cops are easy," Andy broke in. "It's all about psychology."

"Go on, doctor," Ellen said, waiting to be reassured.

"Well, for starters, why does anybody become a cop in the first place? Because they have a desperate need to serve and protect? Bullshit! It's all about power. They want power. They need it. They lust it. They're control freaks."

"You would know," Jeff said wryly.

"What they want is your respect," Andy continued. "But they'll settle for fear. It doesn't matter, as long as they keep control. Most people will tell you they *respect* police officers, but what they really mean is they *fear* them. Whether it's the fear of an expensive ticket, jail, or getting the shit beat out of you, it doesn't matter. Everyone's got something to be afraid of when the blue lights start flashing."

"And your point?" Ellen asked, now seeking closure, or at least movement.

"The point is," Jeff interrupted, "if a cop wants to talk to you, you talk to him. But you only tell him what he wants to hear, something that reinforces his perception of control. They want you to know they have the unquestioned authority to bust your ass, or even your skull, but really they'd prefer not to have to fuck with you at all."

"Here's all you need to know," Andy concluded. "As long as you can convince a cop that his time would be better spent dealing with real threats to society rather than wasting it harassing a productive citizen like yourself, you're fine."

"Is that why you never get busted even though you've been pulled over about a thousand times?"

"Well, yeah. That and the handicap placard. The police don't mess with the disabled. We're harmless," Andy said with a sly grin.

"Fine, you and your handicap placard can drive then," Ellen agreed.

Andy finished packing and snubbed his cigarette in the ashtray before rising.

"At least your parents got their money's worth sending you to school."

"Why is that, Graham?"

"You're pretty good at getting people to do things they don't want or need to do. Maybe you *should* be in advertising."

3

Sundays on Cornwall Street were slow, simple, and recuperative. Most of their elderly black neighbors rose with the morning sun, donned their finest clothes, and enjoyed breakfast at home before heading to the early service at church. Andy and Ellen hardly ever awoke before Bradford's various congregations concluded their recessional hymns and moved towards their post-worship lunches.

Jeff had a different arrangement. He worked *every* Sunday morning for employers with zero sympathy for the ill after-effects of ambitious Saturday evenings.

Although it was often a struggle to rise and shine, Jeff could not be happier. He was among the lucky few who got paid to do what he loved. And what Jeffery Aaron loved to do was sing. He was a vocal powerhouse. From Motown to metal, Jeff could do it all. A country boy from the rural sticks a hundred miles outside Bradford, he'd come to the *big city* school to study vocal performance. And he'd come armed for the challenge with a boatload of confidence and plenty of raw talent.

By his third year in school, he'd done his share of local theatre, including several performances at the Gryphon, the same venue to which he had just helped donate an impressive collection of footwear.

Jeff honed his chops at school and on stage, but that's not where he earned his money. On Sunday mornings and in the early evenings, a couple of times a week, he distanced himself from the sins of Cornwall Street with the three-mile journey to his gig in the House of God.

One of his drama teachers was a parishioner at St. Timothy's Episcopal Cathedral, and when the need arose for an Assistant Choral Director, he'd enthusiastically approached Jeff with the opportunity.

The pay was as good or better than most of the part-time, dead-end gigs his friends held down. Plus, he'd get paid to showcase and develop his true passion and most marketable skill. It was a position that suited him well in many ways, but one he nearly turned down.

Jeff attended Methodist services with his mom all his young life. There, the youth choir had sparked a flame he still carried for singing. But his few years in Bradford, particularly on Cornwall Street, took a toll. He quit attending church regularly. The fire within him had cooled to a tepid stream, which still flowed but with considerably less force. It wasn't intentional, but during those first years of living away from home, rising early on Sundays fell behind sleeping off hangovers on the priority list. And as much as he'd come to love his new group of friends, few among them found the idea of church, or God, appealing in the least.

The prospect of plugging back into a church, especially if it meant getting paid, was genuinely desirable to Jeff. But the offer at St. Timothy's did not come without the burdens of conflict and guilt. Jeff was aware, sometimes painfully, that much of what happened on Cornwall Street was morally questionable. His struggle was real.

He talked a lot with himself, a little with God, and not at all to his roommates or other friends about the challenges such a job might bring. Jeff accepted the position at St. Timothy's, working hard in the beginning, through constant practice, to convince himself he could drive straight down the line separating two such duplicitous paths. And most of the time, if you didn't look too closely, he appeared to be pulling it off.

Over time, it became an exercise in trying to glide back and forth, with as little friction as possible, across a boundary that was steadily fading away. Jeff's belief in God and his intention with St. Timothy's were genuine. And plenty of joy came back to him as he returned to church. But if he was being honest, it was a delicate balancing act, and sometimes, he fell.

A year later, Jeff was basically running the show at St. Timothy's – the de facto leader of a choir of 50 souls, most of whom were old enough to be his parents. That kind of responsibility, and the regular morning hours it required, certainly caught the attention of his roommates. Though, as with most of the shocking behavior on Cornwall Street, it had ceased to be anything abnormal.

Andy found it funny and ironic that one of his roommates worked at a bar and the other at a church. The only distinction he made most of the time was that he'd prefer Ellen be the one to bring her work home with her.

Like so many Sundays before, the local college radio station blasting from his clock radio was Jeff's wake-up call. It was instantly clear his half-night's nap had been insufficient and perhaps even counterproductive. His eyes stung from a lack of sleep as he fought to keep them open.

Jeff inhaled deeply, only to be reminded of the strenuous workout his lungs had taken the night before. His chest burned. His head pounded. A hot shower and two cups of coffee would have saved his life, but he was already running late and would have to do without either.

Jeff approached the mirror modestly, hoping he looked much better than he felt. He found a green rubber band on the dresser and pulled his shoulder-length chestnut hair into a neat ponytail. His blue eyes were tell-tale bloodshot, but the facade would suffice.

He stepped into the kitchen and grabbed a cold Coke from the fridge. He popped the can open and closed the refrigerator door, but not before noticing an unopened twelve-pack of Budweiser on the bottom shelf. It was the last thing he wanted to see, but he lingered. He didn't recall it being there as recently as four hours ago.

Jeff forsook the mystery beer in favor of locating the bottle of ibuprofen above their kitchen sink. He shook three tablets from the bottle, chased them with ice-cold caffeine, and invited the healing to begin.

Seconds later, his face was rudely introduced to the hardwood floor of the home's front room. The full can of Coke flew a remarkable distance, colliding with a bookshelf across the room in an explosion of thick brown carbonated foam.

It happened in a flash and made an awful noise. Graham, who was snoring steadily on the couch, shot upright.

Jeff slowly collected himself and turned his attention to the cause of his accident. There on the floor, slightly crushed by his weight, was a pair of black stiletto high heels, slit down the sides and strung together by a plain white tennis shoelace. The phantom of vague remembrance cruised through Jeff's head, and he cursed loudly.

"God fuckin' dammit!" he wailed, kicking the shoes into the wall.

"Wha…?" Graham groaned through a deep mental fog.

"I'm late for church," Jeff huffed, slamming the door in frustration.

Graham mumbled, recovering a thin, itchy blanket from the disgusting floor, and rolled back over. He was asleep again before Jeff started the engine of his black Toyota pickup truck and sped away.

10

The house remained still for several more hours until the shrill cry of the phone pierced the silence. Andy rolled out from his nest of pillows and blankets and, with eyes closed, tried to hush the screaming beast. In the process, he managed to tip a half-full can of Milwaukee's Best into an overflowing ashtray. The mere stench of his spontaneous creation forced Andy to rise with haste.

"Hello?" He said, equally confused and irritated.

"Andrew Maxwell, please," came the too-pleasant response. The woman sounded young and very awake.

"Speaking," Andy said, trying to focus.

"Mr. Maxwell, my name is Brenda from Creative Credit Services. How are you today?"

"I'm tired," he offered honestly. "How are you?"

"Um, fine." The woman hesitated, surprised by the nonstandard answer. "I was calling about your Visa account, Mr. Maxwell."

His attention was fractious at best. Still shaking the sleep from his brain, he scanned the cluttered bedside table. He rescued a pack of Winstons from the small pool of spilled beer and considered lighting one as he sat up in bed, but decided against it.

"Sir," she continued, now finding her place again in the script, "we show that your account has become dangerously delinquent, and we were wondering if a recent payment had been made?"

"*Dangerously* delinquent?" Andy repeated, amused by the ominous adverb.

"Umm, yes, sir." Brenda was again caught off guard by his reply. "The account is overdue and nearing its limit," she clarified. "Has a payment been made?"

"Well, let's see," Andy said with mock seriousness. "Yes, ma'am," he lied. "That went out just this past Thursday. I paid the minimum balance due."

"One fifty-seven forty-three?" Brenda asked.

"That's right," Andy agreed, as he would have to any figure she offered.

Yes, ma'am, indeed, 'the check was in the mail.' From his grand accumulation of seventeen hundred dollars, the fine folks at Creative Credit would get their due, but like everybody else, they'd have to wait their turn.

"I guess it hasn't gotten there yet," Andy suggested innocently.

At this point, what else could Brenda say? She was a customer service rep. She didn't have—and probably didn't want—any real power. "Well, we'll give it a couple more days to get here, then. Sorry to have bothered you, Mr. Maxwell."

"No problem, Brenda," Andy offered with a hint of snark. "You have a nice day."

As he cradled the phone and again eyed the dampened pack of Winstons, Andy considered what it must be like to have Brenda's job. He imagined spending most of the day, day after day, being lied to by people who couldn't, or wouldn't, pay what they owed. He didn't even have a job, but he knew he'd rather be in that boat than rowing in endless, meaningless circles like Brenda.

* * *

The sound of water came rushing through the pipes in the wall connecting Andy's bedroom to the home's central bathroom. Intrigued and now fully awake, he rolled from the bed. Pulling on a white cotton T-shirt and a pair of black jeans, he went in search of answers. He'd expected to see Graham rambling through the house but was met with a far more charming sight.

Ellen stood before the open refrigerator, ravenously slurping orange juice straight from the jug. In mid-swallow, she looked up to see Andy watching her and smirking.

"Sorry. There's no clean glasses, and I had to get this taste out of my mouth."

"I know. I feel like a beer."

"You cannot be serious," Ellen said with disgust.

"No. I mean I feel as if I *were* a beer, a very warm, very flat beer," Andy clarified.

Ellen was a frightful mess. Though long and straight, her hair seemed confused as it sprawled in every direction. A small stream of juice had slipped down her cheek and splashed onto the collar of her pink and white terrycloth bathrobe. It hung open to reveal a long blue shirt with "I LOVE ROCK 'N ROLL" printed in large black letters. Thick black socks protected her feet from the filthy kitchen floor.

"Damn, you're sexy in the morning," Andy mocked.

"Fuck you," she played along.

"Hey! The bus is gone! Where's Graham?" Andy asked.

"Don't know. But he'll be back. You know he'll be back."

"I know," Andy admitted. "But he's always running off to somewhere else. I just wish he'd stick around."

"Why, so we can take him for granted like everyone else we see every day? Part of why you love him is because he's *not* around," Ellen suggested. She was right on both accounts. Andy appreciated Graham immensely for reasons she and most others didn't even realize.

In Andy's eyes, he and Graham were kindred spirits, brethren united by a shared experience – suffering. In his myopic and supremely cynical view, Andy had come to believe he'd endured hardships that few people his age could understand, let alone rival. In fact, until he met Graham, Andy wasn't sure anyone else he knew had suffered much hardship at all.

Graham was built differently. He carried himself with a mysterious lightness and powered through tribulation in an almost cheerful way, Andy truly admired but could never find. Each time Graham came back, Andy was elated. Every time he left, it was like a light going out, leaving Andy's world dimmer until their next reunion.

"Fuck it," Andy lamented, finally lighting the Winston he'd brought from the bedside table. "What do you say to breakfast? My treat. You don't have to shower, but you can't wear that to Coleman's."

"Coleman's? Hell yeah!" Ellen cheered, already headed for a change of clothes, as Andy searched for his shoes.

11

Ellen piloted Chet out of their neighborhood and to the top of the hill on Paxton Avenue. As the car crested the apex, a sea of flashing blue lights exploded on the horizon. A disturbing number of emergency response vehicles were assembled a quarter mile down on their left. At the intersection of Paxton and Juniper Streets, they rolled to a stop, joining a line of cars going nowhere fast. Traffic backed up several blocks, as each car slowed to a near halt as it pulled alongside The Cactus Club.

"Damn," said Andy. "That's gonna be a problem. Detour around that shit."

Ellen maintained her slow downhill roll and began looking for alternatives. "Don't you want to see what's happening down there?"

"Yeah, but honestly," Andy replied, "I'd rather go see what our shoe tree looks like. Besides, with all those cops, whatever it is will still be there after we've eaten."

"And so will your shoes," she said, executing a U-turn in the middle of Paxton Avenue. "We can go down Firth and take back roads. We gotta stop for smokes anyway."

There was nothing extraordinary about The Cactus Club. Every college town in America has its share of unremarkable dives, and Bradford was no exception. Like most of the 20+ bars within a five-mile radius, The Cactus Club was a shithole. But to the residents of Cornwall Street, it was *their* shithole, like a clubhouse filled with friends. And being the closest belly-up to their house certainly factored in the frequency of their visits. Unlike The Green Room, The Cactus was primarily a music venue. Nightly, someone was onstage making a glorious racket. "Big" acts would play there occasionally, but mostly, it was a proving ground for local bands tightening their chops or blowing off steam in a live setting. And since almost everyone they knew was either in a band, lived with someone in a band, or dated someone in a band, The Cactus Club naturally became a second home.

They knew several people who worked there. Andy started making a mental list of the folks he needed to call—after breakfast, of course—to get the inside scoop on what had happened. If it hadn't been for their own party last night, they and many of their friends would likely already know firsthand.

12

Even with some church release traffic folded into the mix, the journey to Coleman's Diner was straight and short. It was only ten minutes, but that was still long enough to turn their modest desire for grease and carbs into a desperate craving.

Ellen eased into a spot along the diner's east side. A small sigh escaped her tired lips as she killed Chet's engine. A police cruiser crossed the parking lot in front of them. With no lights ablaze, it was uncertain whether this deputy was headed to join the already-stout posse they had just passed.

Coleman's Diner was a glorious contradiction—both a redneck eyesore and a genuine historical landmark. The walls were plastered with 1950s-style advertisements for everything from Coca-Cola to Coleman's own brand of pancake mix (still available at the counter on the way out, by the way). A chronological visual history of Bradford, in the form of aerial black and white photographs, now tinged by decades of sunlight and cigarette smoke, hung on the diner's wood-paneled back wall.

The cool, processed air inside Coleman's offered a welcome change from the hellish humidity of a Bradford summer. Ellen's dark sunglasses loosely hugged her nose as they took a booth in the back. Before they were seated, a lit Marlboro hung from her lips.

"You want one?" she said, offering the open pack across the pleasantly cold marble tabletop.

"Hell no! How can you do that?"

"Do what?"

"Smoke so early in the morning."

"First of all, there are about 45 seconds left in this *morning*. And second, it's called addiction."

"I can't smoke a cigarette until after I've eaten something," Andy said as if this made him somehow superior.

"Shit, sometimes I wake up just to have a smoke and then go back to sleep."

"That's nasty."

"Like *you* never smoke in bed."

"Only after sex," said Andy, with exaggerated suaveness.

"Now who's being gross?" she said, turning to their waitress. The 40-ish-looking woman with voluminous hair had arrived midway through their juvenile exchange and was pretending to be patient.

For them, ordering breakfast at Coleman's had become so practiced that it was nearly a reflex. Years of on-site research in various states of sobriety had revealed the perfect culinary experience. The Coleman's Breakfast Sampler Sandwich was delicious but deadly. Piled high, between signature square-cut pancakes, were two farm-fresh eggs, multiple pieces of grease-laden bacon or sausage, and enough cheese to choke a Frenchman. The true thrill-seekers, those in the express lane to heart failure, could even top it off with a bit of butter or sour cream.

"Who was on the phone this morning?" Ellen asked through a cloud of smoke.

"Brenda, from Creative Credit. She was calling to let me know that my account has become dangerously delinquent."

"Dangerous?" Ellen pondered. "To whom? And how?"

Andy laughed, enjoying the affirmation of his own earlier confusion.

"I'm not sure. Maybe if I don't pay up, they'll send the Credit Mafia to the house to break my thumbs."

"She called on a Sunday morning? What a shitty job that is!"

"I know. But on the upside, she gets paid to sit on her ass all day and harass people she'll never even meet about a bunch of money nobody's ever gonna see or touch. She's probably working from home, throwing back screwdrivers, and watching TV."

"When you put it that way… where do I sign up?"

They smiled and sat upright to greet the waitress as she delivered their food.

Heaven had no pleasure, and hell hath no fury like the Coleman's Breakfast Sampler. It seethed with fat, cholesterol, and every other fabulous tasting wonderfood that will just fucking kill you. It was pure plated hedonism and required the briefest moment of solemn reflection before digging in.

Ellen cut into the culinary monster to see if the egg yolks were cooked solid or runny. Andy reached for one of the four small pitchers of syrup. Seconds later, a river of pure blueberry-flavored sugar flowed over the already-volatile creation.

"Damn. You're going to die," Ellen said, almost gagging.

"Yup. So are you."

"No. You might die right *now* if you eat that."

"What? It's blueberries. I needed some fruit."

"Nice balance."

13

"Take a left. Here. Take a left. We're almost there," Andy demanded, so excited he was almost vibrating.

"Chill, dude. I know where the fuck I'm going. We were here like eight hours ago."

Chet rounded the last corner onto Providence Road. Andy squirmed in his seat, angling for a better view. She headed toward the post office. It was closed on Sunday, and its big, empty parking lot offered the perfect view of their target across the street.

Depending on one's perspective, their arrival was timed perfectly or horribly. Ellen watched with great interest as the parishioners of Bradford Baptist filed out of the sanctuary, many milling casually in the courtyard. Andy hadn't even noticed the people yet. He was transfixed by the spectacle next door. The car had barely stopped before he was out in the parking lot, moving about as fast as Andy ever really did.

"Oh, that's fucking beautiful!" he raved as if viewing a masterwork by Matisse or Rembrandt.

Andy stood on the curb, still radiating, and stared at the massive live oak tree in front of the Gryphon Theater. Ellen would never have caught up to him if not for the DO NOT WALK sign holding him at bay.

"You're not going over there," she instructed, now standing beside him.

"The fuck I'm NOT. Look at it!"

"But look at all those PEOPLE!"

She had to know he wouldn't be denied. The lights switched, and he was off again, moving across the street. "I know. That's the best part!"

Ellen was so busy chasing him that she hadn't seen it yet. Then she looked up.

It was absurd and insane, and oddly beautiful. Hanging from those branches, bathed in the full, glorious light of day, were a ridiculous number and variety of shoes. There were too many to count, although that's precisely what he was doing.

Andy scoured the scene, reveling like a deranged pyromaniac standing next to the hook and ladder truck while watching a vacant building burn. His eyes trailed from the highest branches all the way down. He noticed at least two pairs of shoes lying on the ground. His instinct was to run over and hurl them upward to live with their brethren, but he fought that.

"It's pretty fucking cool, Andy," Ellen admitted, still looking skyward and smiling.

"This is ridiculous," said the bent old lady behind them. She was dressed in her Sunday best and propped on her husband's arm. The youngsters stopped as the octogenarians trudged past.

"Stupid kids," the old man added to his wife's critique.

"Damn," said Andy. "Pretty judgmental for folks who just spent the last hour gettin' 'churched up'."

"Screw 'em. I think it's awesome. Don't let anyone ever tell you you're not creative."

"Thanks."

Her praise left Andy conflicted. Of course, he wanted it, but it also made him feel weird. This shoe-tree installation was easy, yet foolish. The serious business of life was still proving far more difficult.

"I can't believe I forgot the fuckin' camera." Andy groused.

"You can come back and shoot it later. Now, we should go home."

14

The Chevette hit the gravel driveway and stopped behind Andy's green SUV. A small sidewalk divided the drive into two suggested parking spaces, four when you factored that they shared the driveway with their neighbors, the Murphys.

She sprang from the car and made a beeline for the front door. Although delicious, the Coleman's Breakfast Sampler had a nasty habit of repaying its consumers with bouts of severe abdominal distress. Andy felt solid enough for the moment as he hobbled towards his own vehicle. Leaning on its front corner, which had warmed well in the early afternoon heat, he reached for the pack of Winstons in his shirt pocket.

Andy basked in the shade of the giant poplar until the sound of a heavy screen door crashing against its frame broke his peace. Next door, Quenton Murphy loped down the steps to his front yard.

A black man in his early 60s, Quenton was an ideal neighbor. He'd been married to the same lovely woman, the former Miss Lula Franklin, for 39 years. Their four children, three boys and a girl, grew up well in that house and had all moved on. Quenton and Lula had lived on Cornwall Street for more than twenty-five years. They'd probably die there too. The Murphys had suffered their share of neighbors in that time—some good, some anonymous, but probably none quite as interesting as now. Andy suspected Quenton didn't really mind and was perhaps even a little amused at his current situation.

Quenton and Andy had become unlikely associates, exchanging pleasantries in the driveway or across the sad chain-link fence that separated their backyards. Quenton was nearly three times older and surely worked that much harder than Andy, too. Even though he was retired, Mr. Murphy worked his piece of Earth religiously, maintaining his small yard and garden. Maybe it was at Lula's urging or perhaps it just gave him something to do, but he was out there sweating almost daily. The young renters next door had no such attachment to the land they occupied, and it showed.

"Hey Murph," Andy called, bouncing off his SUV. He tossed the butt of his cigarette, taking care not to launch it across the imaginary line dividing their properties.

It was an odd reference, calling a man that much your senior by his last name. But Quenton was unoffended. He preferred the cordial sound of his surname, especially as it ran off the young white tongues of his neighbors. And he definitely preferred it to Lula's saccharine cadence, as she called "Quent-ton Dear...," usually followed by "could you..."

"How are you this fine Sunday?" he asked Andy through thin puffs of a Salem menthol.

"I suppose I'm okay. And yourself?"

"Well, it was either come out here in this damned humidity, and wax down the Caddy," he started, "or wait for the wife to come home from church and start preachin' about how I should be out here waxing the Caddy instead of sippin' on a beer. This way I can do both, and there's no naggin'."

Sure enough, Quenton's wrinkled left hand held a six-pack carrier of Budweiser longnecks, two of which remained. Murphy placed it on the ground, opened both bottles with surprising speed, and stood back up. He may have been in his sixties, and a little wiry, but Quenton was what they called "old man strong." You'd never guess it by looking at him, but years of working with heavy tools—first as an aircraft mechanic in the Army and then later in machine shops and factories—had strengthened and thickened his dark, aged hands. Andy learned the first time he accepted a vice-grip-like handshake from his neighbor that there was more to Quenton Murphy than met the eye.

"Drink up, son," Quenton said, offering Andy a cold beer with a wistful smile. "What's a little more on top of the damage y'all did last night?"

It certainly wasn't his default, but somewhere inside Quenton Murphy, a younger man still lived who would occasionally enjoy sharing a cold beer with his neighbors.

"You know what?" said Andy after downing a mouthful of lager. "I sure have enjoyed living here."

"Have?" Quenton replied, noting the tense. "Sounds like you got plans. Where you going?"

"Well, that's just it. I don't have a clue where I'm goin'. But I think I'm close to done here. I finished school, which is why I came to Bradford in the first place. And I managed to avoid finding a future ex-wife, so it's time to start thinking about what's next."

"Hey, that's aw-right. That's what it's all about. A young man's gotta go out there, look around, and see what the world's got for him. Ain't nuthin' wrong with that."

"Yeah, but that shit's scary," Andy admitted in a way he wouldn't have to his friends.

"Good. It's supposed to be. Nuthin' worth havin' should be easy. And a man who ain't afraid of nuthin' is either crazy, or stupid."

"I guess. So, what about you then?"

"What *about* me?" asked Quenton, focusing more on his big grey Cadillac than on his neighbor as he cracked the seal on the car wax.

"You know? Is this everything the world had with your name on it?"

Andy had meant no offense. He didn't even realize the condescension in his question, inferring that Quenton had made the most of life by living next to a shithole house filled with ignorant kids just passing through on the way to something better.

"In a lot of ways. I got everything I need right here, and nuthin' to complain about. But on the other hand, Hell no! If this was all there was for me, God would have already come down here and gotten me by now."

"So, you're happy with the way it's all played out?"

Quenton emerged from the driver's side door. The windows were down, and the stereo was up. A pleased smile spread across his face as the James Brown cassette tape in his deck switched sides and broke into the triumphant opening of *'Super Bad—Part 1.'*

"See, you gotta relax. You're young. You got the rest of your life to be worried about the rest of your life," Quenton mused through a blast of minty smoke.

"But that's kind of my point. I don't know that I feel very young at all. I mean, I look around, and I see all these people my age or younger who are famous actors and rock stars, and I can't help but wonder when *whatever* is supposed to happen to me, is gonna happen to me." Waves of anxiety built within Andy as he spoke.

"So, that's it? You want to be a rock & roll star?"

"No, not really. I mean, I tried that. It didn't pan out for me. But yes, I do want to be *something*, you know? *Someone*."

"Do I know? Lemme tell you sumthin', Maxwell. When I was your age, what I wanted most in the whole world was to be this dude right here." Quenton threw his thumb over his shoulder at the tape deck as the Godfather of Soul belted out *'I'm real Super Bad. Ain't nobody good enough to take the things I have.'*

Andy wasn't about to argue with The Gospel According to J.B. and silently threw back another long swig of Budweiser.

"You really wanted to be James Brown?"

"Hell yeah!" said Quenton through another blast of menthol. Sweat cursed his dark brow as he made small wax circles on the Caddy's massive hood. "Used to dress like him, too. I even put that relaxer crap on my hair one summer and tried to grow the man's do. I looked at myself in the mirror, hoping to see the Godfather, but you know what? It was still just me. Ain't no point in spending your life trying to live somebody else's. You start doin' that, and before you know it, all that stuff out there, the stuff with your name on it, you miss it. And you only get one shot."

"I know all of that. Besides, I don't really want to be somebody else. I just want to be me, but with more money and less trouble. It's just frustrating not to know what the hell I'm doing with my life."

"At least you're thinking about it. Plenty of people your age are too busy chasing the bottom of a bottle, or getting wasted on junk, to figure out that one day they're gonna have to grow up and actually live life."

Simple wisdom wrapped in a massive dose of irony. Andy leaned against his car and wondered if Murphy knew just how close he'd come to nailing Andy as most of those horrible things he described. At that moment, he was paralyzed. He could try to change the subject, acting as if his neighbor's assessment didn't apply, or he could run. His mind raced in small circles, searching for a friendlier topic, but found nothing.

Then, as if in answer to a prayer Andy hadn't even made, Jeff's black pickup truck came grumbling up the hot asphalt hill. An angel of mercy, straight from his gig in the House of God, Jeff had come to rescue him from Quenton's unintentional inquisition.

"Ah. Speaking of rock stars, here he comes now," said Andy, pointing at the truck. "Now see, Jeff could do it. He could actually make it. But who knows what he really wants, either? He's a mystery. He could pack up his shit and move to New York tomorrow. Or he could stay here forever. Could go either way."

"You're right." Quenton agreed, smiling. "But either way, he'll be *happy*."

"Why is that?"

"'Cause he ain't wasting time or energy fightin' the future. You know, it's all gonna work out the way *He* wants it to, right?"

"He who?" Andy asked, pointing back to the Caddy's dash. "The Godfather?"

Quenton laughed up another billow of smoke and extended his bony black index finger skyward. "That's funny. But don't play, son. The Godfather is the Man. But Father God is the Truth."

"So, how come you're skippin' church to wax the Caddy?"

"Oh, me and God, we have an understanding. Sometimes I go to his house to talk, and sometimes we hang out elsewhere. He don't mind. He's always around – ain't hard to find Him, so long as you're lookin'."

15

Jeff was a sight to behold, still clad in his choir robes of blazing white with royal purple trim. He started across the short front yard to the house, sunglasses hiding the portion of his face not obstructed by the mane of hair that flew in the breeze. Andy couldn't decide if Jeff more closely resembled Jesus or a young Ozzy Osbourne. It wasn't until they met at the foot of the porch that he noticed the small brown paper bag in Jeff's hand.

"So, how was church?"

"Excellent, but pipe organs are loud as hell when you're hungover. I couldn't sing for shit though. Good thing I didn't have any solos today."

"Next time you do, let me know. I wanna go."

"Bullshit! You've been talking smack about goin' to church with me for the past nine months, but you never quite make it. I don't want to hear it anymore."

"No. I will. I mean, I would. I really would. It's just that it happens so early. I think I might be better at talking to God a little later in the day."

"Now God has to work on your schedule, too? You don't ask for much, do you?"

"Forget it. What's in the bag?" Andy asked as they reached the top of the steps.

"In a minute. Gotta find Ellen first."

The stench of spilled beer and wet ashes assaulted them as they entered the house. The front room alone was littered with at least two dozen blue plastic cups.

"Well, so much for hoping you guys would have all this shit picked up by the time I got home."

"Nope. We had to go to Coleman's for the Sampler this morning," said Andy, lighting a Winston and hoping to ignite a little jealousy, too. "Besides, that didn't seem like it would be fair to you."

"Well, aren't you considerate? Now, where is Ellen?"

In the time it took Andy to share a driveway beer with their neighbor, Ellen had at least begun the process of greeting the new day. As Jeff reached the living room, she stepped into the hallway, freshly showered and again wrapped in the pink and white robe she had donned just a few hours before.

"Check it out." Jeff offered.

She walked straight to her bedroom as if neither was standing there.

"Whatever it is, I'm getting dressed first," she declared.

Jeff took the delay as a chance to slip out of his own robe. Andy stood alone at the exact center of their home, silently surveying the damage around him. It was remarkable and widespread. Suddenly, the air inside the house seemed warmer and more humid, nearly unbearable.

To his surprise, after Quenton primed the pump, Andy found himself craving a second beer. The phantom 12-pack in the fridge was unopened and certainly fair game. He grabbed three bottles from the box and trusted the refrigerator to close on its own behind him.

Reaching the Den, Andy took the chair directly opposite the television and waited. A moment later, Ellen entered and lay on the couch beside him. Jeff was a few steps behind, still clutching the brown paper bag. He leaned against the closet door, sweeping a curtain of hair away from his eyes.

Andy tossed one of the unopened Budweisers at him and held aloft the third bottle for Ellen.

"Hell no!" she declined.

Andy placed the unwanted beer on the table. Settling in, Jeff reached into the sack and produced a half-full bottle of 100-proof Smirnoff vodka.

"Double hell no!" exclaimed Ellen, much more emphatically than her last refusal.

"Bravo! Where'd you score the Sunday booze?" applauded Andy.

"It's not liquor," said Jeff, letting the mystery settle and breathe. His roommates waited, knowing he would fill in the blanks.

"Seriously? Am I the only one who remembers last night?"

Andy and Ellen exchanged puzzled glances.

"Apparently," Andy replied.

Ellen sat silently on the couch, confirming that she, too, was in the dark.

"Last night? When we got back? You don't remember? It was the three of us and Graham sitting on the.... Hey! Where's Graham?"

"Disappeared again. Early this morning, I guess," said Ellen.

"No. He was there on the couch when I left for church. He woke up and talked to me."

"Well, he's not there now, so I don't know what to tell you," said Andy.

"Well, that's fuckin' great," Jeff said. "Graham's gone, and you two idiots don't even remember talking about THIS." He shook the small glass bottle furiously as he spoke.

"It's all good," Andy offered. "Relax and start over. It sounds fascinating."

"YOU started it, you dick!" Jeff blurted at Andy. "Remember? When we got back from your little shoe tree adventure? We were talking about doing bad shit. Somebody brought up the question of Hell. And YOU started asking people what the fastest way was to end up there."

"That DOES sound like something you'd say," Ellen agreed.

"You can't even remember what you said last night?"

"I'm probably not gonna remember saying any of THIS later today," Andy admitted. "Stuff comes in, stuff goes out. I dunno." His nonchalance was doing nothing to soothe Jeff's growing agitation.

"Seriously?!" Jeff ranted. "You brought it up. And after we tossed the idea around a bit, Graham came up with… this!"

"So, what is THIS?" Ellen asked, waving her hands in small circles framing the mystery bottle.

"Like I said. It ain't liquor. You honestly don't remember Graham talking about using Holy Water for bong fuel?"

"Wow," Ellen said matter-of-factly. "That would do it."

"Jesus!" said Andy. "That's fucked up."

"Yep! And *your* idea," countered Jeff.

"I thought you said it was Graham's idea," Ellen suggested.

"No. He brought it up, but you're the dick that dared me to do it," explained Jeff, now getting even madder.

"I don't remember that at all," said Andy innocently.

"Really? How can you say something like 'Hey, you're going to church tomorrow. See if you can get us some Holy Water, and then not remember?"

"I dunno. People say a lot of crazy shit around here. If we did everything somebody suggested, we'd all be in jail or dead."

"Or in Hell, apparently," Ellen added.

"Sorry, man," Andy apologized. "I don't remember saying that. And if I did, I definitely didn't think you would actually do it. That's just crazy. Sometimes I talk, just to be talking. Plus, I was pretty wasted, so I could have said anything."

"What? Like 'let's throw a hundred shoes in a tree'?" Ellen asked, laughing.

"Shut up. THAT was a good idea last night, and it still is. You saw how awesome that shit looked." Andy said it to Ellen, but also as a segue for sharing his grand accomplishment with Jeff.

His roommate was having none of it. "So, let me see if I have this right..." Jeff said. "One asshole has a dumb idea, and then another asshole dares me to do it. Then, like an asshole, I do it. The next morning, Asshole # 1 takes off, and Asshole # 2 can't even remember his name... which is 'ASSHOLE'! by the way! Does that about cover it?"

"Wow!" declared Ellen. "I see you're making good use of that *Webster's Cursing Dictionary* I got you for Christmas."

"Have you got to the B's yet?" Andy said.

"Bastard and bitch!" Jeff added for good measure, pointing to each of them.

"Very good," said Ellen, knowing it was time to quit. "So, that really is Holy Water then?"

"Yeah. Or as holy as it gets these days."

"What does that mean?"

"Well, it's just tap water, or in this case, spring water. They have so many gallons in the storage room. The priest blesses it a closet-full at a time. This morning, they left a nearly empty jug on the counter. Honestly, I wouldn't have even noticed it, and would have never thought of taking it, if you and Graham hadn't planted the seed in my head. I figured no one would miss half a pint of water. They probably would have tossed it and started with a new one for the next service."

"So, see? It's not like you stole it after all. That should make you feel better." Andy clearly wanted a little absolution, too.

"So, what do you want to do?" Jeff asked. The three of them sat there, each like Robert Johnson at the crossroads, wrestling with the notion of consummating a deal with the Devil.

"Well, I want to get high," said Andy. "But I'm sure as Hell not smoking through Holy Water."

"But you don't even believe in God, so what do you care?" Jeff argued.

"Just because I don't believe, doesn't mean I can't still be afraid. Who knows? I could be wrong. But there's no sense in poking a bear, just to see if it will maul you."

* * *

Like his roommates, Andy grew up in the Christian church, learning about a loving God and his son, Jesus. Those ideas had been comfortable enough—until suddenly, they weren't.

The defining moment of Andy's youth came during the autumn of his fifteenth year. His brother, Tristan, was eleven at the time. Their age difference didn't keep them from being close. More than brothers, they were genuine friends. But four years is a wide berth, and it created some natural separations – different schools, different schedules, different friends. In their younger years, they were always together. But as they grew, Andy drifted toward new interests, often forsaking his brother to hang with kids his own age.

On a Friday afternoon in the early fall of 1987, Andy left Tristan alone, as he'd done many times. It would only be a few hours until their parents came home. When a neighbor boy, Brock, who was 12, invited Tristan to his house, the younger Maxwell gladly accepted. Brock's parents also worked, leaving him largely unattended in a house Tristan always thought of as much more fun, with better toys and fewer rules than his own. When Tristan arrived, Brock was more excited than usual, quickly ushering Tristan to the basement where many of the best 'toys' were kept. In addition to the pool table and a few real arcade-style video games, there was also a safe roughly the size of a phone booth, to which Tristan had never given any real thought. On that day, Brock's excitement was the product of pure parental neglect. Young, inquisitive, unsupervised Brock discovered the safe his father had failed to secure contained four hunting rifles and two handguns. Brock led Tristan to the safe and pulled open the door, revealing its all-too-alluring bounty.

Both boys stood wide-eyed, perusing the small cache of weapons. Brock, with absolutely no malice of forethought, grabbed one of the handguns and wheeled toward Tristan, brandishing a Hi-Point 9mm pistol. He thrust the gun in Tristan's direction several times, making explosive 'pow' sounds with each extension. It was easy enough to imagine an innocent, ignorant pre-teen boy pretending to be any of the countless armed heroes or villains he'd seen in the movies. Tristan laughed, albeit nervously, as he dodged the gun's barrel. Brock followed him, stabbing at the air between them twice more. The gun produced a noise and violence neither of them could ever have imagined. The discharge forced the weapon from Brock's too-small hand, leaving him stunned. Tristan was rendered speechless, too. From less than six feet away, a 9mm slug entered his tiny torso, ripping flesh and decimating bone before it exploded out of his back.

With his friend lying on the cold concrete basement floor, bleeding profusely, Brock froze. His parents had lectured him often on safety in general and very specifically about the dangers of the guns they owned. But now, when it really mattered, it was all a blur. Several minutes passed as Brock attempted to comfort his still-conscious friend or somehow fix the damage he'd done. Clearly, he was incapable. Eventually, he called 911. Eventually, the paramedics came. But it was too late. Tristan Maxwell, age 11, died in the back of an ambulance, the victim of an accident so random, senseless, and sudden it defied comprehension. As a result, 15-year-old Andy Maxwell's relationship with God perished abruptly and definitively.

* * *

"So," started Ellen, dismissing the Holy Water wholesale, "put that shit away. Let's just desecrate our bodies in the normal, not-go-straight-to-Hell way."

"Yeah, just one problem," Jeff pointed out. "My stash is cashed."

"I got it!" Andy shot out, bounding down the hall. "It's the least I can do."

"It usually is," Jeff replied under his breath. He placed the vodka bottle back in the bag, equally peeved and relieved that his sin of theft was not to be compounded.

"He really can be such a bastard sometimes," Jeff said to Ellen, with Andy well out of earshot.

"Yeah, it's true. But how often are you bored?"

Not two minutes later, Andy returned. Jeff was cleaning the screen in the bowl of his favorite pipe, a little purple piece of PVC about 5 inches tall. It was emblazoned with a shiny iridescent sticker—the kind a child might get from school or the doctor— which said, 'Super Star.'

"Damn! This was a quarter yesterday afternoon." Andy stared at the shabby quantity of marijuana. "We're gonna have to go see Pete again."

They all took turns filling their lungs with smoke as the pipe made its way around the circle.

"I do wonder, though…" Ellen pondered, "if it would have tasted or felt any better."

"I don't know, El, but it's probably not worth it to find out," Andy offered. "Besides, I'm feeling pretty disconnected right now anyway." Warm inebriation washed over him, bringing with it a sense of calm. It didn't last long.

"So, what are you gonna do about a job, Andy?"

Whoa. Where had that come from? As quickly as he began his escape, reality drew tight its leash and yanked him sternly towards responsibility.

"Damn. You sure know how to kill a buzz."

"Sorry, but we gotta talk about this sooner or later."

"I know. And I feel bad about it. It's getting down to the wire. Now that I've graduated, I can't squeeze much more out of my parents under the pretense of job hunting. If something doesn't happen soon, I'm headed back to their basement."

"I thought you had a couple of prospects," Ellen pressed.

"Yeah, one of them fell through. But I have an interview with a real ad agency tomorrow."

It had been a sore subject at the house for weeks. Andy reached the painful realization that where he was and where he was supposed to be might be two different places. Bradford was great. Andy had grown quite fond of its small metropolitan charm. But opportunity, at least the kind he sought, wasn't abundant. Most jobs in town were either with the government or the university. Neither option really applied nor appealed to him. If he was gonna to do anything of "real value," he was facing forced geographic relocation—or so he had decided.

"Yeah, it's either that, or I figure out how to come into a helluva lot of money, and quickly," said Andy.

"Legally or illegally?" Ellen wanted to know.

"Well… TV and movies have taught me that crime is fun, glamorous, and very lucrative. But I can't really see it as a career path."

"Yeah. Take it easy. Shoe Boy here doesn't need that kind of encouragement," Jeff kidded.

"Although I think I have figured out how people do make a lot of money—legally that is," Andy submitted. A cloud of cannabis smoke was now driving his train of thought.

"Shit. And you've been holdin' out on us? Give it up, Einstein."

"No, seriously, check it out. People are stupid, right?"

A combative opening for sure, but intriguing, nonetheless.

"Right," agreed Ellen. "But what does that have to do with making lots of money?"

"Everything. People are stupid, and lazy," Andy resumed. "This world is full of lazy bastards just waiting to buy the next big thing that's supposed to make their lives a little easier."

"Hence the remote control?" Ellen offered.

"Perfect example; the lazy man's best fucking friend."

"So, what are you saying?" Jeff asked.

"The best way to make money is to create something that doesn't already exist. Then all you have to do is to convince a bunch of people—people who've been doing just fine without your help so far—that they couldn't possibly live another day without whatever it is that you've invented."

"Really?" Jeff mocked through a billow of smoke. "Whatever happened to 'woe to he who willfully innovates', Mr. Zen Master?"

After severing his relationship with the Christian God of his childhood, Andy had taken a break from religion altogether. In his junior year, he needed an extra elective. He chose Comparative Religion, as much or more for its favorable schedule than for any genuine interest in the subject. To his surprise, Andy found some semblance of logic in the Eastern philosophies, particularly the *Tao Te Ching*. His interpretations of Lao-Tzu's wisdom ranged from broad and liberal to completely misguided. Still, they were almost always good for a laugh.

"Oh, I've got that covered." Andy beamed.

"Yeah? Lay it on me."

"In fact, I'm glad you asked," lied Andy, whose mind was racing to catch up with his mouth.

"Okay. So, 'Woe to he who willfully innovates', right? Lao-Tzu describes woe as '*the burden brought on man by his preoccupation with his own worldly possessions*.' So, therefore, the man who willfully innovates is destined to incur excess woe, or more specifically, lots of worldly possessions."

"I don't get it," a stoned Ellen admitted.

"And the beauty of it is," Andy continued, ignoring her, not out of rudeness, but to keep his train of thought, "it doesn't even matter what you create, as long as it's new. Bad books, bad movies, bad records, they all make millions of dollars. You could invent a better mousetrap, or toothbrush, or crack pipe, for that matter. It doesn't matter. *Somebody* out there will lay down the cash to buy into it."

"Hey, wait. That might work," Andy pondered, interrupting himself. "What if we created a self-lighting crack pipe? Well not a crack pipe, 'cause crack sucks, but a pipe anyway? It would have a lighter built into the side, right over the bowl."

"Not bad," commended Ellen. "You'd never have to look for a lighter again."

"That sort of thing could save you weeks over a lifetime," Jeff agreed.

"And you'd have a free hand, so you could smoke while you wrote, or ate, or did your homework. And it would sure make driving while smoking a lot easier."

"Well, thanks for making the world safer for all the kids," Ellen congratulated.

"Whatever. What would you invent?" Andy asked, his skull still tingling.

"Actually, I had this thought just the other day at work," she said to his surprise. "Every day, these miserable bastards come in and throw back half their pay in booze."

"Which happens to pay your check," Andy added.

"I know. Not the point." Ellen shut him down. "Check this out. Think about the water company. They've got pipes that run all under this city, bringing water to every home in Bradford. For a small monthly fee, of course."

"Yeah," they both agreed, seeing her conclusion approaching from a mile away.

"So, apply that technology to getting wasted, and what do you get? You take a brewery, run pipes to every home in the neighborhood, and offer people the luxury of continuous beer, mainlined straight into the comfort of their own homes. At a small monthly fee to subscribers, of course, and voila!"

"Damn. That might be even better than cable television," Jeff applauded.

"No. That's not possible," Andy replied curtly. "But it is damned good thinkin', El. Woe unto you."

"Thanks. But wait, there's more," she gleamed. "What does the water or cable company do if you forget to pay them?

"They cut you off until you cough up the dough," Jeff answered.

"Oh my God." The revelation formed fully for Andy. "So, you give people credit, at crazy-high rates, of course, on an endless supply of beer–delivered directly to a population of obese, underemployed bastards strapped to La-Z-Boys. Almost overnight, they'd become used to that shit—dependent on it, like an alcoholic welfare state. Wow! Congratulations, Ellen," Andy said, genuinely impressed. "You just figured out how to take over the whole fucking planet!"

"Except that some people don't drink," Ellen noted.

"Sure they don't," Andy laughed, dismissing the statement outright.

"You know what I'd like to see?" asked Jeff. "I'd like to see somebody make a movie that was real. And not like a documentary, or anything like that. Just a movie where things happen completely realistically."

"That happens all the time. And they're typically very boring," Andy argued. "People don't want to see real shit happen. People go to the movies for the same reason they do drugs—to escape reality. We see reality every day. We need fantasy to keep us sane."

"No, I agree. That's not what I'm saying. Like, I was watching this *Rambo* kind of movie the other day. You know, the ones where one guy, with ungodly luck and a big fat grudge, takes on seven hundred heavily armed bad guys and wipes 'em all out. That's not fucking reality."

"True. So, what are you suggesting?"

"I want to make a movie that lasts about thirty seconds, 'cause that's all it would really take. It'd be called *Bad Guys with Good Aim*. Quick character intros, you know, one guy's wearing the black hat, the other guy's wearing the white hat. Pretty straightforward. Both have guns, but realistically, the Bad Guy just knows how to handle his a little better, cause sometimes, that's the truth. So, he whips out the firepower and puts one right between Mr. Nice Guy's eyes. Dead just like that, with no set-up. Now that kind of shit happens every day, too."

"What a happy little story that is," mocked Ellen. "It's kind of short, though, don't you think?"

"No. That's the whole point. I mean, we could have the Bad Guy steal the dead Good Guy's unfaithful girlfriend if you like. Boom! Now, you've got a love story. We could stretch it to a full two minutes."

"Much better," quipped Ellen. "A little somethin' for the ladies."

"Wouldn't it be great if it were all that easy, though? One big idea, and bang, you're filthy fucking rich. No way. The only way to make any money in this world is to bust your ass or your back, or your brain, or whatever it is God gave you that's worth a damn," Jeff lamented.

"Or you could inherit it," added Andy.

"Or you could marry it," suggested Ellen.

"Fuck. You really *are* a *girl*, aren't you?" teased Jeff.

"Man, this place is wasted. It would be easier just to move." Ellen was finally done procrastinating. She stood and stared at her boys with a look that suggested they do the same.

16

For most people, in most tasks, taking drugs results in a net loss of productivity. For Andy, house cleaning was a notable exception. With a head full of narcotics, he somehow acquired a sense of hyper-focused tunnel vision. Jeff and Ellen had learned that if the job was straightforward and in his best interest, all they had to do was load him up and stay out of the way.

With two overstuffed trash bags at arm's length, Andy walked faster than usual toward the front porch. To his surprise, the door swung inward before he arrived. Standing there in the open frame, mostly blocking his path, was Cricket Lowe. Andy was immediately aware of how bad he must have looked and smelled.

"H-Hey, Cricket." he muttered. "What's up?"

Andy slid past her and dropped the bags in the trash can beside the porch.

"Nothing," she said, entering the house without an invitation or waiting for him. Her tone was a touch cold, but Andy was used to it.

To Andy, Cricket was gorgeous—in a very basic way. She wore no makeup. Her un-styled, sandy blonde hair fell in small curls at her shoulder blades and hung loosely in her eyes when she wore it down. Her long, athletic frame had a lovely curve, but she often wrapped it in flowing ankle-length skirts, hiding her shape too well for his taste. She wore leather sandals or went barefoot most of the time, and Andy thought even her toes were cute.

Like so many other local young ladies, Cricket enjoyed Jeff's company. Surely more so than most of them, she was good at acquiring illicit substances. Many a sober night had been remedied at her hand, so Cricket was always welcome on Cornwall Street. She didn't come calling often, but when she did, it was always for Jeff.

Cricket made her way towards the center of the house. Andy watched her go, the brown suede bag on her shoulder bouncing off her hip with every other stride. He sighed and returned to cleaning.

"Hey, sweetie. How are you?" Cricket purred at Jeff as she swept a blonde lock from her face.

"All good," he said, stepping over the pile of debris at his feet. "But where the hell were you last night?"

"Nobody told me. But it looks like you had a good time."

"Yeah, not bad. Sorry. You're probably the only freak in Bradford that wasn't here last night."

"Not true. The fucking Cactus was packed," she replied.

Ellen's head swung. "You were there? What the fuck happened? Andy, c'mere!"

"It's on the front page of this morning's paper," Cricket said as Andy walked into the Den.

"The shoes!?"

"Shoes? What shoes?" Cricket asked.

"Fuck your shoes, Andy. Tell us about the Cactus," Jeff urged.

"Holy shit! You were there?" said Andy.

"Shut up and let her tell it."

"The place was jammed. You could hardly move. We went to see Cold Gin. You know? The KISS cover band?" Cricket began.

"Shit! We missed that?"

"Sorry," Andy offered sarcastically as if their party was a poor substitute for an evening watching four art school dropouts pretend to be the world's premiere geriatric glam band.

"Anyway," she continued, "it was way late, and I was messed up, but..." Each of them had lit up and settled in for story time.

"We're sitting in the back, you know, by the pinball machine. It's me and Pete, and four or five others. I can't remember. So, the band breaks into *Flaming Youth*, and we head straight for the front."

"So, what happened?" Andy asked, mostly just wanting to say something to her.

"You really don't have *any* patience." Cricket scolded.

No reply was forthcoming or needed from the sufficiently embarrassed Andy Maxwell.

"So, there we are, up near the stage, rockin' out. And then, out of nowhere... BAM!" She punctuated the point with flailing arms and enough gusto to startle her audience.

"Apparently, Cold Gin thought they could set off fuckin' flash pots inside the Cactus. You know, to give it that real KISS feeling?"

Jeff couldn't believe her. "They let 'em bring in flash pots?"

"I guess, 'cause it happened," Cricket explained. "Anyway, the stage is in front of that big window by the street, you know."

"Oh, shit." Andy didn't have to try hard to imagine the resulting carnage.

"They get near the end, and... BOOM! The fucking pots go off, right underneath that window. It might have been the loudest thing I've ever heard. The window went. The whole fucking thing blew up and threw shrapnel all over Paxton Street. Some people got pretty cut up."

"That explains the police convention down there this morning," said Ellen.

"What else does the paper say?" Jeff asked.

Cricket had stalled and was eyeing the unopened Budweiser on the table.

Andy grabbed the beer. "You want one?"

"Sure. Thanks." A small bolt of electricity ran through him as her pinky finger swept lightly across the back of his hand during the exchange.

Cricket opened the bottle and started again. "The blast was loud. I mean, like shotgun loud. In fact, that's exactly what it sounded like. And you know how small the Cactus is. Well, I guess that's what everybody else thought it was, too. When the window exploded, all hell broke loose.

"You guys remember when that guy got shot down at Riley's Pub?" she asked. They all nodded their heads, recalling the botched robbery, which had left one man dead and a whole bar full of people emotionally scarred for life.

"Well, the Cactus is too small for that shit. One person thinks they hear a gunshot and suddenly, you've got a stampede."

"What did the band do?" Ellen asked.

"What *could* they do? Every drunk in the place made a beeline for the doors at the same time. The whole thing was probably empty in three minutes. There was no fire, just the blast from the flash pots. We stuck around 'til the cops came, and I never saw the band come out. They were probably too embarrassed to face the crowd in the parking lot."

"Jesus Christ," Andy said, at a loss for anything else.

"Exactly. Jesus fuckin' Christ man," Cricket agreed, reaching into her oversized hip bag and retrieving the Sunday edition of *The Bradford Exchange*.

"And here's the really crazy part. Listen to this. Margo Hammond, 21, of Willow Creek, has been missing since the incident occurred early Sunday morning. Authorities have not ruled out the possibility of foul play in her disappearance," Cricket quoted.

"Who's Margo Hammond?" Andy asked.

"Like I know," Cricket snapped. "She's just some random chick who went to see a Cold Gin show, like everybody else who wasn't here last night. Except, she wound up slipping off the face of the planet. Could just as easily been me or you."

"Nah-uh," said Andy, "Not me. I was hanging with the shoes."

"What's all this shit about shoes?"

"You can read about that in *tomorrow's* paper," he said to Cricket, quite pleased with himself. He turned to Jeff, still eager to share the tale of their own triumph. "Dude, you gotta come see it. We went earlier and it…"

Ellen cut him off again. "She's not just some random girl to her parents, or her boyfriend, or *somebody*."

"That would be nice," replied Cricket, just under her breath.

"What?" asked Jeff.

"Nothing. Never mind." Cricket said, avoiding eye contact. "Hey. Can I talk to you for a minute?" she asked, already on her way to his room.

The two rose, leaving Andy and Ellen to exchange puzzled glances. Andy leaned back, pondering yet another unfruitful go-round with the enchanting Cricket Lowe.

"What the hell is wrong with her?" Andy asked through a cloud of smoke.

"What? Just because the girl won't sleep with you, she's a psycho or something?"

"I was just trying to tell Jeff… You know, never mind. Fuck you."

"Can't. I'm crazy too, remember?" It was her final taunt as she reached for the broom. A second later, she was gone too.

Andy sulked in silence, but only for a moment. With no audience left, he grabbed another trash bag and joined the battle to reclaim their home.

A few minutes later, Jeff and Cricket emerged. Jeff had changed shirts and was carrying a black backpack on his shoulder.

"Looking good, y'all," Jeff said of the much cleaner room.

"Where are *you* going?" Andy asked, his tone almost parental.

"To Overton. Cricket's in a jam and needs a ride back to her folks' house."

Cricket was waiting in the other room, leaning against the couch that had reclaimed its spot from the drum kit.

"When are you coming back?" Andy wanted to know.

"Tomorrow. Probably early, if that's okay with you, Dad."

"Fine, don't worry about your mother and me," Andy played along, putting his arm around Ellen. "We'll be fine without ya. You just go then."

"Oh, grow up," Ellen finally said. "I swear you two are lovers or something."

Ellen struggled to understand her roommates' unique relationship. Of course, they were friends—oftentimes the best of—brothers even. And like brothers, they fought constantly, incapable of being too close or far apart for long. Mostly, they battled with words, but they weren't above occasional fisticuffs either. Ellen loved them both, also like brothers, but often found it exhausting jumping in or out of the middle.

"By the way," Jeff turned to Andy, "good luck with your interview tomorrow. Maybe you won't have to move," he said, wanting to believe it.

Almost as quickly as they'd closed it, Andy reopened the front door and chased after them.

"Hey, Cricket!" he called from the porch.

"Yeah?"

"Are you holding? We're kinda slim after last night."

"Nope. Sorry." There was a tenderness in her tone that was alien to him, and he thought it was the sweetest-sounding rejection he'd ever heard.

"That's cool. See you later." He yearned for more, but she was already walking away.

Andy watched with fascination as Cricket strode through the tiny patch of too-tall grass in their front yard towards Jeff's truck. Her long blue and white tie-dyed skirt nipped at her ankles as she walked. Her tight cotton tank top became almost obscenely white in the bright sunlight. Jeff was already behind the wheel, fooling with the radio knobs. Andy heard the truck's doors close behind him as he walked back into the house.

17

Ellen was sweeping the front room as he returned, a lit Marlboro between her pursed lips. The house would pass for clean, mainly because they were ready to be done cleaning it. Andy grabbed the last full bag of trash and headed for the door.

"Leave it open," Ellen implored. "It smells like ass in here."

Again, that door collided with the wall behind it. A small circular divot the size and shape of the doorknob had formed in the drywall from many such previous assaults. Two dollars at the hardware store and five minutes of someone's time installing a new doorstop could end the damage, but for the young sobriety-challenged renters, it wasn't even on the radar.

"What are you doing today?" she asked.

"Not a God-damned thing," Andy answered with great pleasure.

"Yeah, me neither. I was thinking of having a few drinks and then working on that damned table."

"Still?" Andy asked as if the matter had been pending for years. He was leisurely thumbing through the Sunday *Exchange*, which Cricket had so kindly donated to the house. He often bought one himself, but today, she'd saved him the trouble and money. As a bonus, he noticed the cheap rag paper still carried a hint of the strange herbal scent she wore.

"Yeah, well, I've been busy," Ellen replied through the wall. She had returned to her bedroom and left Andy alone with the paper.

He sat busily dividing the sections of the gigantic Sunday edition into two neat piles. Only certain ones merited interest, and he liked to separate the wheat from the chafe before reading a single word.

His selections were always the same. Always the front page, the classifieds, and the comics—in that order. Looking for a job, which had become a full-time position itself lately, was awfully depressing, and it helped to chase the defeat with some foolishness. And finally, Sports. This he considered the dessert of the exercise, the cherry on top.

Satisfied with his stacks, he left them and walked to Ellen's door. Poking his head inside, he found her clearing piles off a makeshift wooden table.

Among the things he loved most about her was the diversity of her interests. Ellen had a ton of hobbies, and she excelled at most of them. But she sometimes lacked motivation and follow-through. Ellen painted, played the violin, viola, and piano quite well, and had recently begun trying woodworking. Eventually, she hoped to combine her passions, learning to sculpt fine classical musical instruments.

Her first project was much less ambitious. It was a simple table, qualifying as such by having five uniform legs and a relatively flat surface. It was ugly and kind of wobbly but not too bad as a first shot at carpentry. The two-by-six-foot surface had become increasingly cluttered with random items and had all but disappeared.

"What are you going to do to it?" he asked, leaning against the cheap wood paneling that covered the walls of her room.

"Don't know. But it needs something. I might just paint the thing."

"That's boring."

"I agree. Help me take this bitch out back."

They each grabbed an end of the table and began working it out of her room, into the tiny hallway, and through the kitchen. Stopping at the back door, Ellen propped her end on one knee and reached behind herself to get the door. Andy could lift reasonably heavy stuff but had learned the hard way that his bad balance precluded doing much of anything while walking backward.

"Damn it's nice out here," she said, inhaling the fresh air.

"A helluva lot nicer than in there."

"No doubt. Hey, go turn on your stereo, will you?"

"Groovy tunes comin' up!" He climbed the stairs and took an immediate left into his bedroom, which overlooked the backyard.

Sunday afternoon hangover? Manual labor outside in the warm pre-summer Bradford sun? The conditions begged for Led Zeppelin, and there was no better place to start than *Houses of the Holy*. Andy grinned wide, watching Ellen ponder the table. The din of *The Song Remains the Same* began to wash over the yard as he went to grab his stacks of paper and rejoin her.

18

Jeff's black pickup rolled out of the gas station and turned right. Down the entrance ramp they went, merging onto Interstate 26. Traffic was light and moving fast. Overton was just over a hundred miles from Bradford, about an hour and a half away by Jeff's math.

But time was irrelevant. Things had turned out well for him. Cricket had offered him fifty bucks to drive a hundred miles; well, two hundred, counting the return. Cruising the open highway with a pretty girl and good tunes was a much better deal than cleaning his nasty house at any price.

Jeff rolled down his window and lit a cigarette as Cricket bent forward to retrieve her bag from the floorboard. Mick Jagger was still belting *Heartbreaker*, but not so loudly that she couldn't hear his question.

"You don't waste any time, do you?"

"Sorry, I didn't know you weren't ready," she cooed.

She had gone to her satchel, retrieved a plastic sandwich bag, and began unrolling it in her lap. The pungent stink of the neon-green grass was instant. She reached into her sack and brought forth a book of extra-wide rolling papers. Harvesting the last two leaves, she tossed the empty package out the window.

"I thought you told Andy you were out."

"I did. But don't take it personally, it's all just part of the game," she said with a smirk.

"Why is there always a game? I'd give anything for a normal girl who's just straight-up."

"You think you would. But if you *had* a straight-up girl, she'd probably bore you to death. Men need and appreciate intrigue."

"Whatever," he said, knowing she was right.

"It's fine. We don't have to smoke it now. I just wanted to roll one. I like to roll joints. I find it relaxing."

Jeff drove silently for several minutes. In glances, he half-watched her slender fingers work the large buds into a more manageable shake. Spreading the pieces evenly, she folded the paper and began to roll it atop an empty Girl Scout cookie box she'd found behind the seat.

She held the perfectly round joint aloft for his approval. "Ta Dah! Anytime you're ready, big boy."

"Very nice."

The big green sign ahead announced that Overton was eighty-five miles away.

"Fire it up!" With a devious grin, he reached down and located a pair of silver-framed sunglasses. The radio was momentarily silent as Jeff flipped sides of his road trip compilation tape.

Seconds later, the first galloping bass notes of Swervedriver's *Deep Seat* filled the truck's small cab as Cricket set fire to the joint.

Sweet, stout smoke enveloped Jeff as he activated cruise control. Set at a modest 74 mph, they'd still make pretty good time into Overton.

Jeff lifted the joint to his lips and pulled hard. It burnt his lungs and throat, but was delicious. He held his breath as long as he could and exhaled, passing it back to Cricket.

A warm fuzz filled his brain, accentuating the joy of hearing one of his favorite pieces of music.

"Do you know this one?" he asked her, smiling.

"No," Cricket admitted. She liked music, but not the way many in his circle did. She'd been at plenty of parties that devolved into the boys waxing over how 'great,' amazing,' or 'trans-sonic' a particular song or album was. She sensed he was headed in that direction, but he veered.

"That's some pretty stiff shit, Cricket."

"Yeah. Cold Gin is cheesy, but the real hardcore freaks come crawlin' out when they play, and they're always holdin'."

"That's fuckin' nuts about the Cactus."

"Yeah. After a while, though, you get pretty tired of living in the middle of crazy shit."

"I haven't hit that wall yet."

"Careful what you wish for," she cautioned.

She was authentically eccentric, and Jeff had learned that just about anything was possible with Cricket Lowe in the mix. Even so, he could never have foreseen what was about to happen.

Jeff was busy adjusting his seat and immersing himself in the sonic tidal wave emanating from the truck's shitty speakers. He didn't even notice Cricket fumbling through her bag again. But he snapped to attention when she withdrew her svelte hand, and he saw it was now clutching a silver pistol with a pearl-colored grip. Jeff was forced into an incredulous double-take, which ultimately paid off. On second glance, he recognized the pistol as the toy cap gun it was. It was one of those Lone Ranger six-shooters with the rolls of red caps you loaded on the side. Every boy, and apparently some girls their age, had probably had one growing up, but it'd been years since Jeff had seen one.

"What the fuck is that for?" Jeff asked.

"It's not *for* anything, it's a toy. It's for fun," she said, smirking.

"Guns aren't *for fun*, Cricket. They're serious."

"Not this one," she smiled and pointed it straight at him. "Jesus, take it easy. You sound like tight-ass Andy."

"No, I don't," Jeff deflected. "Besides, he's not *always* wrong, you know."

"Really? So why are you always bustin' his balls about everything?"

"Somebody's got to. I mean, I love the guy, but he's a mess. He's like family. But he's his own worst enemy. If he was half as motivated as he was smart, none of us would be sweatin' his future right now."

"Why do you care?" she asked, spinning the toy gun around her slender index finger. "The future takes care of itself."

"That may be true. But people need to take care of each other, too, even our idiot brothers." Jeff had hoped this little unplanned road trip would be a respite from the mounting tension back home. He tried to think of any other topic, but all he could come up with was "Stop pointing that shit at me!"

Just as he finished that thought, she playfully pulled the trigger. The gun produced an audible click but nothing else as the plastic hammer fell. He knew it wasn't real. Still, Jeff recoiled at the sound.

"Geez, lighten up," she repeated and buried the barrel an inch deep in her mouth, clicking off two more quick rounds of nothing. He knew of his passenger's penchant for drama. But now, like a kid who'd instantly regretted his decision to brave the biggest roller coaster in the park, it was too late. He was strapped in, and the car was already clicking up the first big hill.

She put her hand gently on his knee and squeezed lightly. He smiled uneasily at her, not knowing how else to respond.

* * *

A blood-red Ford Taurus cruised in the right lane ahead of them as they crested a long, gradual hill on I-26. Jeff hit the blinker and changed lanes, looking to pass the slower traffic.

"You've got no sense of humor," she criticized.

Cricket rolled her window all the way down as they pulled alongside the Taurus. Holding the toy gun tightly in both hands, she popped up and leaned out of the window just as the two vehicles drew even. Her long blond hair flapped wildly in the highway-speed wind.

"BANG!" she howled, clicking the gun repeatedly at the unsuspecting driver. "You're dead, motherfucker!"

Jeff never saw it coming.

"Jesus!" he screamed, grabbing a handful of her white cotton top and reeling her back into the cab. "What the fuck is wrong with you?"

The Taurus slammed on its brakes and let the truck fly by. Cricket doubled over with laughter.

Jeff checked the rearview mirror. The Taurus was behind them now, following at a safe distance. The truck's cruise control disengaged when he'd braked to collect her. Jeff eased down on the accelerator, resuming a practical speed. He looked over and saw her studying him. Cricket smiled just wide enough to reveal the two rows of perfect teeth that hid behind her thin lips.

"You have to admit, that was pretty fucking funny."

"I really don't."

She laughed again. "Trust me, it was funny. You shoulda seen his face. I can't believe he hasn't pulled over to check his pants yet."

Jeff rechecked his mirror. Nothing. He turned his head just in time to see the dark red sedan crossing through his blind spot and drawing even again.

"Holy shit! What's he doing?" Jeff blurted.

"Probably coming up to give us the bird."

Compared to what Jeff saw, their victim's middle finger would have been wholly welcomed, comforting even. The driver of the Taurus, a rotund man with thick glasses, held aloft a simple notebook. The license number of Jeff's truck was scrawled quite legibly in characters four inches high.

"He's got my tag number!" said Jeff, not exactly sure what that meant.

"So what?" said Cricket, still unworried.

"Fuck!" cried Jeff as the Taurus stayed parallel.

"What?"

"Look!" he said, pointing to their new friend.

The man was now holding the most potent non-lethal weapon known to man. Clutched in his liver-spotted hand was a cellular phone.

"Fuck!" Jeff repeated. "He just called the cops!"

The smile disappeared from Cricket's face. "Are you sure?"

"Pretty fucking sure."

"What should we do?" Cricket asked, suddenly showing concern.

"Well, for starters, you could put the fucking gun away," Jeff suggested.

Without so much as a whisper, the toy found its way back inside the brown suede bag at her feet.

"Don't worry," she said, attempting to tender the situation. "He probably just wanted to scare us."

"Mission... fucking... accomplished! I *so* don't need this bullshit."

"Just keep driving."

Cruise control, like his sense of comfort and the rest of the joint they'd been smoking, went straight out the window. Jeff was lased-focused on staying in the lines and monitoring his speed.

Seventy-one miles outside of Overton, the situation officially went from bad to worse. As they cleared the top of the next ridge, with the Taurus still in tow, they passed the first police car. The cruiser was backed neatly into the brush on the side of the road, but its front end and ominous rack of blue lights were perfectly visible.

The truck rolled by, well within the speed limit. The Taurus, now at least a hundred feet back, also passed the cop, at which point the cruiser casually entered the highway. Waves of fear crashed over Jeff; unlike anything he'd ever felt.

Looking almost exclusively in the rearview now, Jeff watched as the cruiser steadily advanced. His brain discarded the possibility of coincidence and ran straight into a controlled panic.

"Turn that shit off!" demanded Jeff, uncharacteristically ruffled. He was suddenly failing to appreciate the mammoth, churning, swirling guitars he had been enamored with just moments ago.

Cricket sat beside him, barely breathing at all. "Why hasn't he pulled us over?"

"Careful what you ask for," Jeff threw back at her as it all began to fall apart. As they approached another slope, the three-car caravan crept along at forty-five miles an hour.

There, hidden in the shadows of the overpass, was Cruiser #2. Jeff's speed was low, but his anxiety blasted into the red zone as the second cop pulled in and joined the party.

"We're fucked," Jeff said. "We can't even ditch the weed, Cricket. We're going to fuckin' jail."

"Shit! I forgot the weed."

"Take out the gun," Jeff said, now with an eerie calm. "Take it out and open the cap chamber so they can see it's a toy. Lay it right on the dash."

Cricket did as she was told, emerging from the bag with the gun in one hand and the dope in the other. She flipped up the side panel and set the toy pistol down between two tape cases on the dash.

"We can't hide that, Cricket," Jeff was sure. "We're fucked."

"You just keep driving till they cut on the blues. And roll the windows down to air this bitch out," she said, starting to gather her long skirt up from the bottom.

"You're gonna put it in your panties?" asked Jeff, not having a better idea but not liking that one much either. "What if they frisk us?"

"I don't wear underwear," she said plainly. "And if they frisk me where this is going, we'll sue the whole fucking state."

The rearview mirror erupted in a sea of flashing blue lights.

"Fuck!" Jeff gasped. "Do it then! And make it quick, 'cause this is it."

"Don't watch me!" she demanded.

"Just do it!" he snapped, very aware of what he *wasn't* watching.

She winced slightly as her body accepted the contraband.

The truck slowed. Jeff waited only until Cricket had opened her eyes and let back down her skirt to start pulling over. He fumbled to light a cigarette, hoping to masque any lingering smell from the weed. They exchanged nervous smiles as the vehicle left the road and came to rest on the shoulder.

Jeff barely shifted into park before the vehicle was engulfed. From out of thin air, the first two cruisers were joined by a third, then a fourth. A brown four-door with no official markings approached from the side and stopped a few feet behind Cricket's door.

"Goddamn," said Jeff, in utter disbelief. "Whoever's robbing banks and liquor stores around here has it fuckin' made right now."

A nervous laugh escaped the tightly pursed lips of his passenger. "What now?"

"Whatever they want. Sit still. Don't say shit until someone asks you a question. Answer it honestly and then shut up again."

The irony of it all was not the least bit lost on him. Roughly twelve hours ago, he and Andy had been advising their Shoe Tree conspirators on the finer points of interacting with law enforcement. Their theories, all they were in truth, were about to be tested by fire. Jeff Aaron had confidence in spades, but right now, with Johnny Law bearing down on them, he was sweating bullets and praying hard.

The engine was off, but the keys still hung from the ignition. They sat motionless as two officers approached in cinematic slow motion. Both held their service revolvers drawn high and very visible.

Jeff clutched the hard plastic steering wheel, mindful to keep his hands in plain view. Cricket's arms lay palms up in her lap, uncrossed – the least threatening position she could think to assume. The officers' eternal approach culminated with the sickening thud of a steel revolver butt crashing against the driver's side door.

"Hands up!" the officer shouted at the open window. The doors swung open, and both passengers were snatched from the cab by armed escorts.

A blinding whirlwind of justice crashed down as everything blurred into strobes of blue light and noise. A mix of garbled questions flew at Jeff and Cricket. Police radios buzzed, and the whir of a hundred passing cars filled his ears to capacity.

The two young threats to public safety stood side by side, clutching the truck's tailgate. Cricket's slender fingers held tightly to the sun-warmed metal. Facing the car, they watched helplessly as two new officers approached the vehicle and began searching it. Instantly, the cap gun, still lying chamber-open on the dash, was recovered and brought to an officer who stood somewhere behind them.

In the odd silence at the center of this shit storm, Jeff found himself wondering how all this commotion and drama must have looked to the passersby—the businessmen, couples, or whole families en route to someplace more friendly. Somewhere on that highway, carloads of children bombarded their weary and suddenly uncomfortable parents with questions and stared wildly at the coolest thing they'd ever seen in real, three-dimensional life. The smallest smile crossed his lips, but it didn't stay long.

The crisp sweep of the officer's shoe against Jeff's ankle was enough to break up that daydream. His legs spread wider, leaving him prone to his captor's intentions. Cricket fared no better, as a taller, thinner arm of the law executed the same maneuver on her.

"Ow!" she said, possibly attempting to elicit sympathy or even an apology from her oppressor; neither came, of course.

The frisking began at Jeff's midsection. The officer's ham-fists moved around Jeff's waistband in vain. His pockets were invaded, and their contents emptied onto the lowered tailgate of the truck. One black wallet, one pink plastic cigarette lighter, a loose dollar bill and forty-one cents in change, and three ibuprofen tablets—that was it. No bullets, no drugs, no knives, no nothing. In fact, nothing more dangerous than expired headache medicine was found, which, as far as he knew, was not illegal. So far, so good.

Cricket, on the other hand, had no pockets. Her white tank top hugged her form tightly and plainly concealed nothing more than what God Himself had seen fit to give her. Her attending officer ran his hands slowly and firmly against her curvaceous hips. His fingertips made their way around her middle and checked the waistband of her flowing skirt.

Jeff watched intently from the corner of his eye. He was clean but actively praying that Cricket's secret remained safe. The thin cop bent and patted her ankles. She tensed at the touch of his coarse skin against hers. Reaching upward and under her skirt, he ran his fingers up the backs and outside of her bare legs.

"Hey!" she snapped, not very innocently at all, as his dry, calloused hands neared the curve of her buttocks. The officer stopped short.

Jeff's attention was divided equally by Cricket's frisking and the two officers sifting through his backpack. The bag was being emptied by a gigantic black cop taking inventory of its contents. Cricket's shoulder sack and other items of interest were scattered around the truck's bed.

A snickering laugh that seemed so out of place pierced the tension. It had come from the huge black cop but was deceptively high in pitch. His enormous hands emerged from Jeff's pack, and a little wave of laughter flew around the scene. Held aloft for God and every passenger on I-26 to see was a pair of white cotton boxer shorts lavishly decorated with pink and red Valentine hearts. Any benchmark Jeff may have had for embarrassment was instantly destroyed.

"Those are really cute," Cricket teased quietly.

"Shut up!" came simultaneous demands from Jeff and an officer behind them.

"Mr. Aaron. Ms. Lowe. Sit." The voice was new but authoritative.

The newest cop, a sheriff, directed them to rest on the tailgate, which they did, sheepishly waiting to be addressed.

"What the fuck is your problem?" the sheriff needed to know.

Recognizing a rhetorical question was a valuable skill, and one they both possessed. Jeff scanned the officers' badges and noted they were being addressed by a man named Slocum.

"I've run both your I.D.s," said the sheriff, tossing Jeff his wallet and handing Cricket hers. "Not even a speeding ticket. So why do I have twelve men out here?"

"Because...," started Jeff, apparently losing the ability to disregard rhetoric.

"Because" Slocum interrupted, "somebody thought *this* shit might be funny."

Clearly, the *shit* Slocum was referring to was the cap gun he now held clutched in his fist.

"What you didn't know was that your friend back there in the Taurus, is also *my* friend—off-duty Deputy Sheriff McVee, to be exact."

Jeff looked at Cricket as if to say *you stupid bitch.*

"And really, you're pretty damned lucky," Slocum pointed out, slipping the dark sunglasses from his face for maximum effect. "If that had been me you pointed a gun at, fake or otherwise, I'd have put a bleedhole in both your skulls and filled out the paperwork over coffee and doughnuts on Monday fucking morning."

A pregnant pause followed as the sheriff studied their young faces for a response. He wasn't kidding, either. He was merely explaining, without much exaggeration at all, how close they'd come to being dead for no good reason at all.

"I should haul both your asses in for reckless endangerment. But with no priors, and nothing on you, it's probably not even worth the time. Besides, I think you've both crapped your pants enough from all the attention this little stunt has gotten you."

Cricket and Jeff sat silent and expressionless on the back of the truck.

"Lessons learned?" Slocum asked.

"Yes, sir," they offered in unison, in major disbelief of their apparent fortune. They fought the urge to smile or look at one another. Both were regularly contumacious, but quiet obedience was the way to finish this one.

Slocum turned away and barked at the officers still milling around the scene. "Move on, boys. We're done."

He turned and offered a final suggestion. "Get in your car, Mr. Aaron, and drive away; the further the better. And if we ever see either of you again, you can rest assured that meeting won't have a happy ending."

"Oh, and," Slocum added. They both turned on a dime from either side of the vehicle to hear his parting sentiment. "Happy Birthday, Priscilla."

The words made no sense at all to Jeff. He'd known Cricket for over a year, and the topic of her real first name had never come up.

"*Priscilla?*" Jeff mouthed over the top of the cab, trying not to laugh or even smile in the presence of the police.

"Shut the fuck up," she sneered, opening the door.

"Priscilla," he said once more to himself as he gathered the emptied contents of his pack from the back of the truck and placed them inside.

Jeff collapsed behind the wheel as Slocum and his boys merged into traffic. At that moment, neither he nor Priscilla knew quite what to say.

"It's your birthday?' Jeff settled on.

"Yeah. That's part of the reason I had to go. You know, some things you just gotta do at home."

"So, what do you want for your birthday?" He asked, turning the truck's engine.

Cricket reached across him before he could engage the gears. The motion was swift and catlike. Her hand landed midway up his thigh and slid just a touch upward.

"Kiss me," she said. It was almost a question.

Jeff faltered and pretended not to have heard her. "What?" he faked.

"That was the most exciting experience I've ever had fully clothed, and I want you to kiss me." Her rock-steady, dominant voice further fueled his hesitance.

Cricket saw the look in Jeff's eyes, and she understood. It wasn't often that your best-looking friend of the opposite sex asked you flat out to plant one on her, and he was dazed.

Cricket slid closer to him and watched his blue eyes close as she drew near. They met with a friendly, confused passion, each no doubt recalling multiple instances when such a thing could have happened but never did. It was a short-lived union. Cricket withdrew her mouth and formed a lovely wide smile before Jeff even had a chance to process the exchange.

"Thank you," she whispered.

"Uh, sure," he answered, a bit pink in the cheeks. "Happy Birthday, Cricket."

"It's Priscilla, remember? But if you ever tell another living soul, I'll rip your nuts off and feed them to you," she threatened, still smiling.

"About your name, or about that kiss?"

"Yes," she clarified with a giggle. "Now take me home."

The rest of their trip was downright dull by comparison. The jumbled ramblings of a local classic rock radio station and Cricket's sparse directional commands provided most of the commentary. Thirty minutes after they'd slipped Slocum's noose, Jeff's truck pulled into the Lowe family driveway, coming to rest behind her mom's silver Mercedes-Benz. The house was large and set safely in a posh suburb of Overton.

Including their unexpected visit with the sheriff and his boys, the trip took a little over 2 hours. In time and distance, they weren't worlds away from Cornwall Street. But everything seemed foreign and unbalanced to Jeff.

Somewhere along the way, without Jeff even noticing, Cricket managed to rescue the luckiest plastic bag on the planet. The engine idled, and they shared another silence before she turned to go.

"You'll be alright tonight?"

"Yeah, fine. I'm gonna crash with Vince out in Jasper. It's been a while since I've been out this way. It's not far, and I could use a break from the usual scenery."

"That's cool," she said, flipping the wad of rolled-up plastic into his lap.

"No thanks. I think I just quit."

"Whatever," she replied, dismissing his claim. "But I don't want it either. Give it to Andy. But if you dare tell him where that's been, I'll..."

"Feed me my own testicles?" Jeff guessed.

"Worse."

Gathering her bag, she turned once more to face her friend.

"I love you, Jeff," she said with sweet sadness. It was the most serious thing he'd ever heard her say. She planted another light peck on his lips and slipped out the door.

Jeff sat behind the wheel, trying to comprehend the past few hours. He was tired and confused but not in jail, which he decided was a pretty good trade. He watched her walk up the drive and smiled.

"I'll be back in the morning. See you then," he called through the open window.

Cricket was most of the way up the drive. She was still within earshot but never looked back. Jeff ran his sweaty hands through his hair, put the truck in reverse, and drove away.

19

The front door flew open. Even when Andy was just careless, that poor adjacent wall still suffered. But when he was angry, it took a real beating.

Andy's tantrums had grown more frequent during his recent job search, and he sadistically preferred to share them with an audience. His entrance this morning was plenty loud but also premature. Jeff wasn't back from Overton, and Ellen was still fast asleep.

Unacceptable, he thought. Anger of this magnitude deserved to be witnessed. Several items suddenly found themselves dangerously in his path. Sadly, Ellen knew the score before even opening her bedroom door and facing the storm.

Andy's suit coat lay crumpled on the floor as she entered the living room. Following the sound of crashing cabinet doors and clinking ice cubes, Ellen turned the corner. The freezer door was open, obscuring his top half from her view, but she could tell he was still wearing a tie. She approached with caution.

A second glance revealed the brown paper bag clutched in his right hand; vodka for sure. Apparently, the interview had not gone well.

"Andy?" she said softly as the freezer door swung away from her and bumped shut.

"What?" he asked, not looking at her. He'd meant to snarl but was deflated and couldn't muster the energy.

Andy's eyes were large and wounded, deeper and shinier than usual. He was either remarkably sober or about to break down and cry. His thick dark hair, often held at bay by a dollop of styling gel, now towered disheveled over his furrowed brow as if he'd repeatedly run his angry hands through it.

She watched silently as her roommate poured three fingers of vodka into a tall glass and then searched the refrigerator for a mixer.

"Breakfast?" he asked, lifting the bottle at her.

"No thanks. Do you wanna talk?"

"What the fuck is there to talk about? It's over. I failed, and it's over. I'm outta here."

"Relax. It can't be that bad."

"No, it *is*. I might as well call my parents right now and tell them to get the fucking basement ready."

She watched as he tried to swallow his failure along with the alcohol. Ellen could tell tears were hiding just below the surface, but he was determined not to set them free.

Her roommates may have considered her one of the boys, but Ellen's maternal instincts were strong, and they'd gotten an earnest workout from living with these two. She drew nearer and wrapped her strong arms around him, pressing a kiss gently against his freshly shaven cheek.

"I'm really sorry. I still love you."

She held him and waited, feeling out the pause in his angst. She knew he was hurt, his mind racing a mile a minute processing options and obstacles.

"I love you too, El." He'd said it a thousand times before, in various states of mind, but now, as they hugged in the middle of their nasty kitchen, it felt heavier and more real.

"Enough mush," Ellen said, releasing her embrace and heading straight for the Den. "Come in here and talk to me."

She was already cuddled up on the couch by the time he joined her. Andy eased into the overstuffed rocker across the table and dug for his cigarettes. Breaking his own rule, he lit a pre-meal smoke before extending the pack to Ellen.

"Cancer?"

"Please," she said, not even realizing he'd transferred enough of his anxiety to jump-start her subconsciously tugging and twirling her hair.

Andy grabbed the remote control and summoned the warm, consoling glow of television. It didn't take him long to find what he was looking for. Talk shows, goddammit-that was the answer. Any unemployed person worth their salt knew that.

Talk shows had one major redeeming quality as far as Andy was concerned. They were entertaining, for sure, but that was just gravy. The real meat was in the power of relative superiority. Daytime talk shows offered those who watched them one gigantic comforting truth – *my life might suck, but at least I'm not this asshole on TV*.

Yep. *It could always be worse*, he'd thought on many occasions, and now it was worth repeating. *I AM unemployed and worthless, but I COULD be bitching about being unemployed and worthless on national television.*

The *Mack Riley Show* was Andy's favorite. Nasty, irreverent, and juvenile, it was an ideal backdrop for Andy to share the details of his brutal morning. He forced himself to breathe and to take smaller sips of his disappearing cocktail. "I never saw it coming, El."

20

A hundred miles away, things weren't going any better. Jeff told Cricket he wanted to pick her up as early as possible the following day so he could get back to Bradford. Cricket had never been terribly connected to the concept of time, and Jeff assumed that no matter when he pulled up to the Lowes' house, she'd probably be ready to leave within five minutes.

The late morning air was cooler than usual and very pleasant. The sky was cloudless, and the sun shone bright enough to hurt his eyes. Grateful for sunglasses, Jeff guided the truck along the sharp curve leading back to Cricket's parents' place. A dull ache rose in his stomach as he approached a four-way stop. A black and white Buxton County sheriff's car sat directly across the intersection. While he couldn't think of a single illegal thing he had done since waking up, Jeff was still understandably gun-shy from yesterday's adventure. Then he remembered the small sack of marijuana Cricket had left with him, and minor discomfort became major panic.

Jeff looked both ways twice and waited for the cop to pull through, even though he clearly had the right of way. He rolled nervously past the officer, who took no notice of him at all.

A quarter of a mile down the road, Jeff turned left onto Crescent Circle. Cricket's parents' house was the ninth on the right, as she'd reminded him. Simple enough instructions, except for one thing; as soon as Jeff turned onto Crescent, what he saw made him immediately lose count. The gathering was modest compared to yesterday but no less conspicuous. Down the street, Jeff saw two more police cars, and they were not alone. The obnoxious orange and white top of a county hospital ambulance loomed over the blue bulbs of the cruisers. Jeff instinctively knew he could stop counting houses. The low rumbling in his stomach was now a burning stab bordering on nausea.

He inched toward the house until he reached the perimeter of the response vehicles, then pulled to the curb and cut the engine. It was almost noon on a Monday. Most of their neighbors' homes lay quiet and empty. The Lowes' driveway was filled with cars and activity. Mrs. Lowe's silver Mercedes sat next to her husband's red Audi A8, just as they were when Jeff had dropped Cricket off the night before.

Jeff had never met either of her parents. But he'd heard Cricket bitch about them often enough to make it unnecessary. He couldn't assume they were bad people or even bad parents, but according to Cricket, there was no shortage of screaming, fighting, and drama at home.

Everyone yelled at everyone else. Cricket's mom and dad both yelled at her until she left, and then they kept yelling at each other. Jeff felt terrible for her. He tried to empathize with her situation, but he simply couldn't imagine living in a family where no one seemed to like anyone else. He was one of the few people he knew whose birth parents were still happily married.

Jeff moved closer, walking along the driver's side of the ambulance until nearly colliding with a young EMS technician rounding the front of the vehicle with more speed than focus.

"'Scuse me," said the tech, too casually.

"Sorry." Jeff was still trying to gauge the situation. He noticed the tech was not much older than him.

"What happened in there?" asked Jeff, expecting no answer.

"Just doing our jobs."

Jeff couldn't decide if he was being cavalier or intentionally vague. In either case, the tech's nonchalance suggested to Jeff he might have the berth for a follow-up question.

"Some sort of accident?" Jeff quizzed as the young EMT climbed into the driver's seat.

"No. I'm pretty sure not," the tech said with certainty. It was already more information than a seasoned or sensitive pro would have offered, but he didn't stop there.

He grabbed the door frame by the bottom of the opened window and pulled it to, now sitting a foot taller than Jeff.

"It's a shame, too," the tech added for no reason. "Beautiful young girl."

Jeff was thankful not to have been looking him in the eyes as he heard those words. He was standing so close he could feel the ambulance's hefty engine roar to life. Seconds later, the tech put it into drive and rolled away. None of his lights were flashing.

Realizing he was now standing conspicuously alone in front of what could be a crime scene—one to which he could in some twisted way be connected if the right people asked the right questions, Jeff turned and shuffled back to his truck. He slumped low behind the wheel, almost hiding beneath the dashboard. Jeff needed to believe that the officers from the two empty cruisers in the Lowes' driveway had never seen him. More specifically, he needed to believe that the chance of him answering any questions about whatever the fuck happened in that house was absolutely zero. He raised his head like a prairie dog over the dash and watched the still, empty street before him. Sad, angry tears welled in his eyes, but he managed to get the truck into gear and pull away before losing it altogether. The tech had given him all the information he needed to know she would not be joining him.

* * *

Ninety miles of open road was the best and worst thing Jeff could have hoped for. No co-pilot, no traffic; just caffeine, nicotine, music, and time. Whether he wanted it or not, he had at least an hour of soul-crushing solitude in front of him. Try as he might to vanquish them, thoughts of Cricket invaded his weary head as the tears kept coming.

He wasn't even sure why he was crying. They hadn't been super close, but that didn't matter; death is death. He was sad, but more than anything, he was mad, furious, really. Mad at her for doing it and madder still for involving him. Mad at himself for not seeing it or being able to stop it. There was a time, not long ago, when he'd been clearer and more focused that something like this would not have gotten past him. Jeff found his anger drifting toward Andy, but that seemed misplaced, at least partly. Those frustrations were specific and recent. No, if he was being honest, Jeff's own choices had put him on this road.

He filled his lungs to capacity and unleashed a series of primal screams into the rushing wind as he floored the accelerator.

21

"So, I'm sitting in this guy's office, right?" Andy started again. "And I figure, no big deal, right? I've met him before; it's cool, no pressure. We talked for about ten minutes, about nothing really, which only made me feel more comfortable, 'cause I can talk about nothing *forever*, you know?"

"Oh, I know," she said.

"So, we're talking, right? And from out of nowhere, he says I need to meet with another guy. Well not just another guy; the vice president of the place. 'No problem.' I said, 'I'd love to meet him.' Well, that's where the fucking bottom fell out." Andy paused for a deep breath and another long sip of breakfast.

"So, what happened?" Ellen asked, for what seemed the eleventh time already.

"I fucked it up big time." The volume of Andy's voice grew along with his frustration. "I walked in there ready to tell this guy every reason why I'm smart enough and creative enough to sell every flavor of shit they've got. And then I blew it!"

"He starts asking me all these personal questions. Apparently, he was more interested in my marital status and long-term economic plans than seeing my work."

"He asked if you were married? I didn't think they were even allowed to do that."

"Yeah. I don't know. But I had no idea what to tell him or what he wanted to hear, so I told him that you and I are engaged."

"You what!?"

"I know. How stupid is that?"

"Pretty fuckin' stupid," she agreed. "And honestly, it's a little sweet, but as proposals go, it kinda sucks."

"Ha!" he allowed himself a small smile. "Don't get me wrong, El. I think you'd make a great wife, but we both know that would end with one of us being dead, right?"

"Yeah," she teased. "And people would *really* miss you, so let's not."

They both laughed as Andy crushed the last of his Winston in the crystal ashtray between them.

"And it got worse from there. That one question threw me off so hard, I stuttered and staggered through the whole rest of the interview. To be honest, I don't even remember what else I told them."

"But just because you got a little flustered, you think that's enough to keep them from hiring you?"

"Oh, you didn't see it, El. I looked like an idiot. Nobody wants a guy who can't even tell you if he's married or not to write ads with million-dollar price tags."

"Big deal," she insisted. "So, you don't get this one. That means your life is over? Just go out and find another place to work. It's not like you have to leave town, Andy."

"That's what nobody understands. For as long as I can remember, I've only wanted to do one thing—write. My whole life, people have told me it's the one thing I should be doing. And I happen to agree. Except now, when it really counts, I can't get anyone to *pay* me to do it. I came here to get my degree so I could do what I wanted, and if I can't find that job here in Bradford, then yes, I have to leave." He was near the bottom of his screwdriver and ready for another round.

"But there's got to be somebody else in town you can write for."

"You don't get it. I don't want to work for just anybody. Work isn't fun enough to do for just anyone, especially creative work. I need a place that makes me excited about *getting* to go to work, not *having* to go. Otherwise, what's the fucking point? This was probably the one place in this whole shitty little town that was even close to that for me."

"You love this shitty little town, and you know it." she said, running low on advice and empathy. "So, what are you going to do?"

"Well, right now, I'm gonna pour myself another drink, watch the rest of Mack Riley, and wait for Jeff to get back from kissing Cricket's sweet ass."

Ellen wasn't sure there was anything left for her to say as he turned towards the television and raised the volume.

* * *

"And so, things got worse after he left and took your son?" Mack asked the middle-aged woman who was obviously wearing a wig. Talk about rhetorical questions. Of course, it had gotten worse, or she wouldn't be crying her eyes out on television.

"A lot worse," she blubbered. "I started drinking; well, drinking more. And it really didn't help anything. I know that now."

"She must have been doing it wrong," Andy said, rising to fix the second course of his liquid brunch. "You want one?"

"Not yet. Too early for me." Ellen replied.

"So, what's this one about?" he asked from the kitchen.

"I think it's a bunch of folks bitching about how good their lives used to be and how terrible they are now. Sound familiar?"

"Welcome back," Mack Riley said. "Today, we're joined by some real heroes; people living true nightmares; clutching desperately to the very edge of sanity and somehow finding the will to go on." The hyperbole was ridiculous and masterful.

"Wow. That's dramatic, even for him," said Andy, after downing a mouthful of Orange Juice Plus.

"I don't know. Some of these people are really fucked up. There's this one lady who..., wait, yeah her, listen."

"Eight months?" Mack asked the young lady.

"Yes sir," she answered the smug British host, who was over twice her age.

"You really stayed in your house for eight whole months?"

"Yes."

"Why?"

"It all got to be way too much for me." Small tears began to break from her eyelids as she spoke. "Last year was the worst year of my life. My brother got killed in a factory accident. I quit working, going to school, or spending time with my boyfriend. He got impatient, waiting for me to just 'get over it' and started cheating on me. Then he just left. Then, a drunk son-of-a-bitch with no insurance totaled my car, giving me back problems that the doctor said might never go away. Oh, and my dog Mickey died of cancer." She was really turning it on now as tears streamed down her flushed cheeks.

"Bullshit!" blurted Ellen, now thoroughly sucked in. "No way all that shit happens to one person in a year. No wonder she locked herself in the house. I would, too."

"I just kept thinking it couldn't possibly get any worse. If I just stayed in the house and didn't answer the phone or the door, nothing else could get to me. I got paranoid and withdrew. I just lost faith in general."

"The world can be very cruel." Mack comforted his guest, milking her angst for every rating point it was worth. "I'm amazed you could be here today." The empty congratulations came complete with the obligatory box of tissues, which never seemed too far away.

"Ding! Ding! Oh yeah, we've got a winner!" Andy shouted. "This bitch is *way* more fucked up than I am."

"I don't know, Andy. I think I heard her say she had a job," Ellen teased.

"It got to the point where I couldn't even get up in the morning. I definitely hit rock bottom, and I had to get help." Oh yeah, she was playing it just how the network boys loved it – pathetic but with a glimmer of hope.

"Tell us what happened," Riley urged.

"I didn't see how bad it had gotten. Then, one day, I realized I was sitting around the house, drinking boxed wine and eating ginger snaps. I gained 55 pounds in a year and even stopped bathing regularly." She left a beautifully pregnant pause, allowing the studio audience to paint their own vivid pictures.

"I looked at myself in the mirror and all I saw was this disgusting, fat, drunk shell of a woman who couldn't think of a reason not to drive off the nearest bridge."

"Cause you didn't have a car after that fucker wrecked it!" Andy said smugly.

"You heartless bastard," Ellen accused. "Like you'd be turning cartwheels if all that shit happened to you."

"No. But it didn't happen to me. I just can't get a job."

"Correction. You *won't* get a job," Even before she'd finished the sentence, she regretted it.

"Fuck you, Ellen!" he said with real venom. "What do you know? You dropped out to be a fucking bartender."

"No," Ellen corrected. She was legitimately offended. "More like I went out and found a way to keep living after my parents' money ran out. That's something *you* don't know shit about. So... Fuck you, too! It's hard to feel sorry for someone so good at feeling sorry for their self."

And there it was; the ugly truth. They'd all gotten pretty good at lobbing hand grenades of good-natured bullshit at each other, but they usually knew where to draw the line. Ellen had loaded up a barrel full of absolute, honest-to-God truth and shot Andy right in the face.

"That's what you think of me? Just because I can't make myself work some bullshit, go-nowhere job that means nothing to me? I *do* want more than that, and you should too. You're so smart and talented, and you're rotting away just like I would if I stayed here. Bradford sucks like that. Fuck Bradford."

Ellen stared at him, conflicted. She knew he was only being so mean because he was wounded. But she also knew deep down he might be right about her, which hurt even worse. Still, telling Andy how she saw his situation wasn't exactly the cruelest thing she could have done.

Quiet invaded the Den as they both sucked hard on cigarettes. Neither looked at the other as they waited for the tension to thin. They weren't waiting long when the unmistakable sound of the front door smashing into that poor wall broke the silence.

"Good. They're back," Andy declared, sulking as if Jeff was going to waltz in and start throwing solace at him.

* * *

Somewhere between Overton and Bradford, the blood in Jeff's body had managed to quit flowing to his face, which was now pale and drawn. The beads of sweat dripping from his brow didn't help either. Flying on autopilot, Jeff headed for the Den.

"Jesus!" said Ellen as he broke the threshold.

"You look like french-fried shit," Andy added.

"Didn't get any sleep last night?" Ellen asked with thinly veiled innuendo as she moved her bare legs off the couch to make room for him. He remained standing.

Jeff looked weak and dazed. "I think I might be sick."

"Well don't give it to me. I've had a bad enough day already," said Andy, trying to pull focus back to his own suffering.

"Trust me." said Jeff. "I've got you beat."

"Aw, poor you," Andy whined, eager to start another fire. "You had to miss cleaning the house so you could go out of town with Her Majesty."

"Not now, man." The last thing Jeff wanted right then was to argue with him.

"You're just pissed because she still won't give you any," Andy said with jealousy so thick he may as well have been neon green.

"Fuck you, Andy!" Jeff yelled. He was going to quit there, but the juvenile smirk on his roommate's face was just enough to drive him over the edge. "Cricket's dead, you self-absorbed son-of-a-bitch!"

He didn't even wait to watch it register on their faces before burying his head and starting to cry. He'd only managed a few quiet sobs when Ellen stepped in. She rose to comfort him, but not before shooting serious eye-daggers at her other roommate. She was used to being the buffer between them when it got testy, but this was a completely different level.

"I … uh… What? I…. I'm sorry, man," Andy mumbled. "What the fuck?"

"I don't know," Jeff said quietly, staring at the floor. "She just gave up. She did the one thing you can never do. She gave up. And worst of all, she had me drive 200 miles, just so she could shove that shit in her parents' faces. I didn't see it, but she knew yesterday when she came over here, she was never coming back."

"Oh my God." Andy said. "I'm so sorry." Every bit of his righteous indignation was gone.

Jeff was distant, but not so much that the rare apology from Andy Maxwell failed to register. He looked at his roommate with swollen, surprised eyes and said nothing. He had no interest in sharing the few details he knew from this morning, and he sure as hell wasn't up for sharing their adventure on the side of I-26 just yet. For the moment, there was nothing left to say.

"Well, we've definitely hit our quota for bullshit today," Ellen announced. "You boys need a reset."

"Jeff," she said quietly, wrapping her arm around his shoulder and pulling him close. "If I promise you're gonna like it, are you up for a little field trip?" she asked.

"I don't know," he said. "Anywhere is probably better than here right now. But I gotta take a shower or at least change clothes," he said, already on his way to his room.

"That sounds good," Andy agreed, splitting off to slip out of the rest of his suit.

Ellen stood alone in the small square hallway between the Den and her bedroom. From there, she could hear both her roommates rumbling in their respective corners. It wasn't always easy living between them – literally and figuratively – but it was a place she felt comfortable, secure even. More than anywhere else, it felt like home, a place worth protecting and holding together. And she did. In fact, Ellen excelled at keeping the peace, even if her methods were a bit unorthodox.

Closing her bedroom door, she pulled off her grungy t-shirt. She applied fresh deodorant and donned a racy, luminescent silver rayon disco top with three-quarter-length sleeves and ambitious lapels. Next to her black denim jeans, the flashy silver seemed to explode. Satisfied with the transformation, she was only slightly bothered that she had yet to bathe for the day.

She walked toward the front of the house with the confidence of a girl who knew she was the prettiest thing in the room. Jeff sat crumpled on the ratty couch. She approached with care, placing herself gently beside him and slipping an arm around his shoulder. He twitched by reflex at her touch but then fell into her. His mop of long brown hair fell across her lap.

"Do you want to talk about it?" she asked, stroking the locks away from his face.

"I don't know," he said. "It's not like we were even close friends."

"I get the feeling she didn't have many of those," Ellen suggested.

"But she knew I would take her home, no questions asked."

"Oh, Jeff. You had no idea. You couldn't have known."

"I know. And I know I'm not responsible for her choices either. But it still fuckin' sucks."

"You want to stay home?" she asked.

"No. I need a distraction."

"Perfect. I can do that," Ellen assured. She lifted his head and kissed it before popping off the couch. Only then did he notice her attire.

"Geez. It's a little early for clubbing."

"Depends," she said with a grin.

"What about Andy?" Jeff asked. "What's he all pissed about?"

"Bombed his interview."

"Shit. That sucks… for all of us."

"And now this with Cricket. That's not going to help either." Ellen was considering whether the plan in her head was really the best idea.

"Why?" Jeff asked. "He knew her even less. He just wanted her, but more like an object than a person. For him, it's probably like losing his favorite poster or something. I think he just liked looking at her."

"OK. I'm ready," Andy called from the kitchen.

"Wow!" He marveled as he entered the front room. "That's pretty hot, El." Placing a fresh pack of Winstons in the breast pocket of his blue short-sleeved shirt, part of him wished he had not changed after all. "Suddenly, I feel underdressed."

"You'll be fine where we're going."

Ellen grabbed her sunglasses and made for the door. The boys filed in behind, entirely at her mercy.

* * *

Quenton Murphy stood at the base of their shared driveway, retrieving the empty trash cans from the curb.

"Morning, Murphy," said Jeff.

"Afternoon," he corrected, exhaling a blast of menthol smoke. "You look nice today, Ellen."

"Thanks," she replied. Usually, a girl of Ellen's age would be rightly repulsed by such attention from a man as old as Quenton, but this felt good. In fact, now that she thought about it, in the last five minutes, she'd been complimented on her appearance by three very different men. She had no reason to suspect any of their motives. In fact, it made her wonder if she might want to spend an extra few minutes in her closet occasionally.

"Where are you off to all slicked up?" their neighbor asked.

"We don't know," Jeff admitted, opening the Chevette's passenger door and climbing into the back seat.

"She won't tell us," Andy added, folding back the seat and jumping in shotgun.

"Sounds like fun."

"You have no idea," Ellen said with a wicked grin.

Quenton stood there smoking and smiling as they backed out of the short driveway and headed down Cornwall's gradual southern slope.

"So, what's the big mystery, El?" Andy asked.

She gave them nothing, not a word or a glance. The boys took the hint and kept silent as Ellen guided the car left onto Peters Street. Four blocks down on the right, she pulled to the curb and cut the engine.

"Excuse me?" Jeff asked from the back seat. "You got all jazzed up to come to Dave and Jimmy's?"

She was already out of the car and lighting a Marlboro on the side of the road.

"Chill," she demanded, "it's just a pit stop." Ellen had a plan, and it wasn't up for discussion. She was already halfway up the yard.

22

People came to see Oklahoma Dave and Jimmy the Fish for one reason. They were drug dealers. Most visitors arrived under pretense. They didn't stay long, and they rarely left empty-handed.

Bradford was like most places; if you looked for something long enough, you would find it. Dave and Jimmy made that easy, especially if you were a 'friend.' However, in certain businesses, it can be hard to distinguish those from the people who just want something you have. The residents of Cornwall Street were semi-regulars in Jimmy and Dave's circle, even if the truth stopped somewhere short of genuine friendship.

Andy shrugged at Jeff in silent confusion as they started up the lawn. Ellen was already knocking on the front door. Its two rectangular windows were masked by an American flag. As the boys reached the porch, the door swung open. Jimmy stood shirtless, shielding his squinty, red eyes from the sun.

"Right on," he said, opening the door wider. It was early afternoon, but the house was midnight dark. Every window was covered with something–drapes, blankets, flags, whatever–as long as it looked cool and kept out the light and the curious.

"Nice top," Jimmy told Ellen, his tone just shy of lecherous.

"Thanks," she answered, now beginning to question the extra attention her wardrobe was getting.

Jimmy liked her. Unfortunately for him, he couldn't have been further from her type. She was brighter by light years than the stable of tragically attractive *ladies* he seemed to wake up next to.

"Dave's around here someplace," Jimmy said, speaking to all of them but addressing her. Following him inside, they closed the front door, sealing out the only light in the room. The blare of an acoustic guitar being strummed with more confidence than proficiency came from the back of the house. The group rounded the corner, nearly tripping over Dave, who sat in the open doorway, eyes closed, still plucking away. A thick stream of smoke rolled over and through the brim of his straw hat. It smelled a thousand times sweeter than Marlboro country and was decidedly narcotic.

"Hey, kids." Dave greeted. "Long time, no see." He said that with great regularity, even though he saw most people either quite often or not at all. He reached up to shake Jeff's hand. Informal greetings made their way around the circle in the dark hallway. Dave rose and moved toward the back of the house. As Jeff and Andy fell in line, Jimmy tapped Ellen on the shoulder and ushered her in the other direction.

"What are you guys looking for today?"

"Just the usual," she replied.

"Cool. But, come check this out," Jimmy offered, casually taking her arm.

* * *

As Dave perused the refrigerator, his visitors stood in the kitchen, awkwardly contemplating the many glass aquariums scattered throughout the house. The tank that caught Andy's attention was home to several small saltwater eels.

"When did you get these?" he asked.

"They're not mine," Dave said. "I think Jimmy put 'em in last week."

"I meant *you* in general," Andy clarified.

"I know. I just like to be on record that none of these fuckers are mine."

"I dunno. Having eels in your kitchen is kinda cool, man." Jeff offered.

"I guess," said Dave. "Jimmy wanted to put a porcupine puffer in there, but apparently, blowfish get big and would outgrow this place."

He pulled a cold six-pack from the fridge, walked into the front room, and began fumbling with remote controls. He offered them beers and turned again to address the machines. The house may have been a dump, but clearly, business was good. Top-of-the-line audio and video equipment filled their front room. Their setup put Cornwall's to shame, but the comparison was hardly fair.

* * *

"Belly up," Jimmy pulled the chair out from under his desk for Ellen.

He reached over her shoulder, opened the drawer and retrieved a locked, wooden box. A key chain landed on the desk with a slight bang and jingle. A one-inch-tall plastic Godzilla figurine on one end was connected to an oddly shaped key on the other. She smiled nervously, pulling a strand of long brown hair from behind her ear and beginning to twist.

"Open it," he said, now also smiling. He walked across the room and pulled on a shirt as she lifted the lid and sat back.

"Is that what I think it is?" Ellen asked, the lock of hair wrapping ever tighter around her finger.

Jimmy laughed, reveling in the innocence of someone who couldn't positively identify cocaine.

"Depends on what you think it is."

"Very funny," she said, studying the small glass vial inside the box. "I know it's coke, Jimmy. It's just not something I see every day."

"Huh. I don't remember what that's like," he said honestly. "Do you have any smokes?"

She gave him a Marlboro and held up her lighter. Taking her hand in both of his, Jimmy bowed towards the flame.

"I'm a bartender in a shitty college town, Jimmy," she said. "I can't afford coke. And besides, even if I could, I don't think I'd really be into it."

"I don't recall asking if you wanted to buy any," he clarified. He reached over her shoulder again to grab the box and then around her to snag the first CD case he could reach. He placed it ceremoniously in front of them, unscrewing the vial and spilling a small pile of white powder atop Black Sabbath's *We Sold Our Souls for Rock & Roll.*

"Do you have a dollar?" he asked.

"Wow, that's pretty cheap coke," she joked.

"No. For a straw, dummy." He took a small red rubber band off the desktop and snapped it at her.

She reached into her pocket and pulled out a crisp ten. "You got change?"

The Fish unsheathed a razor blade and chopped the tiny crystals into an even-finer powder. Picking up the rubber band, Ellen wrapped it around the rolled-up Hamilton a few times until it held tight. She placed the straw on the desk and sat back in her chair, unsure what to do next.

"I don't believe you've never done this before."

"I always figured I never would, unless it was like some perfect situation."

"What? Like if you were trapped on a desert island with Hunter Thompson or something?"

"Who's that?" Ellen asked seriously.

"Never mind," he replied. The Fish bent low across the desk and inhaled the fattest of the six white lines he'd drawn on the CD cover.

He was amused to think he could teach her a few things. Whether or not those things were in her best interest never crossed his mind.

Jimmy raised his head from the desk and sniffed heavily, wasting nothing. Ellen gave him a look of strange curiosity as he handed her the straw.

* * *

"Did you hear what went down at The Cactus?" Andy asked Dave as the bong drifted from their host's lips to Jeff's waiting hands. Before Dave could even answer, Andy was marching on. "Cold Gin nearly blew the bitch up the other night."

"Yeah, and…" Jeff added, "there are cops all over that place, asking questions about some girl that disappeared. I think her name is Margo."

"I saw her picture in the paper," said Dave. "She was cute. But who the hell names their kid Margo? That might be a good band name, but…"

"But there's a twenty-five-thousand-dollar reward for whoever finds her," Andy asserted.

"You mean for whoever finds who killed her," Dave corrected.

"Why do you say that?" Andy asked.

"I don't know. People go missing all the time. But Barbie-pretty coeds from nice neighborhoods? What's someone like that running away from? When people like her go missing, it's usually 'cause somebody took 'em."

Jeff found Dave's assessment callous and disturbing. Thoughts of Cricket invaded his head, and he almost said something. But he knew that conversation was more trouble than it was worth.

"Or maybe she pissed off the wrong people or owed somebody a lot of money," Andy suggested.

"Shit. If that's all it takes to get whacked, how come you're still around?" joked Dave.

Jeff only half heard it. His mind was busy replaying Dave's words. It occurred to him that, aside from Jimmy and Dave themselves, there were few people in a town this size to whom it might be dangerous to owe that kind of money. It was unsettling to consider that if Dave was right, Margo Hammond might have spent her last moments on Earth at the mercy of someone not too different from Dave himself. Jeff was also smart enough to realize that Jimmy and Dave probably knew everybody else around Bradford who was even just a little bit like them.

Jeff tried to chalk all this paranoia up to a combination of good drugs and a very bad day. But his brain was intent on drilling the rabbit hole ever deeper. He found himself contemplating his own recent choices. Sure, he dabbled in some debauchery in the free time between his responsibilities–they all did. But these guys were in a different league. He wasn't afraid, but suddenly, all those 'slippery slope' cautions from his parents and mentors about the dangers of drugs seemed to ring in his head. He wondered how far up or down the slope he and his roommates were from these guys and, more importantly, whether that distance was shrinking.

As he sat there, trying his best to enjoy their superb weed, Jeff was ninety-nine percent sure Dave and Jimmy had nothing to do with the mysterious disappearance of Margo Hammond. But the other one percent was driving the bus right now and asking plenty of questions along the way, one of which was: *Where the hell is Ellen?*

* * *

"I don't know," Ellen hesitated as Jimmy held the rolled-up bill out to her. A big, easy smile had settled across his face.

"What's a good reason not to?" Jimmy asked, skipping right over devil's advocate and playing the part of Lucifer himself. He lowered his head and took a second, smaller line of powder.

"I don't know," she repeated. "It seems like there's a big difference between something that grows out of the ground naturally, that really just chills you out, and something some asshole cuts with baby laxative in his basement that eats all of your money and makes you super paranoid."

"Wow. You make it sound so bad," Jimmy said as he wiped the white residue from the stubble under his nose.

"OK, so I may be a little scared."

"Do you really think I would do something to hurt you?" Jimmy asked, taking her hand.

She recognized the line as something cheesy, slimeball bastards said to secure trust they didn't deserve; but she could also sense he legitimately meant her no harm.

A million thoughts raced through her brain. The week had been long, draining, and full of drama, but she wasn't sure it was enough to justify climbing another rung on the drug ladder. Then she remembered why they had come to Peters Street in the first place and where they were going when they left.

She laid her burning cigarette in the ashtray and gathered the hair away from her face. Taking the straw in her hand, she clamped shut one nostril, lowered her head to the tray, and inhaled much harder than necessary.

"Whoa!" It was improbable she would be feeling the rush yet, but her brain didn't know any better.

The line she'd inhaled was pretty fat, and at least a quarter still lay on the plastic CD cover. Jimmy picked up a razor blade and began chopping at what was left.

"Clean your plate, girl," he grinned with sly satisfaction.

"Just a second." She squirmed a little in the chair, unsure of her choice, but now in midstream. "It tastes terrible."

"You kinda get used to it."

"Fuck it," she said, puffing again on her Marlboro. "If you're gonna do something, do it. Right?" She bent again to the tray and deposited the bill squarely in her other nostril. The powder shot up her nose as she swept the tray.

"Bravo," he offered. Jimmy was lying on the double bed, smiling as he locked his hands behind his head.

Ellen rocked back and forth in the wooden chair. Nervous energy pulsed through her body. Lightning storms clicked in her head. Under normal circumstances, her brain was a machine of extreme logic. She was used to thoroughly examining and resolving one thought before moving on to the next. But now, a thousand people and places cruised through her mind, each demanding a sliver of her attention. As she struggled to catch any of them, Ellen had a moment of clarity. She recalled Andy's description of precisely the same feeling—confusion and a longing to concentrate on a single thing. She remembered him saying it was how he felt most of the time. *No, that's not right,* she thought. He said it was the way he felt when he was *sober*, which was considerably less than most of the time. She wondered what it must be like to approach drugs as a way of escaping the very feeling she found herself engulfed in now. The thought of living like that was sad. But, like all the other ideas flying around her brain just then, it stayed for only a moment and was gone.

"Goddamn, you look good in that top," Jimmy said.

"What?" she asked. Ellen again became aware of his presence and that he was approaching.

"I said, you look hot today. I mean, hotter than usual," he elaborated, now standing directly in front of her.

"Jesus. I wish people would stop saying that. I think I liked it better when nobody noticed me."

"That's bullshit," Jimmy said. "Everybody wants to be noticed. I notice you all the time. It's just you look *extra* hot today."

Before Ellen could fully process the situation, Jimmy dropped to one knee and came to rest between her slightly open legs. Bracing his forearm along the top of her thigh, he extended a hand until it met the back of her neck. He advanced. His large, glassy pupils disappeared as he closed his eyes and kissed her full-on. Her heart pounded with a mixture of narcotics and surprise, and any sort of normal response failed her.

His lips were strangely soft and warm, much gentler than she imagined he might be. Jimmy's mouth trailed slowly from the base of her neck, finding her chin and then her flushed cheek. He placed a light kiss on her nose before advancing again. Sheer confusion left Ellen's mouth slightly agape, and Jimmy accepted the unintended invitation.

The touch of Jimmy's tongue snapped her focus back with alarming speed. The moment the wet intruder crept between Ellen's teeth; Jimmy went reeling backward onto the floor from the force of her thrusting arms. Before his ass even hit the carpet, she was standing and gathering her smokes and lighter from the desk.

"Sorry," Jimmy said sincerely. Ellen looked down at him as he leaned on one elbow, making no attempt to rise.

"Don't get me wrong," she said. "That was interesting, but that's never gonna happen again. Thanks for the high…I think. We gotta go."

Moving through the kitchen, she passed various fish and reptiles in their glass houses along the way. Nearing the front room, she heard laughter and could already smell the dope smoke.

"Where ya been, Ellie?" Andy asked.

"Talking to Jimmy. Let's go," she demanded.

"What's your rush?" Dave asked, reaching for the bong again. "Take a toke for the road."

"I think not," she said and repeated her command. "Let's go."

Ellen was hardly ever adamant about anything, and the boys knew it was best to take her seriously when she was. Rising to leave, they both gave Dave a quick handshake and thanked him for the buzz. Ellen was already out the door.

"Hey, Maxwell," Jimmy called out from the porch as they left, "I saw the paper today. You might want to pick one up." He laughed, closing the door and returning to the darkness inside.

Sweeping her hair from her face, she opened Chet's door and got in. Before she could reach across and grab the passenger side handle, Jeff pulled the other door open and folded the seat forward for Andy.

"I got shotgun," he explained, smiling and waiting for his friend to climb in.

"What's with you?" Andy asked from behind her as she made an immediate and awkward U-turn in the middle of the street.

"Nothin'," she said, with too much energy. "We just got shit to do."

23

Doubling back on their route from home, Ellen drove along Creighton Avenue, parallel to Memorial Park. It was busier than usual on a Monday afternoon. The basketball courts teemed with activity in the sticky summer heat. Jeff tracked a golden retriever as its owner launched a pink Frisbee.

"What the fuck is she talking about?" Andy asked Jeff.

Even at their modest speed, the wind whipping through the open windows made it hard to hear.

"No idea. I wasn't listening."

"Never mind. I was talking to myself about something that had nothing to do with either one of you, which makes no difference anymore, because I can't even remember it, and nobody was listening anyway," Ellen blurted in one hurried breath.

"Whoa!" Jeff said. "Slow down. You okay, sis?"

She was vibrating, trying to light a Marlboro. Beads of sweat formed between her hairline and the top of her sunglasses.

"I'm fine, but it's hot as a bitch out here today, and this goddamned lighter won't work and all I really want is a cigarette. Is that too much to ask?" She reeled, tossing the spent lighter on the dashboard.

"Easy," urged Andy, offering a flame over her shoulder. "We need to get you somewhere with A/C and cold beer."

"Don't worry," she replied. "We're almost there."

Hold on. Not much farther now, she kept telling herself. *Talk less and slower. Sweat less and thank God for sunglasses.*

The boys craned their necks, scanning the streets for clues to their destination. As Chet slowed to turn onto the access road, they erupted in cheers.

"No way!" Andy crowed like a 4-year-old whose mom had just pulled the minivan into McDonald's. "Tell me you're serious!?"

"Oh, I think she's for real, man."

"I think I love you," Andy told her.

"I know," she said. "You both do."

24

The Chevette made one final turn and pulled into the parking lot of Wonderland. It was mid-afternoon on a Monday, just shy of Happy Hour, and already the lot was surprisingly full. Bradford was a small town, so when new establishments opened, it usually didn't take long for folks to notice–especially new strip clubs.

"You're 100% serious, right?" Andy asked.

"You had to know we'd get here sooner or later," she replied, taking an extra second to revel in their excitement before killing the engine and collecting her smokes from the dash. "You boys have been busy lately. Graduation. Road trips. Job interviews. You know, all that heavy, grown-up shit. Figured it was time to blow off some steam."

Another of the many things the boys loved about Ellen was her ability to appreciate adult entertainment. Unlike most girls they knew, and certainly any of their ex-girlfriends, Ellen was perfectly willing. It's not like she'd ever go alone, but she enjoyed watching the dancers, and watching her male friends take in the scene, too.

"Shit!" said Andy. "I've got zero cash."

Ellen dismissed the objection, pointing at one of the grand neon signs protruding from the building's brushed metal façade.

Bright tubes of noble gas bent and flashed before them, heralding an unbeatable collection of marketing phrases: "Live Nude Girls," "Beer & Liquor," and the three little letters that made even the most grandiose fantasies seem possible: "ATM."

"Right on!" shouted Andy.

"Right on is right!" she repeated.

Heavy techno dance beats seeped into the parking lot as they approached. Ellen pulled open the door and ushered them into the cold, smoky noise. The whole place glowed with an eerie pale blue that seemed unbalanced.

"Damn. It's like X-rated *Tron* in here." Andy said, amazed and amused.

Jeff grasped his roommate's shoulder. Leaning in, he shouted, "And loud as shit, too."

"What?"

"Never mind." Jeff said, smiling as he turned and walked deeper into the club. Standing in a room full of semi-beautiful, semi-clothed women, he could feel his frustration tangibly dissipate. The lights were low, the music was loud, and T-bone steaks were only $4.95. What was there to be mad about?

"Where's Ellen?" Andy shouted over the speaker right in front of them. Jeff pointed to the bar where their friend was collecting three cocktails.

"Goddamn. She is the best."

"Amen, brother," Jeff agreed.

The crowd was surprisingly robust for a Monday afternoon, but they still had their pick of tables. Less than a minute later, just as Ellen rejoined, a slender brunette girl made her way to the stage right above them. According to the cheesy strip club MC, her name was Tiger, assuming what appeared to be Stage Two.

Right out of the gate, Tiger eased her back into the brass pole and performed a bend so deep it stretched her skin-tight animal print bodysuit to its limits.

"Damn."

"Pace yourself," Ellen advised Jeff.

Black fishnet wound three-quarters of the way up Tiger's long legs. Her equally dark hair was absurdly over-permed. Her deep brown eyes were trained to scan the floor in a constant search for the next big spender.

Several man-boys approached Kelly on Stage One. A well-executed spin on the pole drew wide eyes and exuberant whoops from the newest contributors to her college fund.

"You know what?" Jeff said, nodding at Tiger. "Speed Kitty here isn't really doin' it for me. I think I'm gonna piss and check out the rest of the scenery. Everyone good?"

"Yep," Ellen said, looking elsewhere. Still spiraling, she was committed to the sit-and-sip strategy for as long as it took to steady the ship.

* * *

Song two faded. Tiger and Kelly basked in a moment of mediocre applause. The last number was a bit sleepy, and the tipping had suffered. Surely, the DJ would send something raucous down the pike next. His selection delighted Andy to no end.

After a few seconds of dead air, the chunky, monolithic opening riff of *Sin's A Good Man's Brother* sprung from the speakers. It was an old Grand Funk Railroad tune, but Wonderland appropriately opted for the more recent heavy-as-hell remake by dope rock lords Monster Magnet.

"No way!" Andy extended his hand to Ellen, looking for a high-five that never came.

"Screw the dancers. I might go tip the fuckin' DJ!" he said.

Fuzz-encrusted guitars bolstered Dave Wyndorf's sadistic howl, and there was no question; it was wake-up time. Tiger shot across the stage with renewed energy. In five-inch heels, she managed a near-running start and leaped high, catching the pole near the top and beginning a series of mind-boggling twists, leg flares, flips, and turns.

Ellen was mesmerized. Stunned and stoned, she managed a few words. "Wow. That fucking rocked!"

As Tiger's whirlwind came to rest on the stage floor, she and Andy both jammed their hands in their pockets, fishing for cash to reward the ambitious young girl.

* * *

Jeff stood at the bar. The service was slow, but he was content to hang back and take in the scenery. As the bartender placed three glasses before him, a playful voice crossed his ear.

"You must be thirsty," joked an elfish girl with fine golden hair that reached just past her tiny breasts.

A neat row of beverages separated Jeff from his visitor: a screwdriver for Andy, a Bloody Mary for him, and a rum and cola for Ellen.

"Hi. I'm Swan," she said. "It's a little early to be drinking that hard."

"Yeah, well..." Jeff hesitated as he completed a not-so-subtle visual inspection of the waifish blond. Of all the times to be speechless.

"Hanging out in a room full of naked strangers is like voting," he recovered, hoping she hadn't heard the joke before.

"How's that?" Swan asked.

"You should never do either one sober."

"You're cute...and funny." She tilted her head and smiled, signaling she wanted to continue the conversation. "What's your name?"

"I'm Jeff, and these are for my little party over there." He pointed at Andy and Ellen.

"Nice to meet you." It was something she said all the time but hardly ever meant. In fact, she couldn't remember the last person she was genuinely glad to meet, but she was sure it wasn't at work.

Jeff and Swan had reached the strip club "crossroads," where polite conversation gives way to contract negotiation. His options were limited but clear. "Spend time" with the lady or politely wish her a good day. He took the plunge and accepted Swan's offer of a little company, and the meter started running.

"How long have you been dancing here?" he asked.

"A couple of months."

"What did you do before that?"

"Nothing. I came to Bradford from North Carolina to study Sociology. Just started in the fall."

"How old are you?" Jeff said without thinking. He knew it was something you never asked a lady, or a stripper. It had no chance of being answered honestly and every possibility of being offensive.

"Nineteen," she said, clearly not bothered. "Well, I will be next month."

"So, what would you do if you could pick any job in the whole world?"

"Including stripping?" Swan asked for clarification.

"Sure."

"Probably stripping," she said. Jeff couldn't tell if she was joking.

With Tiger's set ending, Swan knew this was the time to make moves and close sales. Her hand landed on his shoulder. She winked a green eye at him as her fingers sifted through his hair. "Do you want that dance now?"

"Sure. But come meet my friends first."

Jeff was taking liberties with Swan's time. She had made a specific offer – "do you want this, or not?"– and he was pushing his luck by asking for another song's worth of her time. Again, Swan wasn't bothered. Aside from his friends and the frat boys, the rest of the crowd was a homely collection of middle-aged, balding businessmen. She'd heard enough of their stories to know that no matter who Jeff was taking her to meet, it was probably her best option.

"Ahh, you brought a lady."

Jeff wasn't sure if it was a question or a statement. "Actually, she brought us," he laughed.

"Even better. We love seeing girls in here. It breaks up the testosterone. And honestly, they're *way* more fun than you guys."

Jeff was a step ahead of her but stopped abruptly as they reached the table. Swan hit the brakes without spilling a single drop of her gin and tonic.

After buying drinks and tipping the bartender, Jeff had set aside two more twenty-dollar bills from his humble bankroll. He leaned in close to ensure Swan could hear his proposal over the din of the loudspeakers. She smiled and gladly accepted the cash.

* * *

"Your moves are awesome," Andy told Tiger. She smiled just enough to veil how dreadfully weary she was of these meaningless, post-shift interactions.

"I enjoyed the hell out of that," Ellen added. She still felt her pulse racing a little, but at least everything was starting to make sense again.

"Boys and girls," Jeff announced, "this is Swan."

Tiger curled her lip and rolled her eyes at Swan as they performed the changing of the guard. Tiger was now free to seek her fortunes elsewhere while Swan was welcomed into the fold.

"Hi. I'm Ellen," she said, taking the drink from Jeff. Swan gave her a polite, cautious smile.

"I'm An...,"

Before he could finish, the speakers destroyed his introduction with the announcement of the next set. Andy conceded defeat to the sound system, sat back down, and took a long gulp of orange-juice-plus.

A new rhythm began to dominate the club–faster, less rock, more techno. Swan instinctively swayed in response to the frenetic new beat. She was on the clock and ready to work.

Swan sauntered past the boys, giving them ample time to take in the view. Her wardrobe—a white vest and very short, sheer white shorts—complemented her stage name. Her vest was half-zipped, suggesting, but not revealing, her modest cleavage.

Ellen felt a sudden rush of heat as it became clear she was the target locked in Swan's radar. Her face burned through several shades of red as reality set in. Jeff had set her up, but Ellen would be damned if she was gonna give him the satisfaction of publicly embarrassing her. *What the hell*, she figured. It had already been a memorable day full of "firsts." She would roll with the punches and worry about payback later.

Swan raised her arms majestically over her head and, with one elegant sidestep, stood directly in front of the girl who would be playing the part of her new "best friend" for the next three minutes.

As a rule, Swan avoided eye contact with male customers during solo dances. There were only a few stock expressions she ever found staring back—lost drunkenness, demented lust, or smug objectification. None were the least bit appealing and like most of the girls who'd spent more than a day in this game, she had perfected the art of looking "through" people.

What Swan saw in Ellen was different. Her eyes, wide pupils aside, conveyed a mixture of amusement, intrigue, and general willingness. She was good to go.

The song sped into a fever of swirly, processed guitars that perfectly backtracked Swan's silky gyrations. Her long blond locks obscured her face from the boys on either side. Now only inches from Ellen, their combined tresses formed a sort of intimate, two-toned curtain that gave Swan the "privacy" to formally introduce herself. Grasping the back of Ellen's chair, she lowered herself and locked gazes with her blushing dance partner.

"Is this cool with you?" Swan asked, sweet and gentle.

"Sure. Why not?" Ellen was never one to let embarrassment get in the way of a bit of fun.

"Okay, then. Relax. I won't hurt you."

Swan nudged her victim's knees together with her thighs and slid onto Ellen's lap. Ellen resisted the urge to laugh out loud, but it was hard. Swan *might* have weighed 100 pounds, and Ellen couldn't imagine a scenario where the dancer's warning was even plausible.

Jeff and Andy sat like a pair of ridiculous smoking bookends, gawking at the action between them.

Swan straddled Ellen's waist, moving in perfect rhythm to the music and exaggeratedly tossing her hair. Jeff was watching, but was also aware their table had become a focal point. In fact, the most exciting thing in the whole place was happening about two feet to his left. The small group of college guys, who moments ago were patronizing Kelly, now leered at the cute chick getting a lap dance from the thin little blond number they'd previously ignored.

"Lean in and go with it," Swan instructed. "The boys will be disappointed if I don't get a little bit naughty."

Ellen felt her shoulders and legs relax–as much as was possible with 98 pounds of slightly sweaty stripper flesh on top of her. Keeping her legs wrapped around Ellen's waist, Swan bent all the way back, reclining almost horizontally from her dance partner's torso. She found the zipper on her tight white vest and slid it down. The boys leered unabashedly at the spectacle.

In one swift move, Swan unwrapped her legs and bolted upright. To Ellen's surprise and everyone else's delight, Swan's vest stayed behind on the floor. Topless Swan planted a kiss on Ellen's cheek, playfully close to the corner of her open mouth.

Swan stood, not touching Ellen at all now for the first time since the dance began. Ellen used the break to adjust in her chair and take a deep breath. The blue neon lights masked the flush of red enveloping her face, but she still made a conscious effort to avoid eye contact with either of her roommates.

Swan pranced seductively for a few seconds, allowing the boys a clearer view of her assets.

Jeff had selected her, but Swan was Andy's type to a tee, from the top of her blond head to the tips of her stiletto-strapped toes. In fact, Jeff would have thought her 'plain' or 'boring' if he passed her on the street or in the grocery store. He preferred more exotic women—dark skin, dark hair, with bonus points for an accent that might suggest she was something other than the typical American girl next door.

Of course, Andy knew this. He and Jeff could easily pick each other's fantasy girl out of a lineup, especially at a strip club, where such a thing was entirely possible. The gesture wasn't lost on him, even through the haze of chemicals and current distractions.

They both should have been busy committing the spellbinding visuals before them to permanent memory. But looking up, Andy found Jeff looking straight back at him, a devious smile, almost a smirk, on his face. He shot Andy a casual salute. The currency was non-traditional, to say the least, but Swan was a peace offering. It was Andy who had been the biggest asshole of the day, and clearly, Jeff had suffered the most. At that moment, despite all the junk swirling around in his head, Andy was convicted with total clarity.

The gesture revealed an awareness and kindness in Jeff that Andy knew he did not currently possess. The unlikeliest of teaching tools—a silly, seedy lesbian lap dance—had crystalized for Andy that Jeff was currently the "bigger man" and maybe objectively a better human being. Through the sting of shame, he raised his near-empty screwdriver and offered his friend a silent, humbled toast.

The music wound down, and Swan wrapped up her performance. Ellen was long over any embarrassment, and the event had helped her emerge from the depths of her own haze. As the song ended, a hearty round of applause rode through the club. Two other girls had been on stage at the time, but the crowd was lauding Swan's exhibition almost exclusively.

Ellen sat relaxed in her chair, puffing on a Marlboro Red. Swan zipped her vest and gave a quick cheesy bow as punctuation. Another round of applause from the three roommates followed. Jeff had paid for Swan's services in advance. Still, Andy and Ellen were both waiting with additional tips to show their appreciation for her efforts.

"Thanks," she said, inviting them to place the bills in the white lace garter on her thigh.

"Join us for a drink," Andy offered.

Jeff smiled at his roommate. He knew Andy couldn't let a girl so closely built to his ideal specifications just walk away.

"I don't know." she said, clearly ambivalent. "You seem like pretty nice guys."

It was the first time she'd acknowledged him since joining their party. She was friendly and less guarded after spending three minutes of quality time with Ellen, but she was still on the clock.

"Ha! You don't have to live with them," Ellen said.

"Yeah…" the dancer said, now even less engaged. Their transaction was complete, and the speed and ease with which Swan shifted gears was terrific. She had enjoyed her time and didn't want to be rude, but Swan had places to go and dollars to make. It was time to move on in search of the next greener pasture.

Jeff and Ellen were on the same wavelength and fully satisfied. Andy was less clear. It's not that he would have lobbied to stay longer; it just hadn't occurred to him yet to leave.

Swan stood and straightened herself. "Thanks for the good time," she said, waiting as they gathered their belongings.

"Our pleasure. Thank *you*," Andy said, with an over-eagerness that loudly broadcasted his attraction.

Swan stepped to Ellen and gave a surprisingly robust hug. Adding a little sugar to the fire, Swan gave her a quick kiss, full on the lips. "Bye, baby. Take care of these boys."

Again, Ellen was red-faced and speechless.

The boys didn't make out nearly as well. Swan gave Jeff a half-hug and a peck on the cheek and then moved quickly to Andy. She knew a mark when she saw one and was keen to capitalize. "Come back and see me soon," she whispered and walked away.

"Damn," said Andy. "She's good at her job."

"Speaking of jobs," Jeff replied. "Don't you still have to find one?"

And there it was—the ultimate buzzkill. Andy walked out of the air-conditioned, fluorescent blue fantasy and back into Bradford's brutal afternoon heat. Reality was there, waiting patiently to punch him in the gut.

"Fuck." Andy sighed. "Why not? Tweaking my resume is one way to kill a hangover and a hard-on. Let's go."

25

The three of them piled back into the Chevette, each reapproaching sobriety at their own pace. None would admit to being "addicts" in the traditional sense, but withdrawal was a physiological reality. The roller coaster went up; the roller coaster came down.

Ellen became quiet and introspective. Jeff had slight manic-depressive tendencies and was often near-narcoleptic on the backside of a binge. The drive home from Wonderland was about 15 minutes, but Jeff passed out before Chet reached the highway.

Andy was the wild card. His response to withdrawal, irritability, was a constant. The object and severity of his attacks were far less predictable.

Jeff snored in the back seat while Ellen played the part of distant chauffeur. Andy stared blankly out the window. It wasn't until they joined Bradford's rush hour traffic that she considered the time of day. Ellen let out a low sigh as she worked to change lanes.

Andy processed the traffic on another level. For him, it was an instant reminder that whether here in Bradford or somewhere else, the elusive job he had yet to capture would also *capture* him. Almost certainly, he'd become just one more of *these people* – driving to and from work in long, uninspired lines of drudgery. His already half-empty glass drained just a touch more.

Ellen had little interest in creeping along the interstate in prolonged silence, especially with Sleepy & Grumpy in tow. She merged right, aiming for the less crowded surface streets.

"Where are you going?" Andy asked.

"Don't worry. I got this," Ellen said, trying to dodge a follow-up question. Telling Andy not to worry was like telling most people not to breathe—it didn't work that way.

"Can we get some food? I'm starving."

"Read my mind," she replied. Andy assumed she had something specific in mind as he watched several perfectly acceptable options pass by. He *always* wanted to be involved in decision-making, but Ellen was on a roll calling the shots today, so he was content to let it ride.

"Hell, yes!" he exclaimed as they pulled into a cracked and busted driveway in desperate need of repaving. "You're batting a fucking thousand, El."

Andy's joy was sufficient to wake Jeff, who rubbed his eyes and enacted a dramatic yawn-stretch that made him look like a deranged 180-pound kitten rising from slumber.

"You ready to eat, Sleeping Beauty?"

They had arrived at another of Bradford's culinary treasures, Phat Phil's Fine Eats–home to some of the best authentic Southern comfort food in their city or anywhere else. One block down was the Cubby Corner convenience store they frequented for beer and cigarettes. And right next to that, where Paxton Avenue hit Juniper Street, sat the Cactus Club. Even from a distance, you couldn't miss the bright yellow police tape still screaming around its perimeter.

"Hey, I gotta get smokes," said Jeff, starting toward the Cubby.

"I'll come with you," Andy offered.

"Y'all go for it. I'll grab a table."

26

"You had almost a whole pack when we left for Wonderland," Jeff told Andy as they started up the uneven sidewalk. "You hoarding?"

"Nah. I just wanted to take a quick look at the Cactus since we're right here," Andy admitted. "And Jimmy said we should get a paper today."

"That shit's shut down. Roped off. What is there to see?"

"I don't know. But I want to see it. You do your thing. I'll be back in a second."

"Whatever. I might not wait for you."

Andy kept walking as Jeff veered into the Cubby. He knew his roommate wasn't kidding.

27

A cowbell strapped to the crossbar of the heavy glass door announced Ellen's entrance into Phat Phil's Fine Eats. The smell of garden-fresh collard and mustard greens simmering with bacon hung in the air. Another sniff brought hints of fried chicken and baked fruit pies. In total, it was a grand olfactory symphony that blurred the line between pleasant and intoxicating.

Phat Phil's was one of the smallest restaurants in Bradford, offering only a handful of tables. Depending on the day and time, you could have the whole place to yourself. Or you might encounter a line out the door and a lengthy wait.

Today, the place was almost empty, except for a woman in her early 40s and her pre-teen son sitting near the door. Their drinks were empty. A half-eaten piece of pie swam in melted vanilla ice cream between them. Wanting to spare them the storm of smoke and profanity that would likely accompany her roommates, Ellen looked for a table furthest from them.

Serendipity made the decision easier. In the opposite corner of the room, she saw the unmistakable orb of Graham's balding head. He sat in a booth along the back wall intently staring out the window. His gaze remained locked until she slid in beside him with a gentle bump.

"Howdy, stranger!"

"Ellie!" he replied with genuine surprise.

A near-empty plate and a half-full ashtray suggested Graham had been there a while.

"Where are the brothers?" he asked, moving the plate to clear the space in front of her.

"They're getting smokes at the Cubby. Should be right back."

"Good. I'd hate to miss 'em."

"Likewise, I'm sure," Ellen agreed. Before she could ask where the Bus was, she was interrupted.

"Hey, shu-gah."

Ellen smiled every time she heard it. Ms. Philomena Mascoll–Phat Phil herself–stood tableside. At 250 pounds and with a disposition as sunny as her parents' native St. Croix, Philomena was a jolly mountain of a woman. She grew up working in the Caribbean-themed restaurant her parents owned for years, but never really loved the foods of her family's native land.

Phil had lived her entire life in the Deep South and much preferred its culinary traditions. Her parents retired a few years back, leaving her to run their Blue Sky Cantina. She kept the Caribbean thing going for a while, mostly out of respect for the years of sweat her parents had poured into the place. But it was clear to them all she didn't love it. With their blessing, Philomena closed the Blue Sky and transformed the airy, beach-tinged café into a down-home Southern kitchen reflecting her own personal palate.

Within two years, the popularity and profitability of Phat Phil's easily eclipsed that of the Blue Sky. That was a low bar to clear, though. Hung-over college kids will prefer homemade mac and cheese and biscuits smothered in country gravy over jerk-seasoned mahi-mahi every day of the week.

"Hey, Phil," Ellen replied, half-standing to give her a one-armed semi-hug before flopping down again. "How you been?"

"Ooh, slow as honey," Phil said with a mix of flair and exasperation, neither of which was fake. "Dem crazy boys blew up da Cactus. And dat girl went missin'. Lotsa cops. Not lotsa customers. What choo want?"

"I'm gonna wait for the boys. But can I get a sweet tea?"

"Shure ting, baby," Phil said with a smile. "For *real* sweet?"

"Make my teeth hurt. It's been one of those kinda days."

"Ain't *every* day one of them days with you kids?" Phil teased, rolling her big eyes.

Philomena was thirty, not *too* much older than Ellen or any of the other college-aged "kids" who frequented her eatery. But Phil was a grown-ass woman. She'd worked hard for a long time and carved out a respectable place for herself. She called them "kids" partly in jest, but compared to her experience and accomplishments, that's precisely what they were.

"Pretty much," admitted Ellen, proud and guilty. "I'd tell you where we've been today, but you wouldn't believe me."

"Oh, I doan wanna know. But dat's what young is for. You have your fun, girl. Just don't be gettin' no one hurt."

Most people who came into the restaurant probably saw Philomena as just a fat black lady frying chicken and serving lemonade. Ellen saw an impressive woman who'd found happiness in something she'd busted her ass to create. There was genuine respect there, and Ellen accepted the advice in the wise spirit in which it was offered.

"Speakin' a them boys; where dey at?" Phil asked.

"They're up the street. Should be here any minute."

28

Andy walked the block up Paxton Avenue toward Juniper. The shabby gravel driveway, which served as a parking lot for the Cactus Club, was occupied by three vehicles. A red Chevy Blazer, which he knew belonged to their friend, Echo Thompson, a jack of all trades for the Cactus Club, was parked right by the exit doors nearest the street. A few car lengths away sat a white panel van and a police cruiser. A slight breeze slapped the yellow police tape against the building's weathered brick façade. As Andy approached, the reason for the panel van became evident. The large plank of plywood that had been nailed to the rectangular window frame in the club's front wall now sat on the ground outside it.

Andy stopped and studied the two men working to place a new sheet of glass into the void. He guessed it would soon be darkly tinted, like its predecessor, but for now, it was perfectly transparent. Andy could see clear through, past the stage and halfway down the long, narrow galley to the bar along the club's left side wall. He watched them seal the new glass into the frame with great interest until a new character entered from stage right.

Like a Vaudevillian actor trapped in some surreal performance, Peter "Echo" Thompson strode casually into the scene, dragging a broom across the floor that was concealed by the window frame's bottom.

Andy watched Echo swing the broom in small arcs a few times before he was noticed. Looking up, Thompson ran a flannelled sleeve across his sweaty brow and stared at Andy. Usually, he would have stopped and talked. But they were separated by twelve feet and a thick plate of sound-killing glass. Peter let the broom rest against his shoulder, freeing his hands to give Andy a quick wave. He followed with a simple shrug, palms to the sky as if to say: *"Shit happens, man. Whadda ya gonna do, right?"*

Echo's appearance made Andy laugh but also think. He couldn't imagine himself on the other side of that glass, in Echo's shoes. He'd worked shit jobs before, but at the age of twenty-two, still a few years younger than Echo, Andy felt like he was done with that, or at least desperately wanted to be. The prospect of nearing thirty and pushing a broom around a dingy nightclub was terrifying; soul-crushing, really. Why on Earth would anyone settle for a job so meaningless? And yet, by all accounts, Echo was content. Maybe the ability to joyfully do unglamorous work was something you grew out of, or into. Andy didn't get it.

On the tails of his guilt from Jeff's offering of Swan at the Wonderland, this was the second time in an hour Andy had been shown a glaring flaw in his own character. *Damn,* he thought, *selfish AND lazy, every girl and parent's dream.* He often failed to receive these transmissions or simply ignored them. But for some reason, that frequency was wide open today.

"Move along!" The command came from the uniformed officer stationed at the corner. The cop's bark broke Andy's trance. Indeed, there was no reason to be standing in front of a club that was not only closed and damaged but also an active crime scene.

Andy gave a quick smile and a salute to Echo and obliged the cop's request. Head down, hands in his pockets, he turned toward Phat Phil's just in time to see Jeff enter the eatery.

A moment later, Andy met the mother and son on their way out. The door opened inward, and though it required him to awkwardly push past them first, Andy attempted to make the chivalrous move and hold it for her. The brass cowbell clanged again.

"Thank you," said the woman, appreciating the spirit of the gesture, if not its execution.

The restaurant was deserted, save for his two roommates and their surprise guest. He also perked up instantly at the sight of Graham sitting next to Ellen.

Philomena and Andy both approached the table from different paths. He carried a folded newspaper; she had a tray with two tall beverages.

"Hey, Phil!"

"Hey shu-gah. Whatchoo drinking?"

"Oh, man. Can I get an Arnold Palmer?" He'd been thinking about the heavenly mix of sweet tea and lemonade since the first second Ellen pulled into the lot.

"Sure, baby. Be right back."

Andy waited for Jeff to scoot toward the wall and then sat with a heavy thud. He reached down and rubbed his atrophied calves, which throbbed even after the short walk.

"Hello, my friend!" Graham welcomed him, reaching across the table to shake Andy's hand.

"Mr. Lafley." Andy playfully matched his formality. "Pleasure to see you, sir."

Graham reached for the tin rectangle on the table. He popped open the lid and displayed an assortment of expensive clove cigarettes and neatly rolled joints.

"Want one?" he offered, speaking to all of them at once.

"I don't like cloves, but…," said Jeff.

"I love the smell of them," Ellen suggested, "but they give me such a headache."

Andy declined, too, with a simple wave of his hand.

"Do you mind if I light one?" Graham asked.

None of them did. They'd all probably light cigarettes soon enough, too. Still, Ellen was glad the mother and her son were gone, so she didn't have to feel guilty about smoking them out of the tiny place.

They contemplated the menu, each trying to prepare their food orders before Phil returned with Andy's drink.

"Can we get food to go?" Andy asked.

The option hadn't occurred to either of his roommates, but neither had an objection.

"You got somewhere to be?" Graham wondered.

"Nah. I just want to get home. I've got job search stuff to do."

"Oh yeah," Graham enthused. "How's that goin'?"

"Nowhere, and fast."

"That's not the worst way to live, you know?"

Of all the people they knew, Graham would be the trusted authority on that matter. Andy was fascinated by and jealous of the lightness with which Graham lived.

"Speaking of going places…" Ellen interjected. "Where are you headed? And where's the Bus?"

"She's down by the park. It's hard to find a place to put that big ole bitch. I just left her down there and walked."

That park was over a mile away. The mere thought of trudging that far in the afternoon heat made Andy's legs hurt even worse.

"I gotta go back up north, and get closure on some shit," Graham said. There was a heaviness in his voice they were unaccustomed to hearing. None of them asked for clarification, but he obliged anyway.

"I was living on this piece of land up in Appalachia. It was beautiful, the base of a mountain, a running stream, blue skies, the whole package. This guy I met had like a hundred acres up there. Way more than he knew what to do with. We hit it off. I asked him about buying a piece of it. He said he liked the idea and that I could even put a trailer by the stream—you know, set up a real place."

"Sounds great," said Jeff. At heart, he was a country boy who understood the appeal of off-grid life on some smaller level.

"It was. Until a few weeks later when the fuckin' DEA came swoopin' down in helicopters like bats outta hell."

"What!?" Andy blurted.

"No shit, man. Turns out, this dude was using most of his hundred acres to grow weed. Also turns out, The Man can come and just take all that shit away from you."

"But you said you bought some of it," Ellen asked.

"Nope. I was *gonna* buy it. He never got around to making it official. There's no paper trail between me and him, but they still got my trailer. I'm out like 10,000 bucks, but at least I'm not him. That dude's in jail for *years*."

"Fuck" was all Andy could think of to say. It was like everything else in Graham's life. Crazy, dramatic, tragic. But somehow, he still managed to find the silver lining.

With perfect timing, Philomena came lumbering back to the table with Andy's sweet and sour concoction in tow. She pulled a towel from her apron and wiped the sweat from her dark round face.

"What's for suppa?" she asked.

"Ladies first," Andy offered. It was more of a stalling tactic than a courtesy.

"We're gonna get it to go, Phil," started Ellen. "Can I have a veggie plate with collards, mac & cheese, and black-eyed peas, please?"

"Shore thing, baby. Biscuit or cornbread?"

"Cornbread."

"And you, shu-gah?" Phil said, turning to Jeff.

"Mmm. Country-fried steak and gravy, please. With green beans and cornbread." Jeff requested.

"You ready?" Phil asked Andy.

"Yep. A veggie plate sounds good," he said, still following Ellen's lead.

"I'll have mac & cheese, mashed potatoes, fried okra, and a biscuit."

"Ain't no veggies on that plate, shu-gah," Phil corrected, prompting all three of his friends to laugh at his 'healthy' selection.

"Whatever." Andy defended. "That's what I want."

"Okay, y'all. Suppa to go. Be ready in a minute." Phil was still chuckling as she made her way back to the kitchen.

They sat and waited, filling the small restaurant with smoke.

"So, what'd you learn about the Cactus?" Jeff asked Andy.

"Nuthin' we didn't already know. Like I said, I just wanted to look at it. I was only there for a second before some cop made me leave. Echo was in there cleaning shit up. We'll talk to him sooner or later and get the real scoop.

Andy placed his burning cigarette in the ashtray and turned his attention to the newspaper. The Monday edition of *The Bradford Exchange* was meager compared to the pulpy behemoth Cricket had brought them yesterday.

Jeff moved on without him. "So, check it out. These are up on the wall at the Cubby and probably all over town by now, too." He pulled out a white piece of paper and laid it on the table.

Staring back at them was a girl with light shoulder-length hair and a cute, although slightly uneven, smile. "MISSING," read the huge banner above her photo. Below it, in letters not nearly as large: "Margo Hammond." The flyer also noted that she was 20 years old, 5' 3" tall, approximately 105 pounds, with blue eyes and brownish-blond hair.

"She looks so young," Ellen noticed.

"It might be an older picture, but the best one they had for the posters." Graham suggested.

At the bottom, in letters also bigger than Margo's name: "Reward: $25,000", and finally, a 1-800 number.

"Well, there you go, Andy," Jeff suggested. "With that kind of money, you could go much longer without a job."

Andy wasn't listening. He was busy leafing through the thin sections of the *Exchange*.

"My guess is…" Graham said, "Finding a random missing girl is probably pretty close to a full-time job." He hadn't meant it as a joke, but Jeff still laughed.

"It's crazy that someone can just disappear like that, with no trace, and without *somebody* seeing *something*," Ellen mused. She was processing the situation very differently from her male companions.

"Oh, somebody knows something," Graham said. "Somebody knows *everything*."

"That's true," Jeff agreed. "It makes you wonder. I mean, she's been gone 48 hours now. That's when they say most runaways show up."

"Her family, or somebody, came up with twenty-five grand pretty quick." Andy thought. "I'm not sure my family could do that."

"Or *would*, "Jeff teased.

"Fuck you."

"Both of you shut up," urged Ellen. "That girl is gone, and you guys are getting off trying to figure out what happened to her."

The attachment of a face to the missing girl's name had made it more real for her. She was done listening to their theories about her fate.

Ellen was rescued from further conjecture by the sight of Philomena approaching their table with two white plastic bags full of delicious home cooking. To everyone's surprise, Andy offered to pay for the entire meal—even Graham's.

"Why are you suddenly in such a good mood?" Ellen asked.

"Well, your little field trip was pretty awesome," he said. "But I just found the cherry on top."

Andy held aloft a folded page of newsprint for all of them to see, and flashed a giant, shit-eating grin. A full quarter-page in the Lifestyle section of *The Bradford Exchange* was devoted to a photo that would have been intriguing to the average reader simply for its oddity. All of them knew instantly what it was. A pair of dark, strappy high heels connected by a white tennis shoelace hung from the branches of an oak tree. A closer inspection would reveal several other pairs behind it in the blurred background. Andy sat there, basking smugly in the tiny little spotlight while they looked. His small audience, each of them co-conspirators, was almost as enthused as he. Almost.

"No fucking way," Jeff said.

"Yes, fucking way," Andy replied. "And listen." He'd turned the page back toward himself and recited the small caption under the photo. "About forty pairs of shoes were discovered hanging from a tree in front of Bradford's Gryphon Theatre early Sunday. The theatre's owners confirmed the origin of the shoes is a mystery."

He laid the paper on the table and sat back, smiling even wider.

"They shorted you almost twenty pairs," Ellen noticed.

"I don't even care," Andy said, beaming.

"Nice," said Jeff. "You got exactly what you wanted, eh?"

"I totally did." The satisfaction in his voice and face was palpable. After several recent failures, he was gonna take the win and bask in it. He'd started with a blank canvas, added a little flair, and created something that had gotten noticed. He imagined seeing his words in magazines or on billboards one day would feel just like this. He felt somehow justified, or maybe just happy. Either way, it felt good.

"Well done, Maestro," Graham congratulated. "So, what's next?"

And there it was. The brutal reality of fleeting fame, summed up in one statement. No matter what one accomplishes, you're only ever as good as your next act.

"Next, he has to figure out how to get paid for all that creativity," said Jeff.

"You really do know how to piss on a parade, don't you?" said Andy, still plenty pleased with himself.

They collected their belongings and thanked Phil in advance for what they already knew would be a fabulous feast. Retreating to the Chevette, Ellen offered to give Graham a lift back to the Bus. He declined, preferring to put another mile on his shoes.

29

For most of the two-plus years he'd lived on Cornwall Street, Andy had shown little or no interest in the mail they received six days a week. Ellen and Jeff took the lead in keeping the lights, water, and cable TV running, and he'd learned he could depend on them to just tell him how much he owed. Over the past month, though, checking the mail had become another minor obsession for him. Lately, he'd been watching the rusty letter box like a hawk.

In the month preceding his graduation, Andy sent nearly 100 copies of his anemic resume to prospective employers in Bradford and beyond. "Beyond" was somewhat relative, though.

He knew several people with jobs or at least offers already. Some were very excited about picking up and moving to real big cities. That plan held zero appeal for Andy.

If he was willing to think about it honestly, Andy had nearly limitless options. Gripped by fear and anxiety, he really only considered two. Either he would secure a position with one of the few advertising agencies in Bradford, or he'd slink in defeat to the basement of his parents' house in suburban Atlanta and cast his net in that much deeper job market. That was it, as far as he could see.

Andy Maxwell was a 22-year-old man-child who loved the concept of comfort-physically and mentally; and who became nearly paralyzed in its absence. The worst part was, he didn't even know when or how it had happened.

In Bradford, he discovered a level of comfort he'd never known. Initially, he loved that it was a place where no one knew him. The chance to reinvent himself was something he craved after graduating high school with many of the same people he'd known since first grade.

Leaving all that behind for another fresh start was the last thing he wanted. Everything about Bradford was simple. Andy and his friends enjoyed maximum fun, legal and otherwise, without suffering any real consequences, and on a minimal budget. They worked unimpressive, unchallenging jobs that paid just enough to keep the party going. But that was it, really. Unambitious for sure, but simple, and comfortable.

Andy knew he *could* live like that indefinitely. In fact, he knew some people who had seemingly already made the commitment. He could stay in this small pond forever, paying only the price of his own disappointment, and possibly that of his parents, for making the easy choice. Or he could brave the unknown, paths fraught with opportunities to succeed OR fail gloriously. He figured his road lay somewhere in between. For now, he was lost.

30

Jeff opened their front door for Ellen and headed straight to his room, desperate for a little quiet after such an eventful day.

"Holy shit!" Andy gasped from the well-worn couch in their living room. Its upholstery had once been something in the crème spectrum. Years of exposure to heavy smoke and semi-regular staining had left it a grotesque, dingy grey.

Jeff and Ellen stood like patient bookends, about five feet on either side of Andy, waiting for the payoff.

"You plan on sharing?" Jeff asked.

Ellen plopped down on the nasty couch beside Andy and took a long, recuperative drink.

"Holy shit," Andy repeated, this time more sedate but no less dumbfounded. "I think I have an interview."

"What? Wow!" Ellen said with genuine shock. "That's awesome."

Jeff perched on Andy's other side. "Cool, man. What's the gig?"

"I don't know," Andy said, scanning the brief letter again. "It's some company called Firebrand Marketing. The name doesn't ring a bell. I sent resumes and letters to almost every agency in town. There are really only about three *decent* ones in the whole lot, but I sent shit to like 40 places."

"Sweet. So, what's it say?" Jeff asked.

"Dear Mr. Maxwell," Andy began. "Thank you for your interest in Firebrand Marketing. We currently have an opportunity available for a candidate with your qualifications and would like to speak with you to discuss the position. Please contact me at your earliest convenience, and we can set up a time to meet. We look forward to hearing from you. Sincerely, Gina Lavell, Human Resources."

"That's it," Andy said plainly. The letter was four sentences—no longer than most of the form rejection letters he'd steadily received over the last month. Four little sentences carrying a mountain of hope and possibility.

He'd had exactly two interviews, both trainwrecks. The first, before he'd even graduated, was with a "marketing" company that posted a flyer on a job board outside one of his Journalism classes. Andy arrived at his "interview" to find himself among 50 people who had shown up to what the company called an "orientation" for new marketers. Confused, Andy sat quietly amidst the other hopefuls, willing to go along for at least a short ride. Most of his fellow applicants were not "dressed for success." He felt grossly overdone in his charcoal grey suit and red power tie.

The only other person wearing a coat or tie was a slick-looking young man in his late twenties. As the lights dimmed, that man strode to the front of the room and began a presentation called "The Opportunity of a Lifetime." Less than a minute later, Andy realized he had wandered into a heavy-handed recruitment pitch for a 'multi-level marketing organization.' All you had to do was pay $500 for the *privilege* of becoming an 'associate.' You were instantly qualified to start selling 'an array of state-of-the-art, next-generation solutions in water filtration and purification.' But wait, there was more. Of course, you made commissions on *your* sales, but that was just the beginning. The 'real big money' came from recruiting your friends and family into the organization and cashing in on *their* sales.

Had he chosen a seat closer to the door, Andy would have bolted before the lights even came back on. As it was, he sat there fuming for five more minutes while the wonder kid in blue pinstripes regaled the audience with success stories of the many associates who had "become millionaires, working part-time, and completely on their own schedules." As the lights came up, the facilitator made a manipulative appeal to his captive audience. He admitted, "This opportunity wasn't for everyone—only the most bold, confident and truly successful among you." He closed by suggesting they take a quick break, perhaps to use the facilities or get a drink of water, and that all those who were "seriously interested in serious money" should remain to begin their training immediately. Pissed at having wasted part of a sunny afternoon on this bullshit, Andy left immediately. Although, by the time he got home, he wished he'd waited five minutes in the hall and then peeked back in. He wondered how many suckers either bit on the pyramid scheme or simply had nowhere better to be that day.

This sham aside, Andy's only other interview was that morning's debacle with the marriage question. But now, clutching that short little letter, he felt a spring of renewed possibility and purpose. Invigorated, he rose and headed for his room.

"Where you going?" Jeff called.

"Gotta put this up, recheck my portfolio, and see if anything needs to be ironed," Andy said as if some phantom 'responsibility' switch had been tripped in his brain.

"Hey! What about your food?" Ellen shouted. He'd already disappeared through the kitchen and around the corner.

"Fuck it," Jeff said. "That boy's gonna do whatever he wants. I'm not waiting for him. Let's eat."

31

*A*ndy couldn't remember the last time he'd used the alarm clock on his bedside table. For years, he'd custom-tailored his class schedule, and damned near everything else, to eliminate early risings.

This morning was different. He'd gone to bed early, but only after anguishing over his wardrobe and his portfolio of writing samples. His singular grey suit hung neatly from the thin border of molding outlining his closet. His black, faux leather portfolio sat on the chair across the room.

Both lay waiting as the alarm sprang to life, screaming shrill beeps less than a foot from Andy's head.

Most mornings, that sound would have elicited animosity, violence, or profanity–possibly all three. This morning, Andy was well-rested, clear of purpose and uncharacteristically enthused. A foreign energy pulsed through him, urging his brain and extremities to life. It was 8:30 in the morning, and to his great surprise, Andy Maxwell was not only awake but happy and excited to be alive.

His first instinct was to check the bedside table for the tri-folded paper. The letter was, of course, just where he'd left it. Andy unfurled it and reread the short correspondence. In his haste, he may have jumped the gun. Upon further review, he realized their only request had been that he contact them to schedule an interview. Laying out his suit was likely presumptuous. But Andy had already built a head of steam. He was awake and moving forward. It was just after 8:30. By the time he peed, poured a cup of tea, read a bit of the newspaper, and watched a few minutes of "SportsCenter," surely it would be 9:00. Andy was determined that the first thing Ms. Gina Lavell was going to do today at Firebrand Marketing was hear his voice.

He was close. After scanning the morning headlines, he sat upright in the living room's blue recliner, watching the muted TV impatiently as last night's baseball highlights filtered across ESPN. He stared at the clock, watching the second hand inch around the circle. Four more minutes.

Butterflies churned in his stomach. Andy had no intention of eating until after his meeting. But the pack of Winston Lights on the coffee table still looked good.

Andy lit a cigarette and filled his lungs with smoke. The white-grey cloud he released mingled with the early morning sun crashing through the windows. Over the past two years, he would have bet he'd smoked in every seat in their house at just about every time of day imaginable. But this combination of smoke and light was new and intriguing. He stopped fixating on the clock and sent more clouds into the sunshine.

"Oh shit!" Andy muttered as he glanced back up at the clock. 9:01 am. He hastily crushed the Winston and reached again for the letter.

32

Andy sat on the edge of the couch, stiff and hunched like a cathedral gargoyle. He pressed the phone to his ear. The line rang. Like so many others he'd made recently, he assumed this call was bound for voicemail purgatory. Instead, to his surprise, a tinny, not-so-chipper female voice entered Andy's ear.

"Good morning; Firebrand Marketing."

Andy froze. Introducing oneself was simple enough, but the sound of an actual human flummoxed him.

"Hello?" the voice offered.

Say something, idiot! The voice in his own head screamed. That guy was *never* at a loss for words.

"Hi. Yes. Hello." Andy finally managed. He feverishly scanned the short letter for the name of the woman he was supposed to contact.

"Good morning," the voice repeated. "Can I help you?"

"Good morning, ma'am," Andy fumbled. "May I speak with Ms. Gina Lavell, please?" He'd only spoken two sentences, but this phony, formal tone immediately horrified him.

God. This is the EASY part, and you're even fucking THIS up ! he thought as he waited for the voice to reply.

"And who may I ask is calling?" it inquired.

"Yes, ma'am," Andy started again with the same politeness. He made a mental note to stop doing that. "My name is Andy Maxwell. Ms. Lavell sent me a letter asking me to call her about a writing position available there."

Too much detail? She doesn't care why you're calling. She just wants to know which button to press so she can transfer you and then go back to doing whatever you interrupted, before forgetting you even exist.

"One minute. Let me see if she's in."

Ah, Andy loved that one. He'd heard it a hundred times in the last few weeks. The receptionist *must* answer the phone. For everyone else, all bets are off. Most of the people he was trying to reach were "busy." Creative Directors and other agency brass had far better things to do than talk to new graduates begging for jobs. Andy figured once again he was destined for voicemail. Again, he was wrong.

"Good morning. This is Gina."

He was surprised not only to have reached her but even more so by the tone of her voice. It was surprisingly high-pitched and carried an accent he couldn't place.

"Umm, good morning. Ms. Lavell?" Andy half-stated and half-asked.

"Yep. This is Gina," she repeated.

"Hi. My name is Andy Maxwell. I received a letter the other day asking me to call you about a writing position available with your company."

"Okay," he thought. *"That whole thought came out fine and might even have passed for professional."*

"Why, yes, Mr. Maxwell," answered Gina with an enthusiasm that made her already impossibly high voice rise even further. The sounds of shuffling papers and typing were audible through the phone as if she were trying to find some record or context for him as she spoke. "We *are* looking for a good writer. Is that you?"

"Yes, ma'am," he responded as if there were any other answer to a that question. "I would love to come by and show some samples of my work."

Andy had shifted into the next highest gear and entered sales mode. He felt his pulse quicken as he tried to walk the fine line between interested and desperate.

And then, as if solely to disrupt that balance, the door behind Andy opened with a sharp, sickly creak. It startled him, wrecking his train of thought. Jeff lingered in the doorway. He stood, blurry-eyed and confused at the sight of Andy, awake and seemingly productive at nine in the morning. Andy put a raised index finger to his lips, beckoning his roommate to *"shut the fuck up!"* and then waved his arm furiously, attempting to usher him out of the room. Jeff shuffled past Andy en route to the bathroom without saying a word.

"Well..." Gina began again, her shrill pitch reclaiming Andy's attention. "That'd be great..."

Andy's spirits rose in concert with Gina's voice at the prospect of another interview.

"But..."

Dammit! Why was there always a 'but'? Andy wondered.

"You're gonna need to meet with Mr. Forrester, our VP of Marketing. He's our creative guy. But he's leaving this afternoon for two weeks of travel. Let me check his..."

"I can come this morning!" Andy blurted, fully crossing into desperate territory without even considering the feasibility of his suggestion.

"Hmm. Can you hold for one minute?" Gina asked.

"Of course."

"K. Be right back."

Andy had no idea what was happening. Maybe he'd shown some tenacity that was about to grease the wheels. Or maybe he'd just come off as a self-righteous, newbie grad who assumed corporate vice presidents were flexible enough to accommodate his desires.

"Shit," he whispered into the dead air coming from the phone.

"What?" Jeff had finished his business and was sitting bare-chested on the arm of the couch across the room.

"I'm on hold, about a job. Shut up!" Andy said tersely, hoping to correct him before Gina came back on the line. Jeff was content to slump into the couch, puff on his cigarette, and watch in silence.

"Mr. Maxwell?" Gina returned.

"Yes. I'm here."

"Mr. Forrester is leaving at noon for the airport. Can you be here at 10?"

"Uh, sure." Andy stammered. It was already 9:15.

"Do you know where our office is?" Gina chirped

"I've got the address from the letter, but can you give me directions?" Andy asked. He was starting to power-load anxiety as the clock's second hand continued its relentless sweep.

"Sure. We're down in the warehouse district on Century Street, by the riverfront. The complex is called Rayner Industrial Park. We're around back, off the road. It's Suite 134."

"I know where it is," Andy replied. "I can be there by 10."

Luckily for him, it was the truth. The riverfront was less than five miles from their house, and he was certainly no stranger to the warehouses. He'd been there many times, just never for "business."

The district was home to many companies, but his context was totally different. The complex had several vacant spaces, which the landlord was happy enough to rent to local bands as practice spaces. There were, however, conditions. These bands were not allowed to 'interfere with or cause undue hardship upon' the operation of their business neighbors. All this really meant was they couldn't make a shitload of noise or pack the parking lot with intoxicated misfits—at least not during business hours.

To think he was headed there for a job interview kind of fucked with Andy's head. But, as the clock on the wall reiterated, there was no time for that now.

"Okay. Great. We'll see you shortly."

"Yes, ma'am. Thank you, ma'am," he said to no one. Gina was already on to the next thing in her day.

"Oh shit!" Andy blurted as he raced past Jeff toward his room.

Jeff followed him. "What? What happened?"

"I have an interview. In… 42 minutes." Andy said, pulling off his t-shirt. He was frantic but happy. A smile tried to force itself through the shroud of anxiety.

"That's awesome, dude," Jeff encouraged.

"Yeah. Awesome. Except I have 41 minutes to shave, shit, shower, dress, and drive over to the riverfront."

"Go, man! Go! I'm outta your way!" Jeff cheered, retreating to the kitchen to make coffee.

33

It wasn't even 9:30, but Andy could already tell today would be a scorcher. He'd read somewhere that cold showers invigorated the body and mind, brought greater mental focus, and had a way of steeling one's nerves against adversity. It was brutal self-flagellation at first, but it proved to be a solid strategy in the end.

Andy stepped from the ultra-narrow shower stall, naked and dripping. His body balked at the warm, heavy air around him. Wrapped in a big, ripped pink towel, he covered the four feet from the bathroom to his bedroom in two quick bounds. Before the door closed behind him, he was naked again. 9:36 am.

The matter of his wardrobe required no thought at all. He was proud of his choice to iron and prep his ensemble last night.

With every layer he added—underwear and undershirt, pants and shirt, tie and belt, and finally shoes and jacket—Andy's body temperature rose. Four minutes ago, he'd been standing in a cascade of cold, cleansing water. Now, as he pulled on the cheap suit jacket and turned to face himself in the mirror, tiny beads of sweat engulfed his hairline. He bent down, picked up the moist pink towel, and mopped his brow before tossing it over a chair to dry. Andy checked his reflection. He fiddled with the knot of his tie and then declared himself presentable. 9:43 am.

Andy grabbed his portfolio and opened the bedroom door. Thanks mainly to adrenaline and hope, he felt ready—and miles better than usual.

"Want some coffee to go?" Jeff asked as Andy buzzed through the kitchen.

"Nope. I'm already jittery. And coffee gives me the shits. But thanks."

"Okay, then," Jeff said, discarding the unpleasant thought. "Well, good luck!" Andy closed the door, his friend's well wishes widening his smile as he went.

He tossed the portfolio into the passenger seat of his SUV. He sat behind the wheel and draped his suit coat carefully over the top of the case. The vehicle's engine roared to life. The tool-loud stereo produced a blast of musical rage, courtesy of Soundgarden, that punched him straight in the face. With veins already full of natural adrenaline, it was the last thing he needed. Luckily, the tape in the deck was a double-sided, dichotomous mix: mayhem on one side, mellow on the other. Andy pushed the flip button and was instantly rewarded. The beauty of Jimmy Page's Celtic-tinged acoustic masterpiece *Bron-Y-Aur* emerged to soothe the savage beast. 9:48 am.

Twelve minutes to drive four miles, park, and walk into the offices of Firebrand Marketing. It would be close. Andy put the vehicle in reverse, backed out of the driveway, and aimed for the river.

Traffic was light, and his luck with green lights had Andy feeling like everything might work out. This was precisely the kind of last-minute adventure, which he did not orchestrate, that would ordinarily throw him into a spiral of nervous panic. But he'd started to learn it wasn't so much the situations themselves that made him suffer as the anticipation. Once the ball started rolling and he had to react in real-time, he usually did okay. It was when he had time to think, analyze, and over-analyze, that dread fear and paralysis took hold.

Bolts of sunlight bombed his windshield as Andy approached the turn-in to Raynor Industrial Park. Entering the alleyway between two distressed red brick buildings, he saw a sign atop one of them announcing the name of the complex. He'd been here dozens of times but never noticed it. Andy knew this place simply as "the warehouses." 9:56 am.

The narrow, brick-lined canyon opened into a small black-top parking lot. He was surprised by the number of cars there on a weekday morning. A sign ahead ushered him left. Fifty yards down, Andy found Suite 134.

Instinctively, he moved toward the signs designating handicapped parking. For years now, he'd been a member of that distinguished club. Several surgeries on his legs more than justified him legally parking there, but he chose a regular spot across the aisle instead. The difference in distance was negligible; the difference in perception was not. He didn't need anyone at Firebrand Marketing to see him park in a handicapped spot and then walk "normally" into the building. That kind of first impression might earn him more asshole points than his thin resume could overcome. 9:58 am.

Andy parked the SUV and leaned back until his head met the cushioned grey cloth of the headrest. He breathed deeply and deliberately. He closed his eyes and breathed again—slowly, deeply, deliberately. No radio. No engine noise. The last gasps of air-conditioned coolness escaped from the vents and dissipated into the warming air. He could feel a slight tightness in the middle of his chest as the silent car cabin let his beating heart take center stage. He opened the SUV's armrest console. Sifting through pocket change, receipts, and assorted trash, he found a box of peppermint Tic-Tacs. He spilled two oblong mints into his palm and ate them. He'd read somewhere that peppermint was a natural digestive calmative. He didn't know if it was true. Still, fresh breath and the placebo assurance of gastrointestinal serenity seemed like a win-win. 9:59 am.

34

At precisely 10:00 am, as if by some grand design, Andrew Maxwell approached the four small concrete steps leading up to Suite 134 of Raynor Industrial Park.

Reaching the establishment's precipice, he noticed a few non-traditional details. The front door was not glass or wood but a menacing, unattractive metal. A simple placard affixed to the brick wall affirmed this was, in fact, Suite 134, but no corporate name or other descriptors appeared. He half-registered these but was more focused on hitting the lobby before the minute hand finished another lap. As he opened the heavy metal door, it was clear this was no typical office.

Andy was surprised to have entered a small glass portico no bigger than a phone booth. Behind him, the metal door closed with enough emphasis to create an airlock effect that brought on a sudden sense of claustrophobia. To his left, the wall was floor-to-ceiling brick. To his right, thick glass. Straight ahead was another door. Andy reached for its handle. A quick tug revealed it was locked tight, presumably with a magnetized security seal. Only then did he notice the intercom box on the wall to his right. It had a circular red button and a sign that read, "Ring for Service, Please."

Confused by the odd entryway and awash in fresh anxiety, Andy pushed the button not once but twice in quick succession. Instantly, a voice acknowledged.

"May I help you?"

The voice was female and soft but robotic. Andy couldn't tell if it was natural or the result of the strange echo that occurred upon its broadcast into the small glass booth.

"Hi. Andy Maxwell, here to see Mr. Forrester," Andy managed.

"Ah." came the monotonous reply. It was followed by a buzzing sound and a loud click as the magnetic field released. "Come on in." This last bit seemed more human, perhaps even cordial.

Andy pushed the glass door much harder than necessary and nearly fell into the lobby. It would have been an awkward first impression had anyone been watching. No one was.

He composed himself–standing up straight, slowing his breathing, and smoothing his cheap purple tie. A girl with shockingly shiny jet-black hair sat behind a massive reception desk. She had noted him long enough to buzz him through the security door but was otherwise ignoring him from behind the paperback she was apparently being paid to read. Andy was honestly grateful for the snub. He took another deep breath and approached.

"Andy Maxwell. Here to see…"

"Yes. I know," the receptionist cut him off. The intercom in the glass booth had accentuated her disaffected monotone, but not by much.

"Mr. Forrester is busy. I'll ring Ms. Lavell for you." She had yet to look at him.

"Thanks," Andy replied, having clearly received the message from the World's Least Friendly Receptionist.

He watched as she used the phone to announce his arrival. Her death-black hair, alabaster skin, and exaggerated mascara around her intensely green eyes made her look like a bizarre, gothic China doll. She was attractive in a scary, plastic way but completely unapproachable. Besides, Andy had other goals today. He turned and stepped away from the desk, satisfied to occupy another portion of the lobby while he waited.

Less than a minute later, another remarkable woman rounded the corner. She was nearly six feet tall, even without the bonus of three-inch heels. Andy attempted to survey her discreetly, but it was impossible. Pink, textured tights encased her half mile of legs before disappearing beneath a plain black skirt. Her haircut was equally intriguing. Razor-shaven at the back, it increased in volume gradually as it came forward over the crown of her head. The gradient of reds, browns, and blondes was more than he could comprehend in one quick glance, but Andy knew it looked cool. He finished scanning upward just in time to make eye contact as she reached him.

"Hey, Andy. I'm Gina. We spoke on the phone this morning," she said, extending her long arm to shake his hand.

Andy grasped her cool, ringless hand. "Hi. Nice to meet you."

"Thank you, Sera." Gina said to the receptionist, who was no longer ignoring them.

"Sure, Gina. My pleasure," replied the now-not-at-all robotic young girl behind the desk. It was as if someone had pushed a button on the back of her cold ceramic neck, instantly transforming her into a polite, engaging human.

"Thanks for coming in so quickly," Gina offered.

"No problem. I'm just glad I could catch Mr. Forrester before he headed out of town."

"Absolutely," Gina agreed. "Follow me."

She made a turn toward the corner from where she had emerged and led Andy down a hallway behind the foyer. The interior of the space was flooded with artificial fluorescent light. If there were any windows in the suite, he couldn't see them. The floors were cold polished concrete, and all the walls were either stark white or the same natural brick as the building's exterior. *Not exactly warm and welcoming,* Andy thought.

Andy's thin legs struggled to keep pace with Gina as she cruised down the hall. She took a left and slipped from his view. Beyond the corner, he found her standing in a conference room doorway. But, his gaze was transfixed by something altogether different.

Twenty feet behind her stood a gigantic vault door– the kind you would see at a bank or in some Hollywood heist film. Andy studied it in awe as he continued toward the conference room.

"Pretty cool, huh?" Gina said with almost ironic nonchalance.

"Uh, yeah," Andy muttered as he considered the behemoth mystery.

Gina ushered him into the room, which also had no windows. It had a glass wall that provided a perfect view of that giant vault, though.

"Have a seat. Can I get you something to drink? Coffee? Water?"

"Water would be great. Thank you," Andy replied, clearing his throat. He chose a seat on the table's longest side. From here, the safe was still visible.

"Sure. Be right back."

Andy sat calmly in the conference room, silently practicing the presentation of his portfolio. His previous interviews hadn't exactly polished him, but he at least discovered a few pitfalls to avoid. He glanced again at the vault door down the hall, beginning to obsess about what, if anything, was inside.

More anxiety flooded as he second-guessed the seat he'd chosen. Initially, he *wanted* to be staring at that vault, but now it was proving to be a major distraction. He looked at the clock above the door. 10:08 am. He wondered if he had time to change his position at the table. Before he could act on the impulse, it was too late.

35

"Good morning, Mr. Maxwell."

Andy heard the gruff masculine voice before he saw the body it belonged to. He raised his head and instinctively stood at the notion of someone entering the room.

Evan Forrester was a tank-like slab of a man. Roughly the same height as Andy, he appeared nearly twice as wide. He wasn't fat, just solid and oddly square. A high-and-tight box of mostly grey hair sat atop his head. From the base of his nearly non-existent neck and mountainous shoulders down, there was almost no taper to his frame.

Andy would typically have tried to break the ice with a joke or casual statement, like asking to be called 'Andy' instead of 'Mr. Maxwell'. Taken aback by Forrester's stature and assertive entrance, he extended his hand in silence.

Evan came the rest of the way to him, stopping at the corner of the table. He clasped Andy's young, unhardened hand in his, which appeared to Andy to be about the size of a glazed Virginia ham. Andy looked him straight in the eye. Forrester wore a smile in the middle of his square, grizzled face. Still, Andy could tell he was a no-nonsense guy who was gonna do most of the talking here.

"Good to meet you, son. Have a seat."

Andy happily obliged. Gina had re-entered the room and closed the door behind her.

"I'm a busy guy, Maxwell. Too busy, in fact, which, hopefully, is why you're here," Evan started. It took no expert deduction, but Andy guessed Mr. Forrester was ex-military. The chiseled physique, take-charge demeanor, and habit of referring to people by their last names were all decent tells.

Andy glanced back at Gina as if seeking some reassurance. Her eyes shone brightly from behind square-framed glasses, and she gave him the slightest of smiles before turning her attention back to Evan in a subtle but direct manner that suggested he do the same.

"You're a writer."

Andy couldn't tell from the tone or delivery whether this was a statement, a rhetorical question, or an inquisition that required his reply.

"Yessir," Andy said simply, assuming it would satisfy any scenario.

"And you've done technical writing?" Forrester asked.

Andy had learned, the hard way, the dangers of answering questions in too great of detail, or worse, getting sidetracked and answering a question you weren't even asked. He was determined to play this one cooler and more direct.

In any real sense, the truthful answer to Evan's question was 'no.' But like most recent graduates, Andy's resume was an exercise in spin. What he lacked in actual experience, which was substantial, he made up for with clever, vague packaging. In truth, he'd been responsible, since high school, for creating a painfully basic newsletter for a company owned by family friends. On paper, this translated into "Communications Liaison" and "Marketing Consultant." And as for "technical writing?" Sure. Those 200 pages of sales scripting and maintenance catalogs he'd edited for the same company qualified, right?

"I have," Andy replied with intentional vagueness, hoping it would buy him a follow-up question he could attack more squarely.

Forrester paced the conference room floor, maintaining constant momentum.

"So, I'll get to the point, Maxwell," Evan stated bluntly. "You're a writer. And I need one, like yesterday. I had a real smart guy, a reserve in the Marines, doing this job for about a year. He just went active duty, so now I gotta replace him."

Andy was about to break in and ask a question, but Forrester kept rolling.

"You caught me at a good time...and a bad time. I need someone fast. Someone good. We have a lot to do around here, but I'm traveling most of this month. In fact, I'm leaving for the airport in about ten minutes. I'd hate to wait a couple more weeks to hire someone."

"Okay," Andy stated, sure Forrester would continue.

"So, here's the deal." Evan checked the large silver chronograph on his wrist, disregarding the clock on the wall.

"We're what you'd call a specialized marketing company. We deal exclusively with firearms. We create highly detailed technical manuals for various automatic and semi-automatic weapons. Handguns, shotguns, hunting and assault rifles; you name it. If it shoots, we can teach you how to assemble it, disassemble it, fire it, clean it, store it, and care for it."

Andy felt the blood drain out of his face. A wave of cold despair built in his skull and washed straight through his chest to his legs and feet.

'*Fuck*'. The single word was loud and clear in his head. He didn't think he had said it out loud...at least he hoped not.

Forrester kept talking.

"We do some catalog stuff, too, and the occasional ad or booth for local gun shows. But mostly, I need someone who can crank out a ton of mechanical documentation on the latest line of weapons from our manufacturing partners."

"That's what's in the safe," Andy said, this time very much aloud, but to no one in particular.

The nondescript building, the heavy metal front door, the glass booth, the giant safe. It all made sense when you pulled the curtain back. But Andy couldn't have imagined a more disappointing or disheartening grand reveal. He stared again at his portfolio case, realizing there was little chance it would even be opened today.

"Very good," Evan responded in a matter-of-fact way that suggested he wasn't giving Andy much credit for connecting the dots. "There's about a million dollars' worth of firearms locked up in there. We get to hold onto them for 'hands-on reference' while we document them. We send most of 'em back when we're done. I buy some of them—the really cool ones—to add to my personal collection. Of course, there's no ammo in the building, but we can take just about anything we want over to the range and well, you know, blow off some steam."

There was a gleam in Forrester's eye and a much broader, almost maniacal grin as he reveled at the notion of endless gunplay. Andy tried hard not to react at all.

"Okay," Andy repeated, searching for other words and failing.

"I know. It's kind of cool to think about," Forrester assumed for Andy. "In fact, if you love guns, or even like 'em, this could be a bit of a dream job."

Forrester was clearly talking to himself and hadn't noticed Andy's lack of shared enthusiasm. He had a schedule to keep and was simply moving forward.

"Alright. This is a little rude, but I gotta get moving," Forrester announced. He extended his massive hand again to Andy, who stood and accepted it.

"You got some thoughts in your head, son. I can see that. And I'd like to hear 'em, but I'm gonna miss my flight. Miss Lavell here has shared your info with me, and she has all the details of the job, so you can ask her anything you'd like. Here's my card. Why don't you talk to Gina, and call me on Monday, and we can work out getting you started."

"Okay." was all Andy seemed capable of saying as the Forrester Express rolled on.

Evan handed Andy a business card and swiftly walked out of the room. 10:12 am.

The whirlwind had come and gone in less than five minutes, during which Andy had managed to speak only seven words. He sat back down, dazed and very confused. Had he just been offered a job? Gina sat across the table, fingers interlocked, smiling at him.

"So… that was Mr. Forrester." It was almost an apology, but she also seemed a little amused by his shock.

"Can I get that glass of water, please?" Andy answered quietly.

36

In Andy's absence that morning, the house on Cornwall Street was particularly serene. Ellen emerged from her bedroom, a blue and white striped towel piled high like a beehive atop her freshly showered head. Jeff sat quietly on the living room couch, reading a book. Steam from a coffee cup and smoke from a quarter-burnt Winston wafted over the makeshift table between them.

"Hey."

Jeff finished his paragraph before, swept his long hair behind his ears, and offered a slight wave in lieu of words.

"Damn, it's quiet in here. When is Andy coming back?"

Jeff cleared his throat and took a long sip.

"Who knows? I guess the longer his interview takes, the better, right?"

"I guess. He was really excited when he left. So, I guess we'll see. Fingers crossed." Ellen redundantly acted out the expression for good measure.

"Yeah. I hope he finds what he's looking for."

"Me too. I just hope he finds some happiness," Ellen said, taking a cigarette from the pack on the table and continuing to the kitchen for coffee.

"I think it's one and the same," suggested Jeff. "He's spinning his wheels thinking he's gonna find some perfect situation that will magically make him happy."

"Isn't that what most people do?" Ellen asked, knowing she'd probably count herself amongst *most people*.

"Yeah. But that's the problem. Happiness doesn't work from the outside in. That's called 'pleasure'. People confuse the two all the time. Real happiness comes from the inside and shines out."

"That's pretty deep, dude. I believe it, but that's a hard sell. Andy's sure not buying it."

"Yeah. But it would make life a lot easier if he did," Jeff said. "You can struggle against the truth all you want, but there's nothing on that road but demons and misery."

"Well, damn. I don't know if I feel better or worse about myself now." Ellen admitted.

"Oh, you're fine. You…"

The ring of the phone broke the mid-morning calm. Its volume was amplified significantly from the living room's central location as rings could be heard from four phones simultaneously.

"I got it." Ellen moved toward the kitchen.

Jeff's quiet morning of reading was over. He rose from the couch and headed for the front porch to enjoy the rest of his smoke and a second cup of coffee. He left the door open behind him, hoping the slight breeze would cut the stale, warm air inside.

A bright blue garbage truck rolled through the intersection down the block. A brown-haired lady jogged up the hill beside a svelte Belgian Malinois. Jeff offered a friendly wave as she passed, but she never saw it. Scanning left to right; he watched her trudge up the hill until something out of place registered in his peripheral vision.

A bright white envelope was taped to the rusted letterbox on their home's front wall. Jeff exhaled a puff of smoke and stepped toward the box. In blue ink, in handwriting he did not recognize, was a single word: "Friends."

Jeff grabbed the envelope and was about to open it when Andy's green SUV came barreling down the hill, far exceeding the posted 25 mph speed limit. He leaned against the peeling white banister and waited for his roommate's report.

37

Raucous music blared from open windows as the SUV swung hard left and pulled into the loose gravel driveway. Andy killed the engine, flung his door open, and climbed out. The stark contrast between Andy's present appearance and how he looked roughly an hour ago was immediately apparent. The suit coat was absent. Once neatly pressed and tucked, Andy's bright white Oxford shirt hung loose and disheveled. He was still wearing the tie, but it sat sloppily a few inches from the top of his unbuttoned collar. Even Andy's pile of dark hair was distressed. This was not the look of a man who had just succeeded.

Jeff knew Andy like a book—one wrought with a few recurring themes and teeming with caustic language. He knew asking for details was unnecessary. Andy would tell you whether you wanted to hear it or not. Jeff stayed still, leaning against the banister with his coffee and cigarette as Andy approached. At closer range, Jeff could see a powder keg lurking below the surface and a look in Andy's eyes, almost begging for someone to light the fuse so he could go off. Jeff was determined not to be that person.

Jeff tried to avoid eye contact lest he be baited to speak. He also found himself fighting the urge to giggle. Andy was clearly agitated, and laughing would have been plain rude. Jeff knew this dance and how it would play out. He pulled hard on his cigarette, intent on extending the silence, if only for a few seconds more.

Sensing Jeff had no interest in sparking his impending explosion, Andy set a path for the open front door. Before he got there, Ellen emerged. She was still carrying the cordless phone handset.

"Hey! Andy! How'd it go?" she asked with excitement, oblivious to the black cloud around him.

Jeff's lowered and turned his head. He closed his eyes as if preparing to shield himself from the shrapnel he knew was coming.

"GUNS!" Andy blurted, uttering a response neither of them could have possibly anticipated or understood. "It was fucking guns!"

Ellen was shocked by the volume and venom of his reply. She took a step to her left and cleared a path for him. He kept moving and entered the house. Ellen shot a confused look at Jeff and mouthed the word "fuck". Jeff simply shrugged. The pin was already out of the grenade.

Jeff followed Ellen back into the house, the small white envelope still in his hand as he closed the door.

Andy hurled his portfolio case onto the nearest chair. Ellen and Jeff sat together on the nasty beige couch, leaving the recliner vacant for their roommate upon his return. They waited patiently through the clinking of ice cubes and the shaking of the orange juice carton, neither daring to comment on another pre-lunch screwdriver. They waited while he went through the motions of making a drink, finding a cigarette, a lighter, and an ashtray. It was like sitting through the previews before the feature presentation at a movie theater. The dark cloud still surrounded him as Andy returned, but Jeff hoped at least a little fuel had burned off the fire.

Andy took a long, aggressive drink of the pale, yellow poison. He lit a Winston, tossed the lighter onto the table, and dove in headfirst.

"So, I bust my ass to get ready in like no time," Andy started, with a full head of steam. "I drive out to the warehouses, and there's a bunch of shit over there you can't even imagine. I pull up, and this place is like fucking Ft. Knox or something, all locked down, with security doors and cameras and shit. Totally crazy. I get in there, and this jacked-up old Army dude starts telling me about the million-plus dollars' worth of fucking guns he's got locked up in a giant bank vault down the hall. And that's the job. He wants me to write tech manuals about automatic and semi-automatic weapons. That's the whole fucking job—all guns, all the fucking time!"

Andy had worked himself into a lather, flailing his arms and spewing bits of alcoholic spittle as he ranted.

"And the worst part is he made it sound like the job was already mine for the taking."

"How is that the worst part?" Ellen wondered aloud. "Doesn't that solve your problem?"

She knew better, or at least she should have. She knew all about Tristan, about the past he wasn't about to let go–they both did. Andy couldn't change who he was or how he reacted to specific inputs, but neither could she.

Ellen was a "fixer." She was patient when it came to people and their problems. And she genuinely tried, as much as possible, to actually help fix them. Unfortunately, Andy was every bit her equal– and opposite. For every solution, he was able and willing to find another challenge.

Andy reveled in the art of argument and had remarkable stamina for it, as long as someone was willing to play the foil and keep pressing him. He would always have the last word; the worst thing you could do was keep asking him questions.

Jeff figured this out long ago and had grown tired of playing the game. Eventually, he started avoiding these kinds of conversations altogether. But this one was larger and affected them all. Andy's failure to solve this particular problem would mean the dissolution of their little family home. It would also mean a 33% increase in Jeff and Ellen's rent. This was motivation enough to at least have a conversation. So, they both settled in and waited for the next episode of "The World According to Andrew Maxwell" to begin.

"Fuck no," Andy countered. "It doesn't solve my problem. It's a cruel joke."

"I know exactly what I want to do, and I've been trying for weeks now to get someone to give me a shot. I know I can write. I have good ideas, and I know how to work with other people to make shit happen."

"Like throwing 80 shoes in a tree?" Jeff asked.

"Exactly!" Andy defended. "That *was* a good idea. That shit got put in the newspaper. It got noticed and talked about. People are *still* talking about that."

Jeff and Ellen were fighting a losing battle, trying not to laugh at the detour Andy's explosion had taken.

"Screw you, though," he blasted, determined to finish his point. "You know that's not what I'm talking about. All I want to do is write. But so far, the only break I get is the fuckin' Gun Palace?"

"So, there's no way you'd even consider..." Ellen started.

"Are you fucking serious? You know how much I hate guns. They only have one function: to kill a living thing. So no, I don't think I could spend my whole day extolling the virtues of the evilest thing ever invented."

"But don't people in advertising have to sell shit they don't believe in all the time?" Jeff asked.

"Yes," Andy admitted. "But there's a sliding scale. I know cigarettes and alcohol are bad for you. But I could write about those all day long. I could find a way to justify peddling those brands of death. They help certain economies. They're non-violent choices that harm users more than others. Hell, it'd be hypocritical of me to blast those things. Even politics I could stomach. But guns? I can't do it. I just can't do it."

He stopped and took another gulp of screwdriver. Andy stared at his black leather wingtip shoes. He focused on slowing his breathing and suddenly found himself with nothing to say. Ellen and Jeff sat likewise silent across from him.

Ellen looked at the blue plastic clock above their kitchen doorway and was reminded she had somewhere to be. She promised Traci she would meet her at the restaurant in 30 minutes, and she still needed to dry her hair and finish getting ready.

Bartending at The Green Room almost always paid her rent and basic living expenses. But she also had a solid backup plan to help pay for incidentals and "extracurricular activities." Ellen had plenty of experience in the restaurant business, doing everything from hostessing and waiting tables to tending bar, prepping kitchens, and working as a sous chef. Her former roommate, Traci Nixon, was the daytime manager of Bradford's gaudiest Mexican cantina, El Lagarto Guapo—*The Handsome Lizard*.

From time to time, when any of the many slackers who staffed the kitchen or bar called in 'sick,' Traci would call Ellen and see if she wanted to pad her pockets with a bonus shift. For Traci, it was easier than constantly firing mostly reliable people and hiring unknowns who wouldn't be any more reliable. For Ellen, it was easy, non-committal work.

"Andy," she said gently. "I don't want to walk away from this, but I gotta help Traci get through lunch at the Lizard. Can we talk more later?"

Jeff turned his attention back to the strange card he'd found taped to their mailbox. He'd opened the envelope and was reading the note inside during the awkward silence following Andy's tirade.

"Yeah," replied Andy, dejected, but not by her. "I don't know what else there is to talk about. It's cool. Go do your thing."

"Hold up," Jeff implored. Ellen was already walking toward her bedroom. "There's something else."

Jeff held up the little white note card. "This was on our mailbox this morning."

"What is it?" Andy mumbled through an ice cube.

"Dear Neighbors," Jeff began. "Quenton and I would love if you could join us for dinner on Friday. 6 pm. Bring nothing but yourselves. Signed, Lula Murphy."

"What the hell?" Andy replied.

"Okay. That's weird," Ellen added, now walking back into the room.

"I know." Andy joked. "Who the hell is named Lula?"

"No, dumbass. The whole thing. We've been here for like two years, and I don't think I've said 100 words to either one of them in that time."

"Really?" said Jeff. "I talk to Quenton, all the time."

"Me too. I drank a beer in the driveway with him just the other day. But I don't think I've ever even met Mrs. Murphy."

"Looks like you're about to," said Ellen.

"Wait. Did that say Friday?" Andy asked. "*Today* is Friday."

"Uh, yeah," replied Jeff. "So, what do you wanna do?"

"Fuck it," said Ellen. "I say let's go. I mean, I gotta do the lunch thing with Traci, but I'll be back by five. I don't have to be at the Green Room until nine. I'm in if you guys want to go."

"Really?" asked Andy.

"Sure," Jeff agreed. "First of all, *whatever* Lula's cooking is way better than what we're getting otherwise. And second, we got nuthin' better to do. Bailing would just be rude."

He was right on both accounts. And so, it was settled. At six o'clock, they would join their elderly black neighbors for an evening of conversation and cuisine none of them could have foreseen or would soon forget.

"Well, shit!" Ellen said. "Now I'm gonna be late."

"Nobody's caring how your hair looks at the Lizard. Traci's gonna make you wear a net anyway," Andy teased. Both boys laughed at her expense as she slipped on her shoes and worked a brush through her still-damp hair.

"As for you and me…" Andy continued, pointing to Jeff as he walked towards the Den. "We better get busy."

"Busy with what?"

"We've only got a handful of hours until we must be sober as church mice. Better top off the tanks."

38

With Ellen gone, the boys migrated to their respective sides of the house, but only for a moment.

The vodka Andy wolfed down was beginning to work. He took a few deep breaths and finished trading his interview clothes for athletic shorts and a cleanish T-shirt. He didn't need to dress to impress for his next appointment.

Andy reclaimed his near-empty glass en route from the living room to the Den. Jeff was already waiting. A telltale rosewood box lay on the table between them.

"I was gonna ask if you wanted one, but it looks like you found your way onto the train all by yourself," said Andy, eyeing the fresh screwdriver on the table.

"Sometimes you *do* have good ideas," Jeff joked. "And here's *mine*… Grab the Hydra."

"That's a great idea," Andy agreed.

Jeff tested the hookah's airflow, pulling deeply on one of its hoses until tiny bubbles appeared in the chamber. All systems were 'go for launch.'

Andy scanned the surface of the coffee table. He found the remote control peeking out from under an old issue of *NME* magazine and clicked the TV to life. He didn't care what was on or that the volume was muted.

One or both TVs at Cornwall Street were almost always on and almost exclusively on Andy's account. It might not meet the clinical definition of "addiction." Still, Andy had a psychological relationship with, if not an actual dependence upon, television. He'd been self-conditioned, first as a latch-key kid, and now as a less-than-ambitious quasi-adult, to view television as a source of comfort. It was an ever-present companion, like a good friend, a frequent entertainer that often bolstered his self-esteem and only occasionally told him things that made him angry or uncomfortable.

It was 12:30 in the afternoon, which meant another dose of *The Mack Riley Show* was gracing the airwaves. Even with the sound off, Mack made it easy to follow along. The episode's title was always superimposed in can't-miss letters along the bottom of the screen. Today's episode was called "I Was Better Off in Prison."

Andy watched the silent screen with strange delight as Jeff packed the Hydra's bowl and finally announced, "We're ready."

They each grabbed a tentacle and touched the rubber-tipped ends to their lips. Jeff lit the huge bowl, and they inhaled. A standard, one-person bong could be fogged and dispersed in a single breath. The Hydra required considerably more effort. In fact, partakers often exhausted their lungs just by filling the large chamber with smoke. Once it had reached capacity, it was wise to pull back, cap the hoses with a thumb. Seasoned Hydra pros learned to take a few deep cleansing breaths and let the smoke float over the tarwater for a second before proceeding.

"One. Two. Three," Jeff counted. In lockstep, the synchronized smokers dove back toward the hoses, filling their lungs with the ice-cooled, super-potent smoke. They both did their best to hold their breath before gasping out thick billows of smoke. Before they'd even exhaled, the chemicals were working their magic, firing certain synapses and inhibiting others.

Andy turned back to the TV. He had been half-watching the silent drama brewing as Riley's panel poured out their angst. He reached for the remote and notched up the volume. A scrawny white dude with a shaved head and several neck tattoos was blabbering in an exaggerated ghetto accent about how bad his life was now that he was 'free.'

"Serious, man. At least in the joint I had food, clothes, a roof, some TV. I'm outside now. Ain't no jobs. Ain't no money. I gotta hustle a new place to sleep all the time. For what? I'm sp'osed to go outta my way to stay clean and to try, when there ain't nuthin' in it for me? Might as well knock over another store and go back inside. I know it in there. It's easy. Don't cost nuthin', ya know?"

"Damn," Andy said, his head pulsing pleasantly now. "That's fucked up."

"What?" Jeff asked, not really paying attention to Andy or the TV.

"This guy. He'd rather go back to prison than try to get a job and live straight."

"Yeah. I don't recommend that for you."

"Ha. Funny," said Andy. "But think about that for a minute. For that dude, his standard of living was better *in* prison than outside it. At least, that's what he thinks, which I guess makes it true for him. He had someone giving him everything he needed. Now, his 'freedom' is like a burden because it comes with the cost of being responsible for himself. He'd prefer to have no responsibility, even if it means giving up all his rights. That's crazy, but there's a weird logic to it."

"So, that's what you'd prefer?" Jeff asked, now engaged.

"Not *that* exactly. But think about it. Think about how we live. Shitty little house; shitty little jobs. We pay a few hundred bucks a month in rent and piss the rest away having fun. Some people might look at that and say, "Screw it. Why does it *ever* have to get any better than that? I have everything I need. I could do better for myself, and I probably should, but that would mean I would have to *try*. So, why bother?"

"So, now you're living in a prison?" Jeff concluded, trying to connect his roommate's dots.

"Aren't we all? I mean, we can all be content to stay where we are, where we know what's gonna happen and what's probably not—where we know our limits. The only other alternative is to try doing something else. Try harder, do more, put yourself out there. Risk getting hurt learning something or doing something new. That's what we're all living in."

"I could stay here and just keep doing what's easy. I'd have to get another bullshit job to pay the rent. But the world—my parents, my professors, my gut, and even the bullshit commercials on daytime TV-tells me I'm supposed to do more than that. I just don't know if I want to."

"Wow," Jeff said through a billow of grey-white cigarette smoke. "You really spend a lot of time thinking about shit like that, don't you?"

"Sometimes, shit like that is *all* I can think about. It makes my brain, and my stomach hurt."

"So, if that's 'not enough' as you say, what do you *really* want?"

"I just want to be happy," Andy blurted. The answer came fast, like a reflex.

"See, that's your problem," Jeff diagnosed immediately. "Happiness isn't something you can *get*. It's something you have to *give* yourself. It comes from being content with what you have and with who you are as a person."

"Dammit. Graham said almost the exact same thing the other day." Andy offered.

"And Graham's smart," Jeff answered.

Usually, Andy would want to argue. Maybe it was the creeping calm of the weed flowing through his brain. Or maybe Jeff had struck a chord. Either way, Andy was at least willing to hear more.

"Can I be honest with you?" Jeff continued, now looking him square in the eye.

Andy was instantly uncomfortable. He recognized the sincerity in his friend's tone. Still, he also knew nobody asked that question and then followed it up with anything nice.

"Sure," Andy said, almost out of defeat.

"You *are* living in a prison," Jeff stated. It wasn't what Andy expected.

"And it is mostly one of your own making. But, like the rest of us, you've had help building it."

"You've had some bad shit happen to you, I know. We all have. But in a lot of other ways, you've had it kinda easy. Your parents put you through school and didn't ask that much of you in return. You just graduated from college with almost no debt. Most people don't get that. I didn't get that. Ellen sure as shit ain't getting' that."

"What's worse…" Jeff continued, "is you've got all the talent you need, and more, to do exactly what you want to do. I've seen your work. I've seen you do your thing, and you're *good* at what you do. You just can't get out of your own way."

"I think you're afraid to step up and do what you gotta do on your own because you've never *had* to. Your parents were doing what they thought they should be doing, making it easy for you to succeed. But maybe they made things too easy. Now, you're up against having to do it alone and you're scared. You're locked in a prison of self-doubt, scared to death of disappointing people, including yourself. And *that's* the worst prison of all."

Even if Andy had *wanted* to argue, there was no response to Jeff's surgically precise assessment.

"Your biggest problem is that you honestly give a shit about what people think about you."

"Damn." Andy finally broke in, taking issue with that last critique. "*Everybody* cares what other people think, man."

"No. They don't," Jeff corrected, not missing a beat. He'd been waiting a while to say some of that to Andy, and now, he was letting it fly.

"Most people *notice* what other people think about them. Some might even adjust based on those opinions. But there's a world of difference between that and *caring* what they think, especially to the point that you actually live your life trying to please other people. 'Cause guess what? That's fucking impossible. *That's* the thing that's pointless to even try.

No matter how smart or good you are at whatever you do, somebody will always be dying to tell you you're not good enough. Chasing happiness through other people's approval is a fool's game. You can't win."

By the time Jeff finished his lecture, Andy had subconsciously curled himself into the corner of the couch—defensiveness personified.

"So, you just don't give a fuck what anyone thinks?" Andy asked.

"I didn't say that. I care what some people think. Like you. I care what *you* think, believe it or not. But I don't get my self-esteem or confidence from it. Mostly, I live my life doing what makes me happy. I try not to hurt anyone. If that's not good enough for other people, then it's not good enough for *them*. Fuck 'em. But the best part is, I'm not responsible to *them* for anything. I don't owe anybody their happiness. And neither do you."

"Think about it, Andy. I do a lot of 'weird' shit people could easily make fun of. And maybe they do, who knows? I do theater. I sing and dance, for God's sake. And speaking of God, I work at a friggin' church. You think people think that stuff is *cool*?"

"I think a lot of people think it's cool the way *you* do it," Andy had to admit.

Jeff was surprised by the odd compliment.

"And it's cool that you think that" Jeff acknowledged in return. "But that's the point. The *way I do it* is with total joy for myself. And if what I do makes other people happy, that's a bonus. But if it doesn't, that's on them."

"Even the church part?"

"Especially the church part."

"I thought you just did that as a job, to make money singing."

"No. I really like church," Jeff said. "And believe it or not, I *love* God," he added emphatically.

"How can you say that?" Andy demanded. Jeff had been playing offense the whole time, and the shift caught him off guard.

"Why? Because He lets bad shit happen? How can I love Him for that?"

"No," Andy said plainly. "Because you're just as much of a degenerate as me, sometimes worse. But you go to church and *love God*, so it's all good? How does that work?"

Andy wasn't looking for a fight. Truthfully, the shot was more of a random, blind deflection than some carefully planned body blow. But Jeff felt the sting of the hypocrisy his roommate's assertion implied and was compelled to counterpunch.

"I thank God every day for the gifts He's given me," Jeff defended. "I may not wear that love on my sleeve like some people, and I certainly don't put it in other peoples' faces, like the friggin' zealots that give God a bad name in the first place."

Andy remained quiet.

"It's not something I need to talk about. I know how I feel about God and what that relationship is for me personally. I also know that most of the people we hang out with don't have that same experience, so I just don't talk about it."

"But isn't it more complicated than that?"

"What do you mean?"

"I don't know," Andy started. He really *didn't* know where he was going. "Isn't it hard trying to live in both camps like that?"

"It used to be," Jeff admitted. "Until I realized that all of it makes me happy."

"So, as long as you're happy, that's all that matters?" Andy continued.

"Wouldn't you agree?"

"Yes. But I'm not trying to please God at the same time. Wouldn't He expect more from you?"

"You know what?" Jeff said, now glassy-eyed and miffed. "Why don't you just shut the fuck up?" He scoffed and lit a cigarette, looking to dismiss his friend's pointed assertion. Maybe with a clearer mind, he'd have had a better answer. For now, Jeff had nothing.

"How did we even get here?" Andy asked.

"Now, *that's* a question for God," Jeff joked. "The question for you is, 'why don't you stop talkin' shit and hit that again?'"

Already sufficiently damaged, Jeff offered one more solo pull from the Hydra to Andy, who was all too willing to oblige.

39

Alcohol, marijuana, failure, and self-help sermons can all be potent depressants. But now, Andy's brain was swimming in a warm bath of euphoria. In truth, the extra hit was probably too much. They were both giddy and lethargic, nearly incapacitated at the hands of the Hydra.

They'd stopped talking. The nonsensical rambling from the television meshed with the humming in their heads. Andy couldn't remember telling his legs it was time to move, but suddenly they were. He was almost in the kitchen before he realized he was up and walking toward the back of the house. From somewhere deep in his subconscious, his brain sent signals to his extremities, demanding they cooperate in making sleep the next order of business.

The final toke of weed was clearly overkill. Andy was profoundly intoxicated, past the point of comfortably numb. Making it to his room by muscle memory alone, he eyed the sweet sanctuary of the bed just a few feet away. Before Andy could get there, his equilibrium failed. His legs ceased to support his weight, and he stumbled forward. Burdened with a head full of static, liquor sloshing in an otherwise empty belly, and lungs burning in his chest, his knees buckled. He went down hard.

The last thought that crossed Andy's challenged mind as he slipped into the semi-consciousness of sleep was a simple, perhaps unintentional prayer: "God, help me."

40

Nearly six hours had passed since Ellen left them alone and unsupervised. Her roommates' cars were parked just as they had been, suggesting neither had left while she was gone. The front door was unlocked, as it always seemed to be.

Ellen was rarely at home alone. She entered, expecting to be greeted by smoke and/or noise. Instead, she found herself standing in the front room, surrounded by absolute still.

The door to Jeff's bedroom was closed. Being so near the front entrance, Jeff correctly assumed this was the best way to protect his privacy while he was home and his belongings while he was not.

In the silence, Ellen was reminded how the shabby, loosened floorboards creaked with her every step. As she reached the kitchen, the groaning of the hardwoods was replaced by a grosser, more depressing combination of sounds. That floor was covered by a sad layer of buckled and cracked linoleum, which might have originally been something close to white in color. With each step down, the floor seemed to release some quantity of air trapped between the linoleum and the subflooring. And with each step up came a grotesque ripping sound of shoe soles breaking the grip of a sticky film that seemed ever-present.

She placed a white cardboard box on the kitchen counter and continued to the back of the house. She expected to find Andy's door closed, too. But it wasn't. What she saw, Ellen could not immediately process. Andy was face down, touching the bed, but not on it all, and slightly fetal. He was still wearing the white undershirt and black socks from his interview, but now with dark blue athletic shorts. The rest of his suit lay strewn across the stuffed tan chair in the corner.

Seeing someone passed out was nothing new, but this made her uneasy. As Ellen approached, she heard the unmistakable sound of muffled breathing—a half-snore. A gear in her brain shifted, moving her from concern straight to agitation.

Only seconds ago, she would have knelt beside him and carefully checked on his condition. But now she had a much less gentle technique in mind. Placing the kitchen-sticky sole of her shoe against his shoulder, she kick-pushed him onto his back.

"Wake up, bitch!" she said, with no kindness.

"Huh?" Andy raised his hands to his still-closed eyes.

"Get up. It's after five. We have to be next door by six."

"Fuck," Andy groaned.

"Fuck is right," she continued. "That's what I was saying as I walked in here after working an extra shift to find you passed out when we're supposed to be going to the neighbors' for dinner. And where the fuck is Tweedle Dee?"

"I dunno," Andy said, struggling to shake off the webs. Tired and incoherent, he was still clear she was pissed. "He's probably sleeping, too."

"Whatever. Get up and get dressed. Be ready and happy about it by 5:45," she demanded and walked out the door.

Andy sat on the floor, listening as she turned on Jeff. A door opened indelicately, followed by more of Ellen's loud and clear voice. Andy assumed his roommate was also now awake.

"Whatever..." she repeated, plenty loud enough to be heard across the house. "...he doesn't know his ass from his elbow lately, but you should know better." Clearly, she was mad at them both, but for different reasons. "Get up!"

One door slammed. Seconds later, another. If Jeff wanted to shower before heading to the Murphys, he was in line behind her.

Andy looked over at his bedside clock. 5:11 p.m. For the second time in eight hours, he would have to scramble to make himself presentable. He'd already completed the same drill once today. His evening appointment was far more casual, which relieved the stress he typically felt in time-sensitive situations.

In fact, he felt tangibly less stressed in general. He rose, surprised at the looseness in his shoulders and back, surprised he genuinely felt 'good.'

Throughout the day, the heat stacked like layers, adding weight and a sense of burden to the air inside their home. The smallness of the back bathroom and its lack of any ventilation only compounded the problem. With the door closed, the heat and humidity created a thick, choking atmosphere, like being sealed in an eight-square-foot Tupperware container.

Once again, Andy opted for the wakening punch of a colder shower. The sting of the cool water on his sweat-covered skin was brutal for the first few seconds. As his body regulated, the feeling turned from agony to ecstasy. The heat rose through him, pouring from the top of his head like a demon being forced from his body. He lingered, basking in the total refreshment of the cold cascade. He could have stayed there much longer, but they were on the clock. Andy turned off the water and again grabbed his ripped pink towel.

5:30 p.m. He was right on schedule. Andy slipped on a pair of khaki pants, the ones he used to wear working the desk at Howard Johnson's, or whenever his parents would visit and take him to a 'nice' dinner. He added a short-sleeved button-down shirt in green, white, and yellow plaid. Andy hated wearing a belt but acquiesced. Slipping on a pair of brown topsiders, he decided he was presentable enough.

Andy found Ellen in the living room, brushing her hair and staring out the window. She was a jeans and T-shirt kind of girl. But there she stood in a greyish-blue, knee-length skirt and a simple black top that was sheer and stylish. Black hose wrapped her suddenly shapely-looking legs. Andy wanted to crack a joke about someone letting a girl into their house but based on his last interaction with *that girl*, he wisely thought better of it.

Instead, he offered, "Wow. You look awesome."

"Thanks," Her tone was neither angry nor friendly, leaving Andy unsure how to proceed.

"Sorry about earlier," he said. He didn't even know what he was apologizing for but figured it was a safe play.

"Yeah, me too. There's a lot of tension around here, and I had a shitty time at The Lizard today. I didn't even want to go, but I did it anyway. Then I got home, and you guys looked like you'd had a little party without me. Kinda rubbed me the wrong way."

"Sorry," Andy repeated. "You know, I love that about you."

"What's that?" Jeff asked, emerging from his room, clean and polished in some of his better clothes. "When she plays sexy dress up?"

It was precisely the kind of barb Andy had resisted throwing just a moment ago.

"What?" she asked Andy, ignoring Jeff's adolescence.

"I love that you're willing to do shit you don't *want* to do to help other people. I kind of suck at that."

There were several things she loved about him, too. But his apology and the unprovoked kindness that accompanied it caught her by such surprise that she blanked.

"You don't suck..." she started.

"Oh no, I do," Andy interrupted. "Mostly, I don't really do anything I don't want to do. I've gotten away with that for a long time, but it's probably not sustainable."

Ellen was confused. Apparently, she'd missed more than just a random round of bong hits while at The Lizard. She glanced at Jeff, who gave her a 'We'll talk later' look...

"We gotta go," Jeff said. "We're gonna be late."

"Oh shit!" said Ellen, walking back to the kitchen. "I almost forgot the pie."

"Pie!?" Andy said with great enthusiasm. He loved pie.

"Yes, pie. You can't just show up empty-fuckin'-handed to a dinner party. So, after my shitty afternoon at The Lizard, I stopped at In Your Face and got a pie."

"What'd you get?" Andy asked with the bouncy excitement of a third grader.

"Mocha banana crème,"

"Damn. Not apple?"

"It's not about you!" said Ellen, inching toward pissed again. "First of all, when your lazy ass is the one that spends time and money to go get the pie, you can pick apple. But just so you know, apple is boring. Everyone knows banana crème is the most socially interesting of all pies."

Not *everyone* knew that—clearly, not even everyone in her own house. They both looked at her as if she was speaking a foreign language and laughed hard.

"Fuck you both," she snapped. "And secondly, you pricks both owe me eight dollars. Now say thank you, and let's go."

"Thanks, Mom!" they cheered in unison, still laughing and heading for the door.

41

Roughly 100 feet separated their front porch from their neighbors' next door. Jeff and Andy fell in behind Ellen as she led the boys on the short walk. Where their cracked walkway met the even more fractured sidewalk, she turned and headed up the hill, carrying that pie like some sacred artifact. Ellen reached the door and waited for her straggling roommates to join her. Then, she had a horrible realization.

"Oh shit," she whispered, wheeling around. Jeff failed to anticipate her about-face, and they collided with enough force to buckle the pie box slightly between their midsections.

"What?" Andy asked at full volume.

"Did either of you tell them we were coming?"

Stares went around the circle as it became clear they had not bothered to RSVP. There they stood, dressed and shiny, in nearly 100-degree heat, on their neighbor's porch, with a pie, quite possibly about to find themselves unexpected and unwelcome.

"So, what?" Andy asked, now adopting a hushed tone and taking a step back. "Should we bail?"

"Fuck that," Jeff said. "I'm hungry. Just ring the bell. They invited…"

"Yeah," interrupted Ellen, "they invited, but we never accepted, so they probably think we're total …"

The door opened behind her.

"…assholes," Ellen finished, still facing away from the house. Andy's face plumed red with embarrassment for her. Jeff bore a passable shit-eating grin.

"Well, goodness! Hello, y'all," said a voice none of them had ever heard. "Quenton, they're here!"

Miss Lula Murphy, all five feet of her, stood in the open doorway. She smiled enthusiastically, revealing a set of impossibly white teeth. They stood on the porch, grinning back at her. A rustling approached from behind Lula as Quenton came to the door.

Lula wore tailored navy-blue pants and a peach-colored top. At six-foot-three, Quenton towered over her. Lula was short but appeared solid and confident–the kind of woman you'd think twice about messing with.

"Hey, y'all," said Quenton, his hands resting on Lula's shoulders.

"Mr. Murphy," Andy acknowledged, extending his hand. "Mrs. Murphy," he added politely as Quenton received him.

"Hi," Ellen said tentatively to them both at once.

"Hello, sir." Jeff followed Andy's lead and shook Quenton's hand. "Ma'am," he added, with a simple nod carrying the perfect amount of Southern white boy charm.

"Y'all come up off this porch," Lula insisted. "It's hot out here."

Quenton held the glass storm door until each had entered. The first thing Andy noticed was the air conditioning and the sense of physical relief it brought. A/C was a luxury they had to leave home to enjoy. The second stimulus, the heavenly smell of home cooking, was equally pleasant.

"This is my lovely wife, Lula," Quenton offered, presenting her at arm's length like the prize she was to him. They'd all seen her before in passing, but none had ever spoken to her.

"Andy Maxwell, ma'am. Pleased to meet you." He reached out, expecting to politely shake her dainty hand. The strength of her grip was shocking.

"And these are my friends… Ellen Norris and Jeff Aaron."

"Hello," Jeff said, still smiling.

"Hi." Her acknowledgment of Jeff was warm enough, but really, she was focused on Ellen, who was becoming increasingly self-conscious about the large white box she was still clutching.

"We brought a pie," Ellen said nervously.

"Aww. Ain't you sweet?" Lula pined. "Now, you know you didn't need to do that."

Those were her words. What Ellen knew she meant was *I sure am glad your momma raised you right enough to know you needed to do that.*

"Yes, ma'am," Ellen said, smiling and relinquishing the box to Lula with some relief.

"Quenton, take these boys on into the living room. Me and Miss Ellen will be in the kitchen." Lula directed. As Mrs. Murphy walked away, Ellen looked at the three men. Quenton gave her a friendly smile. Her roommates were both trying hard not to laugh. She threw eye-daggers at them as she turned to follow Lula.

The men retreated to the living room, where Jeff and Andy continued to take in their unfamiliar surroundings. Seen from the street, the exteriors of their two homes were similar enough to be unnoticeable, but the interiors weren't even from the same universe.

The Murphys kept an immaculate home. The living room's light, cloth-covered furniture sat above dark, rich hardwood floors polished to a glossy shine. A tall curio cabinet of nearly the same finish stood in the corner. Behind thick glass doors, it held pieces of antique China, a few old books, and an ancient-looking rag doll.

Quenton moved with the pace and unevenness befitting a man his age. Methodically, he crept to a light blue, high-backed chair. Lowering himself into place, he propped his feet on the matching ottoman and ushered the boys to the couch opposite him.

"Welcome to our home," Quenton offered with outstretched arms and a healthy grin. Behind him was a small fireplace, which seemed too shallow to function safely. The mantle over the hearth held a few neatly framed family pictures. Above them hung a large needlepoint primer proclaiming the Scripture, "As for me and my house, we will serve the Lord. – Joshua 24:15."

Andy couldn't quite reconcile the spectacle. This was the same man he had just watched skip church to wax his Cadillac while enjoying a beer and cigarettes.

"Y'all wanna drink?" Quenton asked. "Mrs. Murphy makes the best sweet tea you ever had." He paused; hands folded in his lap. The full translation was, *'Y'all know I got beers, but this ain't one of them kinda nights.'*

"I'm fine. Thank you," Jeff declined.

"I'm good, too," Andy lied with a thirsty throat. "Dinner smells amazing by the way."

The aroma of authentic Southern cooking filled the house. Plates, silverware, and glasses clanged across the hall. The men could hear the two ladies exchanging bits of small talk. Most of it was directional on Lula's part as they brought the steaming dishes of food to the table.

Jeff was conflicted by Quenton's request for company. He knew it was just an excuse to stay out of the way until the kitchen work was done. But he'd been raised to know he should be helping. Neither Andy nor Quenton seemed to be sharing his struggle.

"Quenton, dear…" came the sweet call from across the hallway, "Bring the boys. Supper's ready."

The boys hopped up much more quickly than their host and were several steps ahead of him on their way to the dining room.

"How can we help?" Andy asked as he reached the table. He knew perfectly well the ladies had already done everything.

"Y'all have a seat and get what you want to drink," Lula chirped, setting down a basket of golden-brown yeast rolls. Two pitchers, one full of iced tea and the other with lemonade, sat near the center of the large oval table that dominated the dining room. A bounty of serving plates and bowls overflowed with meatloaf, mashed potatoes, macaroni and cheese, turnip greens, and spiced apples.

The plates were fine China, the silverware might have even been real silver, and the glasses were actually glass. Worlds away from the paper plates and Dixie cups in their kitchen next door.

Andy watched Jeff, who was watching Quenton, for a cue on how to proceed. Quenton stood at one head of the table behind his still tucked-in chair. The boys assumed correctly that the chair at the other end of the table, the 'I'll get it' seat, nearest to the kitchen, was reserved for Lula. They stood together on one of the oval's long sides, leaving Ellen alone opposite them. Quenton waited patiently until Lula placed the last dish on the table. Only after she was seated did he pull back his own chair. The boys followed suit, waiting for Ellen to sit before doing the same.

Eager to compliment their hosts on the glorious spread, Andy began, "Thank you, Mrs. Murphy, this loo…"

"Just a minute, son," she corrected. "We thank the Lord first in this house. Let's pray." Lula folded her wrinkled hands together and bowed her head.

"Heavenly Father," Quenton began. His voice was gravelly but confident. "Thank you for this home and for these friends who have come to it to share in the fellowship of this bounty You have provided. May this food nourish our bodies as Your Word nourishes our souls. Keep us safe as we travel the path You would lead us on and give us the wisdom to always seek and welcome Your company as we go. In Your Son's holy name, we pray… Amen."

"Amen," they all concurred.

Andy was again stunned by his old neighbor. The prayer was an eloquent, stark contrast to the jive-infused smack they traded in the driveway or over the shoddy fence between their backyards.

Even before he stepped away from God, Andy had always felt awkward around those who prayed openly. To be fair, most of those were street preacher types, aggressively spewing brimstone at heathens. Still, even in less intimidating situations, the practice still made Andy very uncomfortable.

But this felt different. Quenton's words were simple and humble. They were full of grace and thankfulness and, more noticeably to

Andy, devoid of any judgment. He wondered if the words had been practiced or simply delivered. Andy was still contemplating as the warmth of the breadbasket Jeff passed his way registered against his forearm.

"Thank you again, Mrs. Murphy," Andy finally completed his compliment.

"Oh, y'all are more than welcome," she answered. "But it's Quenton you should be thanking. It was his idea to have y'all over."

"Thank you, sir," Ellen offered. "This is so nice of you both."

"Yes, thank you," Jeff echoed as the serving dishes circled the table and plates began to fill.

"The pleasure is ours," Quenton beamed. "It's overdue. Y'all been right next door a couple years now. And I get the feeling Andy over there might be movin' on. Seemed like the right thing to do."

Andy felt the heat of an unwanted spotlight. A quick scan around the table confirmed they were all looking his way.

"How's that going?" Quenton asked pointedly. "Still lookin' for a job?" Andy hadn't expected the topic to follow him to this supposedly neutral arena.

So be it, he thought. The questions about his future were constant. Maybe airing them publicly would bring some closure, or at least a fresh point of view, to a subject he'd grown tired of addressing, and avoiding. In any case, hashing it out in their elderly neighbors' home guaranteed the exchange would be a civil conversation instead of a fight.

"It depends on your perspective," Andy stated cautiously.

"Everything does," Quenton agreed, passing the breadbasket to Ellen.

Andy dished a healthy scoop of Lula's mac and cheese onto his plate. He watched the steam rise as he paused and sipped his sweet tea. "I do have an option or two. But I don't really like them very much."

"What do you mean?" Lula asked. Having heard this story, Ellen and Jeff gladly let their neighbors grill Andy while they dug into the food.

Andy wasn't sure where to start. Not knowing how much either of them cared to know about his situation, he rewound to nearly the beginning and pushed play.

"So, I just graduated, and I've been looking for a job where I can really *use* my degree."

"What's your degree, and what do you want to do?" asked Lula.

Jeff and Ellen continued to shovel Lula's delicious home cooking into their mouths as Andy covered this well-beaten path for a new audience.

"Advertising, ma'am. I want to be a writer."

"Oh, that sounds exciting," she replied with legitimate interest. "Good for you. I would never be able to do something like that."

"I'm guessing it's not as glamorous as it sounds," Andy admitted, mostly hoping he was wrong. "Besides, writing's not that hard or impressive. It's just putting words together. All the answers are in the dictionary."

"Careful, son," Quenton said with a seriousness that surprised all three of his young guests. "It's one thing to be humble, but don't you be glib about the talents God gave you. He gives everybody some kinda gift, something that makes you like nobody else. Some people know exactly what theirs is. Other people search their whole lives trying to figure out what they got from Him."

There was a tension in Quenton's voice. It wasn't quite anger, but at least a frustration that suggested he might be one of those 'other people'.

"If you know what you love to do, and you happen to be good at it, you best count yourself as blessed, 'cause that's rare in this world."

Andy had only meant his comment as a joke, but Quenton wasn't playing. His point wasn't lost on Andy either. "Yes sir," Andy answered, feeling like he'd just been admonished by an older, blacker, slightly kinder version of his father.

"He's right, dear," agreed Lula. Her voice was much softer and sweet but just as firm. "What you think is easy, someone else might find impossible. There's true blessing in that."

"Besides," Lula continued, now showing her own quick wit. "You're right about one thing. There *is* a book with all the answers in it, but it's not the dictionary."

Andy stared at his plate, feeling the weight of their well-meaning criticism.

"Now, continue," she said with a smile.

"So, I know *what* I want to do. It's the *where* and *how* I just don't have figured. I've had a couple of interviews, but those were total failures. And then just this morning, I think I got offered the worst job in the history of the world."

"Oh, I seriously doubt that" Quenton said, still not back to the friendly tone to which his young neighbor was accustomed. Clearly, the Murphy home had a lower tolerance for hyperbole than he enjoyed next door.

"You ever dig a hole for a latrine, Andy?" Quenton asked. He and everyone else already knew the answer. "Or work 15 hours a day on the railroad in the hot-ass Alabama sun?"

Quenton was a good, kind man and a friendly neighbor. But he didn't have a lick of patience for a spoiled-soft, white boy college graduate who wasn't *happy enough* with *all his options*. He'd grown up in a different time when you only had *one* choice—find a way, doing whatever you had to do, to make enough money to take care of your family. *Happiness* was a luxury you thought about after the bills were paid.

The point was sufficiently made, so much so that Andy knew to skip the part about his backup plan being a return to his already-too-helpful parents. This safety net, which had become a real option for so many of Andy's age, was obviously not standard issue in the Murphys' generation.

"Quenton," Lula reprimanded her husband, "there's no need to..."

"It's fine, ma'am." Andy admitted. "He's right. About all of it." He kept his gaze locked on Quenton. It was partly out of respect but at least as much about not having to see the looks on the faces of his roommates, who had to be loving every second of the verbal beatdown he was taking.

"Here's all I'm sayin'," Quenton continued, finally softening his tone. "I've had a lot, probably more than my share, of what you might call the *'worst jobs in the world'*. I didn't like them, but I did 'em and was glad for them. Every one of them was part of the road that led me to where I am today, and I wouldn't change that; not for nuthin'. There ain't a lot of fun or happiness in doing crappy jobs, but there's a sense of pride and self-worth in it you can't get from skippin' over all the hard stuff."

There was nothing for Andy to argue with there.

"I'll just say one last thing, then I'll hush, so you and me can both eat this fine meal that's getting' cold on us." He took a sip of lemonade and pointed his wrinkled index finger across the table at Lula.

"I met this here lady when I was about your age. Didn't have no money, no prospects, no future, and no faith. I was goin' nowhere. Didn't even know where I wanted to go. All I knew was I wanted to go with her. She said she wanted that too, but she couldn't go through life with a faithless man. She told me if things were gonna work, I had to trust her and trust God. I told her I would try, and I don't even know if that was the truth at the time. In the beginning, I faked it, cuz I just wanted to be with her. Over time, though, I don't know. Maybe she wore me down. Maybe some of it sunk in. Who knows? But I felt as lost as you do. Thinkin' there was no happiness comin' my way. But she never stopped encouragin' me. Used to read me Scriptures all the time. Most of it went over my head, or straight through my ears. Every now and then, one would catch me the right way and make me feel better. But there was one that hit hard and stuck."

Quenton's eyes widened, and his voice raised a touch as he reached the peak of his sermon to Andy. Taking his hands from the table, he slipped one into the back pocket of his dress pants. It re-emerged, clutching a brown leather money clip.

"Turns out, this is everything I ever needed to know about working and being happy." He put the wallet on the table and slid it over to Andy. As Quenton removed his dark, bony hand, Andy could clearly see the lettering stamped into the hardened, leather-covered hinge of the clip. *Proverbs 16:3*

"Turn it over," Quenton said.

Andy sat looking at the well-worn clip for what seemed an eternity. Again, he dared not look at Jeff or Ellen. He ran a hesitant finger along the stitched edge of the leather. Approaching as if the leather rectangle were a poisonous viper, Andy quickly flipped it over. More words were stamped on the facing side.

Commit your work to the Lord, and your plans will succeed.

Andy didn't put much stock into divine intervention. Still, it was hard to deny the surreal, perhaps supernatural, relevance of what Quenton had produced.

"Now," Quenton said, slower and much more like the guy Andy was used to seeing puffing menthols on the porch, "Lemme see that."

As Andy returned the money clip, a rush of uncomfortable heat flowed over him. He was embarrassed to be emasculated—laid bare before his friends. And he was rightly ashamed of the ugly truths Quenton had exposed about his attitude, work ethic, and myopic worldview.

Quenton took the money clip in his work-worn hands and freed a small stack of bills. Stuffing the cash into the pocket of his dress shirt, he turned the clip over a few times, contemplating it, and then held it out to Andy.

"Here. This belongs to you now. I already learned what it was supposed to teach me."

"I can't take your…"

"You can, and you should," responded Lula, who'd been silently watching her husband educate their young neighbor. Her eyes were wide, soft, and welling with pride.

"Took Quenton more years than he or I'd like to admit for him to embrace that lesson it doesn't matter *what* he does, so long as he finds joy in it and does his best. God rewards that, and good always comes from it. Same is true for helping people. So, you let him help you, and you listen; cuz when you listen, you can understand, and when you understand, everything gets different."

Andy took the clip from Quenton and thanked them both for the gift and the wisdom that went with it. His roommates had cleaned their plates while school was in session. Ellen sat quietly, her arms folded on the table, looking at Andy. She wore a smile he couldn't quite read. It wasn't judgmental or mocking; it was more like pleased amazement. Jeff had used the distraction of Quenton's sermon to reload his plate and was halfway through a second helping. Andy didn't even have to look at him to know he was probably smiling, too.

"I don't want *everything* to be different," Andy said quietly. "I just don't want to feel like I'm choosing between bad options, just because I need the money."

"So, what would you do if money didn't matter?" Ellen asked. They were the first words Andy could recall her speaking since they sat down.

"I think I'd stay here," Andy said without much thought or delay. "But that's probably the easy way. I guess I don't know. What I do know is I would take my time and not rush into anything, just to be *doing something*. I'd look around and find where I'm supposed to be. I think that's what I was supposed to be doing for the past four years. But I was too busy having a good time to think ahead. This place has been great for me—the best time of my life. But I wasted a lot of opportunities. If I had more time, I'd probably think differently about it."

"We've all been *there*," Quenton admitted. "Just about everybody would take a second chance at somethin' if they could get it. Good luck with that, though. Most of the time, He's trying to move us forward, even if it's not what we want."

"That's enough of the heavy talk, Quenton," Lula chastised. "I'll tell you what we *do* want right now… some of that pie Miss Ellen brought. C'mon girl. Let's go get it."

They laughed, and Ellen rose to follow Lula back into the kitchen. Andy looked at his plate and realized he'd done a lot of talking and little eating. As plates and dishes starting disappearing from the table, he hastily jammed forkfuls of meatloaf and mac and cheese into his mouth.

They sat at the Murphys' big oval table for a while, leisurely enjoying cheap coffee and Ellen's over-priced, highly decadent banana crème pie. Ellen and Jeff each shared various details of their lives and how they ultimately found themselves in Bradford. Andy, by contrast, was largely silent. He chimed in occasionally with the answer to a question or a half-hearted laugh at a good joke. But mostly, he spent dessert quietly, almost sullenly, contemplating his exchange with Quenton. The money clip sat on the table beside his plate, staring him straight in the face. As if repelled by some unseen force, he couldn't quite bring himself to take ownership of it by picking it up and putting it in his pocket.

Two cups of coffee and one and a half slices of pie later, Ellen noticed the clock. She was due at the Green Room in less than an hour and still had to change into clothes she'd accept drenching in bar swill and cigarette smoke.

"Ma'am," she spoke politely, turning to Lula. "I have to work tonight, so I need to get ready. Can I help you clear the table, or with the dishes?"

"Absolutely not," Lula said with a smile. "Cookin's my job. Clearin' is manly work."

Jeff and Andy looked up from their pie and saw the grin emerging on Quenton's face.

"Sorry, boys," Quenton lied. "Shoulda gave you a heads-up on that. This one's on us." He rose from the table and gathered the dessert plates and forks near him. The younger men were still seated but quickly realized their host wasn't kidding about the division of labor.

"You go on and get to work. I'll send these boys home when I'm done with them," Quenton said.

Ellen smiled back and placed her napkin by her plate. Andy and Jeff were grateful that at least she couldn't, or more accurately, wouldn't mock them openly in front of their hosts. But they were sure they'd hear it again from her later.

"Okay. If you're sure," Ellen said, now milking it just for the sake of it. "See you later, boys. Are you coming to the Room tonight?"

"Nope," Andy said without pause. "Doc's having people over. We'll be there, probably late. Meet us there."

Lula took a step backward and created a path. As Ellen passed, Lula opened her arms wide, inviting her young neighbor in for an unexpected hug. Ellen was surprised but went with it. She offered Lula a quick embrace and reiterated her gratitude for their hospitality.

"The pleasure is all ours. Hopefully we'll keep seein' you 'round for a while."

"That'd be nice, ma'am."

She thanked Quenton from across the table and headed for the door.

Looking at the used dishes and glasses on the table before him, Andy took a deep breath. He grabbed the money clip, stuffed it in his back pocket opposite his current wallet, and started clearing.

42

Lula Murphy sat at the head of her table like a contented statue, hands in her lap, looking out the windows across the room. Andy stacked plates and gathered used forks, trying not to stare at her. Her silent motionlessness was oddly captivating. Clearly, she enjoyed watching her husband and his two young charges move the mountain of dishes she'd dirtied in their service.

Jeff shadowed Quenton in the kitchen, rinsing bowls and platters and handing them to his host, who arranged them with precise expertise in the dishwasher. Along with air conditioning, this appliance was another modern convenience Jeff was grateful his neighbors possessed.

A minute or so followed with little more than minor instructional exchanges between them. But as soon as Quenton was confident his assistant knew the drill, he resumed his teacher's pulpit. Now, he aimed at Jeff.

"You know," Quenton said with a slight chuckle, "that boy in there has a lot to learn."

Jeff misread the trajectory and confidently agreed, "You don't have to tell me."

"Oh, but I do," Quenton said, flashing the grin of a master reveling in the folly of a too-sure student.

"We ALL have plenty to learn. Y'all might be graduating, but real school don't never end."

Jeff knew there was more coming. He handed another platter to Quenton and fixed his attention on his neighbor.

"See, you might think you got it all figured out; got yerself right and all that. But I see something else…"

Quenton's "taking to task" tone, which had been amusing to Jeff a bit earlier, now caused an unfamiliar tension to course through him. He couldn't remember the last time someone spoke to him that way–not even his parents. And it wasn't like it was one of his asshole friends giving him shit, which was easy enough to shut down. This was different. Jeff was gonna hear what Murphy had to say, whether he wanted to or not.

"I see you in them choir robes every week. You look the part when you come and go. But what about the rest of it?" Quenton saw conflict in his young neighbor's eyes but not confusion. He could tell Jeff was following along just fine.

"That wallet was talkin' to Andy in there. It's pretty clear that boy's got at *least* one demon chasin' him. That wallet said what HE needed to hear," Quenton continued. "God's got something different for you."

The old man stood tall, maybe to stretch his aching back or to sharpen Jeff's attention. He wiped his hands with a damp dishtowel and extended his bony finger. Jeff followed the line it drew. Amongst a jumble of pictures and reminders affixed to the stark white refrigerator, he found Quenton's target. Another needlework primer, this one no larger than a Post-It Note, hung from a magnetized metal hook.

'*Revelation 3:15-16*'

"Do you know that one?" Quenton asked, giving Jeff the benefit of the doubt.

"No sir," Jeff replied, now even more uncomfortable, "not by heart."

"That's okay," Quenton reassured him. "I'm sure you got a Bible over there, right?"

"Yessir."

It was the truth. It hardly saw the light of day anymore. Still, the very copy of the King James Version he had received at his childhood Confirmation was sitting on a shelf in his room next door.

"Good," Quenton said. "You read it on your own then. But I'll tell you this much… That one I gave Andy? That was mine," Quenton pointed back at the primer on the fridge. "This one here is Lula's." He scanned his hand across the kitchen until that finger led straight to his bride.

"See that lady in there? She's the best woman I know."

Jeff could feel Quenton's pride as he lauded his wife, but the old man wasn't done complimenting her.

"But better than that? She's also the best Servant of God I've ever seen. And do you know why?"

"No, sir?"

"'Cause, you might not know it just to look at her, but she's got a *fire* in her for God that burns like nuthin' I ever seen. Ain't a lukewarm bone in her body. Puts me to shame nearly every day."

"Yessir," Jeff agreed, finding no other response.

"Anyway," Quenton relaxed, returning to the dishes, "You read it. I think you'll see."

"Yessir," Jeff repeated, handing the last platter to Quenton just as Andy entered the kitchen with a stack of dessert plates.

"Hmm," Quenton said with surprise. "More plates. Ain't a lick a room left in the dishwasher."

The boys looked at each other with a shared fear that his next directive was going to be that they finish the remainder by hand.

"Tell you what. You boys have probably had enough for one evening. I'll finish these up once y'all go, while Miss Lula's gettin' into her night clothes."

A great relief swept over them both as they accepted their release. Jeff wiped his hands on the dishcloth and offered a dry hand to Quenton, who shook it earnestly. Andy responded in kind as they departed the kitchen.

Lula was still seated at the dining room table but rose as they prepared to leave.

"Thank you again," Andy offered.

"Not at all," Quenton replied. "Thank y'all for comin', and for listenin'. Y'all be safe and have a good night now."

43

As soon as they stepped foot on the sidewalk, Jeff desperately lit a Winston. He turned back to offer one to Andy and couldn't help but be amused by the sight of Quenton on his front porch, a billow of smoke emerging from his own menthol stick. As punctuation to the surreal visit, Quenton held aloft the cold beer in his other hand as if offering a toast to cap the evening. Apparently, things were back to whatever *normal* was.

"So," Jeff said as they walked down the gravel drive. "You've been talking shit about going to church with me for a while now. How'd you enjoy that?"

44

"What time do you want to head to Doc's?"

The two boys pushed through the front door, shoulder-to-shoulder like adolescent brothers battling for supremacy.

"I don't care," Jeff said. "I'm in no hurry."

"Fine by me. I'm definitely getting out of these, though." Andy was already unbuttoning his shirt as he walked and talked. The idea of changing hadn't even occurred to Jeff, but he embraced the suggestion in stride.

Andy traded his dinner costume for a pair of worn jeans and a black Sun Studios T-shirt. He added ratty sneakers to complete the transition and instantly felt more like himself again. He picked the khakis up off the floor and reached for a hanger. No plans to wear those again any time soon.

Grasping the pants near the waistband, he felt his wallet in one of the back pockets. And then also the gift he'd received. He pulled out both leather squares and tossed them together onto his desk. Andy stood considering the pair of money holders. He knew he would need to take one with him tonight and found himself rationalizing a choice between them, until he chose not to. He stuffed his old wallet into his jeans and left the money clip alone on the desk.

"So, Ellen's gonna meet us there later?" Jeff asked.

"Maybe. Guess it depends on what time she finishes."

"Do you wanna just walk to Doc's?"

"No." As if Andy ever really wanted to *just walk* anywhere. "I need a pack of smokes. I'll drive us up to the Cubby and then over to Doc's."

Doc's house was a mere three blocks from their own, a relatively easy walk. But the distance was irrelevant to Andy. "If we drive there, we'll have a car if we need it. If we get too fucked up, we can always leave it and walk home."

"Sure," said Jeff, certain that wasn't happening either.

45

En route to the Cubby convenience store, Andy chose the longer, downhill route along Paxton Avenue. He assumed it would offer the best view of whether the Cactus Club was still encased in bright yellow police tape. It was.

"You coming?" Jeff was already out of the car.

"Chill. You know I'm slow."

"You buy smokes. I'll get beer."

"That works. But get something good," Andy clarified. "I'm not drinking PBR tonight."

"Whatever, snob. Get a pack of Winston Reds and a pack of Lights. Oh, and a lighter. I lost mine."

"Anything else?"

"No, that's good."

It took less than three minutes for them to reconvene at the register. Jeff held a twelve-pack and two 40-ounce bottles of Crazy Horse malt liquor.

"Damn. That's ambitious. Big plans tonight?"

"It's Doc's house, so you *never* know. It just seemed right."

"Maybe for you. I can't drink the Horse anymore. It makes me angry."

"Dude. *Everything* makes you angry. What's the difference?"

"Whatever. Just get 'em."

Andy forked over a ten to cover the smokes and moved down the counter. Perusing the winning lottery tickets taped to the wall above the register, he spotted an utterly different payout. Plastered over some of those tickets was a new take on an increasingly familiar face.

A stark white flyer, printed in full color, bore a young girl's beautiful, smiling face. Her dirty blond hair was different-shorter-and her dimples were more pronounced. Still, it was unmistakably Margo Hammond. The word "MISSING" was pasted in huge black type on a yellow field. Under the photo, in letters nearly as large as the headline: "REWARD: $50,000!" and then, much smaller, her name and pertinent details.

"Holy shit! Look! They doubled the reward for her."

"I wonder if that's good, or bad?" Jeff wondered aloud.

"It can't be good," said Andy. "She's been gone almost a week now. At some point, the odds of finding her go *way* down."

"Is that new?" Jeff asked the clerk.

"Yep. Just today. $4.13 is your change. Y'all have a good night."

Apparently, the clerk had no interest in starting a conversation about Margo Hammond.

"Damn, man," Andy grumbled on the way back to his SUV.

"What?"

"$50,000. Finding her would solve all my problems."

"More likely to solve *her* problems," Jeff corrected. "Besides, most of your problems, money can't solve."

"Shut up."

Andy put the SUV in gear and headed back up the hill. Two blocks down onto Providence, they turned left. The street was lined with parked cars 100 yards ahead of Doc's house.

"Well, we waited long enough."

"No shit," Jeff agreed. "By the time we find a place to park, we could've walked here faster."

"I'll find one," Andy said as they rolled past their destination. The party had already spilled outside of the two-story white house. Clusters of people dotted the small yard, laughing, drinking, and smoking.

Andy found a space just big enough to squeeze in the SUV. The back of his new vehicle half-blocked a neighboring driveway as he put it in park.

"You'll *probably* be okay here," Jeff cautioned, registering a preemptive 'I told you so' if Andy's new car got towed or dinged.

46

The murmur of small talk and muffled music mixed as they approached the house. Between the sidewalk and the front door, they were acknowledged more than once. Jeff stopped to say hello to two girls. Andy was carrying both bags from the Cubby. More interested in offloading his cargo than chatting, he kept walking.

The spine of Doc's house was a long hallway opening to rooms on either side. People filled the corridor, a few lingering on the steps that led up to the bedrooms. Andy moved through the crowd, veering left at the stairs and into the kitchen. He knew he should have handed one of the monstrous bottles of malt liquor to Jeff before they separated. Unattended, those bottles would be gone before the social butterfly fluttered as far as the fridge. Andy had to move a few things around to make it work, but he found room for the now-open twelve-pack and tucked one of the two big bottles of Crazy Horse into the vegetable crisper. Carrying a Heineken in one hand and cradling the forty-ounce like a baby along his other forearm, he returned to the front door. He would take one lap around the perimeter, and if he didn't spot Jeff by then, all bets were off.

Halfway down the hall, Andy found his roommate leaning against the wall, holding court. Jeff had his arm around a girl Andy didn't know and was telling some story to her and a couple of friends. Andy said nothing. Instead, he interrupted Jeff's flow by reaching through the huddle and jamming the massive bottle of malt liquor within inches of his face.

"Thanks!" said Jeff.

"Yep. Drink up, homie," Andy teased. "You guys seen Doc?"

"Nicky's upstairs, I think," said the girl under Jeff's arm. She was cute and already drunk.

Andy looked at Jeff, entertaining two thoughts at once. The first, whether Jeff intended to pursue the wounded game already in his clutches, was answered by his roommate's slight, devilish smile. The second was more of a puzzled amusement as he mouthed the word *"Nicky?"*, about to laugh out loud.

Their host for the night was Nick Haygood, known to many of them simply as "Doc" and apparently to some others as "Nicky." A year younger than Andy—the same age as Jeff—Nick was still in school. In fact, he planned to be there for a while. Nick was three-fourths through his undergraduate studies, which would lead to a few more years pursuing an advanced degree and ultimately to a career as a pharmacist. His moniker was intuitive but also duplicitous.

Nick Haygood was bright, and he would likely achieve his goal of becoming a Doctor of Pharmacy. But he was smart in a way that could be unsettling. While Andy and most of his friends may have claimed to *know* a lot about drugs, the truth was most of them had a lot of *experience* but very little *knowledge*. Conversely, Doc had a deep, impressive understanding of the pharmacology of the substances they often took, and many they'd probably never encounter. He'd spent countless hours researching the chemical makeup of narcotics and hallucinogens, working to understand their effects from a biological and academic standpoint. He could—and often would—explain to people who'd ingested various drugs precisely what was happening to them chemically. Depending on the substance, its potency, and the user's level of comfort, that extra knowledge could be entertaining, fascinating, or a very scary buzzkill.

Some people distrusted Doc, suggesting his passion for pharmacy didn't truly extend beyond his interest in the inventory. Others allowed themselves to believe some or all the many salacious rumors that swirled around him. The most popular of these was that he'd set up what amounted to a mad scientist's lab in one of the house's empty bedrooms. If you subscribed to all theories, Doc was churning out everything from bathtub crank to high-grade LSD or whatever else the gossip mongers believed could be manufactured in the privacy of one's own home.

"C'mon, let's go," Andy encouraged, attempting to replace his roommate's agenda with his own.

"Yeah. In a minute."

Andy took the hint and moved down the hall, leaving Jeff to finish his conversation. As he neared the base of the staircase, he was hit squarely by a compact female missile that shot around the corner without warning. Andy didn't even have to see her to positively identify the projectile as Traci Nixon. Barely five feet tall, she might have been the shortest adult he knew.

"Damn, girl. Slow it down," he said, spreading his arms and hunching forward to dodge the splash of beer their collision had caused.

She giggled as she steadied herself and came to a complete stop. Already outstretched, Andy wrapped his arm around her and pulled her in for a quick half-hug. She lingered there for a second and then retreated. Andy didn't fixate on Traci physically the way he did so many other girls. But tonight, dressed in very tight cut-off jean shorts and a black tank top that showcased her toned shoulders and arms, she was exceptionally noticeable.

"Where's Ellie?" Traci asked.

"Working the Green Room," said Andy. "Sort of a double for her, after helping you at The Lizard." He was surprised she didn't know this.

"Oh shit. That sucks. She told me she had a dinner thing tonight, but not that she had to work. I shouldn't have…"

"That's Ellen for you, though. She's never gonna say no, even if it's a pain in her ass. She's just built that way."

"Now I feel bad."

"Don't worry. She'll be here. Besides, she earned a little extra cash. Everybody likes money, right?"

"So, what? You want me to hook you up with some shifts at The Lizard, too?"

"Yeah, that's not my scene," Andy said. "Also, I'm very good at saying no."

"Nice of you to join us." The voice came from behind but was unmistakable. Andy and Traci pivoted to greet the Good Doctor himself.

Nick's eccentricities were plentiful, and his wardrobe for the evening was no exception. His black ten-hole Dr. Martens merged into a ridiculous pair of green, yellow, and black Scottish tartan pants paired with red suspenders over a plain white V-neck shirt. Black, thick-framed glasses peeked out from the chin-length veil of reddish-brown hair that cascaded across his face. A quarter-bent, squat bulldog pipe he'd inherited from his grandfather was clenched in his teeth. He perpetually rotated between smoking potent weed and a blend of cherry brandy tobacco from that pipe to the extent that traces of both could always be smelled no matter which currently filled its bowl.

"Doc!" Andy was happy to see him again after almost a month. They were both a little reclusive. Unless one was in the other's house, they might never cross paths.

"Hello, old friend." It was an odd greeting, something a much older man might say. "Where's the rest of Cornwall Street?"

"Jeff's hunting wounded fawns in the kitchen," Andy betrayed. "Ellen's working, but she should be here later."

"Good deal. Grab Jeff and meet me upstairs in five minutes. I've got something to show you."

And like that, he was off. They watched him weave through the thickening crowd with the agility of some deranged leprechaun. Andy scanned the scene over Traci's head in search of Jeff. He found him propped up against the kitchen sink, captivated by the one and only Eddie French.

"Beer?" Andy offered, headed for the fridge.

"No thanks," said Traci. "There's some crazy strong punch on the counter over there. I'm sticking with that."

"Good call," Andy agreed. "Doc always whips up some wicked shit."

Approaching from behind Eddie, Andy gained Jeff's attention and mouthed the words, "*Come with me.*" Andy cupped his hands onto Eddie's unsuspecting shoulders. Eddie nearly buckled as he turned.

"Eddie! Good to see you again."

Jeff took the opening and joined Traci as she kept moving toward the punch bowl.

"Hey, Shoe Boy!" Eddie chuckled, vibrating with a mischievous energy Andy usually loved. "You know, most of them are still up there?"

Andy heard the whole sentence but really one word. *'Most'?* Why did he say *'most'?* Had some of them fallen? Were they being taken down? How many is *'most'?* His masterpiece was intact just the other day. Now, he found himself fixating on the welfare of his project, as if the shoe tree was his legacy to the city itself and deserved some kind of protection from decay or dismemberment.

Andy had to balance his desire to ask follow-up questions with his need to not get sucked into another conversation. He had a Doctor's appointment to keep, after all.

"Yeah, man," Eddie chugged along, "that shit still looks crazy cool though."

"It does," Andy agreed, in full transition. "Crazy. Hey, I'm gonna grab some punch, and I gotta ask Jeff something. Can I catch up with you later?"

"Sure, man." Eddie said, "I..." Andy was already gone.

Traci and Andy filled red plastic cups almost to the brim, assuming the punch bowl would be empty by the time they returned to it. Jeff stood behind them, nursing the massive bottle of malt liquor and studying the tattoo of a half-sun-half-skull face on Traci's right shoulder.

"What's new, Traci?" Jeff asked.

"Just workin'. I don't get out much anymore. But I still try to tear it up on the weekends." She flashed the devil horns hand sign to give some rock-n-roll credence to her declaration.

"I hear ya. Glad you made it out."

Jeff tilted his bottle of Crazy Horse until it touched the rim of Andy's cup. "Cheers! So, what's the deal?"

"I don't even know," Andy confessed. "Saw Doc a minute ago. He told us to find you and come see him upstairs."

"Ooh. You know something good's gotta be waitin' when you get summoned to the Doctor's Office."

They all laughed. Traci snorted as she choked down a mouthful of potent punch.

"Well, let's not keep him waiting," Jeff suggested.

The crowd thickened by the minute. Smoke and a mass of sweaty bodies filled the kitchen. As they reached the stairs, Andy realized Doc had requested he fetch Jeff but did not mention Traci. He'd said it plainly in her presence, though he failed to acknowledge her. Was Andy supposed to bring her or not? He let it be, deciding Doc could dismiss her if he preferred.

A few people were hanging out on the lowest couple of steps, but no one was beyond that. Perhaps, at least for now, the upstairs was off-limits. Andy led as they ascended. Jeff followed, and Traci brought up the rear. Directly across from the landing was a half bathroom. Its door sat ajar, a candle flickering on the back of the commode in the otherwise small, dark room. To the right, two doors—both closed. To the left, another, also half-open. As they all reached the landing, Doc's voice rang from inside.

"Jeffery Aaron!" he called as if mocking a schoolteacher taking roll.

Doc emerged from the master bedroom, leaving the door open behind him. The room was dimly lit, and there was music. He shook

Jeff's hand and gave him a quick bro-hug. Doc saw Andy and then Traci. His joyful smile flattened, replaced by something slightly suspicious. Andy jumped to the defense.

"Nick, you know Traci..."

It seemed he did not.

"Good friend of ours. She's totally cool," Andy asserted. Jeff nodded in affirmation.

"Okay then," he allowed, apparently accepting their endorsement. "Good to meet ya. Call me Doc."

"Hey, Doc," Traci offered cordially but confused. She'd met Nick Haygood on at least two previous occasions and seen him in passing countless times. Doc had become increasingly reclusive, but she was still offended that he didn't recall her. Even worse, he seemed wary of her for no reason at all.

He looked her over once more and moved on. "Wait here a second."

Nick passed by them to the other side of the hallway. Digging into the pockets of his garish pants, he pulled out a collection of keys. He selected one and approached the last door on the right. With the protectiveness of a hoarding squirrel, he addressed the deadbolt that had been added to the otherwise standard interior door. He unlocked and opened it only wide enough to dart inside and closed it quickly behind him. The others stood in the hall, puzzled but amused by his cartoonish mannerisms.

Seconds later, he reappeared, just as animated. Now, he carried a tan metal lock box–the kind you'd see holding money at a school bake sale.

"Follow me," Doc ordered with a bit of hushed paranoia. The drama was intriguing but did little to dispel all those rumors.

As soon as the four entered Doc's bedroom, he shut the door behind them. Doc sat on the floor, using the foot of the bed as a backrest, and ushered them to join him. He waited until they were all settled before making his next move. With enough grandeur to suggest they were about to see inside the Ark of the Covenant, Doc inserted another small key from the chain into the lockbox and turned it.

Doc held aloft two plastic sandwich bags filled with a spongy brown mass. "Boys and girl," he announced, "magic mushrooms."

"Are you kidding?" Jeff howled. "Thank God! I thought for sure you were gonna bust out some homemade meth or something."

"Fuck that," said Doc. "Meth is dumb all the way around. Dangerous as hell to make. Dirty as fuck to take. Chemically speaking, it's like emptying a toxic waste dump into your body. I *could* cook that shit, but I would never do it. Never. The younger kids move toward that shit 'cause they don't know any better. They're start tweaking out on cough medicine 'cause it's cheap and easy to get, but that's like a little meth starter kit. All that shit is bad news. The high is okay, but coming down is a bitch. If those idiots want to fry their brains and livers, whatever. This is so much nicer."

Doc was rolling the plastic bags in his fingers as he spoke.

"They're fresh too," he continued. "A couple of my boys from the sticks out near Kirkwood came through on their way to the beach. They were looking for a change of speed, so I traded 'em these for some other stuff I had."

Sitting on Doc's left, Jeff had received one of the bags. He was fully engaged, pinching the still-springy caps. Out of habit, he held the bag to his nose and sniffed.

"Smells like shit," Jeff proclaimed.

"Grade-A, grass-fed cow shit, to be exact," Doc laughed. "One of those guys' dads owns a fuck-ton of land out in Kirkwood. He's got cows, so he's got 'shrooms. Probably doesn't even know what they are. Those boys are swimmin' in 'em, though. These are just the extra ones I pulled off the sale pile. I figured I needed to try 'em before I take anyone's money. Who wants to go for a test drive? You never know; it could be a completely religious experience."

"Andy may have had enough of those already tonight," Jeff suggested. Doc and Traci were out of the loop, but Andy got the joke and rewarded his roommate with an ironic smile and a robust middle finger.

Andy sat quietly to Doc's right, contemplating the offer. He was about to speak when Traci beat him to it.

"It's like acid, but not as strong, right? Do you have any acid?"

Andy and Jeff were both shocked by her question and request. They'd known Traci for years, and while she did have a reputation for being particular, this was poor form. Asking what else was on the menu when somebody offered you free drugs was like being mad that the $20 bill you found in the gutter was dirty.

Again, Andy defended her. "I think what Traci meant was…" He shot her with a perturbed look as he completed his address to Doc. "How is this different from acid? I was wondering the same thing because I totally don't do acid."

"You've never done acid?" Doc asked with no judgment but total surprise.

"Never have. Never will," Andy declared. "I'm not into synthetic chemicals. Actually, I've never taken 'shrooms either, but I'm inclined to trust the natural shit."

"Yeah, 'shrooms are a good bit mellower and almost always friendly," Doc said. "But not disappointing by any stretch compared to acid. And they don't last as long, so I prefer them. But I always tell people, don't do something you don't want to do." This last point seemed aimed at Traci, suggesting she was welcome to pass on his hospitable offer.

"How long does it last?" Andy asked.

"Depends. But let's just say, if you eat these, you're not driving tonight."

Andy started doing math in his head. Their house was only a few blocks from where he sat, and Ellen was probably coming later anyway.

"That's cool," Andy said, feigning confidence. "I'm in."

"Me too," said Traci before quickly adding, "Thanks. I appreciate it."

"Ordinarily, I'd mash these up and brew some tea, with a little peppermint to cut the taste. But there are about a hundred people in my kitchen right now, so that ain't happening. Looks like we're scarfin' 'em down the old-fashioned way."

Doc had taken four decent-sized mushroom caps and passed one bag on to Andy. Jeff followed his lead with the other bag. Before Andy or Traci had even selected their caps, Doc stuffed the entire handful into his mouth and began chewing.

Jeff did the same without hesitation. Andy thought about taking them one at a time but decided not to prolong the process. Traci took only two, holding the others in her hand.

The four sat in a circle on the floor, chewing and exchanging glances. Doc reveled in what was clearly not a new experience for him. Jeff oscillated between excitement for himself and anxious empathy for Andy. Traci stared at the floor. Her puckered mouth chewed furiously, attempting to down the first half of her portion as quickly as possible. She gasped as if holding her breath and took a long gulp from her cup of punch.

"Blah!" she said, louder than intended. She popped the other two caps and took another swig.

Now came the fun part. Or for Andy, the worst part. He'd just taken something for the first time, which he was pretty sure would fuck with his head in ways he couldn't even imagine. For someone prone to anxiety, the wait for the impending trip to begin could be anguishing.

Doc wasn't specifically aware of Andy's plight, but he did have exceptional drug etiquette. He'd learned just before takeoff that two of his passengers had never flown, and he instinctively launched into his role as attendant for their maiden voyage.

"There's nothing to worry about." Doc's voice broke the silence. "Like I said, this should be a totally mellow trip. But the most important thing to remember is... you're the one in control. Your trip is totally influenced by your state of mind. It's just going to take you deeper into where you already are. So, if you come into this happy, you should stay there. If you find yourself confused or tense, focus on the last comforting thought or experience you had. And if you start freaking out, try to remind yourself it's like a roller coaster ride. It might get bumpy. There's gonna be some turns. You may even go upside down for a minute. But no matter what happens, you're eventually gonna come to a nice gliding stop back here at the platform. So, don't worry. Enjoy yourselves. Let go and have fun."

"Damn," Andy said, "You should write down every word of that. Print that shit on business cards or something, and hand it out to folks before they trip. That was like a perfect pre-game pep talk. I was nervous, but that helped."

Doc laughed. He'd been where they were, and he'd been where they were going. "Just a heads-up." he said, "you've got about twenty minutes 'til the world goes a little loopy."

With that, he got up and walked out. Given the dramatic secrecy with which he'd greeted them, Andy thought it odd he would just leave them alone in his bedroom. He shrugged it off, content to focus on the adventure ahead. Traci was laying down, her back flat on the carpet, her eyes closed. It was way too early for her to be feeling anything. Still, she seemed to be meditatively waiting for the fireworks to begin.

Andy turned to Jeff. He fidgeted through lighting a smoke. Jeff could see the nervous energy building within him and the fear hiding behind his forced smile.

"I'm glad you're here. I want to do this together."

Jeff knew his friend meant: "*Don't leave me. I don't want to be alone.*"

"Don't worry. I'm not going anywhere."

"So, you've done this before, right?"

"Yeah. We've talked about this," Jeff reminded him. "I grew up out in the country; lived on farmland; had neighbors with cows. It's not like I've done it a million times, but yeah."

"So, what's it gonna be like?"

"Doc's right. It's different than acid–more peaceful. You might see some weird shit like tracers and bursts of color and light. You're probably not gonna see somebody's face melt off."

Traci, still lying motionless with her eyes closed, let out a snicker at the thought of what Jeff had described.

"So, he said like twenty minutes, right?" Andy pondered aloud. "What time is it?" He was notorious for never wearing a watch but always being interested in the time of day.

"It doesn't matter now," said Jeff, pointing to the green LED display on the clock by Doc's bed. Sometime in the next hour, Andy figured Ellen would arrive, just in time to find them tripping on hallucinogens. He made a note to remember this in case he needed a tether to sanity later in the evening.

"I think I'm gonna pee and get another drink before shit gets crazy and I forget."

"That's a good idea. You hit the head first. I'll run downstairs and grab a few cold ones. Meet you back here in five minutes."

Andy loved having a plan; it made him feel safe, like he was in control. Deep down, he knew it was bullshit, but he clung to the mirage.

"Yeah. Do it. But seriously, hurry back." Andy knew it sounded weak.

"You need a drink, Trace?" Jeff asked, getting up and walking toward the door. She lay on the floor, making no attempt to move or respond. "Guess not; back in a minute."

Andy continued to make mental notes as he watched his friend disappear around the corner. He noted the music playing on the stereo—something classical he didn't recognize but liked. He noted the layout and contents of Doc's bedroom. Then, he noted that the master bedroom had its own dedicated bathroom. At that moment, he decided. At least for now, he was bunkering down right here.

Traci still hadn't moved. He contemplated her for a second but then moved on. Andy got up and walked across the room, closing the door that led out to the hallway. He figured any of the randoms downstairs who wandered up to the second story would see the closed doors as 'do not enter' signs. At least, he hoped.

Andy moved toward the master bathroom. It was tucked into the end of a terse hallway created by closets on either side of the passage. The closet doors were mirrored panels, creating a strange 360-degree effect when you stood between them. Andy recognized the mind-bending potential and reminded himself to avoid this zone when he returned. Before approaching the bathroom, he addressed Traci and his growing concern about her lack of movement.

"Hey, Trace. You okay?"

Three full seconds passed before she replied. "Yep. Just chillin'."

"Cool. I'm gonna take a piss. I'll be right back."

He got no response.

Andy flipped the switch, bathing the room in pale yellow light. The floor, and roughly half the height of all four walls, was plastered in shockingly white ceramic tiles. The ones on the wall were standard 4-inch squares; nothing remarkable. The floor was far more interesting. It was covered by a sea of equally white but smaller tiles, each about the size of a quarter. The sheer number of those tiles and their color exaggerated the dimensions of the bathroom. He entered and closed the door.

47

Jeff Aaron was a man of the people. He possessed exceptional social skills but an appalling sense of time. If either Andy or Traci had thought it through, they'd have known he was unfit for a speed-run through a crowd like the one downstairs. In theory, asking Jeff to find the kitchen, grab fresh drinks, and head straight back to Doc's room was totally reasonable. In reality, it was fatally flawed.

If he really concentrated, Jeff could have navigated the social minefield without getting trapped in a conversation. The drugs were only half of his challenge. Jeff was magnetic. People were just drawn to him. He almost made it downstairs without losing his focus. At the bottom of the steps stood two lovely coeds, members of a sorority for which he had recently done a photo shoot. Flanking him on both sides and sliding into the crooks of his arms, they redirected him toward the quieter back of the house, intent on talking about some follow-up portraits. He never stood a chance.

48

Traci opened her eyes. Everything was still. The only sound was the calming procession of notes from the stereo across the room. Piano and violins weaved around each other, babbling like fluid from the speakers and washing over her. The music was pleasant, in a foreign way, and she was content to lie there, staring at the ceiling and bathing in the sound. As she contemplated the texture of the rough plaster pocks above, she became more acutely aware of a growing sense of vibration coming from the floor beneath her. It was as if the collective energy from the people on the first floor was rising with tangible force. The longer she lay there, the more buzz she could hear and feel. At the same time, she lost her connection to the soothing influence of the music. Doc's selection had ended, and nothing rose to take its place. Traci's comfort level nosedived, motivating her to move. Sitting up, she was surprised to find herself alone. A few minutes ago, she was part of a small group, a member of an expedition into the brave unknown. Now, she was alone, abandoned in a strange, quiet room. Replaying what Doc had told them before he'd departed reminded her, she was working with a ticking clock. Traci was not where she wanted to be if things were going to get weird, and she wasn't sure how much time she had to create a better situation for herself.

She decided priority one was lighting a smoke, thinking the simple action might bring some comfort. What it brought was a startling confirmation of the path ahead. A cigarette hanging from her lips, Traci flipped open her silver Zippo lighter and rolled the wheel. A spark ignited the pool of fuel vapors swirling around the wick. The result was a mini fireball erupting in Traci's hand. The flame was much larger than she expected. It engulfed the lower end of her cigarette. She over-corrected, pushing the lighter to arm's length. The flame was also remarkable for the visual effects that now accompanied it. A tiny rainbow of light hovered over it in an arc. Traci felt the metal in her hand begin to warm and realized she must have been staring at it for some time. She slapped the lighter shut, dousing the fire.

It seemed Doc's fantastic fungi were beginning to take hold, but she wanted a second opinion. Traci took a deep pull on the cigarette and exhaled. She opened the Zippo again, holding the lighter at a safer distance.

Yep. Things were about to go sideways.

The wick burst to life, again with the mini rainbow arcing and floating above the flame. But now, tiny sparkles of light joined in the dance. Then, she did what any person in that situation would. Traci started moving the lighter, slowly at first, then quicker across her field of vision. As the burning fuel mixed with a rush of oxygen, the flame extended itself from the wick. But Traci saw much more than this. A full-fledged tail of light emerged from the flame, creating the same effect one would see from making paths in the air with a sparkler.

Traci's reaction was mixed. She was freaked out, but pleasantly, by the impromptu light show she was orchestrating. Then, the realization she was now actively tripping brought anxiety. This was compounded by the fact she was still alone in the upstairs bedroom. She tucked the lighter and her smokes into her small black clutch and moved for the door.

Opening it was like breaking a vacuum seal. Traci was instantly exposed to a rush of noise and activity. She inched toward the steps, her head filled with a mix of garbled conversations, now supernaturally amplified in volume but not clarity. Traci's goal was singular; find a familiar, friendly face in the crowd and hang on for the ride.

49

Andy didn't see it coming either. He'd walked into the bathroom, intent on using the facilities and returning to the safety of Doc's room, where he expected to be reunited with Jeff. He'd closed the door and was about to lift the lid of the toilet when he noticed his feet. An unassuming glance down revealed his shoe was untied. Rather than bend down, Andy chose to spin and take a seat on the throne.

Leaning over to address his shoe, Andy's face drew closer to the small white tiles covering the bathroom floor. His hands completed the mundane task of forming and fastening the loops of his shoelace with no help from his eyes. They were focused elsewhere.

From closer range, Andy could see that the tiles he first thought were squares were tiny hexagons offset at a slight angle. The result was a far more interesting landscape than a simple, straight grid. Still doubled over with his chest to his knees and his hands resting on the tops of his shoes, Andy contemplated the floor. He counted the sides of a single tile twice, confirming the uniform nature of the six-sided shapes. Each white tile was separated by a thin line of black grout.

Somewhere in the back of his mind, it occurred to him he was obsessing over the shape and layout of a random bathroom floor. His next thought might have been to shoot upright and return to his friends. But then, his brain took a detour.

As Andy stared at the floor, his field of vision began to expand. He stopped considering single tiles on a micro level and viewed the whole floor through a wider lens. Then, his peripheral vision picked up the first bit of motion just to his left. He could have sworn he saw something move on the floor, rising dimensionally from the surface, almost jumping. He even detected the slightest noise, like a tiny click, in accompaniment. He looked, expecting to see a cricket or a roach. The stark white floor was bare.

Still hunched over, palms against his shins, Andy stared. In his periphery, now to the other side, the same sense of motion. This time, it came with a double click. Andy glanced to his right; sure he would find something. He saw something alright, but not what he expected.

As he scanned from left to right across the floor, the grout lines separating the tiles came with him. Like the hyperspace jump scenes in *Star Wars*, the fixed points elongated with great speed and then ended abruptly in another place along the same line. Andy rubbed his eyes in disbelief. *Holy shit. Did I just see that?*

He swiped his head back to the left. Again, the grout lines moved with him, blurring across the floor before coming to rest on the other side. Andy's instinct was to flee—to run from the bathroom screaming—hopefully into the company of Jeff on the other side of the door. But his body did not comply. Andy closed his eyes, knowing he probably *had* just seen something crazy. He channeled Doc's pre-flight words of wisdom. This was a journey he had chosen. More importantly, it was something he could *control*, at least he hoped.

Andy sat upright and locked his neck, attempting to lose the disconcerting tracers. He opened his eyes. The motion was gone, but the weirdness was just beginning.

He stared straight ahead. The plain square tiles on the walls were precisely that. Nothing moved. No tracers. The world in front of his face appeared normal. This was not the case below. Even without looking down, he could sense bits of motion on both sides of his feet. With growing anxiety, Andy lowered his gaze. Clear as day, he saw several tiles in random placements across the floor, expanding dimensionally upward and out. The tiles were percolating–rising for a second, separating themselves slightly from their neighbors, and then falling back into place. Surprisingly, his fear was replaced by sheer wonder. The visuals were stunning. Though this was clearly a break with reality, nothing seemed threatening about a tiny ballet of dancing floor tiles.

Andy decided, with whatever portion of his brain he currently controlled, he would embrace Doc's words and this experience. Maybe it was an instinctual understanding that he wouldn't overpower the chemicals. Or perhaps he was exhausted from fighting for control. Either way, at that moment, sitting on a toilet in a strange bathroom, Andy decided he was going to try to do the one thing that came the hardest for him. He would try to let go–to simply exist, as Lao Tzu suggested, to *be the rushing river*, to do no work but to allow work to be done through him. The decision was rewarded almost instantly.

Andy kept watch over the bathroom floor. In direct correlation to his choice to loosen the reins, the floor responded, elevating its activity to a new level. It wasn't just single tiles piping up to say hello before retreating. Now, groups of hexagons collaborated to form other simple shapes. Inexact squares, lines, and larger mega-hexagons began to form. The previously dark grout around them bloomed into bands of colored electric light. Remembering Jeff's claim that his experience was likely to be tame compared to acid, Andy confirmed his resolve to never go near LSD.

He watched with delight and horror as the shapes paraded across the floor. With their glowing outlines, he thought they looked like the crude, boxy tanks from the earliest video games. Then, suddenly, he recognized what they really were—puzzle pieces.

As if by the sheer power of his will, the tiles responded to his unspoken thoughts. No longer moving from left to right, the electrified shapes began to ascend away from him toward the door leading back out to Doc's room. Reaching the threshold, they slid into the crack between the floor and the bottom of the door. A handful of these shapes escaped into this crevice before everything suddenly ceased. Just when Andy decided to go with the flow, the flow had stopped. Everything was still. But, before he could even worry about what might happen next, the answer came.

Andy was still scanning the baseboard for signs of activity when it began again. Now, a single shape, a capital "L" lying on its side, crept from the void under the door frame. It fell slowly toward him, taking several seconds to travel the four and a half feet between Andy and the door. A few inches before the shape reached his toes, it came to rest but continued glowing to distinguish itself from the other tiles around it. He stared at it, but only briefly, as he detected more motion.

Scanning back up the floor, Andy saw another shape, a simple square, slip from underneath the door and start to inch toward him. He watched it proceed along the same line and come to rest in the crook of the "L" that had fallen before it. Then another shape, a longer straight line, appeared. It took him a serving of at least three shapes, but finally, the epiphany came. His psilocybin-soaked brain had transformed Doc's bathroom floor into a game of psychedelic Tetris. As he watched the long, thin bar slowly descend toward his feet, he realized it followed the same baseline and would come to rest stacked widely upon the other two.

Andy recognized the problem and its solution. If only the shape would…

Holy shit! As soon as Andy expressed the desire mentally, the shape responded. Like a dog answering the call of an unheard whistle, the long, straight shape sat up vertically and moved over two columns to the left. It came to rest perfectly aligned next to the two stacked shapes beside it.

Oh my God! Andy thought. Not only did the bathroom floor just turn into Tetris, but *I can totally control this shit with my brain*? His fear disappeared entirely. The shapes kept coming. Andy was amazed at how quickly and thoroughly they obeyed his mental commands. He could flip, rotate, and slide them at will and much faster than in the video game. There did seem to be two constraints, though. The "game board" boundary was apparently defined by the width of the door frame in front of him. He could flip or move the shapes as fast as he wanted, but no matter how hard he tried, they would not travel beyond those sidelines. He also couldn't make them stop or even pause. Otherwise, it was exactly like he was playing Tetris at home–except he wasn't. He was sitting on a toilet, tripping his balls off on psychedelic mushrooms.

The shapes continued, and faster. The game had leveled up in response to his growing comfort. Putting the pieces in their ideal places was getting more difficult. Andy maneuvered another long thin piece into a perfect vertical hole, completing four lines of tiles. The puzzle's satisfied portion did not just disappear as it might have in the actual game. Instead, the tiles exploded into a bright mini-fireworks display of light, scattering dramatically across the whole bathroom floor. The light show was spectacular; psychedelic bonus points provided plenty of motivation for continued success.

Andy plowed forward, directing and arranging the shapes as they fell. He had been doing fine but knew the game was moving faster. The task was still manageable, but the wall of shapes grew higher as the perfect piece came less often. Just as in the real game, the natural response to this was an uptick in anxiety. Andy knew that normally, the game simply ended when the shapes reached all the way to the top. He began to wonder what would happen if the shapes piled all the way back up to the door frame. Clearly, there was some supernatural, less-than-normal shit going on here. Andy became hyper-stressed about what "Game Over" might mean in this scenario. He'd been enjoying his experience so far. Now, he feared something unpleasant, even sinister, might befall him if he failed.

Andy doubled his concentration as the pressure built. The shapes were piled almost halfway up from his feet to the Doorway of Possible Doom. He couldn't be sure, but he thought the outlines of the stacked shapes glowed faster and brighter the closer they got to the top. Pieces continued to fall, faster and faster. His anxiety rose right along with the wall. He could feel his portion of control slipping away as the blocks ascended.

I can't do this! He thought, nearing panic.

A strange humming had been growing in his head. It got progressively louder and became more of an obstacle to his waning concentration. Andy was about to surrender.

You can.

He hadn't said it. He hadn't even thought of it. But there it was. He heard it as clearly as if someone had whispered it directly into his ear. *You can.*

Auditory hallucinations were one thing and maybe even something to be expected at this point. But what came next was entirely unmanageable for Andy's mind.

He'd hunched back over, clenched with the stress of the rising wall before him. He realized how tight his body had become. Then, in what HAD to be another hallucination, he felt the slightest weight being applied to his right shoulder. It was not forceful or aggressive in any way. It was, in fact, calming, like the simple, reassuring touch of a friend's hand upon his back.

You know you can.

Andy was afraid. He was hearing voices and feeling the presence of things unseen. This was deep in uncharted territory and way more than he'd bargained for from Doc's gift.

Relax... Trust.

Andy panicked. The train was flying off the tracks. He was out of control and out of options.

"Okay!" Andy said, very much out loud.

Again, he felt the pressure on his shoulder, this time slightly different – almost a squeeze. Then everything stopped.

The shapes remained, but the 'game' had been paused. But not by him. Then, the pieces began to move differently. Each piece appeared as usual from below the door and then hovered, flashing in the center of the open space. As if being clicked and dragged by an unseen hand controlling a mouse, each of the next ten or so pieces was placed precisely where necessary within the puzzle to clear the corresponding rows. With perfect resonance, one final long straight piece careened down the board, sliding like a dagger into the single void left for it. As it connected, completing the remaining rows, the fireworks returned. The pieces scattered across the bathroom floor, disappearing as they reached the boundaries on all four sides.

Andy sat up straight, still afraid but also relieved. Nothing moved, not on the walls and not on the floor. The humming was gone too. He sat alone in the stark white, silent bathroom. A burst of emotion ran through him like the electricity that had surrounded the floor tiles a minute ago. He felt the prickly burn that preceded tears welling up in his eyes.

He sat there for a minute, breathing, waiting to see what other craziness might come for him. Nothing did. Wiping his face, he lowered his head into his hands and exhaled. He was exhausted.

50

ndy had forgotten why he'd gone into the bathroom in the first place, and his bladder had become uncomfortably full while playing magic-floor-Tetris. As he rose from the seat, he was startled by the burning and tightness in his quadriceps and hamstrings. Apparently, he'd been there long enough for his thin legs to fall asleep, long enough to require some shaking and a few deep knee bends to restore the blood flow to his strained muscles. Completing his callisthenic routine, he wheeled around, lifted the lid of the commode, and relieved himself.

As he approached the sink, new feelings of dread surfaced. He was afraid to turn on the faucet. Snakes, or laser beams, or some other ridiculous shit might come pouring out. He was scared to look in the mirror. This much he managed, though, as it was unavoidable from where he stood. What he saw staring back at him was ugly but not surprising. His face was flush and blotchy red from heat, pressure, and tears. His hair was predictably disheveled, too.

Andy took a deep breath and gave the faucet handle a half-turn. Nothing but clear, cold water sprang forth. He formed a bowl with his hands and splashed the cool liquid against his hot face several times. He turned off the faucet and reached for one of the small hand towels Doc had stacked on the basin. He laughed at the notion of even owning hand towels, let alone having three clean and ready in case you had company.

Feeling much closer to normal, Andy walked across the floor, which had moments ago been part of an alternate reality. He was glad it didn't suddenly transform into gelatin this time or simply collapse under his weight. Andy reached for the door handle and re-entered Doc's bedroom. He couldn't have been happier to see what awaited him.

51

"**D**amn, dude!" Doc howled. "Have you been in there the whole time?"

"What?" Andy asked. "I just went in to take a piss."

"That was like an hour ago!"

The fact that Ellen was now sitting next to Doc on his bed, laughing her ass off at Andy, was solid corroboration. Jeff sat Indian style on the floor, his back against the foot of the bed. Head-in-hands, a cascade of brown hair hung halfway to his navel.

"Oh my God!" Andy gasped. "El! I'm so fucking glad to see you."

Hallucinogenic euphoria accounted for part of his enthusiasm. But an equal portion came from the recall of the mental note he'd made earlier about her. Jeff and Doc were probably just as fucked in the head as he was, but surely Ellen was sober. *She can be trusted*, he thought—she was the safe harbor he needed after the storm he'd endured.

"Are you as whacked out as these two?" Ellen asked, pointing at the others as she lit a fresh smoke.

"Maybe worse. Can I have one of those?"

She handed the lit cigarette to him and retrieved another for herself.

"Really?" Doc laughed. "Are you seeing crazy shit too?"

"You wouldn't believe me."

"Oh, he might," Ellen suggested, amused and perturbed. "I got here about ten minutes ago. I walked up the block and found Doc on his hands and knees, crawling through the bushes like an animal."

"I have that beat," Andy wagered.

"It's crazy, right?" Doc asked, giggling. "I don't even remember who I was talking to, but I ended up outside on the porch. From there, shit got very weird. I started seeing things in crazy shades of red and blue, like when you put on 3-D glasses. All the houses and cars looked so fucked up. I couldn't take it. I walked down the block toward the park, where there's no houses. I looked up into the trees, and they started talking to me."

"See?" said Ellen. "Fucking nuts."

Andy found it strangely comforting that he and Doc were at least in the same ballpark. "What'd they tell you?" he wondered aloud.

"They just kept saying, '*Come find me.*' It was some creepy little girl's voice, too. You know, like in a horror movie or something."

"And so, you figured you should walk *toward* the voice? You know how that usually works out, right?"

"I don't know, man." Doc continued, "It was hypnotic. Before I knew it, I was walking down the street. I have no idea how I ended up in the neighbor's bushes."

"Speaking of finding people..." Andy said, looking at Jeff. "Where did YOU go?"

Jeff remained shrouded in a cloak of hair and silence. He sat motionless and stared straight at the floor.

"He's been like that since I got here," Ellen said. "He won't talk to anyone. He's breathing, and he looked up at me when I asked him to, but he's somewhere else right now."

"He'll be fine," Doc laughed. "He's still in it, but he'll come back, just like you did."

"So, wait…" Andy asked, "is it over then?"

"Probably not. Maybe. It's hard to tell. 'Shrooms are a pretty inexact science. Sometimes you're gone for a while. Sometimes you go up and down. It's always different, and you never know. That's part of the fun."

Andy couldn't think of a worse definition of 'fun.' Every one of those things Doc described was the opposite of the predictable, comfortable consistency he loved.

"You okay, dude?" Andy tried engaging his roommate.

Jeff remained still but finally spoke. "I want to be alone." His voice was a shaky shadow of its usual confident tone.

"Yeah, that's not happening," Ellen said. "You don't have to talk. But we're not leaving you."

"Hey, wait…" said Andy, "Where the fuck is Traci?"

"Oh shit, dude!" Ellen exclaimed. "That's the even worse part. So, Nature Boy here tells me she went tripping with you guys, too."

"Yeah, she did. Why? What happened?"

"Apparently, before I even got here, shit went bad for her, too. I ran into Eddie downstairs, and he had a front-row seat for the freak show.

"He always does," Doc said, chuckling.

"Shut up," said Andy, flashing a rare streak of empathy. Also, he might have been the last person she'd seen before shit got weird for her, and he wondered if he was responsible in some way. "What *happened*?"

"Eddie says she came downstairs, looking all glassy-eyed. He didn't think much of it, cuz who hasn't seen that a hundred times before? So, he's standing there talking to someone and says he keeps seeing these flashes pop up. Apparently, she's playing with a lighter, you know, a Zippo. She was probably getting cool tracers off it or something. I don't know. But then, Eddie said she noticed the little bits of thread hanging down off the ends of her cut-offs."

Andy was glassy-eyed, too, but listening like a schoolboy at story time.

"I guess she couldn't resist the urge to see what those frays looked like when they burned. Eddie said the fringe ignited and just kept going. Before she knew it, half her damned leg was in flames!"

The boys started snickering. "She set herself on fucking fire?"

"Yeah! And it's seriously not funny. It's bad enough it happened at all. Imagine that shit while you're trippin' balls. Eddie says she lost it. Dropped to the floor and started rolling around, screaming like a goddamned banshee."

"So, what did Eddie do?" Andy asked.

"He dumped a full cup of beer on her," Ellen said matter-of-factly.

The boys exploded in laughter.

"Now, THAT'S funny!" Doc offered.

"It's a damn good thing he wasn't drinking the punch. I think that shit had jet fuel in it. She'd have gone up like a dried tobacco barn."

Ellen had to admit that, with the hindsight of knowing her friend had escaped serious injury, it was a spectacle she wished she had seen. Instead, she'd be one of the countless people who would share the story later. Most of those probably weren't even at Doc's house that night, but would claim to have been 'standing right there when it happened.'

"Oh my God," Andy said. "I had no idea. Is she okay?"

"Yeah, lucky for her, she had some other friends here. They took her home and are gonna hang with her until she comes down," Ellen explained. "Speaking of which, I guess I get to babysit you dumb fuckers for the rest of the night now."

"Thanks, Mom," Andy teased.

"Yeah. Fuck y'all." Ellen replied. "I think you've both had enough fun for one night. It's too late for me to start drinking now, and I gotta drive. Let's go home. You're both gonna pack me the biggest fuckin' bong hits ever."

"Fine with me," Andy said without pause, knowing he'd reached his limit. He turned again to his tunnel-visioned friend on the floor. "Can you walk outta here?"

Jeff said nothing but surprised them all by rocking forward from the bed and standing in one fluid motion. The veil of hair swept away from his face, and as he turned toward Ellen, she saw something in his eyes she never had before. His cheeks were red and swollen, like he'd been crying, and his deep blue pupils were drowning in fear. Jeff returned his gaze to the floor and took a step toward her. Ellen met him and gently took his hand, ready to guide him the rest of the way.

"Thanks for the fun, Doc," Ellen said with massive sarcasm.

Doc offered a nervous smile but no words as Andy fell in behind his roommates and followed them out the door. They spoke to no one as they walked from the house to her car down the block.

52

"Where's the Chevette?" Andy asked as they left the front yard.

"About three blocks." She pointed up the street, opposite where Doc had returned from his nature expedition.

"Fuck," Andy complained, "the house isn't much further than that."

"So, walk home," she suggested.

"Fuck that," Andy said, wrestling to release the carabineer key chain from his belt loop. "Here." He tossed his keys at Ellen, who couldn't have expected the move any less. They bounced off her chest and fell to the ground. She just stood there.

Andy covered the three paces between them and stooped to pick up the fallen keys. He placed them gently in her hand. "Sorry. Here. Drive mine. It's right over there."

Ellen knew Andy was under the influence of psychotropic drugs. Still, his suggestion floored her. Even before he got a sweet new ride, Andy *never* let anyone drive his car. Sure, it was her and only a few blocks, but it was still a shocking offer. Highly motivated to be home, Ellen accepted. She wasn't worried at all about leaving her own shitty car there for the night. Nobody was gonna mess with sad little Chet.

Approaching Andy's SUV, Ellen pushed one of the buttons on the small key chain remote. All the doors unlocked simultaneously. This was not a standard feature on the '82 Chevette. Andy took the co-pilot's seat while Jeff piled in back.

"There's a little lever on the side of the seat to move you forward or up," Andy offered.

Ellen found it and began to toggle the switches. She imagined it was fucking up Andy's world pretty hard to see someone else at the controls of his car. The seat glided forward to accommodate her much shorter legs and she smiled with glib satisfaction.

"Ooh, fancy!" she teased and started to tweak the angle of the rearview mirror.

The trip back to their driveway took less than five minutes from where Andy had parked. It was over almost before it began, but Ellen reveled in every second. She knew fatigue and drug-induced trepidation were behind Andy's concession, but she still viewed his surrender as a small victory—for them both.

She pulled the SUV into the driveway and all the way up to the corner of the house, where her own car usually sat.

"End of the line. Everybody out," she called, killing the engine and keeping the keys Andy was notorious for losing. She waited until both passengers opened their doors to push the lock button on the driver's side armrest. Still using Andy's keys, Ellen unlocked the front door and let herself in.

"Den. Bong hits. Two minutes," she commanded.

The boys hobbled up the porch steps, each nursing their own wounds. Andy had no idea what was happening inside Jeff's head, but every time he closed his eyes, he was still haunted by an endless procession of those damned hexagonal puzzle pieces. They were no longer speeding toward him but simply cycling through his head. The thought they might keep him from sleeping, or invade his dreams, was unsettling. He was determined to find something to take their place in his brain.

Jeff stopped just inside the front door and looked toward his bedroom. "Go get your stash."

It was the first thing Jeff had said to him since before they'd hopped on Doc's Crazy Train. Andy objected to the authoritarian tone, but that wasn't his biggest issue. "I don't think I can put any more shit in my head right now."

"Me neither. Trust me. But we owe her."

53

Andy shed his shoes and slumped into the chair by his desk. As he reached to open the drawer, his eyes and brain began to fuck with him again.

His room was dim, lit only by the faint blue glow of a small stained-glass lamp hanging from the ceiling in one corner. Most of his surroundings were obscured in darkness, but one object seemed unaffected. Right before Andy was the money clip Quenton had given him earlier that evening. The side with the Proverbial text faced up. Nearly all the etched writing was illegible in that light. Still, a few choice words glowed inexplicably as if filled with luminescent gel. Clear as day, the words "*the Lord and your plans*" stared him straight in the face. It happened in a flash—the kind of thing you definitely saw but might be able to convince yourself you hadn't.

Andy looked away. Training his gaze on the desk drawer, he opened it. The small plastic bag he sought was there. He briefly considered joining Ellen for a night cap, but his gut offered much better advice.

Closing the drawer, he raised his head. Andy wanted to look again at the money clip before departing, perhaps to check his sanity. But fear forced his eyes closed. He counted slowly. At three, he snapped his eyes open and stared down. The money clip lay there, harmless and inanimate. By now, his eyes had adjusted to the level of light in the room, and he could read the entirety of the inscription equally well. No glowing, liquid-lighted letters danced or distinguished themselves in any way. Relieved, he exhaled deeply and stood to join his friends in the next room.

54

Ellen had demanded they reassemble in a mere two minutes. Jeff knew this was unrealistic. He also assumed that if Andy kept his part of the bargain and attended to her need for weed, they wouldn't care if he was a little tardy or absent altogether.

Jeff placed his palms flat upon his face and focused on breathing. He took his wallet from his back pocket and put it on the wooden table beside his bed. He was about to sit and remove his shoes when he noticed the scrap of blue paper on the nightstand. He recognized it instantly as having come from Quenton and Lula Murphy's kitchen counter. Written in Quenton's atrocious scrawl was the homework assignment he'd been given a few hours ago. *'Revelation 3:15-16'*

Fueled partly by curiosity and much more by his experience at Doc's house, Jeff walked across the room to the makeshift cinder block and lumber bookshelf. The well-worn leather cover of his King James Bible was easily located among the other more glossy paperbacks around it. Jeff scooped up the book and returned to his bed, already flipping toward the back. It only took him seconds to locate the passage.

"I know thy works, that thou art neither cold nor hot. I would thou wert cold or hot. So, then, because thou art lukewarm, and neither cold not hot; I will spue thee out of my mouth."

Even in his clouded state of mind, the words hit Jeff like a sledgehammer to the heart, penetrating in a way that tangibly constricted his chest. His eyes were free from the psychedelic haze and the terrible visions it brought. They saw with perfect clarity, even through his huge, warm tears.

55

"You made it," Ellen said from the stuffed easy chair next to the couch where Andy lay stretched out with his eyes closed. Ellen's two-minute mandate had come and gone. She had shed her work clothes and was now sporting a pair of grey sweatpants and a bright yellow T-shirt featuring the cartoon superhero Mighty Mouse.

"Uh huh," Jeff replied, swiping Andy's legs from the couch and collapsing beside him. Andy's stash lay on the table like a sacrifice awaiting royalty.

"Excellent," she proclaimed. "Fire that shit up."

"Help yourself," Andy replied. He'd meant to suggest that she was welcome to proceed without him, but it really came across more like 'F*uck you. If you want to smoke it, you pack it.*'

"I'm seeing shit I can't even explain."

"I'm done too," agreed Jeff, lighting a Winston and passing the pack.

"So, tell me what you saw," she asked them.

Andy looked at Jeff to gauge his inclination to share. Jeff waved it off, inviting Andy to have at it.

"I don't even know," Andy began. "...what's real or not. I went into Doc's bathroom, just to take a piss, right? Next thing I know, the floor turns into some alternate dimension game of Tetris. Shapes were coming out of the floor and moving around and shit."

"Really?" Ellen asked through a billow of smoke. "That sounds kinda awesome."

"Yes and no. Scary at first, then mind-blowingly cool, then scary as fuck again at the end. It got to where I couldn't control it anymore, and I thought I might die if I lost the game."

"Yeah. That's fucked up," Ellen agreed. "So, how'd it end?"

"I gave up," Andy admitted. He was moving his lit cigarette at variable speeds across his field of vision just to see if he was still hallucinating. Nothing at the moment.

"What do you mean by 'gave up'?" Jeff asked, now intrigued.

"I don't know. I think I knew it was more than I could handle, and I just let go. Kind of like standing on the edge of a bridge and finally deciding to jump. I just let go."

"So, what happened?" Ellen asked.

"Something else took over. I can't explain it. All I know is one second, I thought I was master of the universe, and the next, I was very sure I wasn't. Everything got fucked up and panicky. But then, when I let go, it all just sort of worked out. Like I said, scary and weird."

"Maybe you should let somebody else drive more often," Ellen suggested.

"That *is* pretty fucking weird," Jeff agreed, "but it doesn't seem all that scary."

"Oh, no?" Andy asked, more than willing to enter a pissing contest over the comparative insanity of their hallucinations. "So, what did you see?"

Jeff was closer to his normal social self but obviously still holding back.

"It's okay," Ellen offered, trying to reassure him he was safe. "It sounds like everyone got screwed by that batch of 'shrooms. You can tell us. It's not like it's real anyways."

"Everything is real," Jeff replied, pondering the carpet. He still resisted making eye contact as he began.

"It started out fun, like a regular party. I was surrounded by lots of people. I was in a yard, outside. There was music. It stayed like that for a while. Warm. Happy. Upbeat."

Andy and Ellen sat silently, listening and smoking as he talked.

"But then it all fell apart," Jeff said with real heaviness. "The lights went out, and everything got pitch dark. I mean, it was outside, so there should have been at least some light from the moon or something. But no. It was pitch-fucking-dark, like I was locked in a closet."

Jeff constantly shifted his gaze between his roommates. His eyes were wild, wide, and full of dread.

"Then there was a flash of blinding light, but only for a second. After that, I could see again, but it was still dark. The music stopped and was replaced by this mechanical grinding that was still rhythmic, but horrifying."

"That sounds terrible," Ellen consoled.

"It gets worse," he cautioned. "I realized I could see again, but only because of the fire."

That brought his audience's attention to a whole new level.

"And it wasn't like a wall of fire, either. I stood there and watched as a river of lava rose from the dirt to surround me. Everything, and everyone, around me was vaporized, just like that!"

"Ho-ly shit," Andy muttered. "You win."

Jeff continued.

"I was the only one left, standing alone, on a dark island, floating in a sea of flames. I heard crying but also laughing. And the smell… the smell was awful too—like charred flesh and sulfur gas."

Now, it was Andy and Ellen whose eyes were wide.

"I closed my eyes, trying to make it stop. When I opened them again, there was a path, a single path leading off that island, back toward the house. I ran. I ran as fast as I could. I got to the house and ran inside. It was empty. I ran through the house, up the stairs and into a room. I slammed the door, and when I did, everything was still. No sounds. No smells. No fire. Nothing. I sat down on the floor, afraid to move, and I hid. The next thing I knew, Ellen was shaking me, and Doc was standing over me with a big stupid Cheshire Cat grin, like he'd done me some big fucking favor or something."

"I'm never taking 'shrooms again," Andy said, as a matter of fact.

"I've eaten plenty," Jeff said, "but I've never seen anything like that. Even acid has never been scary like that before."

"What does it mean?" Ellen asked. Two tokes of potent weed had wrapped her brain in a warm blanket of philosophical fuzz.

"My shit was all about control," answered Andy.

"Isn't it always?" she said, returning her attention to Jeff.

"I'm all alone," he muttered.

"That's bullshit," Andy rejected. "You're the least alone person I know."

"No," said Jeff. "Tonight, I was all alone. Everything else got stripped away. Destroyed. Maybe I'm supposed to get away from everything that's around me."

"Good luck with that," said Andy, finding the suggestion unrealistic. "Demons travel. No matter where you go, shit's the same everywhere."

"Not really," Jeff replied, smiling for the first time since they embarked on Doc's Magical Mystery Tour. "There's still one place I have all to myself."

"You can't just lock yourself in your room," said Andy. "You'll end up like those fuckers on *Mack Riley*."

"Very funny. It's not here. It's much bigger than that."

Ellen and Andy weren't following. He might still have been hallucinating, imagining places unreal and speaking nonsense.

"What the fuck are you talking about?" Andy asked.

"I don't know. I've been in Bradford for a while, and I'm okay here. But this isn't really me—it never *has* been. I forget sometimes where I come from."

"You come from the fuckin' sticks, man," Andy teased. "You've said it yourself a thousand times, there's nothing out there."

"That's exactly right," said Jeff. "Nothing at all. No distractions, no expectations. None of this drama or bullshit, for sure."

"No way," Ellen said. "Everyone's got drama waitin' at their parents' house."

"I'm not talking about my parents' place, either," Jeff corrected. "I've got this little piece of land out in Fairview that my grandfather left me. It's about an hour from here but it's half a world away. It's no good for farming, or anything else really, but it's mine and it's quiet. Nothing to do out there but sit and get right with the world."

"That sounds boring as hell…" Andy started before trailing off.

"It is..." Jeff laughed. "…in the best possible way. Back when I first got here, I used to go there all the time, even tried to fix the shack and fields up a little. But it's been a while since I've been back. Too long, probably. Maybe that's why I saw all that shit tonight. Maybe it's just my brain trying to remind me where the center of my universe is."

"I'd like to go to the Center of the Universe," Ellen said in a dreamy fog.

"Maybe you can catch a ride with Eddie and Graham." Jeff teased. "My place ain't Stull, and we're sure as hell going nowhere right now."

"I didn't say right now, stupid," Ellen replied. "But we should go. It'd be good for all of us. Right, Andy? … Andy?"

Andy's head slumped on the armrest of the couch. The remnants of his Winston burned in the ashtray as he snored.

56

Ellen was unsurprised to be the only one stirring at 9:30 on a Saturday morning. Given her roommates' exploits the previous night, she had no expectation of seeing either soon.

Last night's shift at The Green Room was neither remarkable nor taxing. She had arrived at Doc's house to find she'd inherited the role of babysitter and designated driver to her damaged brethren. Intentionally or not, she had gone all yesterday without ingesting alcohol. And even with the bong-hit nightcap, she felt awake and energized. She replayed the evening in her head as she swung her bare legs out of bed and sat up. A few feet away, a semi-clean pair of jeans hung over the back of a wooden chair. She grabbed the pants, slipped them on, and rose to meet the day.

Ellen swept long strands of hair behind both ears as she approached the door. From the hallway, she could see Andy had left the Den at some point. She slid into the bathroom, now less concerned about making noise, and brushed her teeth. Cupping her hands, she took several swallows of cold water and then splashed a handful across her face. She wiped the sleep from her eyes, turned off the faucet, and checked the mirror. She hadn't showered, and her face was ruddy from the smack of cool water. Her hair was mussed, and she was wearing a ridiculous t-shirt. Ellen smiled, deciding she looked plenty fabulous. She didn't need to be lovely or even clean to accomplish her immediate goals.

Ellen was determined to leave the house without waking anyone. Her black leather tote sat on the freshly painted coffee table. Her blue Chuck Taylors lay underneath it. She grabbed the bag, thinking she had everything she needed.

Well, almost. In Ellen's hyper-efficiency, she had forgotten a key detail. Only when she stepped out onto the porch did she see Andy's shiny green SUV sitting where her Chevette usually did.

"Aww, fuck." she muttered.

It would be ass-hot in a few hours, but the air outside was still pleasantly cool. Ellen realized Chet was only a few blocks away. The prospect of a short walk didn't seem unbearable. She filled her lungs with oxygen and headed up the hill.

After several minutes of walking, Ellen was a sweaty mess. The elevation in her heart rate sent fresh stores of adrenaline through her veins. She turned at the corner of Pryor and Maple. Doc's house was just across the next intersection. A small fleet of parked cars lined the street. She wasn't the only one who had abandoned ship last night.

Doc's front lawn was littered with souvenirs of the evening's debauchery. Empty bottles, busted cardboard beer boxes, and discarded cigarette packs were strewn about. A green plastic lawn chair lay upside down in the grass. By comparison, the house next door featured a well-manicured lawn, and neat beds of purple and yellow flowers tucked snuggly in fresh wood chips. Doc's property would be 'presentable' again by sundown, but that probably did little to lessen his neighbor's frustration. It occurred to her that the Murphys might feel roughly the same about them.

A small patch of Chet's unmistakable mustard-brown coat peeked out from behind a big white pickup truck. As she approached, Ellen rifled through her bag. Keys, a small change purse wallet, a pack of Marlboros, and a lighter.

She wasn't the heaviest smoker in their crowd, but she packed enough garbage into her lungs to make even the short walk a decent workout. She took a deep breath and fell behind the wheel. Seconds later, she coaxed the little Brown Beast to life. It wasn't a clunker, just old, and not unlike them most days, it took some warming up to run right. Ellen waited for Chet's engine to level and considered lighting a smoke. Deciding against it, she put the car in drive.

Chet's original in-dash clock had stopped running even before she had acquired the car. The small black circular replacement sloppily Velcroed to the dashboard suggested it was 9:49. On a Saturday morning, it would take her just a few minutes to reach her destination.

A hundred yards away, she could see the traffic light at the intersection with Juniper was turning yellow, which justified her slow coast down the hill. It also allowed for a long look at the Cactus Club as she cruised past. Sometime in the past twenty-four hours, the police tape disappeared. The huge plate glass window had been replaced and re-tinted, and all the structural repairs to the façade seemed to have been completed. Anyone who hadn't passed by in the last week might never have known anything had happened there. Soon, the drunkards and music lovers would return. Relatively few would remember its temporary closure and fewer still would recall the troubling details surrounding it.

The light turned green, and Ellen moved again, taking Chet under one of Bradford's many train trestles. Around the next bend, her destination appeared on the horizon.

57

'T' raci Nixon lived in a massive red brick apartment building a few miles southeast of downtown Bradford. It was a short drive between her place and Cornwall Street, but the two homes couldn't have been further apart in many ways.

Milltown Place was rather uncreatively named in homage to the building's prior purpose. A century ago, the structure had been a thriving textile mill. A few recessions, some lousy management, and a devastating fire later, the hulking brick shell that was left had become an eyesore to the city. It was nearly razed a few decades back. With a bit of inventive rezoning, the building was reborn. In the middle of Bradford's industrial and commercial base, Milltown Place rose from the ashes to provide affordable housing for a few hundred less-than-affluent residents. Ultimately, it became a glorified off-campus dorm for middle and upperclassmen or dropouts who couldn't afford anything better. Traci fell squarely into the second category. She lived modestly, with no real responsibilities and no big plans. And none of this bothered her in the least.

Ellen pulled up to the security booth at the opening in the brick wall surrounding the complex. The gate designed to keep unauthorized vehicles out appeared to be broken. Its arm cocked upward at a strange angle that rendered it useless. Ellen slid Chet underneath and found a space near to the front doors.

The clock on Chet's dash read 9:57. Ellen cut the engine and lit a Marlboro. She had time and was happy enough to relax and enjoy a cigarette. But then she caught a flicker of movement in her rearview mirror.

Milltown Place also had magnetized security doors–the kind that required authorized key cards to open. Without one, you were at the mercy of the call box, which, though justified from a security perspective, was still a nuisance. When Ellen saw the two young men approaching the entrance, she knew it was time to move.

Chet's door opened with a creak. Taking one last drag of smoke, she tossed the butt on the ground and crushed it. She drew a bead on the two boys, locking in like a heat-seeking missile from about fifty feet. She measured her approach perfectly, arriving just as they reached the landing.

"Hey," one of them said, slowing and inviting her to take the lead.

"Thanks," Ellen declined and ushered him through. "You go ahead."

Both boys ascended the steps. The leader dug his wallet out of his baggy jeans without acknowledging her. He placed the leather square against the pad on the brick wall, and a small red light switched to green. An audible click signaled the door's release, which the second boy opened and held for her.

"Thanks," she repeated as both boys followed her inside. Again, the leader ignored her, maintaining his momentum and nearly launching himself up the concrete stairs next to the elevators. His follower was less energetic but more social.

"Have a good day," he said with a simple, friendly wave.

"You too."

Ellen was a quick 2-0 against the security measures at Milltown Place and now turned to the elevators. In a minute, she'd be knocking on Traci's door, and her friend, who should have had at least one warning by now, would be caught completely off guard by her arrival.

The elevator doors opened, presenting an empty car. Ellen stepped inside and pushed the button for the fourth floor. She had been operating in silence for most of the morning, and there was something pleasant about the muted hum of the elevator's mechanics as they churned away.

The ride took only a few seconds, but this elevator was a portal between disparate worlds. The entrance of Milltown Place was well lit and welcoming, with large windows and brightly painted white walls. The building's innards were not. The doors banged open, ushering her into a long, dim hallway. Florescent lights bathed the cold concrete floor in a sickly, uneven pall at 10-foot intervals. The lack of natural light created the same dreadful effect of Las Vegas casinos. It was impossible to tell the time of day from inside those halls.

Apartment 413 was seven doors down on the left-hand side. As Ellen neared, she heard faint music through the door. Someone was awake inside, which would only make things easier. She knocked four quick times and waited. Within seconds, the door opened. Traci stood in the frame, dressed in men's boxer shorts and a long-sleeved grey t-shirt. A mint-green towel hung across her shoulders. Fresh from the shower, she appeared sound of body and mind.

"Wow. Hey," Traci offered with clear surprise. "I never heard you..."

"Yeah, I busted in. The security in this place sucks."

They stood opposite each other in the doorway. Traci was backed by the hospitable glow inside her home while Ellen lingered in the dim of the gloomy hall. At a very average 5' 5", Ellen was still a head taller than her friend.

"Come in," she finally invited.

Ellen moved toward the light that burst through the huge window across the room. It was the television she had heard through the door.

"No roommates?"

"Nope. Krista brought me home last night, but she's working early this morning, and Steph probably spent the night at her boyfriend's. Whatever."

"I'm just glad you got home okay," Ellen said, sitting at the bar that separated the small kitchen from the apartment's small main living space. "I heard what happened."

"Yeah. Shit got crazy last night. Not my best work."

"So, you're alright though?" Ellen probed. "You feel okay?"

"Yeah. I feel fine. No hangover at all from the shrooms. In fact, I feel really peaceful this morning. I know I made an ass of myself last night, but I kinda don't care. Fuck it, right?"

"Absolutely," Ellen agreed, even though she knew Traci cared more about her reputation than she let on. Nobody wants to be known forever as 'the girl who set herself on fire.'

"Are you working today?" Ellen changed the subject, quickly moving back to her original agenda.

"Fuck no. I just did six days straight. I might have to do Happy Hour through close tomorrow night, but my ass is off 'til then. Thank God."

"Perfect. Put your non-workin' ass in some pants and go pack a bag for overnight. I'm taking you away."

Ellen wasn't usually bossy or manipulative, but she'd learned a thing or two living with Andy. Her roommate could be a colossal prick, but he was good at getting people to do what he wanted.

"What? Why? Where are we…"

"Less askin', more packin'." Ellen interrupted. "Go. We're leaving in ten minutes. Oh, and I need to use your phone." She walked around the bar and helped herself to the cordless handset, denying Traci the opportunity to challenge the request.

"I have to dry my…"

"Ten minutes," she repeated, already dialing, as Traci retreated toward her room.

58

It was just after 10:00 when the cry of the phone blasted Andy from slumber. By the third ring, he realized neither of his roommates were getting it. He rolled over and plucked the receiver from its cradle.

"Hello?"

"Good. You're home. Don't leave," urged the excitable female.

Andy was confused. He recognized Ellen's voice coming through the phone, but his brain discounted the possibility. Surely, she was asleep in her room no more than 40 feet away.

"El? Is that you?"

"Yeah. I need you to…"

"What the fuck? Where are you?"

"Listen," Ellen said, now slowing her delivery. "I'm at Traci's. I'm fine. She's fine. Everything's fine. I'm coming home. I didn't want to get there and find you guys gone."

"If you hadn't called, you could have come home and found me fucking *sleeping!*"

"I'm sorry. Is Jeff still home?"

"I don't know!" Andy was getting more agitated by the second. "He's probably still *sleeping*, like I was, until you called."

"I know. I said I was sorry." And truly, she was. "But I need you to do me a favor."

There was no reply. Andy simply waited; eyes closed.

"Go to Jeff's room. Make sure he's still there. Then, don't leave–either of you–until I get back."

"What the fuck is happening?"

"You'll see. It'll be fun. And it'll start with breakfast."

Still, Andy said nothing. But now, at least, she'd struck a chord. There was very little in the world Andy Maxwell loved more than a good breakfast, especially after an evening of self-abuse.

"Fine." He was about to hang up on her, but the suggestion of food had started his engine. He added one more word. "Hurry."

59

Ellen had given Traci ten minutes. She only used a couple of those talking to Andy. As she watched her friend flutter from bedroom to bathroom and back again, Ellen grinned at her success in getting Traci to comply. Traci had finished drying her golden copper hair during Ellen's phone call. She'd also pulled on light blue jeans and traded the long-sleeved t-shirt for a tight white tank top under a plaid flannel.

Ellen noticed the coffee pot on the counter was one-third full and still warm. She helped herself to half a mug of jet-black liquid.

"Pack layers!" Ellen called out, casually sipping her coffee. "Something warm too, like a sweatshirt!"

A minute later, Traci entered the kitchen. She placed a blue backpack on the bar and laid a black zip-up fleece on top of it.

"Done." she said, grabbing her own coffee mug and taking a swallow. "You want to tell me what we're doing?"

"Nope," Ellen teased. "But, you're probably gonna want sneakers instead of those sandals."

Traci gave her an exasperated look, kicked off the flip-flops, and turned.

"I'll kill the coffee pot!" Ellen yelled.

"Anything else I need to know?" Traci asked, returning with updated footwear.

"Nope. You're good. Let's go."

They downed their last gulps of coffee and placed the dirty mugs in the sink.

"Oh, by the way, can you drive?" Ellen added. "The Chevette's suckin' lately."

Traci grabbed the keys to her Jeep Wrangler and headed for the door, uttering an audible sigh as the orders piled up.

"Thanks!" said Ellen. "We just have to make one stop on the way."

60

Andy put his feet on the floor and rubbed his eyes. He sat on the edge of his bed and stared at his bare knees. Fragments of memory floated through his brain, but he couldn't quite recall how last night ended. This type of next-morning confusion usually came with a splitting headache or other hangover symptoms. But his mind was clear, and he felt unusually right. His brain didn't hurt. He wasn't even ill-tempered. Mostly, he was still sleepy and confounded after talking to Ellen on the phone.

Her instructions came back to him but added no context. Andy stood and inhaled deeply. The cheap linoleum popped, and the warped floorboards creaked as he moved across the house. From the living room, Andy could see Jeff's door was open a few inches. No light came from his room.

Suddenly, the absurdity of his approach occurred to him. He'd been trying to tread lightly as he approached Jeff. But really, there were only two possibilities. Either he would find Jeff in bed and wake him, per Ellen's request, or he'd find him absent, in which case he was home alone. Neither scenario required silence at all.

He sped up and pushed Jeff's door with less care than he would have a few seconds ago. The ambient light revealed a Jeff-shaped lump lying stomach-down, facing the wall. Waves of brown hair splashed over his bare shoulders. Andy realized he was just standing there, watching his roommate sleep. The awkwardness of it forced words from his mouth.

"Hey, dude," he uttered with little volume or conviction.

Instantly, he knew it sounded stupid, creepy even. Jeff remained motionless, undisturbed. Andy was grateful for a redux, but he wildly overcompensated with his next pitch.

"Yo! Wake the fuck up!" he yelled, walking straight at Jeff. That did the trick. Jeff convulsed and became more entangled in the navy-blue sheet that half covered him. Locks of hair swept across his bearded face.

"What the hell?"

"Sorry," Andy apologized, now swinging back towards neutral.

"What are you doing?"

"I don't know," Andy answered honestly, still not sure exactly why he was there. "The phone rang a second ago. It was Ellen. I think she said she was at Traci's and was coming back here now. She told me to get up, make sure you were still here, and for neither of us to leave."

The mention of Traci's name brought Jeff further out of slumber. Flashes of last evening went through his head, including how that had ended for her and him. He sat upright in bed.

"Fuck. Is she okay?"

"Yeah. Ellen said they were both fine. Why?"

Jeff stared at Andy, wondering if he would have to fill in the blanks for him.

"Oh yeah. The whole fire thing," Andy recalled. "No, she's fine. I think."

"And since when do you do *anything* someone tells you to do?" Jeff further questioned, now freeing himself of the sheets.

"Whatever," Andy said, stepping backward as Jeff rose. It occurred to him that a retaliatory punch for having been woken was a real possibility. "I was confused. It didn't make sense she was calling, or that she wasn't here."

"Unbelievable."

"I'm gonna go have a smoke," said Andy, walking towards the door. "Get up."

"Shut up," Jeff replied, still pissed to even be awake.

"She's bringing us breakfast!" Andy called from the living room.

It helped a little, but Jeff wasn't ready to be cheerful.

61

"Are you hungry?" Ellen asked, climbing into Traci's ride. She closed the Jeep's door and fumbled for the seat belt as Traci tossed her bag in the back.

"I could eat," Traci admitted, thankful for the question instead of the series of commands preceding it.

"Okay. Let's hit Bubba's. I told the boys I'd bring them breakfast."

Traci started the Jeep and reached across Ellen to open the glove box, retrieving her sunglasses. "I can do that," she affirmed, assuming her ownership and control of the car gave her at least a voice in the process.

Her immediate goal accomplished, Ellen contemplated the next phase of her master plan. Traci realized Ellen wasn't open to questions regarding this plan and resigned herself to finding something pleasing on the radio. A song and a half later, the Jeep blew through the yellow light at the intersection of Juniper and Townes. Traci had no interest in sitting parked for two more minutes, staring directly at their destination. She swung right, guiding the Jeep into the parking lot of Bubba's Biscuit House.

If there were an award for accuracy in branding, this establishment would win hands-down. Bubba's Biscuit House was precisely that, an old house converted into a glorified food stand owned by a guy named Bubba, which served almost nothing but biscuits.

Bill "Bubba" Greer was smart. He knew what he was good at and what made him happy. And he'd figured out how to turn the combination of those two things into a very profitable business. Bubba was good at making breakfast—specifically his grandmother's famous 'cathead' biscuits, so named for their relative size and weight. What made him happy was working less than full-time.

Bubba's Biscuit House was open Monday through Saturday, from 6:30-11:30 am, and not one minute longer. Greer busted ass, slinging biscuits 30 hours a week, and then went home with as much or more money in his pockets than some of his fraternity brothers who were working entry-level jobs at investment houses and law firms.

Exactly to Bubba's liking, people filed in, chose from a menu of less than ten items, paid him, and left. And to his credit, those people came back. They almost all came back, and they brought friends. Because Bill Greer's mam-maw knew how to make a biscuit so good, it made you mad at your own grandma for not being able to match it. Fat, flaky, and moist, Bubba would stuff those catheads with your choice of bacon, eggs, sausage, cheese, or country gravy. That, plus grits, was basically the whole menu. Everything cost $3, but those biscuits were priceless. They were perfect as a greasy sponge to cure the college kids' raging hangovers or as a dense carb bomb to fuel the working class through to lunchtime. And at lunchtime, it was over.

Traci parked the Jeep and cut the engine. They had made it on time but would have to wait in the near-closing-time line. If you got there before 11:30, you wouldn't get shut out of the building. But you might get shut out of the supply. Greer estimated his output for each day and made exactly that many biscuits. When they were gone, they were gone. 'Sorry folks, we'll have more tomorrow.' Ellen once saw a guy pay the lady in front of him $40 for the $9 breakfast she'd just bought her kids.

Ellen reached the door first and held it for Traci, who scooted inside and settled into the line about eight customers deep. At the counter stood another girl their age and a guy, perhaps her boyfriend. The girl was wearing mirrored sunglasses, so it was impossible to know for sure, but Traci sensed she was looking straight at her. The distance between them was roughly ten feet. Through the ambient noise of the other conversations in the small space, Traci could still mostly hear the girl.

"Damn. I think that's her. It is. It totally is!"

Now, the boyfriend was looking their way, too. Traci pivoted and returned their stare, only to find them laughing and the girl now pointing straight at her. She heard the words' fire' and 'crazy' louder and more clearly than the rest of their garbled exchange. The hot rush of embarrassment ran through Traci's face as she swung back around and looked at the floor.

The line moved, and the gawkers shuffled toward the door. As they passed, the mirror-shaded girl chuckled and addressed Traci without stopping.

"You're so hot," she teased with a condescending giggle.

Traci kept her head down and said nothing, hoping they would just keep walking. They did. Ellen had missed the full context. Having only heard the girl's final statement, she turned to Traci with a Cheshire grin.

"Did you just get hit on by some bi-girl, *in front of her boyfriend*, at the fuckin' Biscuit House?" she asked, a little too loud.

"Uh, no," Traci corrected. "I'm pretty sure they were at Doc's house last night." It took Ellen a second to connect the dots on the cruel pun.

"Damn. That's fucked up. Sorry. She's lucky I didn't hear her. I would have busted those stupid sunglasses in her stupid, skankus face."

Traci laughed at the thought of Ellen making good on that threat and prodded her friend forward. "We're next. Go."

Ellen responded like a pro. With zero hesitation, she ordered three Bacon-Egg Bubbas, a sausage and cheese biscuit, and one Messy Cat Head—a fat biscuit smothered in country gravy.

"And what do you want?" she asked Traci.

"Bacon, egg and cheese, please."

"$24.16," said a stoned-looking kid, who was definitely not Bubba, from the other side of the counter.

"Here," Traci offered, attempting to shove a few dollars at Ellen.

"It's on me," she replied, smiling as she plunked down cash.

"Thanks."

Just as Ellen intended, Traci was starting to feel better about how their day was shaping up.

62

Jeff used one hand to lift and pull the other high over his head. Extending it as far as he could, he stretched the muscles in his arms until his elbows elicited little pops. He bent, touching his palms to the floor. Tiny crackles raced up his spine as the tension in his back released. Lifting his head, he let out an aggressive yawn followed by a deep, chesty cough.

As his mental fog cleared, he distinctly remembered Andy saying something about food. Jeff was ravenously hungry. He was glad Ellen was on her way back, but also disappointed she'd left without brewing coffee. He filled the pot with water and impatiently waited for hot caffeine. Out of habit and boredom, Jeff opened the refrigerator and was instantly rewarded. Through the veil of a white grocery bag, he spotted liquid gold in the form of a single can of soda. Jeff pounced on it like a gator snatching a fawn from the banks of a river. He closed the fridge and left the coffee to brew as he moved back toward the Den.

From the couch, Jeff reached out and grabbed the box of Winston Lights off the table. Another single cigarette rolled toward him from behind it. It was a Marlboro Red–Ellen's brand. He popped open the box of Winstons, revealing half a pack. One of the ten cigarettes inside had been flipped upside down–a signature Andy used to identify his packs. With no supply of his own, Jeff faced the dilemma of stealing from his two equally absent roommates. Nine times out of ten, he'd have chosen to disadvantage Andy before Ellen. But the thought of the more robust Marlboro was simply too appealing. He closed Andy's pack and tossed it back on the table.

"Good morning, sunshine. Whose are those?" Andy asked, pointing at the box of Winston Lights.

"I don't know. This one is mine," Jeff lied, twice, for no good reason.

He sat up, exhaled, and reached across the table as Andy sat beside him. Grasping the small purple bong, Jeff spun it until the wooden bowl faced him. He tamped at the lump of charred mass inside it with his pinkie finger.

"Shit. This thing is still alive. Hit that." He passed the bong to Andy, who took it without thinking. Andy lit the bowl and vacuumed smoke through a few inches of spoiled water.

It was alive indeed. A hefty helping of smoke wafted upward. Andy released the carburetor, shot-gunned the dose, and passed the pipe back to Jeff, who set the bowl ablaze again. Jeff put the bong down on the table and held his breath. In that second of silence, just as Andy considered another helping, the front door opened loudly.

"Rise and shine, bitches!" Ellen barreled into the house.

"In here!" Andy called from the Den.

A surprising ruckus approached as more feet than expected trampled the floorboards. Ellen advanced several feet into the Den, leaving room for Traci who was following just behind. The boys were hungry and glad to have her home. They didn't seem to mind the extra company.

Ellen held up two big brown paper sacks, already stained with grease from the inside. Andy hoisted the Super Star in their direction as if to offer a toast or trade.

"Breakfast?" they asked simultaneously.

63

The girls' retreat from the room signaled their declination of a narcotic appetizer. They'd probably all agree the Den was not a suitable environment for eating. The boys got up and followed them back to the living room.

Andy moved instinctively for the remote control.

"Nope," Ellen reprimanded. "Keep that shit off. I want to talk to you guys." She assumed he would comply and started unpacking the sacks of food.

"Who wants coffee?" Jeff asked from the kitchen.

"Me," Ellen called.

"Yes, please," said Traci.

"Nope. I've got a Coke in the fridge."

Jeff stopped, trying hard not to laugh. He calmly returned to the Den and picked up the opened soda. He snuck another healthy sip from the near-full, icy can and returned to the living room. He handed it to Andy.

"No, you don't," Jeff said, turning to hide his wide, shit-eating grin.

"God dammit!" Andy fumed. That he'd only been robbed of an ounce or two of liquid at most was not the point.

"Sorry, man."

"But look," Ellen said, redirecting her roommate's rage. The lovely aroma had already started filling the room. Ellen handed Andy a big, warm wad of cellophane as consolation.

"Oh, I do love you," came the second half of his bi-polar exchange. "She brought us Bubbas!" Andy chirped at Jeff.

"Good call," Jeff agreed.

As Andy unwrapped his prize, Traci realized he was holding the bacon, egg, and cheese biscuit she had ordered. There were several in the bag with just bacon and eggs, and she figured it wasn't worth fighting an already-edgy Andy Maxwell over a stupid piece of cheese. She watched as he took a big smiley bite of her biscuit and silently cursed him as he chewed.

Ellen dumped the rest of the bags' contents on the table and started passing out napkins. She was bubbling with an energy she found hard to contain as she patiently waited for Jeff to rejoin them. Andy continued to devour the biscuit in his hand, oblivious to her hidden agenda.

"Ooh! Sausage gravy?!" Jeff said, immediately eyeing the Messy Cat Head. "Can I have it?"

"Sure," said Ellen. There was plenty to go around, and she had chosen all of it, guaranteeing the boys could please themselves and she'd still be happy with whatever was left.

Ellen and Traci took the chairs at the head and foot of the table while Jeff and Andy crowded together on the ratty sofa behind it. Ellen smiled. Her friends were deeply engaged in the free breakfast that had miraculously appeared. Hoping they were drenched in satisfaction and appreciation, she began her presentation.

"So, nobody has to work today, right?" Ellen asked, pretty sure she already knew the answer. She'd clarified Traci's schedule earlier, and Andy's perpetual availability was already well-documented. That only left Jeff. Unbeknownst to him, he was the linchpin in her whole plan, and she tried not to look right at him while waiting for their replies.

"I'm clear 'til Monday," Traci said.

"I've got that beat," Andy boasted with sarcasm.

"Jeff?" Ellen coaxed.

He raised his index finger, punctuating that his face was jammed with coffee and food.

A few seconds later, he answered. "I've got church tomorrow morning, but nothing today. Why?"

'Oh, shit!' Ellen thought with dread. She'd totally forgotten to account for the obvious obstacle. Masking her panic with a coffee mug, she took a long, slow sip and attempted to stall. There was no Plan B.

"So…" Ellen began, more timidly than she would have liked. "… it's been crazy around here for a while now, especially this past week. Everyone's on edge. I think we all need a change of scenery and pace."

"Are you breaking up with us?" Andy teased. Traci giggled as Ellen's opening statement did have that 'we need some space' feel to it.

"Shut up. I'm trying to be serious."

"Sorry. Continue."

Now, all of them were intrigued. What Ellen said next, none of them would have ever guessed.

"I want to go camping," she blurted out.

"What?" Traci and Jeff said almost in unison. Andy nearly produced a spit take of cold Coca-Cola.

She had planned a much slower reveal of her master plan. But now that the cat was out of the bag, it was time to backpedal and rebuild.

"See, here's the thing," Ellen reset. "I don't know if you guys even remember the conversation we had before you both passed out on me last night." She'd been talking to all of them but now turned and looked Jeff straight in the face.

"You were talking about all of that Center of the Universe shit and getting right with the world. That really hit me. I couldn't stop thinking about it as I tried to sleep. And when I woke up this morning, it was still there."

Jeff was listening. They all were.

"I might have been joking at first when I said I wanted to go to your place out in Fairview, but the more I thought about it, the more I'm sure we should all go. I think we all need a reset."

Jeff was giving her plea his full attention, and she could tell he was working on a reply. As usual, Andy felt compelled to assert himself. "Yeah, but camping sucks," he complained.

"Actually, it's kind of fun." Traci countered. "If you do it right."

Ellen and Jeff held a silent conversation of glances as their friends engaged in the sidebar.

"It really is a bit of a shithole," Jeff admitted, now downplaying whatever attractiveness he may have previously given his meager country acreage. "It's a shitty little one-bedroom shack. Busted plumbing. Iffy generator. Middle of nowhere. It ain't great."

"Yeah, that sounds rustic," Andy bitched.

Ellen was getting peeved and started to press.

"Damn it, Andy. I'm not talking about a week in the wilderness; I'm talking about one fucking night." Her change in tone was noticeable, and Andy stopped. He shut his mouth and let the smirk unwind from his face. But she wasn't done.

"You know…" there was real emotion in her voice, "… it's pretty hard to ignore that things are about to change around here." Now, she was talking straight at Andy.

"I know you're not happy about how things are going. But, in case you hadn't noticed, I'm not all that happy either. I don't know about Jeff; he can speak for himself…"

Jeff had no intention of derailing her momentum.

"... but I've been trying my hardest just to sort of let you be during all of this job search shit. You make a lot of choices I wouldn't, and that's fine. It's your life. But sometimes, those choices impact other people, too. I've been trying to ignore it, but it looks like you're pretty much leaving. And that makes me mad and sad."

She wasn't crying, and she wasn't going to, but from the sound of her uneven voice, she was drifting in that direction.

"So, last night, when Jeff started talking about clarity and getting right with the world... it hit me. Suppose we really are coming to the end of this, whatever *this* is. Wouldn't it be nice to slow down and spend some time just enjoying each other's company without some big-ass party or the constant noise of the TV and video games and all this other shit? We're damn good at having a good time, but when was the last time you sat back and really appreciated what we have here?"

It was true. Neither Jeff nor Andy could argue the bottom line with her. Ellen had deviated wildly from her planned presentation but still made a compelling argument.

"That's sweet," Traci said, crumpling her empty biscuit wrapper. She had plenty of time to finish breakfast during the conversation that didn't involve her. She also now understood why her Jeep was sitting in the driveway with a backpack full of clothes. "But, if you really wanted quality time with *them*, why am I here?"

Ellen didn't hesitate for a second.

"Cuz, you've had a pretty shitty run lately, too," Ellen said bluntly. "Sitting out in a field looking up at stars is a good way to get your head straight, and you could probably use some of that right now, too."

"Besides, you think I want to go out to the middle of nowhere *alone* with these two assholes?"

They all welcomed the joke. Ellen took a breath and turned back to Jeff. "Can we go?"

"I do still have church in the morning. I've got solos. It's not like I can skip."

"What time do you have to be there?" Ellen asked.

"Ten, at the very latest. Probably more like a quarter 'til."

"And you said it's like an hour away?"

Ellen was chipping away, breaking down the wall brick by brick.

"Something like that."

"So, you'd just have to leave Fairview by like 8:30, right?"

"Maybe," Jeff sort of agreed, avoiding any commitment.

Andy finished breakfast and lit a fresh Winston as the negotiation continued. He wasn't buying her plan, but he also knew she'd have to sell Jeff on the idea for it to matter. He leaned against the side of the couch and puffed away, waiting to see how things would shake out. He sat there, watching Jeff, and could pinpoint the second it happened. Even through the veil of hair covering much of his face, Andy could see that smile widen as he gave Ellen's plan further consideration.

"But you guys aren't gonna want to get up that early and drive back," Jeff thought out loud.

"Probably not," Andy muttered.

"We'll take two cars. I've got the Jeep."

Andy craned his neck in disbelief to look at Traci, who'd unexpectedly stepped in to solve the problem. Apparently, she, too, was now on board with the expedition.

Damn, he thought. *This is gonna happen.*

"I don't know," Jeff continued to stall. "You up for it, Andy?"

Jeff had given Andy a window of opportunity to express his dissent, but Ellen slammed it shut.

"C'mon," she interrupted, now addressing them both. "I hardly ever ask you guys for anything. You guys are always making plans, and I go along with whatever, just about all the time. When's the last time you did something I really wanted to do?"

"What? You took us to the strip club just the other day," Andy said.

Traci aimed wide eyes at Ellen.

Yeah," Ellen blasted back. "Right. Cuz, that was for *me*."

She stared at Jeff, waiting for an answer like a young girl asking her father's permission to borrow the family car. Traci smiled as she gathered up the spent napkins and biscuit wrappers. Jeff studied the tabletop as if looking for the answer there. He raised his head; wild intrigue stamped in his eyes.

"Why not?" he proclaimed, failing to find a reason to deny her request. "Let's do it."

A small part of Jeff was excited to show his friends one of his favorite places, unimpressive as it might be. Mostly, though, he just wanted Ellen to be happy. And now she was.

"Thank you!" she burst, rising from her chair to hug him. And then, after the quickest of celebrations, she was back in planning mode.

"Awesome! You guys get cleaned up. Traci and I will gather supplies. We can be out of here in under an hour.

There was nothing else Andy could say. It wasn't even noon, meaning he could still have been asleep if the phone had never rung this morning. But his day, and at least half of tomorrow, had suddenly been planned in full detail for him. He knew he only had two options: be a completely selfish, astronomical prick or go camping. Unpleasant as it was, the choice was clear.

64

Andy had already showered but wasn't about to mention it. He knew if he admitted to having extra time, Ellen would gladly plug him into one of the many jobs on the 'let's go camping' scorecard in her head. Having no interest in following her and Traci around checking shit off that list for the next hour, he grabbed his near-empty can of Coke and headed through the kitchen to his room.

"Where are you going?" Jeff called.

"You grab a shower," Andy replied. "I guess I gotta pack."

"Long pants and sleeves!" Jeff called out after him. "Snakes and mosquitoes!"

"Fuck!" he grumbled, disappearing around the corner.

"Really? Snakes?" said Ellen, with some caution.

"No, not really," Jeff admitted. "Well, maybe, it's the woods. But probably not. I know he's agitated. I just wanted to fuck with him a little," he said, chuckling.

"He does sound pissed," said Traci.

"I don't care," Ellen offered rather coldly. "He'll bitch for a while, and then he'll get over it. He just doesn't like people making decisions for him. He'll make it seem like it's about whether he's gonna have any fun, but it's really about him not getting to control shit. I'm a little over that."

Traci had always assumed Ellen was easy-going, compliant even. The last hour or so had shown her a side of her friend she'd never seen. Nothing about Ellen scared her, but this new assertiveness was a little intimidating.

Jeff was halfway to his bedroom when Ellen called him back.

"So, what exactly do we need?" The sheepish grin on her face betrayed her ignorance. At best, she didn't have everything figured out. At worst, she had no idea what the hell she was doing. But she did know well enough to wait until Andy had departed to reveal it. Jeff had no problem rolling with the punches; he tended to enjoy it.

"It's one night of camping," Jeff said. "We won't need much."

"Sleeping bags. Pillows. Cooler. Beer. Water. Food. Oh, and lighter fluid, bug spray, and toilet paper."

Jeff and Ellen looked at each other in stunned silence. The list had fallen out of Traci's mouth as if she'd been waiting her whole life for someone to ask her that exact question.

"What the fuck, Daniel Boone?" Ellen teased.

"What?" she replied. "My dad took us camping all the time when I was a kid."

"Damn," said Jeff. "I can see I'm not needed here. We'll have the shack to sleep in, too, but that list sounds pretty solid. We have a lot of that shit here, except food. We can stop along the way for whatever else we need. Start gathering. I'm going to take a shower."

65

Andy stood by his bed, stuffing random clothes into a black duffel bag. Taking Jeff's advice at face value, he gathered twice as many garments as he could possibly need for less than 24 hours in Fairview's 'rugged wilderness.' Adding socks, underwear, and a faded baseball cap, he was satisfied enough with his wardrobe to advance to the next phase of packing.

Now, he moved to what he considered his critical survival gear. He reached for the carton of Winston Lights on his desk and shook out two packs. Andy stacked the two gold boxes and placed a white Bic lighter on top. From the bottom left drawer of the desk, he pulled an old cigar box. A robust fragrance escaped, leaving no doubt about the box's contents. Inside was his current stash of weed–at this point, a few mere grams-as well as all manner of paraphernalia: rolling papers, two one-hitter pipes, and another lighter. Discarded stems and seeds littered the bottom of the box, along with a few sticky globs of resin harvested from cashed bowls and clogged pipes. These little balls of scavenged second-hand hash were the literal bottom of the barrel-the last resort when everything else was gone. Smoking that stuff was a dirty, unsatisfying high, but it was better than nothing in a pinch.

He grabbed the smaller of the two pipes and the rolling papers and placed them with his cigarettes. From the same drawer, he pulled a purple velvet bag–the former sheath of a bottle of Crown Royal Canadian whiskey. Into it went one pack of smokes, the lighter and pipe, the rolling papers, and the paltry quantity of pot. Andy pulled the thin gold strings tight and placed the bag into the side pocket of his duffel. He was sure Jeff was performing a similar ritual as part of his packing detail.

Andy tucked the other pack of Winstons into the breast pocket of his shirt, and that was it. It took him less than ten minutes to gather everything he thought he'd need. The faint sound of water rushing through the pipes indicated Jeff was still showering. Andy did not hear the girls' voices or any other activity in the house. He considered reconvening with Ellen and Traci when one more opportunity to delay presented itself.

A cursory scan of his desktop revealed a latent reminder of yesterday's escapades. It was strange enough not to have to search for either his keys or wallet before leaving the house. It was even more unlikely to find both items sitting neatly side-by-side in a place as logical as his desktop. But what really caught Andy's eye was the other leather rectangle sitting right next to them. He approached the desk again and sat. Of course, he knew what it was and how it had come to be there. But still, he stared at it as though for the first time.

Andy picked up the money clip that had recently belonged to his neighbor. It had the softness that came from being well-used but was still in excellent condition. The leather was faded and worn in places, but the stitching was still sound. Andy turned it over repeatedly in his hands, considering the inscriptions on both sides. Condemning and comforting, Quenton's gift of wisdom left him as conflicted now as it had last night.

Upon further examination, Andy discovered there was more to the gift than he had previously realized. In addition to the money clip on the exterior, there was an opening along the short top edge to accommodate cards. Andy grabbed his wallet, wondering how his present resources would fit into this new vehicle. He examined his driver's license. The picture was three years old. He was listed at 6'1", 195 pounds. In truth, he was barely six feet tall and now weighed closer to 220. He took the card out and placed it on the desk. Next was his Visa card, which, thanks to constant reminders from their billing department, he was aware was delinquent. Andy's mother had given—or, more accurately, let him borrow—a second credit card from BP gas stations when he first left home for school. Her intention was good, to help cover the cost of fuel and make it more affordable for him to come home more often. Neither one of them had 'forgotten' he had it. He saw it every time he filled his car, and she got the bills every month. He had simply neglected to return it, and she never brought herself to ask for it back. Three years later, he was still letting them pay for his gasoline. But it was worse than that. Like every other service station, the convenience stores at BP also sold food, sodas, beer, and cigarettes. Nearly every time he got gas, he stopped the pump a few dollars short and selfishly padded the bill with 'incidentals.'

Andy stacked the two cards next to his license and continued to forage through his wallet. There was little else of value besides an auto insurance card. He set aside the empty leather sheath. Without even having to get up, Andy grabbed last night's jeans from the floor. He rescued a crumpled wad of bills from the left front pocket and spread them on the desk. A twenty, a ten, a five, and three ones. $38 was no kingly sum, but it was more than the average of what he walked around with, so finding it was a pleasant surprise.

Andy organized the bills from largest to smallest, turning each one to face the same way as he built a small pile. He hadn't noticed the shower had quit running, but it was hard to ignore the slamming of the front door and the mini stampede that followed. The girls were back and moving through the house noisily. The interruption honed his focus as he considered what to do next. All his pocket money and identification lay on the desk, stacked neatly between his old wallet and the Scripture-emblazed money clip.

Andy knew he was pushing the boundaries of how long he could hide from helping before someone called him on it. He stood and moved to his closet. On the top shelf, under a pile of sweatpants and sweaters he hadn't considered since last winter, Andy found a massive green fleece blanket. He'd gotten it as a high school graduation present from an aunt and uncle who mistakenly believed he was attending college in the Arctic Circle, not the Deep South. The blanket was nice but heavy as hell, and he had never once come close to needing the kind of warmth that thing provided. Andy laughed as he hauled the green wooly monster from its perch, figuring it would at least get one good use in its lifetime.

He threw the blanket onto his bed next to the duffel bag and moved two of his three pillows on top of it just as Ellen peeked around the corner.

"Hey. How's it coming?" Her enthusiasm was palpable.

"Good. I'm packed, and I pulled some supplies together. I was just headed out back to grab the big cooler," Andy lied. "I think we're in pretty good shape."

"Awesome," Ellen said, boomeranging around the corner and out of sight again. "Finish up, and let's go."

Clearly, they were on the clock. Walking back to the desk, Andy made a quick, conscious decision. Instead of reassembling his old wallet, he placed his things into Quenton's old clip. He folded the meager stack of bills once, pried up the tension bar on the money clip, and slid the stack underneath it. He'd never owned a money clip before and didn't know anyone else who had. If Andy was being honest, he thought it looked kinda cool. He grabbed and straightened the small handful of cards. As he slid them neatly into the top slot, the Scripture stared up from his palm.

"Commit your work to the Lord, and your plans will succeed."

'Well, I guess that's one way to put your life in the Word of God,' he thought, turning the now-loaded money clip over again. He jammed the clip into his back pocket, grabbed the gear from the bed, and headed for the living room.

66

The girls were rifling through white plastic grocery bags in the kitchen. In testament to Ellen's motivational skills, it had only taken them half an hour to get to and from the Cubby with a first wave of supplies.

Andy entered, his arms full of pillows, the blanket, and his duffel. He got a partial look at their score as he walked past–one bag of marshmallows, a pack of hot dogs, and a case of Miller Lite beer.

"Nice haul."

"Where's that cooler?" Ellen called after him.

"Just a second."

From the porch, Andy saw Jeff scrounging through the small storage area behind the bench seat of his black pickup truck. Jeff emerged, hugging a large square of black canvas to his chest. Approaching the side of the truck, Andy blindly swung the duffel bag over the side rail and into the bed. It was already in flight when Jeff blurted out his caution.

"Careful!"

Too late. Andy's bag crushed two small fishing rods Jeff had already loaded. It was light enough and bounced off the rigs without discernible damage.

"Damn. Watch what you're doing."

"Sorry."

"Whatever. Help me with this," Jeff replied, unfurling and shaking out the truck's snap-on bed cover.

"We can fit everything we need back here, then cover it." Jeff explained. "I don't know what room Traci has in her Jeep, but this way, nothing will get wet or fly out the back."

Andy cared very little about the details but was at least glad to know Jeff had a plan. He laid the blanket and pillows in the truck bed and grabbed an edge of the liner, holding it steady as Jeff fastened one row of snaps on the far side of the truck. Andy hadn't even considered the possibility of rain. Surveying for clouds, it now occurred to him that there was something that could *further* decrease his interest in camping. For now, the sky above was blue and calm.

"Toss it back over," Jeff called. "I'll snap it down once we load it all."

Andy gave the canvas a mighty heave and launched it back at his roommate. Deciding he was done with that task, Andy walked away. He continued past the porch, along the side of the house nearest the Murphys, on his way to the backyard. The weeds that passed for grass in their yard had grown mid-shin high. Streams of dew slid off them onto his shoes and the bottoms of his jeans. Andy expected to see the large blue and white cooler peeking out from behind the concrete steps that led back up to the house. It was not there.

"Son of a bitch."

He took a quick look around the yard and trudged up the back steps. He re-entered the house to find the girls busily packing beer and bottled water into that elusive blue cooler.

"Thanks for the cooler, Andy." Ellen said dryly. "Hey though, can you take those bags of ice out back and bust 'em up?"

"Sure," Andy agreed.

"I think we're about ready," Ellen decided. "Where's Jeff?"

"Right here," he announced from behind her.

Ellen pivoted and leaned against the counter. She extended an arm toward Jeff, offering him a hug. Jeff slid in and hoisted his arm over her shoulder. She lowered her head to his chest and gave him a solid squeeze. He knew it meant 'thank you' and could tell she was probably smiling. Jeff hugged her back, then released.

Andy returned to the kitchen with a dripping, ten-pound bag of ice at the end of each arm. Traci lifted the cooler's lid, revealing several neat rows of aluminum beer cans and far fewer plastic water bottles. Once the cans and bottles were covered in ice, Ellen came behind and started dumping assorted perishables on top. Hot dogs, a pack of cheese slices, a bag of deli-sliced lunch meat, a small jar of bread and butter pickles, a carton of six large Hershey's chocolate bars, four apples, and four bananas.

"Food's set," she announced. "Sandwiches for lunch. Hot dogs for dinner. Chips to snack on, and stuff for s'mores later. Fruit and Pop-Tarts for breakfast. It's at least as good as you'd get if we stayed here."

"The only things we couldn't get at the Cubby were lighter fluid and bug spray. I thought they'd have both, but nope," Traci added.

"That's cool," Jeff suggested. "We can stop along the way. I've got two sleeping bags in the truck and probably two more in the cabin. Plus, there's the futon bed, with blankets."

"I brought a blanket," said Andy. It sounded roughly as lame as his actual contribution to the process had been so far.

"I think we're good. I threw in some fishing poles, too. I know a little place where we can get some worms or crickets, along with the other stuff we need."

"Awesome," cheered Traci. Her enthusiasm for live bait seemed odd, but they said nothing.

"Let's do this," Ellen urged.

"I gotta pee before we go," said Andy.

"Everybody goes before we leave," Jeff encouraged, slipping into Dad mode. "If we just make one stop, we can be there in about an hour and a half."

"Perfect," Ellen agreed. "Girls in the Jeep, boys in the truck." It wasn't clear whether her statement was a question or a mandate. It didn't matter–it was the most logical division between the two vehicles.

"Hold on," Andy called to his friends from the porch. They were already waiting at the cars. "Can someone lock this door? I'm not driving, so I'm not even bringing keys."

"I guess if you don't bring 'em, you can't lose 'em," Ellen teased.

"Exactly," Andy admitted.

Traci and Jeff were talking at the back of his truck. He was fastening the last snaps over the back panel as Traci asked questions from behind.

"Yeah, it's simple. Turn left on Paxton and follow it across 19. We'll get on the highway there and head east. Once we get off, it's country roads through a couple of tiny towns, maybe the last ten miles. Just follow me. You can't get lost."

"I can keep up with you," Traci said with a smile.

"Maybe." Jeff teased back, climbing behind the wheel. It was close to 1:00 as the doors slammed shut and the engines roared to life.

67

"Well, no!" Traci howled over the Jeep's radio. "That's just sick!"

As Bradford drifted into the distance, the girls laughed and told stories. Eventually, they became engrossed in a game called "Would You?" Simple and crass, it consisted of each person asking the other whether they would do certain things. The only rule was you had to be 100% honest, no matter what the question. The clear object was to inflict maximum embarrassment. The questions always started out innocently enough; stuff about stealing and other ethical conundrums. But without fail, they turned quickly to topics like sex. The two girls were now taking turns grilling each other over which of the various people in their shared world they would sleep with.

Traci's loud denial was in response to Ellen invoking the landlord of their house on Cornwall Street, a slovenly man in his mid-50s prone to wearing ill-fitting carpenter pants and sweat-stained t-shirts. Ellen had no trouble believing Traci would, in fact, not sleep with him.

"What about the fat dude working at the Cubby today? I think his name tag said Chuck. Would you fuck fat Chuck from the Cubby?" Traci asked with a heavy dose of mock sensuality.

She was already cracking herself up, but when Ellen played along, answering, "Oh God, yes. I'd ride that big bull all day," they both lost it.

They were still catching their breath when Jeff suddenly turned without warning or signal. Traci caught the detour in time, but she still had to hit the brakes to keep from crashing. Collision averted, she took a deep breath and burst into laughter again, causing Ellen to do the same.

The two cars entered the parking lot of a place called the Dutch Creek Outpost. Jeff had mentioned making one stop, and this must have been it.

Andy's head jerked. His body lurched forward against the seat belt as the truck came to a stop. With no navigational duties, Andy had drifted off to sleep almost as soon as they had left Cornwall Street. Raising his head, he felt the stream of drool running down his cheek. Jeff had left him alone in the truck and was standing on the curb in front of a country store that looked like it had been there, unaltered and unkempt, for decades. He was waiting by the front door for the girls, who were now climbing out of the Jeep. Andy moved to meet them, but slowly.

"See? That was easy," Jeff told Traci.

"Easy as pie. How close are we?"

"A few minutes. Everything we need should be here."

Part log cabin trading post, part nostalgic convenience store, the Dutch Creek Outpost was like countless other mom-and-pop shops dotting the back roads of America. It catered to populations more distanced from strip malls or the ubiquitous Wal-Mart.

"C'mon," Jeff ushered the girls inside. "I hope he's here."

The door of the Outpost opened with a rusty creak. Andy was only a few paces behind the others but far enough back for the door to crash back upon its steel frame before he reached it. He pushed it again and entered. The place was dimly lit and almost as dirty inside as out. At first glance, the store's layout was a mystery, with no apparent flow or logic. Jeff had already navigated a maze of crowded shelves and random displays and was nearing the back of the room.

"Fitz!" they heard him call out with some degree of joy.

Ellen and Traci were distracted by a rack of sunglasses. They took turns rotating the circular stand and plucking off gaudy selections that were at least a generation out of style. Andy was still getting his bearings among the hodgepodge. Jeff's callout was enough to gain their attention. They turned to see him embracing a stocky young man wearing an orange and white mesh trucker cap.

It was no surprise Jeff would know some folks in the area where he'd grown up and still visited occasionally. Hell, Jeff seemed to know someone *everywhere* he went. The others made their way toward the reunion.

"Jeff Aaron," proclaimed Fitz, now shaking his hand and smiling with great pleasure. "Look at the long-ass, girly freakin' mop on you, boy! Get a fuckin' haircut, hippie!"

The first words the others heard Fitz speak were drenched in a thick country drawl, delivered through the kind of muffle you can only get from a cheek full of chewing tobacco. Realizing they were now all together, Jeff dispensed with the introductions.

"Y'all, this is Patrick Fitzpatrick. His dumbass, Irish-as-hell parents call him Patty. His grandma calls him Pat-Pat, but he hates that shit. Makes all his friends call him Fitz."

Fitz's fair complexion turned ruddy around the cheeks from the embarrassing explanation. None of them noticed it surrounding Fitz's gigantic, grotesque smile. Two rows of snaggled teeth stained a deep, nasty yellow took center stage in the middle of his acne-pocked face. Little tufts of his super-curly golden blond hair popped up from under the band of his hat.

"I thought this was the cutest lady I'd seen come in here in a long time…" Fitz attempted to emasculate Jeff, "…until I saw you two." He aimed the awkward compliment at Traci and Ellen, leering at them and still smiling. They laughed nervously, embarrassed either by or for him, and avoided eye contact.

"These are my friends from Bradford," Jeff explained. "Ellen, Traci, and that's Andy. I've known Fitz since middle school, and he's still hanging around these parts."

"Yup," Fitz confirmed. "But why the hell are y'all way out here?"

"Just gettin' out of the city for a day. They wanted to see the old farm, so we're making a quick run."

Jeff had left out any mention of camping or spending the night.

"We needed a few supplies before heading over there."

"Hell yeah. Whatcha need?"

"Lighter fluid and charcoal," Ellen started.

"Right over there," Fitz pointed. "What else?"

The girls gladly distanced themselves from the Redneck Romeo. "Bug spray," Traci called out, not looking back.

"Two shelves over, on the right, at the bottom." Clearly, he'd mastered the location of every item in the store.

With the girls mobilized, Jeff added, "I need some bait. Crickets, or crawlers, or something. Whatcha got?"

"Both," Fitz answered, walking back behind the counter. "Fresh, too." He turned around and slid back the top panel of what looked to be an old ice cream cooler. Dipping his sweaty hands inside, he returned with two plastic tubs the size of medium soup containers from a Chinese restaurant.

"Crickets and crawlers, bro," he smiled. "What else?"

Jeff took a quick glance around before asking his next question more quietly.

"You got any .22 shells?"

"Shit! Ain't nobody else in here today, man." Fitz laughed at what was obviously a measured precaution on Jeff's part.

"Cool," Jeff replied, relieved but still hushed.

"Lemme see what I got," he said, disappearing around the corner and into a back room.

* * *

Andy was busy rummaging through a rack of cheesy t-shirts emblazoned with deer, American flags, eagles, camouflage, or some combination thereof. Amused but unsold, he returned to the counter where the girls had placed their chosen items.

Andy's eyes drifted to the mélange of notices posted on the wall as he approached. On the bottom right, nearest the register, was a helpful reminder to whoever was manning the counter. In scraggly letters three inches tall, scrawled in heavy black magic marker, were the words, 'No Checks from these Shit Heads!' Below these were photocopies of several driver's licenses, their pictures badly obscured by poor reproduction. Andy considered pointing out to Jeff's friend that 'shithead' was in fact one word but decided the spelling lesson might go unappreciated.

Scanning upward and left, Andy saw five state-issued flyers featuring missing persons. They included four children (two white boys, a black boy, and a black girl, each between the ages of 10-16, and one older adult female appearing to be in her early thirties). The flyers were the kind of thing most people never even noticed. The similar posters and billboards all over Bradford in the last week, broadcasting the disappearance of Margo Hammond, had conditioned Andy to pay closer attention.

The Dutch Creek Outpost was deep in the sticks. Fairview was a hundred miles from downtown Bradford. Andy wondered if the fact that Margo's photo was not on the wall here was a matter of proximity, timing, or something else. The thought lingered only for a second, replaced by his general amusement at the assortment of crass, redneck-themed shot glasses by the front counter.

* * *

"I had about half a box sitting back there. Got more at home. I can spare this if you want it." Fitz said, laying a battered carton of .22 caliber ammunition on the counter.

Jeff slid the box open, checking the quantity. "Way more than I need. But I'll take it if you're serious."

"Serious about you buyin' it," Fitz clarified. "Twenty bucks, and it's yours."

"What?" Jeff bucked. "I can get a whole box for less than that."

"Not anywhere close. And you're already here." That same toothy, shit-eatin' grin of Fitz's that was so repulsive to his female companions was now starting to piss Jeff off as well.

He knew he was being taken. He also knew there was a good chance Fitz was gonna take that $20 and use it to score some cheap meth or crank.

If he'd thought it through, Fitz might have realized he'd have been better off just giving the shells to Jeff. State law frowned mightily on the sale of ammunition without a license. The Dutch Creek Outpost was a lot of things, but a licensed firearms or munitions dealer was not one of them. Jeff would never turn him in, but if this was a regular racket, it was only a matter of time before Fitz tried to fleece the wrong sheep and got what was coming to him.

"Whatever. I'll take 'em." Jeff conceded. He dug into his pocket and brought out the cash. He tossed a twenty on the counter and curled the box in his palm.

Fitz grabbed the bill and stuffed it in his pocket as he moved toward the front of the store. Jeff shadowed him along the other side of the long counter.

Andy and the girls organized a small cache of supplies at the register: beef jerky sticks, more sodas, lighter fluid, charcoal, and bug spray. Fitz took stock as he began ringing up the items.

"Y'all planning to cook and camp?"

"Nah. Just a day trip. Back home again late tonight," Jeff lied.

Ellen glared at Jeff. He subtly shook his head, waving her off with a look that begged her to let it go.

"Too bad," Fitz said. "I'm outta here around dark and coulda swung by."

"Yeah, too bad," Jeff echoed, with a tone that gave her all the information she needed.

"Can I get two packs of Marlboro Reds?" Ellen asked.

"Of course," Fitz replied, oozing more charm at the girls. They were likely much cuter and cleaner than anything he'd spoken to recently.

"$24.16," Fitz announced, jamming the items into two brown paper bags.

Ellen unshouldered the small bag she was carrying and brought out her wallet. Traci stood ready with a crisp $10 bill in her hand. Andy reached into his back pocket and laid his wallet on the counter like he'd done countless times before.

No less noticeable than if it had been flashing in bright neon letters, the inscription stood there screaming silently on the countertop. 'Proverbs 16:3.'

"Uh, nice wallet," Traci mocked. "Pretty funny. Where'd you find it?" She was sure it was a joke the rest of them were already in on.

"Actually, a friend gave it to me." The seriousness of his reply stifled any further commentary.

Andy pulled $10 from the money clip, matching the girls' contributions, and jammed the wallet back into his pocket. He headed for the doors, fighting the frustration he felt rising. The first public display of the gift from Quenton had brought precisely the kind of attention he did NOT want. It embarrassed him and made him angry. He said nothing and kept moving.

"Y'all have fun," said Fitz. "Good as hell to see you, man. We need to hang out a little. Let me know when you're coming back up. We'll go tear some shit up."

"Will do," said Jeff as they gathered their bags and left the Outpost. It was evident to all, except maybe Fitz, that Jeff had no such intentions.

Traci opened the Jeep, and they placed the supplies in the back.

"Colorful dude," Ellen said, unimpressed and glad to be back outside. "We're still spending the night, though, right?"

"Of course," Jeff reassured her, "just not with *that* guy. We go way back, and he's alright enough, but he's his own adventure, and this trip ain't about that at all."

She gave him a thankful grin as they moved back to their vehicles.

"A couple miles down the road, we'll take a left, past this big ol' burned out barn. You can't miss it. Then it's just a couple winds through the trees. We'll be there in like ten minutes."

"Cool. We'll see you there," said Traci, cranking the Jeep.

68

"See? I told you. It's kind of a piece of shit."

"Eh," said Andy in apparent agreement as the truck crept over the last few yards of the tire-worn path in the grass and stopped in front of a threadbare shack. His expectations had been unfairly low from the get-go, so the fact there was even a standing structure on the property was a pleasant surprise. Traci had been tailing him like a bloodhound since they'd left the Outpost, and it was mere seconds before the Jeep pulled in behind them.

She stepped out and quietly surveyed the modest parcel of land. In contrast, Ellen nearly flew from the vehicle, bounding the twenty or so feet between her and Jeff's truck. He'd hardly opened the door before she was there.

"This is fucking awesome!"

He smiled, not knowing how else to respond to her enthusiasm for his sad little kingdom. Andy scoffed, though under his breath. He was amused at her energy, even if unsold on her joy.

Cupping her hand over her brow to shield out the bright afternoon sun, Traci scanned the terrain. The house rightly occupied the highest point on the lot, with the land sloping gently to the left. Behind the house, a small pond had formed in what was probably a natural rain basin. Although, to call it the world's biggest mud puddle would also have been accurate. No more than a hundred and fifty feet across, its water was stained a dark reddish-brown by the southern clay below, and it couldn't have been very deep.

There were a few trees near the house and a few more near a flattened structure—an old barn that had buckled and fallen sideways like a cardboard box folded at the seams. One gnarled, grandiose oak rose high near the foot of the pond, but otherwise, they stood on an expansive clearing. There was a tree line about a half mile away.

Legions of loblolly pines stood tall, forming a wall of sorts around the perimeter of the property. And that was it—a shack, a mud hole, a fallen barn, and a big-ass field.

"This is really nice," Traci said, walking to join the others leaning against the front of Jeff's truck in silence.

"Thanks. It ain't much, but it's mine. Y'all want the nickel-tour before we unload shit?"

"Yeah. Show us around," Ellen decided for the group. Traci and Andy were both less excited, though for different reasons. Being outdoors was nothing new for Traci; she had grown up on a decent-sized piece of land herself in the foothills of northeastern Tennessee. Andy, who had not, was still unsure he even wanted to be there.

Jeff exhaled a cloud of smoke and stomped the cigarette butt into the soft clay of one of the tire ruts worn into the field. With a spring in his step, he waved them on as he moved toward the small clapboard house.

He reached the rickety porch first, avoiding the single step leading up to it. He knew it was already rotten and unstable. From the landing, he turned and offered a hand, first to Ellen and then Traci, helping them chivalrously to ascend the extra 18 inches. He offered no such help to Andy but did make a verbal warning as he approached.

"Don't use the step. It's rotted. I need to tear it out and rebuild it, but I haven't. Just climb over it. It would suck to bust your ankle out here."

Andy grabbed the banister and made the extra-large step over the compromised wood. Jeff propped open the rusted screen door as he worked a key into the deadbolt. Swollen from humidity, the front door stuck but opened with a slight nudge.

The house was dark and smelled terrible. "Whew! How long's it been since someone was in here?" Andy complained.

"A while," Jeff admitted, propping the screen door and joining them inside. "I'll open the windows to air it out. Shouldn't take long."

That much was true. The house was tiny. It was more of a shack, with one central area and another room at the back, which was concealed by a closed door. The main space held a small, carved wooden table with two matching chairs and an old futon couch, which looked remarkably clean aside from a layer of dust. Off to the side, but still technically in the same room, were a countertop with a sink, and a miniature refrigerator.

"I thought you said this place had no water or electricity," said Andy.

"It doesn't," Jeff assured him. "It used to, but that shit's been turned off for ages. Why pay for something that never gets used."

He had to fight with each of the two small windows along the front of the house. Eventually, both relented and allowed fresh air into the place. Jeff moved across the room to the closed door and pushed it open.

"Tiny little bedroom. And one bathroom back there, but it doesn't work either. And that's a closet." Jeff said, pointing to a second door along the wall.

With that, the tour of the house was complete. He entered the bedroom and opened that window as well. Both girls peeked into the room without entering. It was barely wide enough to hold the twin-sized bed along the wall with the window. A simple two-drawer nightstand beside the bed rounded out the furnishings.

"So that's it. Pretty impressive, huh?"

"Shit. This is awesome!" Ellen maintained. "We don't even need tents. We can all crash in here."

Andy supposed she was right, *if* they could get the smell out of the place. The prospect of not having to pitch a tent—something else with which he had no experience—was a pleasant thought.

"It'll keep the food away from critters, too," Traci added.

"That's true," Jeff said. "Let's let it air out, and I'll show you the rest of the land. Then we can bring the stuff in."

He pulled the front door open as wide as it would go and placed one of the wooden chairs against it to keep it in place. Holding the screen door, he waited for them to exit, then leapt off the porch.

"Let's go!" he called, moving towards the pond. They followed him to its bank. Closer to the water line, the clay dirt was noticeably softer. Andy felt disquieted with each mushy step.

Jeff stopped and surveyed the small body of water.

"What?" Andy asked as he caught up.

"Just watching the surface."

"For what?"

"Snakes," Traci said plainly.

"Yup. Water moccasins dip in there sometimes," Jeff explained. "I would tell y'all you could go swimmin', but it's not worth it. Bottom's sludgy as hell, and you just come out brown."

"Yeah. Thanks for the warning," Andy griped. "I'll pass."

"There's usually some fish in there, though," Jeff offered. "Small brim and whatnot. I've got rods in the truck and house, and I grabbed some bait back at the store."

"That sounds fun," said Ellen.

"Except for the snakes," Andy reminded.

"Oh, there might not be any. But we'll shoot whatever we see," Jeff suggested.

"Shoot 'em? With what?" Andy wanted to know, having never considered the possibility of firearms. "You have a gun?"

"Relax," Jeff said, sensing his friend's agitation. "This is the country. Everybody out here has a gun. Most folks have several. A lot of people hunt; some are into the idea of protecting their land or livestock, and some just like to shoot shit for fun, but everybody out here is packing something."

"What are *you* packing?" Andy asked.

Knowing full well his roommate's feelings on the topic, there had never been any reason for Jeff to share his ownership of a firearm with Andy. Besides, it never left the farm anyway.

"There's a little .22 rifle in the closet in there. It's great for plunking squirrels or taking out a copperhead. Not much more than that, though," Jeff explained. "I'd have to shoot you with it ten times to hurt you," he laughed. That wasn't true, but he suspected Andy wouldn't know the difference, and it might make him feel better about the whole thing.

Andy said nothing. Traci held her breath and her tongue.

"Who wants a beer?" Jeff offered, successfully changing the subject. Laying his arm across Andy's shoulder, he turned him around and pushed back toward the cars. The girls fell in and walked beside them.

69

Jeff lowered the tailgate and began unfastening the snaps on the truck's bed liner. About a third of the way up, he stopped and folded the loosened portion of canvas on top of itself. There was plenty of access to retrieve the few items they'd stowed.

He grabbed Andy's duffel and tossed it at him, which freed his path to the object of his real desire. The blue and white cooler slid easily out from under the cover. Packed chiefly with ice and cans of beer and soda, it was heavy enough to justify asking for help. But Jeff declined, happy to display his manly strength for the two girls as they considered what to pull from the Jeep. He lugged the hard plastic treasure chest with gusto, emitting just enough of a labored exhale to punctuate his struggle as Traci and Ellen walked past carrying sleeping bags.

"You want help with that?" Andy half-offered from the porch.

"Naw. Just take your bag. I got this," Jeff said, letting out a short grunt.

Andy knew the display was intentional, but he didn't care. If Jeff wanted to haul that heavy bitch all by himself, he was welcome to it, along with whatever marginal gain it earned him from the ladies.

The cooler met the rotting wood of the porch with a loud thud. Jeff stood tall, straightening his back and stretching his arms. The girls had brought the few sacks of non-perishable groceries to the kitchen's small countertop and lingered. Jeff returned, holding a crumpled brown paper bag in one hand and a six-pack of beer in the other. Andy experienced a strange sense of déjà vu as he watched his friend once again enter a room carrying both intoxicants and a mystery.

Jeff laid the paper bag on the table, freeing his hands to distribute the cans of beer. He walked to the small closet and opened it, emerging with two white and red fishing poles.

"Good," he said. "These are much better than the shitty ones I brought from home. And they're already rigged." Jeff placed them against the wall and ducked back inside the closet. What came next got their attention—Andy's in particular.

Clutched in his right hand was a gun–a .22 caliber Winchester model 77 rifle, to be exact. Andy recoiled involuntarily at its sight while Ellen gazed with moderate interest, sipping her beer. Jeff shut the closet door, walked toward the futon, and sat down. With the gun lying across his lap, its business end pointing away from the rest of them, Jeff checked first to ensure the safety was engaged. He then turned the gun belly up in his lap and pulled free the 8-round magazine clip from in front of the trigger guard. Placing the rifle on the floor, with its muzzle now aimed at the back bedroom, Jeff addressed the paper bag on the table in front of him.

"Can I smoke in here?" Andy immediately sought an outlet for his growing anxiety.

"Cigarettes," Jeff replied. "You're gonna wanna stay sober for this."

"For what?" Andy asked. He was already lighting a Winston.

"Winchester?" Traci inquired. She sat on the edge of the futon, eyeing the gun on the floor.

"Yup," Jeff confirmed. "Early '60s. It was my dad's, but he gave it to me when I was twelve." He had revealed the contents of the paper bag to be the partial box of shells he'd gotten from Fitz at the Outpost. He dumped a handful of bullets onto the table as they continued to talk.

"Nice," Traci said. "I had an old one too growing up, but mine was a bolt."

"You what?" Andy asked with disbelief.

"Oh yeah," Traci explained. "Been shootin' since I was tiny."

Andy thought about suggesting she still was, but he let it go.

"We grew up in the mountains. Daddy wanted boys. He got two girls. My older sister was princess-pink from day one, not the least bit interested in dirt and trucks and football and guns. When I came along, Daddy knew he wasn't getting a boy. He started training me early. Hunting, shooting, fishing, you name it. I was basically raised as a bird dog."

Andy *could* be very perceptive, but only when properly motivated. If he had paid more attention to Traci over the years, he'd have learned more than enough to be unsurprised by her current revelations. But she wasn't high on his radar. And it wasn't just her. Andy was painfully self-aware but often struggled to retain even basic details about others.

Jeff grinned in appreciation of her rural upbringing. "When's the last time you shot?" He asked, feeding the rifle's magazine.

"It's been years," she admitted. "I'm rusty, but I'm sure it's like riding a bike."

Andy and Ellen sat out of this impromptu meeting of the Fairview chapter of the NRA. She had joined him by the open front door, where they stood silently, smoking and draining their beer cans. Traci held the rifle as Jeff finished loading the magazine. She handed it to him, and he jammed the clip into the breach of the gun.

"C'mon," he commanded, sweeping the bag of ammo off the table. "School's in."

Andy figured there was little or nothing Jeff had to teach Traci on the present topic and correctly assumed he was talking to Ellen and him. He had no interest at all in firing the damned thing, but he followed Jeff and the others outside, nonetheless.

Jeff's long hair flapped wildly as he sprung off the porch, carrying the rifle like an eager militiaman.

"Grab another six!" he called back to them. Andy had finished his first beer and gladly obliged the call for more. He reached into the cooler and dug past the hot dogs and condiments stacked between him and the alcohol below. The others were already several paces ahead, moving toward the folded barn across the field. Andy walked slowly, knowing the teacher would wait for his straggling student.

Jeff prepped the rifle, smoke billowing from his cigarette. Andy plucked a beer from the plastic six-pack holder and passed the remainder to Ellen. She did the same, as did Traci, until Jeff stood in the open field with a smoke in his mouth, a rifle in one hand, and three beers in the other.

"Perfect," he approved and started walking away.

Twenty yards downwind, Jeff reached the first of two massive tree stumps. He placed an unopened beer on the stump and continued to the next, another 15-20 yards further down range. He put the other can on the second stump and marched back toward his troops.

"So, now you're gonna 'blow some shit up'?" Andy asked.

"Nope," Jeff said with a wicked grin. "You are."

"No fucking way," Andy declined emphatically.

"It's the *only* way," Jeff replied, with the calmness of someone who already knew they were getting what they wanted. He walked straight at Andy, his rifle-toting hand extended. "This is one of the reasons I agreed to come out here in the first place."

"For what?" asked Andy. Ellen was intrigued as well.

"Here's my guess." Jeff began. "You've never shot any kind of gun before, have you?"

"Hell no," Andy confirmed. He had moved past agitated straight to full-on mad.

"Right," Jeff replied, now tendering his presentation a bit. "I get that you hate guns. And of course, I know why. But I thought this might be a chance for you to see things from a different perspective."

Andy felt hurt and betrayed by his roommate's apparent lack of sensitivity. He was taking the short, literal view of Jeff's proposal, failing to see any larger picture his friend was attempting to paint.

"At some point, we all have let go of the anger and fear we're holding onto. That shit kills you slowly from the inside." Jeff moved closer, relaxing his tone and lowering his voice beyond the girls' ability to hear him. He *was* talking about the gun, but this was about something much more significant, too.

"You think I can just *let go* of Tristan, and all the…" Andy's temper and voice were escalating.

"No," Jeff said, placing his arm around his friend's shoulders. "Of course not. I don't have any siblings. And I don't know the first thing about the pain of losing a brother. I can only imagine it would be like losing you."

Those words were unexpected. They soothed Andy to some degree. Still, they cut deep, unleashing fresh feelings about his past and present relationships.

"But here's the other thing I *do* know about…" Jeff continued. "You came home the other day with a potential solution to your job problem. Someone wants to pay you to write. The problem is, they want to pay you to write about guns."

Tears and angst welled within Andy, but he held his tongue.

"I know this shit makes you anxious," Jeff acknowledged, "but what if you took a chance and made yourself do something completely uncomfortable. There are two ways it can go. Either you move forward, or you don't. Maybe you try something heart-breakingly hard, and maybe you come out stronger on the other side. Or you try it and find out you still feel the same. The worst thing that could happen is you gain nothing from the experience."

"No," Andy replied, finding a footing to counterattack. "The *worst* thing that could happen is that somebody could get fucking shot and die."

Jeff took Andy's dramatic response in stride.

"Okay. That's clearly not going to happen here," Jeff said, attempting to infuse a modicum of reason. "If you can, think about it in a completely different way–a totally utilitarian way. I know it's hard, but if you put all that other stuff aside, is it possible to think about a gun as just another tool?"

"A tool whose only job is to kill something?"

"Maybe. But it's also just a collection of moving parts that does a job, like a lawnmower, or a chainsaw? Those things can kill people too, if the people who use them don't read the manual somebody writes."

Andy said nothing.

"I don't know. I guess I thought there was a chance you might be able to let go and actually *let* yourself do that job, instead of just throwing it away on principle. I thought it was at least worth a shot."

"I want to shoot it," Traci blurted, interrupting Jeff's speech but also offering Andy a possible out.

"You will. And Ellen, too, if she wants. But Andy should go first."

"Fucking fine," Andy caved. He was still mad and unconvinced, but they'd reached an impasse. "I'll shoot the damned thing. Show me how."

"That-a-boy," Jeff congratulated his roommate as if he was a 7-year-old finally mustering the courage to plunge off the high-board at the neighborhood swimming pool. The girls walked to the wreckage of the fallen barn and propped themselves against the last of its upright walls.

"I can't believe that worked," Traci said of Jeff's sales job.

"He played it perfectly," Ellen replied, less shocked than impressed. "The surest way to get Andy to do something is to let him go over the edge like that. He needs to vent and to be heard. But then you can usually reel him back in with a little guilt. It's not easy, but it works if you do it right."

"Now, take the butt of the rifle and bury it here, against your shoulder," Jeff instructed. "This gun barely kicks at all, but you always want to make sure it's firm against you before you fire it. Now, this hand comes underneath, and leaves the other hand for…"

"I'm left-handed," Andy reminded him.

"That's cool. So, just switch it."

The gun was light, roughly six pounds. The combination of steel and wood didn't feel terrible to Andy. Still, he bristled at the sensory experience of holding the thing. He begrudgingly made the adjustments and brought the butt of the rifle to rest against his left shoulder. As his right arm extended forward to accept the barrel's length, he moved his left hand toward the trigger mechanism.

"Not yet," Jeff cautioned. "Never put your finger on the trigger until you are locked on your target and committed to firing the gun."

"I'm *not* committed," Andy grumbled, still shouldering the weapon.

"Okay. Now, the sights are a little off on this thing; shoots high if I remember. So, you're gonna wanna line your target up with this notch here but aim a few inches low."

Andy stood tall and motionless.

"Wait," Jeff interrupted again, "forgot to take the safety off."

Andy lowered the rifle, unsure how to make the adjustment.

"Always good to have this thing on," said Jeff, showing him how to disengage the safety. "But you gotta take it off before you shoot. Now, you should be ready."

Andy raised the rifle again. He stared down the barrel, attempting to place the sight on his target. He was surprised at how small a can of beer looked from sixty feet. Still trying to figure out what came next, he stood there holding his form. The muscles along his right forearm began to announce themselves as he worked to keep the barrel level and still. After nearly ten seconds of inactivity,

Jeff realized Andy was awaiting further instruction. He chuckled to himself as he leaned in over his roommate's shoulder.

"It's ready when you are," Jeff explained. "You can put your finger on the trigger, and when you're ready, I want you to pull it towards you with good, even pressure. Don't…"

BAM! The .22 exploded, startling all of them for different reasons.

Everyone but Andy had expected Jeff to finish his sentence—especially since he was giving gun safety training, and that sentence had started with 'DON'T.'

For Andy's part, the physicality of the experience shocked him. He now had a better understanding of Jeff's advice. The gun did kick a little, but it wasn't any great force; Jeff had punched Andy in the shoulder harder than that many times.

"Holy shit!" Andy wailed, now swinging toward Jeff and bringing the gun barrel with him as he went. "That bullet flew right across my face!"

Jeff deflected the barrel as it approached, clasping it and pushing it toward the ground.

"That was a shell casing. The bullet went straight out; the casings come out here," Jeff explained, now pointing to the ejector slot along the rifle's body. Most people shoot right-handed, and the spent shells come out away from your body. Because you go lefty, the shell came across you. They usually go straight out, but sometimes they can come up like that. Sorry. I shoulda mentioned that."

Jeff expected another assault from Andy. But none came. He was still busy processing the visceral experience of having shot a real, live gun. In fact, they were all so surprised Andy had fired the damned thing that none of them had even bothered looking down range to see the result. Both cans remained undisturbed on their stumpy perches.

"Go again," Jeff encouraged. "There's eight shots in there. No one ever gets it on their first try." That was a lie, but why not give him some hope, Jeff figured.

Andy hesitated but didn't decline. Jeff took this as a tacit acceptance and returned the rifle to him. He stood quietly, waiting to see if Andy would remember the set-up or need to be guided through it again. Andy turned the gun slightly and peered at the safety.

"Red means ready?" he asked.

"You're good to go," Jeff confirmed. "Aim for the closest one."

"Fuck you. I was." Andy raised the barrel and set the butt of the gun into his shoulder.

"You'll get it this time. Remember, aim a little low, like right at the base of the can."

Andy didn't respond; he was locked in. If he *had* to do this, he *had* to succeed. He regulated his breathing, working the nearest can into the sights. Andy brought his index finger to rest on the trigger. His friends stood silently, anticipating he might fire at any time. They were all looking down range, hoping to see a beer can explode when it happened.

BAM!

"God dammit!" Andy howled, flailing both arms wildly upward and out. He began shaking the right one violently as if he were being attacked by some invisible, rabid dog. In the commotion, he hurled the gun. It arced several feet away from him and crashed into the clay with a metallic thud. Thankfully, the barrel stayed down range, and there was no discharge.

"What the fuck?" Jeff screamed, rushing toward him. The girls followed.

Andy clawed at his flannel, which suddenly seemed glued to him. After a few seconds of flailing and cursing, Andy freed himself of the shirt and spiked it with real anger into the dirt. He straightened, clutching the inside of his arm.

"What happened?" Ellen asked.

Andy moved his hand. A small but nasty burn mark, a dark red splotch the size of a penny, had bloomed about halfway up the inside of his forearm.

"Shit, man," said Jeff. "Shell must have shot right up your friggin' sleeve. That sucks."

The initial shock was over, and it wasn't like he'd been severely wounded. There would be a mark for a while, and the burning wouldn't fade fast either, but Andy's pride hurt the worst. Looking down range, he saw the two cans standing tall and mocking him. It was confirmation the lesson had been every bit the failure he expected it would be.

"I'm guessing I shouldn't have thrown the gun," Andy scoffed, trying his best to make light of the clusterfuck.

"Yeah," said Jeff, "don't ever do that again. Next time, roll your sleeves, or just don't wear any."

"Fuck *next time,*" Andy said. "I think I've had plenty of that."

"Aw, c'mon. That's just what you get for being left-handed," Jeff teased. "The world ain't made for you people."

Andy was about to light a smoke when another rifle blast erupted behind them.

By the time the boys had ducked and spun around, a second shot screamed out, this time followed by a loud popping sound. All three of them now watched as Traci took aim at the further can of beer, having just dispatched the nearer one with her second shot. A third shot rang out, causing the second can to explode with a magnificent 'thunk'.

Traci lowered the rifle and switched the safety back on as she turned to face the trio behind her. At 40" long, the Winchester 77 was only about a foot and a half shorter than her.

"Damn. Nice shootin', Tex," Jeff said.

"Thanks," she grinned. "Once a bird dog, always a bird dog. You were right. Comes off a touch high. Pretty easy adjustment though. That was fun. Who wants to go fishing?"

Like the cigarette in his hand, Andy fumed. He wasn't about to volunteer to be shown up by her again in the aquatic portion of the Redneck Olympics.

"Me! I do," Ellen piped up.

"No thanks," Andy declined.

"That's cool," Jeff said. "I've got two rods set up there on the porch. There's a tin of night crawlers and one of crickets in a bag on the floor of my truck. Looks like Chinese takeout."

"You girls go for it," he added, addressing Traci. "I'm guessing you know your way around a rod and reel, too?"

"Of course," she beamed.

"It's gettin' toward late afternoon. You might get some bites. Catch and release, though. Nothing in there is worth cleanin' or cookin'."

"Will do."

"You want to keep the gun, in case there's a snake or two over there?"

"Yes," Ellen blurted, although she knew she had no intention of shooting it.

Traci hoisted the rifle and started to walk back toward the house with Ellen.

"Thanks," she said, with a flirtatious grin at Jeff as they passed.

"Sure."

"Where are y'all going?" Ellen asked.

"It'll be dark soon enough. We'll go get firewood and see y'all later. Have fun."

70

A hundred yards from where they stood, the open field gave way to the first bits of dense tree line beyond. Jeff walked toward those trees, assuming Andy would follow. Less than halfway there, they passed the first can dispatched by Traci's sharpshooting. Its frothing carcass lay in the yellowed grass, still bleeding a slow trickle of beer into the ground.

"Leave it," Jeff said. "We'll grab it later."

"It's a shame two perfectly good beers had to die for that display," Andy grumbled.

Jeff laughed. "You probably wouldn't feel like that if you'd hit one of them."

"Yeah, well, we'll never know, will we? I feel pretty alright about this, though…"

Andy had decided to award himself a consolation prize in the form of a small joint he'd rolled during his packing detail. He inhaled with gusto as they kept walking. "What also feels good is not having to even think about getting busted way out here."

"Not having to think about much of anything is the best thing about being 'way out here'."

"Yeah. I don't know if I could live like this though. Seems like it might get boring pretty fast."

"It all depends on what you're looking for," Jeff said. "I don't want to be out here all the time either, but sometimes, I love just doing nothing."

"Hell. We didn't have to leave the house to do *nothing*," Andy argued.

"Yeah, but this is a different kind of nothing. You can really *think* out here. There's no distractions."

"I like distractions," said Andy. "My problem is that sometimes I can't *stop* thinking. The only way I've found to make that shit stop is to turn my brain off or at least shift it into a different gear." He held the smoking joint aloft as if it illustrated his point and offered it to Jeff.

"You know, I think I'm gonna take a little break," Jeff declined. "My brain's been in some crazy fuckin' places lately."

"Whatever," Andy said. "Your loss."

"There is another way to stop thinking about shit." Jeff suggested. He stopped near the edge of the brush as they reached the shade of a massive tree. Its trunk was twice Jeff's diameter, and as he crossed behind it, he vanished from Andy's sight.

"Yeah? What's that?"

"The best way to stop *thinking* about something is to start *doing* something." Jeff stretched his back against an old park-style bench that had sat in the shade of that poplar for as long as he could recall. He sent a puff of cigarette smoke skyward and invited Andy to join him.

From this perch, they could see the farmhouse across the field and the rolling hill that rose again behind it. They watched the girls walk away from the porch, each holding a fishing pole and a plastic grocery bag. As they traversed the gentle slope toward the pond, the girls began to disappear, like two tiny suns setting below the horizon. The actual sun churned westward, taking with it the clear-blue brightness and leaving a sweep of faint pink that signaled the coming dusk.

"You're right," Jeff continued. "You *have* been thinking a lot lately. Probably too much. And it might be time to start moving toward doing. I mean, aren't you getting to the point where you *have to* make a decision? To figure out what you're really gonna *do*?" He took a drink and waited for Andy's inevitable rebut.

"You mean like the decision *I* got to make to come out here?" Andy said sarcastically. "Or like the decision *I* got to make to shoot that stupid gun? Like all those decisions *I've* been making today?"

"I'm sorry," Jeff offered sincerely. "Trust me. No one's trying to make you mad or get you hurt. By wanting to come out here in the first place, Ellen was trying to help. And so was I. In fact, we've both been going out of our way to help you lately. We know you're struggling. We listen while you rant. We give you advice, even when you don't want it. We've tried to be patient while you work through shit and make decisions. But now? Now you're stalled out, parked at the crossroads. We've just been trying to give you little pushes to jump-start you."

"That's the thing, though," countered Andy. "I'm tired of people trying to push me to do things I don't want to do."

"We all have to do shit we don't want to do, Andy."

"Yeah, but lately, I'm getting it from everywhere. You. Ellen. My fucking parents. That thing with the Murphys the other night. Everywhere I turn, people keep trying to tell me what to do and how to do it."

Andy was worked up, alternately ranting, smoking, and drinking. This felt like some sort of uber-rural intervention–a planned attack by those closest to him, orchestrated to isolate and force him to make uncomfortable decisions. Like a threatened animal, his base instincts kicked in. He struck back in self-defense, motivated by fear. Jeff was unsurprised by all of this, except for the next target of his roommate's ire.

"And now," Andy continued, "over the last week or so, I can't help but feel like even God has been following me around, telling me what to do. And I can promise you, I don't recall asking Him His opinion about any of this shit!"

"Wow," Jeff said in disbelief. He paused, considering what his friend had shared.

"And you think that's a *burden*?" Jeff asked. "That, my friend, is the very definition of a *blessing*. Whether you *asked* for it or not is irrelevant. If God is bothering to get involved in your life, the last thing you should do is build a wall against that. Millions of people pray every day for that kind of guidance. They *beg* for God to speak to them, for Him to *tell them what to do*. If you're hearing that and thinking it's some kind of *hassle*, you really don't know God at all, and I feel sad for you."

"Don't you feel sorry for me," Andy shot back.

"I didn't say I felt sorry for you. I said I feel sad for you. The God I know is not some mean old dude following you around like a grumpy grandpa, riding your ass and telling you what to do all the time. God loves us and wants us to be happy. When He sees us unhappy, He reaches out to comfort and guide us. Sometimes, it's so subtle you'd never even know it's Him. But sometimes, it's like He's right inside your head, telling you with painful clarity what you should do–usually when it's shit you're convinced you *don't* want to do."

Like the humid Fairview air, the silence was thick and a bit uncomfortable.

"So, what has He been telling you to do?" Jeff finally asked.

"I don't know," Andy admitted. "I've spent so much time being mad at Him that I'm not even really listening. It's like being pissed at your dad. He can yell at you all he wants; even if he's right, it doesn't matter. It's all just noise if you're not listening. Eventually, my dad gives up and stops trying to pound sense into me for a while. I just assumed God was gonna work the same way. Besides, after He left me, I've been doing fine enough alone."

Jeff's sadness grew with every word. He tried to temper his frustration with Andy's stubbornness as he continued.

"See that's the thing…" Jeff said, "God *never* leaves us. You can turn your back on Him all you want, but all that means is He's behind you. But when you do that, it's on *you* to turn back around again. He's patient as hell. He'll wait as long as you want."

"I don't know…" Andy started. Jeff wasn't finished.

"And just so you know. God's not *chasing you down* either, trying to make you do stuff you don't want to do. Those are demons.

And trust me, I feel those, too. God is about giving us clues and letting us figure it out on our own. He's always trying to help, but you gotta be willing to listen."

"Damn," grumbled Andy. "I didn't ask for a sermon."

"Yeah, you kinda did," Jeff replied, now smiling. "You're the one that brought up being mad at God. I'm not into preaching or getting in people's faces. I try to leave people alone and let them get where they're going on their own. But if you're gonna be *that* wrong about what's going on here, I owe it to you to at least get you a little closer to the Truth."

71

"I'm guessing this wasn't about firewood, then?"

"Not really," Jeff admitted. "There's probably a year or more's worth of split logs piled up on the other side of the barn over there."

"Piece of shit," Andy was folded over, forearms across his thighs, looking straight down at the barren earth as his roommate continued.

"Sorry, man. I know this whole day wasn't what you wanted. But I swear, I'm not trying to piss you off. I'd love to help you see things differently.

"I know. And I'm sure it seems like I hate that, but I don't. What I hate is hearing stuff I don't want to hear."

"Yeah. You and everybody else."

Jeff was good at reading a room and knew there was little left to gain here. "I wonder if they caught anything?" he said. Andy was grateful for the change of subject.

"Traci probably emptied the pond and shot a bear while she was at it." he joked.

"Ha!" Jeff laughed. "Doubt it. There's nothing much in there at all, but I'm sure Ellen's having fun trying anyway. Besides, I really wanted to hang out with just you for a minute. I'm glad we got to talk."

"It's all good," said Andy, stopping short of full reciprocation. Stomping his feet to plant them, he stood and stretched. "Let's head back. I'm hungry."

Jeff suddenly realized the afternoon had come and gone without lunch. It had been ages since they'd polished off the biscuits with which Ellen had bribed them.

"Yep. But let's grab those cans Traci wasted before we forget 'em."

Cleaning Traci's kills was the last thing Andy wanted to do. He'd rather forget the incident altogether, but the mere mention of the cans forced it right back into his head. It also reminded him of the souvenir from his first shooting lesson–the one scalded into his right arm. He looked down and rubbed the red splotch, which had ceased to burn but was still annoying as hell.

72

Andy's head was packed, and the silent walk through the field was a welcome break from all the earlier confrontations. Two beers and a few pulls from the joint were doing their job. A sensation approximating happiness enveloped him as he neared one of the stumps. Jeff had walked ahead, leaving Andy the closer and easier of the two retrievals.

A few feet ahead, Andy saw the glistening metal reflecting what was left of the afternoon sun. He reached down and grabbed the can, thoughtfully inspecting the small, precise entry hole the .22 bullet had made. Rotating it revealed the exit wound in the backside–a far larger and much more vicious tear. A stream of warm beer flowed over his hand as he turned the can upside down to empty it.

He held the can, inspecting its damage. Seeing what those tiny bullets had done to pressurized aluminum, he could only imagine the kind of havoc they, or more aggressive projectiles like the .45 that had ended Tristan's life, could do to human flesh. There wasn't much to begin with, but any possibility of him accepting the job at Firebrand Marketing was instantly eviscerated.

Andy turned toward the house, shaking the last drops of beer from the can as he walked. As he approached the vehicles, the girls were still nowhere to be found. The tailgate of Jeff's truck lay open, the bed liner still partially peeled back. Andy noted that everything except Jeff's bag and the camping chairs had already been unloaded. With some malice of forethought, he flung the decimated beer can into the back of the truck, smiling as it slid and banged all the way to the back.

Andy pulled Jeff's duffel from the truck bed to make room for firewood and moved toward the house. Ellen and Traci returned from the pond, carrying the fishing poles and plastic bags, but no fish. Andy couldn't hear their conversation but could tell they were laughing and happy.

"Do we have any trash bags?" Andy asked as they joined him on the porch.

"We've got the plastic bags from the Cubby and that other place," Ellen suggested, having forgotten the name of the Dutch Creek Outpost.

"We might need those as we start getting food and piling up beer cans," Andy offered, not mentioning the one he'd just deposited in Jeff's truck.

"Speaking of food," he continued, "it doesn't look like you guys pulled dinner out of the pond."

"We figured you were out bagging a deer or something," Traci returned, digging at his recent failure with the rifle.

"Damn," Andy replied. "I wasn't even…"

"Don't sweat it," Ellen interceded. "We had fun. I actually caught a fish."

"Seriously? Nice!"

"Yeah. It wasn't very big or anything, but it was a real fish."

'Wasn't very big' was a massive understatement. The tiny brim Ellen wrestled from the pond's murky shallows couldn't have been more than a few inches long. Traci was smiling and trying not to laugh. Ellen had indeed caught a fish, and as Traci correctly assumed, it was her first. Traci had accomplished that feat around age 5, landing a much larger trout in her granddaddy's stocked pond. Unlike Ellen today, she had taken it off the hook and even helped clean it herself. But Traci figured the pride and elation were relatively the same, so she stayed silent and let Ellen have her glory.

"That's cool, El. Good for you," Andy congratulated.

"So, yeah. What about food?" Jeff wanted to know, joining them with the second of Traci's cans in his hand. "What do we want to do?"

"First, I need to get the fish slime and cricket guts off my hands," Traci said. Ellen hadn't thought about it, but she could use a good washing, too. "But you said there was no plumbing, right?"

Jeff grinned. "You're in luck."

Returning the fishing poles and rifle to the closet, he came back with a tube of antibacterial hand wipes and an unopened gallon of water. Ellen immediately popped open the wipes and began to disinfect her hands.

"Damn," Andy said again. "What else you got in there?"

"Just a few basics," he smiled, walking back over to the sink and opening a drawer from which he pulled a combination corkscrew can-opener. "Most of my Boy Scout training stuck."

"Perfect," Traci concluded. "With the hot dogs and snacks, we should be more than good. Now we just need a fire."

"We'll do that, while y'all get cleaned up," Andy suggested.

"Fine by me," said Jeff. He walked to the open front door and extended his arm toward the field. "See that circle of stones out there in the middle? Come meet us when you're done."

"Got it," said Ellen, tossing the wipes to Traci and picking up the jug of water as she followed both boys outside.

"Save some of that water for drinking," Jeff reminded. He surprised Andy by walking to his truck instead of past it. He opened the door and climbed in without considering the open tailgate or any cargo still loaded inside.

"C'mon. Get in."

Their destination was at most two hundred yards away. Still, Andy was never one to choose walking when an alternative was available. Jeff parked along the far side of the fallen barn, with the truck's front end resting in a bank of grass as tall as its hood. They both piled out and moved toward the store of split, well-aged wood that lined the back wall of the barn.

"I'd guess about twenty pieces would get us through the night," Jeff said. "Let's just load it up once and dump it by the pit, and we'll be good to go."

"That works."

"We're still gonna need some kindling pieces though. Do you want to load or bust up the branches of that big-ass limb right there?"

Andy was unaccustomed to choosing between two kinds of manual labor and was inclined to answer 'neither.' Instead, he quickly tried to figure out which job was better.

"I'll bust branches," Andy picked.

"Cool." Jeff would have been fine doing either task.

Jeff filled his arms, taking four or five pieces at a time back to the truck.

"Make sure you get a handful of sticks good for cooking hot dogs or marshmallows."

"Fuck." Andy muttered. Somehow, he was sure he still ended up with the shittier of the two jobs. He surveyed the giant wooden appendage, a gnarled old arm of oak severed by either weather or disease. He stood there trying to identify the most skewer-worthy of its branches before finally just attacking the chore of dismantling it with his bare hands.

It took Jeff less than ten minutes to load twenty pieces of firewood. In that time, Andy had amassed a reasonable pile of kindling. With a noticeable sigh, he bent down and gathered the stack, hugging it to his chest as he moved toward the truck.

"Make room for this shit," he called to Jeff, who was leaning on the back of the tailgate.

Jeff slid and stacked a few logs to ensure Andy could dump the whole armful in the nearest corner.

"Nice job," Jeff said. "That's more than we'll need."

"Good. Let's go."

The girls followed Jeff's lead, using the vehicles to mule their supplies to the fire pit. As the wood-laden truck swept around the far side of the barn, the boys could see Traci's Jeep parked near the camp chairs set around the circle of stones. The girls stood talking in the middle of the field as the sky drew ever darker behind them.

Jeff pulled up next to the Jeep. Working together, they emptied the bed in no time, creating a small square pile of wood stacked within easy reach of the fire pit. Again, Andy hugged the bale of brush and transported it to the ground beside the logs.

"Where's the lighter fluid?" Jeff asked.

"Shit," Ellen said flatly. "We brought over the cooler and most of the stuff, but I think we left those bags back in the house."

"No worries," Jeff said. "I gotta grab a few things. And I bet all the windows are still open. I'll go move the truck over there and be back in a few."

"I'll come with you," Andy said. "I need my bag, too."

"I put your pack in the back of the Jeep," said Ellen.

"Well, fuck it then. I'll stay here." Clearly, Andy's offer was utterly self-serving.

"I'll help you," Traci offered.

Jeff was already saddled up. "Cool. Hop in."

"We'll be back," Traci announced, heading for the idling truck.

Andy turned to retrieve his bag from the Jeep. Ellen had taken up residence in one of the neon blue canvas camp chairs. She was staring across the field, lost in thought, enjoying a smoke.

He wanted to join her and would. But first, he had something to prove.

73

Andy dropped his pack in the chair beside Ellen and turned to the woodpile. Most of the pieces were thick, dense wedges that might need lighter fluid to catch and hold a flame. Towards the bottom of the stack, he found what he sought-a few logs much thinner than the rest. He pulled four from the stack as Ellen puffed on a Marlboro, watching him with interest. Perched on one knee, Andy carefully laid two wedges of wood against each other upright. Having balanced those, he grabbed two more and repeated the process, creating a small pyramid. He turned to the heap of brush he'd collected and grabbed two handfuls of smaller branches. Ellen watched in fascinated silence. She'd never seen Andy show aptitude or initiative for anything even remotely related to the outdoors.

Andy packed the pyramid's interior with smaller twigs but was still unsatisfied. He returned to the Jeep and retrieved a brown paper grocery bag and one of their two rolls of toilet paper.

Ellen had changed her stance. She now sat hunched over, forearms on knees, engrossed by his endeavor as if some silent movie were unfolding before her.

Andy ripped the brown bag into strips and stuffed them inside. Still insecure about its combustibility, he proceeded to wrap the entire structure in toilet paper. Three circuits around, and it looked like someone had mummified a tiny scarecrow. He turned to Ellen, patting the pockets of his jeans but coming up empty.

"Lighter," he said, with the seriousness of a surgeon demanding a tool from a triage nurse.

The smile widened across her face as she plucked hers from the cup holder of her camp chair and tossed it at him.

"Light that bitch!" she encouraged.

Andy knelt at the fire pit's base. A trail of paper led away from the mini mummy, like the wick of a bomb. He lit the paper and watched as the flame crept–slowly at first, then much quicker. He walked to the other side of the structure. The toilet paper smoldered briefly, then sprung to life as the oxygen between its layers was consumed. The outer shell fully engulfed; it was momentarily impressive. Still, it would all be for naught if the kindling inside failed to catch. Andy took a long stick and wrapped its tip in toilet paper, fashioning a crude torch. He lit it and thrust it into the heart of the pile, working to touch as many pieces of brown paper as possible. Andy knew he had succeeded as the pyramid's center began to smoke and glow. Small bits of crackling signaled the smaller twigs giving up their ghosts as the fledgling fire grew against the creeping dusk.

"Impressive."

"Thanks," Andy said. "I'm not completely useless."

"Not completely. You want a beer?"

"Yep." Andy's attention was split between tending the growing flames and retrieving the stash from his duffel. Unzipping the side pouch, he dug in and brought forth the purple velvet bag.

Andy was determined to build the fire before Jeff returned. He saw it as a salvo in the escalating exchange his roommate had begun with the cooler stunt earlier. Ellen returned with two cold beers. Andy handed her the pipe loaded with a dense, bright green bud she could smell above the smoke of a growing campfire in the middle of a wide-open field.

"Thanks!"

"My pleasure."

Andy took back the now-smoldering pipe as he glanced toward the house.

"Where the hell did they go?" Ellen asked.

Jeff and Traci had been gone at least ten minutes, plenty long enough to close every one of the shack's four windows and reclaim whatever gear could possibly still be there.

"Who knows? Maybe she's in there blowing him or something."

"Nice," she said with sarcasm and disgust.

"It might be," Andy half-joked. "Although, after that display with the gun, I'm a little more afraid of Shorty."

It was mean but not enough to keep Ellen from laughing.

"Are you having fun?"

"You know, I am," Andy admitted. "I started out hating the whole idea. I really didn't want to come. But yeah. I'm actually digging it a little bit."

"Good. That was mostly the point, you know?"

He said nothing but was genuinely grateful.

The fire was fully established and radiating impressive light and heat. Ellen and Andy heard the screen door slam, announcing the return of their friends as the last bits of light slipped under the seam of the horizon.

"Hit that pipe again," Andy urged. "Finish it."

Even after two or three hits, that dense little bud still had some love left to give. She inhaled hard and held it. Sliding the pipe into her pocket, she chased the hit with a pull from a cigarette and exhaled just as the others arrived.

"Damn," Jeff exclaimed. "Nice fire, Ellen."

"*I* built that shit," Andy professed, equally proud and indignant.

"He did," she confirmed. "Every bit. By himself."

"Well done," said Traci. "Looks like it's ready for a few more big logs."

Andy couldn't decide if that was a criticism or endorsement, but his default was to assume the former.

"You didn't even need this," she said, reaching down and placing a white plastic quart of lighter fluid on top of the cooler.

"Oh, we'll use it," Andy said. "Hey, Jeff, grab a couple more logs."

As Jeff worked to balance another set of wood pieces against the structure without toppling it, Andy grabbed the jug of fluid and tore away its plastic safety seal.

"Why not?" Ellen asked. "Jenga's way more fun when you add fire!"

"Most things are," Andy laughed. "Back up!" It was a reasonable request, and they all complied, particularly Traci, who was still understandably skittish regarding the topic of fire.

Jeff bent down and opened the cooler. "Who wants one?"

"I'm good," declined Andy.

"Me too," said Ellen, holding aloft her cold fresh can as she stepped backward.

"Hit me, bartender," Traci said. Andy couldn't help but think maybe he just had, but he wasn't saying anything.

"Three... two..." Andy began counting, as Jeff was still in questionable proximity.

"So, *now* you're gonna count?" he teased, getting in one more barb about the rifle incident before springing out of the path of destruction.

"One!" Andy squawked with deranged glee as he blasted the open flame with a stream of lighter fluid. A massive plume erupted in the middle of the now-dark field. Jovial shouts went up around the circle.

"Where are the cooking sticks?" Traci asked.

"There's a pile of longer ones right there," Andy pointed, realizing it would have been worth having a flashlight to illustrate his directive. "We're gonna need some more light out here."

"We're gonna need some more *drugs* out here," Ellen suggested.

"Y'all go ahead," Jeff deferred. "Like I said, I think I'm taking a break."

"What does *that* mean?" Ellen asked, having missed his earlier decree.

"Nothing," Jeff suggested, trying to downplay it. "Do whatever makes you happy."

74

Jeff and Andy reclined in camp chairs on opposite sides of the stone circle, quietly sipping beers and staring at the fire. Ellen crouched by the stones, poking at the inferno with a thick, gnarled branch, while Traci unpacked items from the cooler. The absence of conversation made it easy to notice all the other noises around them—the crackling flames, the rustling of ice and plastic packaging, and, further away, a chorus of frogs and insects warming up for their nightly performance.

"You okay with the fire?" Andy asked Traci. He meant it in a concerned way, but she could have taken offense if she'd been so inclined.

"I'm fine," she replied. "It is a little weird though, ya know?"

She paused briefly and then continued without looking up from her task.

"We know a lot of people who aren't exactly masters of self-control. But I don't feel like that. I've never been one to freak out about stuff, ya know? I'm very even tempered. Even when I get blitzed, I still somehow feel like I have things under control. Not last night though. I lost it big time."

"I know how you feel," Andy butted in. This sentiment was well-meaning but potentially overused across all of Andy's relationships. As one who considered himself all-too experienced in the art of suffering, Andy had a bad habit of telling others he 'knew how they felt'. Too often though, it wasn't out of genuine empathy, but rather a shortcut he'd discovered to pulling focus during conversations. If you were really paying attention, this little parlor trick also carried the slightest twinge of condescension, making it extra annoying. Of all the people in Andy's world, Ellen was most attuned to the defect, and the quickest to call him on it. Jeff called bullshit on Andy so often, for so many different things, it was sometimes hard to distinguish the exact source of his ire.

Traci was less practiced, and frankly, less interested in such nuances. She was typically fine letting others hog a spotlight, so his interruption went unchallenged.

"My trip was totally different from yours. But I was way out of control too. At first, I dug it, but when the wheels came off, I wanted out. But I couldn't make it stop. I had to ride it all the way to the end."

"And, the weirdest thing is," Traci said, "my trip seemed to stop almost immediately. One second, I'm seeing an evil wall of fire creeping up my legs, and the next thing I know, I'm lying on the floor soaking wet, and people are gasping and laughing. But by the time Christa got me into the car, I think I was already down."

"I don't know," said Jeff. "I think I'm with Andy on this one. I've done my share of 'shrooms' before, and every trip is unique. Mine lasted longer than I wanted, and my head was still fuzzy this morning. And I was *totally* out of control. It's weird. Usually, that doesn't scare me. In fact, I kinda like it—most of the time. The idea of something else pulling the strings doesn't bother me at all. It kinda gives me peace."

"So, now we're back to God again?" Andy asked.

"Or demons." Jeff replied casually, but ominously. "But I told you–we're never really *away* from God."

Ellen was as uninvolved in this conversation as she was in last night's hallucinogenic escapade. She knew she was missing something, but equally sure she may have gotten the better end of the deal by abstaining.

"Right. And when you take your hands off the wheel, that's when bad shit happens," Andy argued.

"No," Jeff countered. "Bad shit happens all the time anyway. It's gonna happen, no matter how hard you fight to hold the wheel or whether you let it go altogether."

"See, that's not cool though. After a while, if enough bad shit happens to you, you're gonna get pissed off. I mean honestly, if somebody kept disappointing you over and over again, how long would you just be okay with that before you got fed up and cut them loose?"

"I don't know," Jeff chuckled. "You and I are still friends."

Both girls, and even Andy, laughed at the well-played barb.

"All I'm saying is that maybe most of the people who still trust God just haven't had enough bad shit happen to them to break that trust yet."

"I believe it works the other way around," Jeff said. "If nothing bad ever happened to you, it would probably never even occur to you that you might need more than yourself in this world. The more adversity we face, the more reassurance we need that things are going to be okay. Faith in something larger than yourself gives you that."

"And some people are just more resilient than others, too," Jeff continued. "I mean, look at Graham. That dude's like fuckin' Job." He paused, waiting to see if the reference brought clarity or confusion.

Sensing condescension, Andy defended his modest knowledge of the Old Testament. "I know who fuckin' Job is. What's your point?"

"If you didn't know any better, you might think Graham's got it pretty good. But he's had to go through Hell to get there. I can't really think of anyone who's had more taken away from him. And yet, somehow, he keeps soldiering on, taking it all in stride. I don't pretend to know what his relationship is with God, but if I had to guess, I'd say he knows Him for sure. And for all the hardships he's suffered, you'd have to say that guy is still living right. People love him, and through all the bullshit he still manages to be pretty fucking happy. I don't think that's an accident. I don't think you make it through all of that without a little help and the ability to let shit go. I mean, think about it. If he tried to control every little aspect of all that craziness, he'd lose it for sure."

"Like Cricket?" Andy asked.

Jeff took a breath. Evoking her here was supremely insensitive but not necessarily off the mark.

"Yes, Andy," he said curtly. "Like Cricket."

"Who's Cricket?" Traci asked.

"That cute blond hippie chick Jeff was friends with," Andy clarified.

"What happened to her?"

"She died," Ellen said without hesitation. The directness of her delivery was intended to shield Jeff froms having to expound.

He didn't need or want the protection.

"What really happened was she gave up," Jeff corrected. "I don't know what her demons were, but clearly, they were more than she could take. That happens all the time. I guess that's my point, Andy. Bad shit happens to everybody. Some people, like Graham, have big shoulders. They can carry a mountain of bullshit, but usually only with a little help. Others, like Cricket, get buried. But the truth is, nothing is ever over until you give up. And the only thing worse than giving up might be deciding not to try at all."

Andy's callous reminder of Cricket had exhausted Jeff's patience. Clearly agitated, he rose from his chair and headed toward the house without the aid of a flashlight. "I'll be back in a minute."

"But I was just getting ready to roll that other joint," Andy called, trying to back-peddle.

"You do that," Jeff encouraged and kept walking.

"Damn," said Andy, turning to both girls. "I didn't mean to…"

"You *never* seem to mean to," Ellen scolded, now also frustrated.

"Actually, sometimes I *do*, but definitely not then."

"Whatever. I'm gonna go talk to him. I'll be back."

Andy sat in silence, not even 100% sure what had just happened. He looked at Traci, who returned a shoulder shrug that telegraphed ignorance, apathy, or maybe both. He reached beside his chair and started fumbling through the dark for the velvet bag in his pack.

75

"You wanna get high?" Andy asked, knowing her response would not alter his plan to stoke the fire slow-roasting his brain.

"Whatcha got?" She tilted her head toward him and smiled.

The question surprised him. Anyone who knew Andy at all knew that he was a one-trick-pony when it came to drugs. He'd consumed several bales worth of marijuana during his time in Bradford but very little else. Of course, everyone drank to the point that none of them even considered alcohol a 'drug.'

"Just weed," he said, flattening out a double-wide rolling paper on top of a box of graham crackers. "Why? What were you looking for?"

"Oh, I'm not *looking* for anything," Traci said matter-of-factly. "I like weed. Weed is good."

He kept his eyes on the task in his lap, sprinkling a generous portion of his remaining stash onto the paper.

"I've got something just as good, or better."

As Andy sealed the seam of the joint, he was startled by an unexpected noise. In her left hand, clamped between her thumb and middle finger, Traci held a prescription bottle. The amber plastic was nearly invisible in the faded light, but the white top shone. The sound when she shook it was unmistakable.

"What is that?" Andy asked, with no real expectations. He'd known tons of kids, all the way back to middle school, with prescriptions for various anti-depressants and anti-anxiety medications. Xanax, Buspar, muscle relaxers, and ephedrine-based speed were all common where he came from, and certainly in a college town like Bradford. So was the knowledge that students could walk into the campus health center, present a series of well-rehearsed symptoms, and walk out with a script for something to take the edge off. But Andy never developed a taste for those kinds of chemicals. Strangely, pills, whether straight from the pharmacy or off the street, always felt somehow sketchy and unreliable to him. In reality, the weed he smoked daily could just as likely be laced with PCP or God-knows-what, but he falsely assumed it was more trustworthy than pharmaceuticals.

"Oxycodone," she said, giving the bottle another little shake before opening it.

"Like Codeine?"

"Not exactly. It's similar. They're both painkillers and opioids, but the chemistry is different."

"Now you sound like Doc."

"Nah, I don't know shit about science," Traci admitted. "But I asked the doctor the same question 'cause I'm supposed to be allergic to codeine. He told me I had nothing to worry about. All I know is, they *totally* fuck you up."

"How'd you get painkillers?" Andy wondered. His legs and lower back hurt almost constantly. His intake of weed helped for sure, and even though he'd never really considered pharmaceuticals as a solution, he was intrigued.

"Car crash. About a year ago. I fucked up my neck and shoulder and started getting headaches." She had opened the bottle and shaken at least one of the pills into her palm. Tossing her head back, with enough gusto for Andy to question if she still had lingering neck issues, she popped the pill and chased it with a long swig of beer.

"Are you supposed to take those with alcohol?

"No," she said bluntly. "I've been taking 'em for a while, though, and I've kinda got that figured out. My headaches were so bad I was taking like 6-8 of these a day. They're mostly gone now, but I like the way they make me feel, so I keep going back to the doctor and telling him I have the same symptoms. He keeps giving me scripts. Now, I take maybe one a day. It's kind of like mood maintenance."

"That sounds 'kind of like' addiction."

"Said the pot to the kettle," she admonished. "It's no different than you, who smokes weed *every single day* and probably gets irritable if you don't. You know? Mood maintenance."

Andy did know. He also knew there was no reason to argue. He was already pleasantly stoned and probably on the wrong side of the logic.

"You want one?" she asked, aiming the open bottle at him.

"I don't think so," he rejected on principle.

"Go ahead. There's plenty more where this came from."

Addled or not, Andy's brain was always working the angles, and he quickly found one he liked. He had no intention of taking the pill, but in their economy, drugs were drugs. You could probably trade or sell anything you had to someone else who wanted it more than you did.

"Sure. Why not?"

Andy held out his hand, and Traci tapped the bottle until she sensed something fall out. Andy felt two pills tumble into his hand and immediately closed his fist around them. Drawing his hand near to his chest, he emptied the pills into the breast pocket of his flannel shirt behind his pack of Winstons.

"I'm going to hold onto it for a little bit," he announced. "I've been drinking and smoking most of the day, and I'm not sure I want to pile it on right now."

"Probably a good call. I wouldn't push it. And when you do take it, break it up and start with half. See how that makes you feel before you commit to the whole thing. You're not used to it, so half will probably do you fine. Then you'll have more for later, too."

"Thanks," Andy said, sure he would never take them.

"You gonna light that thing or stare at it?" she teased, eyeing the joint in his hand. Apparently, she'd built up enough tolerance to not worry about stacking multiple depressants, even though she'd just applauded him for not doing the same.

"I was gonna wait on Jeff, but it sounds like he jumped on the wagon for some reason all of sudden."

"Either way. It doesn't matter. Here they come now."

Andy shifted in his chair and looked back toward the house. He couldn't make out their bodies in the shadows. But the alternating flares of light coming from two cigarettes as they bobbed and weaved across the field were a dead giveaway.

76

Andy grabbed the lighter, sparked the joint, and toked hard as his friends arrived.

"I'm sorry," he said to Jeff, offering his hand.

Jeff drew Andy close, completing a quick bro-hug before breaking apart again and continuing toward the fire pit.

Ellen looked at Traci, wondering if she might have somehow influenced the apology. Traci shrugged, taking none of the credit or blame.

"That was a pretty dickish thing for me to say. I shouldn't have gone there," Andy continued. "I've actually been kind of a dick most of the day. I know Ellen was trying to do something nice, and I know you didn't even have to bring us here in the first place. I didn't really want to come, but not because I don't want to be *here*, or because I don't want to be with you guys. The truth is, I don't know what I'm gonna do without all this."

The joint made a full lap around the circle as he spoke, with Jeff continuing to abstain.

"I'm stuck between choices I hate. I have no idea what I'm supposed to do, and it sucks!"

Jeff knew exactly what he wanted to tell his friend because he'd already told him several times, as recently as that afternoon. Life is full of trouble. If Andy could 'let go and let God,' he might find more than comfort. He might find 'the answer,' too. But Jeff also knew they'd covered that ground enough times that bringing it up again, especially now, would just start another argument.

"It does suck," Jeff consoled. "It sucks for you, and it sucks for us. None of us like seeing you pissed. But you know how we feel about it. In the end, it's up to you." Jeff turned and put his hands on Andy's shoulders in a show of brotherly support.

"And I'm still gonna love your dumb ass, even if it's sittin' in your parents' basement in Atlanta. It's just gonna be harder for me to love you the way you want me to." As the last words broke from his mouth, he slipped behind Andy, hugged him tight, and ridiculously gyrated his pelvis several times at his roommate. As Jeff had hoped, the comic display effectively broke the tension between them.

"Jackass!" Andy wailed, shooting to the other side of the fire pit to escape any further 'assault'.

"Get a room, boys!" Traci teased, reclaiming the joint from Ellen. "Can we just hang out and enjoy what we've got out here."

"Best idea of the night," proclaimed Ellen. "Y'all sit and shut it."

And so, they did. The next few hours played out almost exactly as Ellen imagined when she'd first hatched her plan. As a fat, full moon rose high into the night sky, their spirits sailed with it. They left the talk of an uncertain future behind, retelling and embellishing stories that connected their various journeys through Bradford.

Even with as much effort as he had put into getting obliterated, Andy could still see all this for what it was—a last hurrah. This adventure was great, but no matter how hard he fought against the march of time, morning would come. And after that, as little as he wanted it to, Monday would, too. About thirty hours from this high-water mark of nostalgia and joy, the tide would roll back. There he would be, phone in hand, making the call to Firebrand Marketing, declining their offer of employment, and effectively ending his time in Bradford.

There, under the surface, lay the ominous truth. This was goodbye. Andy would laugh at their jokes and stories and share a few of his own. But he knew this evening was essentially a wake. His closest friends were gathered to honor a past while trying hard not to acknowledge a future that would never be the same. It was bittersweet, and he kept trying to drown it. Maybe his friends felt the same. Maybe not. Either way, they were all unified in trying to exit sobriety—an endeavor in which they were succeeding. Their voices grew louder and more slurred. Ellen sloppily poked at the dying fire. Traci and Jeff huddled together under Andy's huge green fleece blanket. Her head lay on Jeff's shoulder, her face a mix of drunken glee and emptiness. Jeff sat low in his camp chair, staring into the dark distance. Andy studied him in silence.

He couldn't decide if his roommate was sleepy, drunk, or processing the shitty reality of having to drive back to Bradford in just a few short hours. Noticing Andy staring back at him, Jeff clarified the matter.

"I gotta go the fuck to bed," he bellowed with regret.

"Take me with you," Traci slurred. Her request may have been amorous in nature, but it sounded more like the desperate plea of a girl who was done getting shitfaced in the woods.

77

Jeff stood up, robbing Traci of her support and causing her to slump forward. She was headed for the ground but somehow transitioned to a wobbling stand without falling. Jeff attempted to wrap the green fleece monster around himself, but it proved too heavy and big. Admitting defeat, he dumped the blanket across the two empty chairs.

"Fuck it. Let's go." Jeff's words were drenched with alcohol and resolve as he moved toward the cabin.

Like mice behind the Pied Piper, both girls fell in line. Their exit was sudden, and unfortunately for Andy, it also coincided with his decision to step away and empty his aching bladder. He was understandably pissed to find the circle deserted upon his return and to realize the "after party" appeared not to include an invitation for him to join. Equally bothersome, none of them seemed concerned about what else they were leaving behind.

Andy knew almost *nothing* about the outdoors. But even he knew leaving a live fire and half-eaten food unattended was dumb, irresponsible, and dangerous. For a second, he considered not caring right along with them. Fuck it. It wasn't his land, right? But then, images of untold creatures slipping out from the dark to snack on their leftovers rolled through his mind. He knew none of them were coming back.

Whatever buzz Andy had left was getting progressively diluted as he started making a mental list of what needed to be done. His friends had disappeared into the darkness. Andy tried desperately not to fixate on the mess surrounding him. He spent a long moment considering his options before finally realizing that the mess would still be there after the few minutes it took him to bring them back to do the right thing.

Andy took a few steps toward the house and then broke into a sprint for no good reason. After just a few yards, he stopped. Andy was a sedentary creature with questionable legs who got almost no exercise and who had ravaged his lungs and liver for the last half-decade. He pulled up and slowed to a walk, heaving for breath as he closed in on the house.

By the time he reached the porch, they were already inside. The front door was closed as if they'd simply forgotten him.

Andy entered the house, which, save for the faint yellow beam that spread from his dying flashlight, was quite dark. The small central room was more cluttered than he remembered in daylight. The futon couch had been lowered to its flatbed position, and Ellen was already sprawled face down in the exact center of it. She was still wearing her jacket and shoes. Apparently, Jeff and Traci were together in the small back bedroom. He moved to the closed door and banged on it aggressively.

"Dude!" he shouted, much louder than necessary in such a small space. "What the fuck? We still have to…"

"Tomorrow," came Jeff's singular reply. The unmistakable sound of Traci giggling followed which instantly raised his ire.

"Seriously. We can't just…"

"Fuck it," Jeff reiterated, now also laughing. "I'm done."

Andy didn't need the extra help of the closed door and their playful laughter to know that 'I'm done' meant 'Go away; I'm busy getting rewarded for coming out here in the first place.'

Now, Andy was plain mad. With Jeff and Traci checked out, he turned to his only other option. He wheeled around and shone the flashlight at Ellen. She hadn't moved an inch, but he figured she could still be roused.

He approached the futon and planted himself on the one corner of the surface she managed not to cover. Entirely on purpose, he allowed his momentum to carry his forearm straight into the small of her back. She moved but never stirred. Now leaning in, he tried jostling her, pressing against her hip and shoulder. She made some muffled noise but remained largely non-responsive.

"Ellen. Get up," Andy said. "Jeff and …"

"Uhhhnnn." It was a desperate groan, the sound of someone willing themselves not to be disturbed.

"Come on!" he barked at her.

The tiny house was silent. He sat there staring at her, wondering whether to hound her until she woke up or to mercifully remove her shoes and let her be. As he contemplated, the largest, most bear-like snore he'd ever heard from a female human escaped his now-slumbering roommate.

Andy huffed, assured of defeat and beginning to seethe with resentment.

"Dammit!" he growled, pushing himself up off the futon and training his beam of light toward the front door. "You people fucking suck!" he proclaimed, plenty loud enough for the couple he assumed were still wide awake in the next room to hear. They tried unsuccessfully to suppress their snickering, which only angered him further. Andy walked to the front door, opened it, and slammed it behind him as he walked back alone into the cold, dark morning.

78

Andy seethed. Lurching across the creaky front porch, he pulled out the pack of Winston Lights and freed one from its golden box. Standing on the top step, he frisked himself, searching for a lighter. Running his hand along his chest, he felt the strange relief of two small circles sitting at the bottom of his breast pocket. Digging in, he rediscovered the two white pills Traci had given him. He grasped one between his index finger and thumb and pulled it out. Andy sat on the stoop and inspected the perfect white circle in his palm. In the waning glow of his flashlight, he could still make out the simple inscription "512" etched into the pill's surface. Flipping it over, he noticed it was neatly scored along the center. The clinical markings on the pill suggested to Andy it was a legitimate pharmaceutical and not some homemade trucker speed or God-knows-what-else.

His anger at being abandoned came with a spike of adrenaline, which only heightened his false sense of sobriety. In truth, he'd been drinking most of the day and had smoked at least his usual per diem of marijuana. But he coursed with energy and the dangerous mix of bravado and outrage that was the forebear of countless bad decisions.

"Fuck it," he declared to no one, least of all his bedded-down friends in the cabin behind him. "Maxwell, party of one, your table is ready."

He popped the whole pill into his mouth and chased it with a swig from a mostly full can of beer that, like him, had been forsaken on the porch.

Andy hopped up, more resolute than ever. In his natural progression, immediately after anger and righteous indignation came martyrdom and grudge-holding. If they were going to leave him alone to clean up, the only *logical* response was to clean so thoroughly and fervently that they'd have no choice but to recognize and, more importantly, feel shamed by his monumental effort. Yes, he'd bust his ass to make a point of picking up the mess they'd thoughtlessly left–that would show them.

He plowed across the field, trailing puffs of vitriolic smoke. It was easy to trace the straight line back to the circle of stones, but the fire was almost dead by then.

Andy shuffled back into camp, thoroughly steamed. He located an orange plastic flashlight on the armrest of the camp chair next to him. He pushed its button and delighted in the robust, bluish-white beam that sprang forth. He scanned the scene, considering it as perhaps a detective would, pouring over the scattered debris of what they'd consumed.

On second glance, the damage seemed less severe than he'd made it out to be. There were a couple of open bags of chips and many empty aluminum cans, but the truth was, it wouldn't take that long to fix. Andy had gotten mad on principle without reality-checking the problem he'd chosen to inherit. His friends probably weren't overly delinquent in their willingness to let it all sit until tomorrow, except for Jeff. Andy could see him sleeping until the last possible second and then just jumping in his truck and hightailing it back to Bradford. He would say, "he forgot," but they would still be left to deal with the aftermath.

Andy pulled a last drag of smoke from his Winston and flicked the butt into the fire. He decided only three quick jobs needed to be done; pack up the open food, put out the fire, and haul the few pieces of abandoned clothing and blankets back to the cars or house. Then he'd be satisfied. Then he could sleep.

The food was easy. Andy found a spare plastic grocery bag on the ground, stuffed all the open items into it, and tossed it in the passenger seat of Traci's Jeep. Collecting the beer cans took a few more minutes but helped accomplish the second task of killing the fire. Hot, alcoholic steam rose from the pit as Andy doused the embers with unfinished beers. It didn't finish the job, but one extra bottle of water from the cooler was all Andy needed to feel like he'd mitigated any real fire hazard. All that was left now was the laundry. At some point during the evening, Traci had shed at least one layer of clothing in favor of hiding under a blanket with Jeff. Her black zip fleece hung over one of the chairs. It was already slightly damp with the coming dew. A t-shirt belonging to Jeff, which had been used haphazardly as a communal napkin, lay on the ground. He gathered these items and tossed them in the Jeep, too.

He'd purposely left the two remaining objects for last. The massive green blanket was still draped over the chairs where Jeff and Traci had been snuggling. Underneath it was a decent pillow. Andy knew he'd be sleeping on the cold wooden floor of the cabin, and these two items would definitely help soften the blow.

He rolled the green monster several times to make its mammoth girth easier to carry. Even compacted, it required two hands, forcing Andy to awkwardly bear-hug it and the pillow to his chest while holding the flashlight as he plodded back to the house. The fleece was hot against his face, which he noticed was awash with fresh sweat. Andy was surprised by the profuse perspiration. He also began to feel dizzy in a very foreign and uncomfortable way. He'd drunk away his equilibrium countless times before and the dizziness of alcohol was a feeling he knew well—a spiraling right between his temples, around and behind his eyes. But this was something altogether different.

Close to the house now, Andy began to struggle in a way that made him wonder if he was even going to make it. There was tangible warmth rising from the base of his neck. It ran flush across his face and seeped from the top of his head. A disconcerting pulse rose in his brain as if his skull were filled with fluid and someone dropped a pebble, causing endless waves to ripple outward. He began to swoon, floating along a decidedly non-linear path.

Andy reached the truck parked just to the right of the front porch. Its lowered tailgate offered a first resting place, and he embraced it. Mostly falling, Andy landed hard on the tailgate and used the pillow and blanket to soften his impact as he rolled onto his side. He let go of the cargo and instantly popped up, as if loaded by a spring, and reset his focus on the steps. He staggered up, half launching himself and half falling across the porch. Andy thudded against the screen door. Its metal grating was cool to the touch, but the screen was abrasive as his face slid along it. All he had to do now was open the front door and fall onto the futon next to, or even on top of, Ellen. He was going to make it.

79

Locked! The fucking front door was locked. Maybe he'd done it himself as he slammed it. Maybe it was one of the others, before or after he'd come and gone the first time. Maybe it was an accident or a coincidence. In a different frame of mind, the hows and whys might have been more relevant. The door was locked. This was all he could process and all that mattered. Andy leaned, both trapped between and supported by the screen and wooden doors of the cabin. It never even occurred to him to bang on them in hopes of rousing his friends.

The alcohol and weed he was so used to were now collaborating with the pain killer Andy had thrown carelessly into the mix. His eyes got heavier as pulses of warmth spread further down his neck and shoulders. With waning coherence and strength, Andy pushed himself off the door frame and spun back toward the steps.

80

The sound of sparrows in the morning can be unpleasant, with their high pitch and relentless delivery. Rural Fairview had way more of these birds than Bradford and far fewer competing sounds.

On an otherwise quiet Sunday, the avian symphony surrounding the cabin was the only sign of life, inside or out. But it was sufficient to rouse Jeff from a tenuous sleep.

His eyes tightened in response to the light of day. He felt a dry burning under his eyelids, then the coarse itchiness of the bedding against his bare chest.

Jeff had no desire to move. But the incessant bird calls and a full bladder were beginning to force the issue. The quarter turn from lying on his right side to flat on his back brought another revelation. He was not alone in the tiny twin-sized bed. Jeff's arm came to rest on the soft, unconscious lump that was Traci. He instantly achieved a whole new level of wakefulness.

Memories of the previous day and night flooded in. He fast-forwarded, skipping through the general merriment of the evening, and tried to replay the last chapter. Traci had stumbled back to the cabin, clearly damaged but willingly amorous. He recalled her determined pursuit of him, a strangely aggressive passion tempered or perhaps emboldened by blurriness. Jeff recalled his surprise at finding her nearly nude, lying in wait before he even removed his shirt and shoes. Then he remembered the most shocking detail–that he had spurned her advance.

Around Bradford, Jeff had rightfully earned a reputation as a Lothario, amassing a body count many of his friends surely envied. He was known for many things, but saying no to the ladies wasn't one of them. Traci was cute, and she was among the shrinking number of girls in town he had not yet gotten around to bedding.

Jeff would have scoffed at declining such an opportunity just a few days ago. But this had been no average week. The escalating turmoil with Andy, and in particular their adventures at Quenton and Doc's homes, had planted seeds. His relative sobriety yesterday made it easy to see how unfair a conquest Traci would have been under those circumstances. For the first time in a while, moral clarity prevented him from doing the wrong thing. Honestly, he was more than okay with this outcome.

Jeff swung his legs off the bed and stood. A wave of atypical modesty washed over him. With impressive quickness and quiet, he gathered his jeans from the floor. He stepped into them and zipped the fly before turning to face the bed.

He expected to see Traci staring back or laughing at him. Nope. She remained curled on her side, facing the wall mere inches from the edge of the bed. Her head was buried in a pillow; her face obscured by her hair. His exit from the bed peeled the covers enough to reveal the entirety of Traci's bare back. He stood silently, surveying the brief landscape of opalescent flesh. At the end of the trail, just before the coverage of the blankets resumed, a swatch of pink and purple fabric screamed in contrast against the stark white sheets. Otherwise nude, she retained a pair of shiny satin panties featuring a wild paisley design. Jeff considered peeling the blankets further back to steal an extra glance but refrained. Instead, he chose to find the rest of his clothes.

As his focus intensified, the real priorities of the morning reasserted themselves. He had to piss like a fire hose, and he had to find out what time it was. He knew it was well past dawn from the light beaming through the thin, gauzy curtains. But just how mad of a dash he was in for was unclear. Jeff pulled a clean shirt from his bag on the floor and slipped his bare feet into a pair of beat-up Converse sneakers. He knew he had socks and church shoes in his bag, and he could slip those on at the last minute back in Bradford.

Jeff hastily crammed a few items into his pack and, without zipping it, made for the bedroom door. It creaked slightly, but not enough to wake her. He peered at the plastic clock near the cabin's front door. 8:28 am.

"Motherfucker!" he said, loud enough to wake both women sleeping within ten feet of him.

Ellen didn't move. She lay almost exactly as she had fallen last night, fully dressed and snoring. Traci finally stirred, shocked into partial awakening by the blunt, expletive alarm.

"Huh?' she mumbled, turning slightly.

Shit. Thought Jeff, wanting to get out of there as fast as possible. *I don't have time for this.*

"It's okay," he reassured her, turning around. "Go back to sleep."

Traci was caught somewhere between passed-out bliss and a rude awakening. She rolled toward Jeff's voice, disturbing the bedding that partially covered her. She adjusted, but not before treating Jeff to an extra look at her, wearing nothing but that small swatch of psychedelic satin.

"You're fine," Jeff said, softer and now smiling. She was still responding only to sounds and hadn't opened her eyes.

"What time is it?" she asked, rolling and tucking herself deeper under the blankets.

"Early," he said. "Keep sleeping." He thought about leaving it there and was about to walk out when decency reared its ugly head again.

He stepped closer and whispered, "Do you know where you are?"

"Uh huh," she replied sleepily after a second of pause.

"Can you get home from here?"

"Uh-huh," she repeated.

Jeff, who was now under extreme pressure from both his bladder and the ticking clock, took the semi-lucid girl at her word. He closed the bedroom door and kept walking past an unconscious Ellen. Creeping out the door, Jeff alertly kept the screen from banging behind him. He turned and made a beeline to the edge of the porch, where he unzipped his pants and relieved himself onto the dry grass and red dirt below. The most pressing of his needs now managed, Jeff walked back towards the steps, fumbling in his open pack for his keys. He stopped short of the steps and opened the bright blue cooler. Bobbing in still-cold water were several beers and sodas. He said a small prayer of thanks for the bounty, grabbed a can of Coca-Cola, and stepped off the porch.

Jeff's black pickup truck was parked fifteen feet away and already pointed toward the exit. Now racing, he tossed his pack in the passenger seat, closed the door, and sped toward the back of the vehicle. Only the last snap on each side of the bed liner was unfastened, which he deemed acceptable given his hurry. He turned the corner of the truck, slammed its tailgate shut, and sling-shotted toward the driver's seat in one sweeping move.

Jeff hopped in and revved the truck to life. The clock on his radio showed 8:32 am. He would have to cover nearly a hundred miles of road, change shoes, slip on his choir robe, and be in line for the processional in less than 90 minutes. Thankfully, he had plenty of fuel. There were no scheduled stops on this express trip to God's house. Without a visible police presence, STOP signs and traffic lights would be relegated from mandates to mere suggestions.

81

Traci lay there for several minutes, eyes closed, trying hard not to think. Jeff's whispered directives to go back to sleep lingered in her head, but that ship had sailed. Her body was content to remain still, but her brain was moving.

Gradually, she became aware of her skin and body temperature. She felt a sudden chill, not like a wave of horror, but more of an electrical impulse adjusting her internal thermostat. Traci knew without sight she lay in a foreign bed, nearly naked, but she was neither alarmed nor ashamed. She slept fully nude most nights at home, so the sensation of the cool, course sheets against her bare skin was nothing shocking. With growing clarity, she recalled the events that had landed her here. She had harbored an interest in Jeff for some time and had been perfectly willing to be bedded by him under a thin guise of mutual inebriation. It was here that her train of thought, driven by assumptions and an ignorance of Jeff's relative sobriety, had jumped the tracks and wrecked.

Traci knew eventually she would have to leave the room, where she would no doubt encounter the others. In her original plan, the discovery of them together by Andy or Ellen was something she relished, an opportunity to bask in the triumph of *her* conquest of Jeff. But now, as she sat alone in the bed, a sense of sick dread arose. She hadn't considered the possibility of this ending, and now the tables were cruelly turned. Now, it was more likely she would be considered not as the conqueror but the plundered treasure. And worse, she'd be condemned for committing a sin she hadn't even gotten to enjoy.

Traci sat up, the sheet tucked under her armpits. She reached a few inches to her right and peeled back the drape. The morning sun cut a sharp diagonal line in the field beside the house, dividing it into very different shades of greyish green. Aside from the birds twittering in the berry bushes, nothing else stirred. She relaxed her arms and then raised them slowly, stretching to relieve the tightness from a night of sharing a too-small bed. The covers fell into her lap, exposing her bare torso to nothing more than those birds and a patch of pleasantly warming sun.

Rolling over, Traci lodged herself against the wall under the window and looked down. The object she sought was lying on the floor in the tiny space between the bed and the wall. Traci shot her arm into the crevice to retrieve her bra and rolled back to the center of the bed. She sat up, strapped her cold-hardened chest into the garment, and scanned the room for the rest of her clothes.

She grabbed her shoes and tiptoed toward the bedroom door. It opened smoothly and with less noise than expected. She stopped and scanned the main room. Her worst-case scenario was coming face-to-face with a wide-awake congregation, smugly waiting for her to perform some unspoken walk of shame. Instead, she saw no one. The front door was closed, and the room appeared empty.

She snuck about five steps before seeing the ends of Ellen's legs hanging over the edge of the futon. Though at least shoeless, Ellen was fully dressed and looked like she slept the whole night on top of a blanket. Andy was not there.

Smiling at her good fortune, she slipped past her snoring friend like a cat burglar. The front door required a decent pull which produced a loud pop when it finally gave. The noise didn't phase Ellen a bit.

Damn. Thought Traci. *That bitch can SLEEP! Good for her.*

She carefully closed the screen door, leaving its wooden mate ajar behind her.

Jeff's truck was gone. Given the foggy exchange they'd shared before he left, she wasn't surprised. He'd made it clear before they even came, and they all knew he had church this morning. But like everything else so far today, Traci thought it would play out differently. She stood silently in the farm's vast front yard. Knowing Jeff had left the three of them and driven back to Bradford only compounded how alone she felt.

82

Traci walked toward her Jeep, motivated to make a few hygiene and clothing adjustments. She knew she would find Andy, likely smoking or sulking next to an extinguished or possibly rekindled fire. Now, outside the cabin, or more precisely, Jeff's room, she had no issue encountering him.

She reached the Jeep and opened the driver's side door, tossing her shoes and socks across to the opposite floorboard. Slipping her muddy bare feet into a pair of sandals, she noticed her fleece from last night and what appeared to be a bag of half-eaten food piled randomly in the passenger seat. It seemed odd but not grossly out of order. She left the door open and headed toward the back of the vehicle. Everything there was as she recalled.

From behind the Jeep, Traci could see the fire pit. It was deserted, as the whole farm seemed now to be. Even the birds had ceased their chattering. No birds. No squirrels. No crackling fire. No Andy. Everything was quiet, and the scene of their party last night was surprisingly tidy–her first real clue that something was amiss.

She rummaged through her pack and found a small makeup bag, a misnomer here as she only sparingly used cosmetics. Instead, the case carried a few more practical items–a toothbrush and paste, a hairbrush, some deodorant, and the amber prescription bottle, half full of Percocet tablets. Traci had spent many a day and night in the woods of Tennessee and was unfazed by the absence of plumbing. But she was also cosmopolitan enough to want to knock the stink off her breath and armpits if given the chance.

Shouldering her pack, she moved back to the Jeep. She grabbed a nearly full bottle of water from the driver's side cup holder and headed for the outskirts of the field. Ten feet past the tree line, she stopped in the thin underbrush. From here, Traci could see the firepit and the house's front porch, but she was concealed from both.

Traci dropped her pack and unbuttoned her flannel. She used the deodorant and changed into a fresh t-shirt. She brushed her teeth, leaving a froth of spat foam on the pine needles to her left, and placed the toiletries back in their case. Before closing it, she pulled out the pill bottle, unscrewed the lid, and emptied a white circle into her hand. She tossed it into her mouth and washed it down with a long drink of water. It was barely 9:00, but she could already tell she would benefit from a little 'mood maintenance.'

She stuffed everything into her pack and stood. The slight crunch of dew-moistened leaves under her sandals was the only sound. Satisfied she was still alone in the woods; she unfastened her jeans. Traci dropped her pants and underwear and squatted. She was amused to see a fat, fuzzy caterpillar making its way across a leaf by her feet. She smirked, watching him wriggle along as she relieved herself.

Traci popped up and zipped her pants. She was 'camping clean,' with an empty bladder and what would soon be a head full of painkillers—in prime condition, she figured, to face whatever came next.

83

What came next was Ellen emerging from the cabin. The screen door banged behind her and echoed loudly in the crisp morning air. So did her strained voice when she tried to speak for the first time since waking.

"Hello?"

Her grumbled, woozy call was followed by the unmistakable bark of a smoker's hack. She was more than 50 yards from where Traci stood concealed in the bushes, but the sound really carried. Traci appeared at the edge of the field, carrying her backpack and meandering toward the front porch, eyes to the ground. Preoccupied with lighting the day's first cigarette, Ellen didn't see her. The influx of nicotine gave Ellen a jolt. The chemical remnants of last night's intake had the opposite effect. She was jittery yet lethargic and not ready to welcome the day.

"Good morning," Traci offered gingerly, sensing the damage. "You okay?"

"Mmmm."

"You slept hard as hell last night."

"Yeah. No shit. I fell out like a ton of bricks. How are you?"

"I feel pretty fucking great," Traci said with a level of cheer that was almost assuredly annoying. She had no real hangover, and the dose of narcotics was beginning to make its presence felt in the form of a warm wave of euphoria.

"Well, good for you," Ellen mocked.

"Hell, at least you beat Andy. Looks like he's still passed out."

"Where?" asked Ellen. "He's not in there."

"What do you mean? Are you sure?"

"Positive. I checked the back room and bathroom before I came out here. It's not like there's anywhere to fucking hide in there."

"Well, shit," Traci replied frankly. "I just went out to my car to get clean clothes, and he's not over there or by the fire either."

The mention of cars triggered Ellen's brain to another level of awakening.

"Jeff's gone," she realized.

"Yep. Left in a hurry, maybe thirty or forty minutes ago. I think he was running late for church."

"He'll make it. He always does."

"So, where the fuck is Andy?" Traci asked.

"Maybe he's passed out in a ditch in the woods somewhere."

"Or maybe he got up early and went to church with Jeff."

Ellen scoffed, choking on the last drag of her cigarette. "Seriously? Which of those two scenarios do you think is more likely?"

Traci scanned the horizon, now questioning her choice to load up on painkillers first thing in the morning.

"Fuck," she proclaimed with a sigh. "Put your shoes on. We gotta go find him."

84

Jeff was making exceptional time. The country roads of Fairview were far behind as he hummed along the highway at more than eighty miles an hour. Traffic was light, and as hoped, he hadn't seen a single cop. The digital clock on the truck's dash read 9:17 am. In about fifteen minutes, he'd reach the exit back into Bradford. Another ten minutes on city streets, and he'd be pulling into the parking lot of St. Timothy's Episcopal.

Far too often recently, Jeff made the trek to the church through a dense mental fog. Balancing Saturday night sins with faithful Sunday service was getting more difficult, and honestly, less enjoyable. This morning couldn't have been more different. The commute was extreme, but he wasn't bothered at all. For the first time in a long time, he felt genuine excitement, a joy that *compelled* him.

The last time he was alone on the open road, just a few days ago, was Jeff's return from Overton. That ride was devastating, full of anger and sadness, and the need to numb himself to the pain and confusion of Cricket's inexplicable decision. This stretch of highway was far kinder. With nothing but desolate blacktop and time ahead, Jeff achieved greater clarity with every passing mile. His head was unburdened by chemicals. His chest was light yet full of anticipation. The past week's revelations had crystalized in his heart and mind; he was headed home. And with any luck, he would make it right on time.

85

"When's the last time you saw him?" Ellen asked.

"Same as you. Last night. We all gave up at the same time, didn't we?"

"I don't remember a whole lot about how last night ended. To be honest, I'm not even sure how I got back to the house."

"I thought we all walked back together," Traci said. "But then Jeff and I went straight to his room, and…" She stopped mid-sentence. Trying to recall seeing Andy in the house last night, she realized she'd also just incriminated herself.

Ellen looked down at her from the porch stoop with wry amusement. It wasn't necessarily judgment, but Traci went on the defensive anyway.

"What?" she asked, smiling though trying not to.

"Nothing," Ellen replied. Her dismissive tone confirmed they were both dancing around the same subject. "Again, good for you."

Traci saw the opportunity and seized it by the simplest of means—saying nothing at all. If Ellen wanted to think she and Jeff crossed a threshold last night and would let it go without further comment, she was willing to play along.

In truth, Ellen couldn't care less about who Jeff slept with, or about Traci's place in that vast universe. All of that was drama for another time. Right now, her focus was elsewhere.

"Anyway," Traci said, "I don't remember if I saw Andy or not."

"Well, there are only two possibilities," Ellen surmised, slipping on her shoes. "Either he's here, out in the woods somewhere, or he's not. Let's walk the perimeter and see if we find him. If we don't, I say we grab our bags and bust ass back home."

"What about the rest of the stuff?" Traci asked.

Most of what they brought had come in Jeff's truck, which was also gone. The camp chairs, the cooler, and the few remaining things might all fit in the Jeep if they tried, but it would be tight.

"If we pack it all," Ellen countered, "there won't be room for Andy when we find him. We can leave most of this shit here. We can come back for it later, or make Jeff deal with it, since he's the one that left us without talking to anybody."

The notion of repaying Jeff for rejecting her last night and deserting her this morning was just fine with Traci.

Ellen bent and put her cigarette butt into an empty can next to the cooler. On the way back up, she lifted the cooler's white lid. Like Jeff earlier, she was pleased to find a few non-alcoholic options floating alongside the leftover beers.

"You want one?" she asked, popping open a soda.

"I'm good. Let's start by the pond and get the worst-case scenario out of the way."

If Ellen were still struggling to wake up, Traci's suggestion was a brutal slap in the face. For the few seconds she'd spent thinking about it so far, their search for Andy was little more than an inconvenient game of hide-and-seek. She fully expected to find him propped up against the back of the house or under a tree somewhere in the shade. Traci's implication was far more ominous.

Holy shit, she thought. *What if he's fucking dead?*

That thought, and then the next, discovering the lifeless body of one of her best friends floating in a pond or lying in a desolate field, scared the shit out of her.

"How can you even say that?"

"What?" I was just… never mind. He's fine. C'mon."

They cleared the edge of the house and moved toward the sludgy pond. Ellen's imagination had kicked into overdrive, and she now somehow *expected to* see Andy's dead body floating face down in the shallow mud hole. A few feet down the slope, they gained full sight of the small body of water. The sun had burned off the mist that hung just above the surface earlier this morning. There was nothing in the pond.

"See?" Traci reassured. "I guess we should walk along the tree line? Make a lap around the field and see if we spot anything?"

"I'm following you," said Ellen. Based on yesterday's performance, she trusted hunting and tracking were also squarely in Traci's wheelhouse.

Twenty sweaty minutes later, they'd walked the entire perimeter of the field. They checked behind clusters of trees and peered into the deeper brush. Each of them called his name at intervals, hoping for a response. None came. Circling back to the house, they walked by and around the collapsed barn building. They looked inside and again called out to him. Again, there was no response.

Both girls were worried at this point. Both had assumed they would find him, and neither had a plan now that they hadn't.

"Let's go," Traci urged. "We have to go. We can be back in Bradford by noon."

"We can't just leave him out here," Ellen demanded, more frantic and agitated.

"He's not *out here*," Traci answered. "We looked. You wanna look some more?" She thought about waiting for Ellen to respond, but they both knew the question was rhetorical.

"Besides," she continued, "when we get back, he's either gonna be with Jeff; or if he's not, Jeff will know what to do—who to call, where else to look; something. We don't know shit about this place."

Ellen didn't want to admit that she didn't have a better plan. And standing around staring at each other in an empty field wouldn't help either.

"Fine. We'll go. Fuck!" Ellen cursed loudly, creating a vulgar echo that would have been comical under just about any other circumstance.

"My stuff's in the Jeep already," Traci said. "Go get your shit out of the house." In stark contrast to yesterday morning, Traci was now giving the orders.

The girls walked in opposite directions. Then Ellen broke into a run. Her mind raced, filling with fear and anxiety as her eyes welled with tears.

86

St. Timothy's was unlike any other building in Bradford. It looked more like a Spanish fort than an Episcopal church. The cathedral's walls, grand slabs of terra cotta-tinged marble, rose more than a hundred feet into the sky.

The church loomed at the corner of Gault and 11th Streets. In the late mornings, the shadow of the squared-off spire towers blocked the sunlight, creating a veil of shadow that enveloped the intersection of the two roads.

Jeff made one final left turn onto Gault and eased the truck into the parking lot. The spots nearest the side doors, where the ministers, deacons, and choir entered, were already occupied. He was not the first of the cast to arrive, but he might still have had a chance of not being the last. The first empty space he saw came at the exact spot where the building ended, and the chest-high, red brick wall surrounding the church's cemetery began.

9:49 am. With or without him, the morning's processional would begin in eleven minutes. The parishioners would never notice if he wasn't there. But many among the choir were likely sweating Jeff Aaron's absence right now.

Free from his seat belt, Jeff reached for the robe draped over his passenger seat and the black leather slip-on shoes on the floorboard. Both hands full, he bound from the truck. He shut the door with an awkward thrust of his bony ass and ran for the doors, his long, unclean hair flapping behind him.

87

Traci's Jeep crept slowly up and down the dusty, unpaved road along Jeff's farm. The girls had traveled the half mile on either side of the property three times, desperately scanning the alternating swatches of dense trees and open fields for any sign of their friend. With dread, they resigned themselves to leaving without him.

Traci clutched the steering wheel, fighting the slight spin of Percocet. Her eyes were glassy, and she probably should have let Ellen drive. But as they called off the search for Andy and decided to head home, she saw an even more troubling look from her passenger.

Ellen's eyes were distant, empty orbs filled with fear and sadness. Traci may have been inebriated, but Ellen was incapacitated. Traci gripped the wheel and forced herself to concentrate, knowing, for better or worse, she was piloting the ship.

During the first few minutes, fueled by the hope of finding Andy on or near the farm, the drive had been wrought with nervous energy. Now, they were flying down the highway, no less tense but completely drained. The radio was low and all but drowned out by the wind whirling through the Jeep's open top. Ellen sat despondent, looking out the window and chain smoking. They'd left a good portion of the gear back at the farm, and she couldn't help fixating on the empty space behind her where Andy was supposed to be sitting but wasn't. Neither of the girls had spoken for a while when Traci abruptly broke the silence.

"Fuck!" she blurted, slamming both her hands against the steering wheel for punctuation. Ellen sat up.

"We're not gonna make it." she said. "Goddamned gas light just came on."

"Seriously? What the fuck?"

"I'm sorry." Apologizing was the first and only thing she could think to do. "I had no idea we'd be in such a hurry to get back. How was I supposed to know?"

"How far out are we?" Ellen asked.

"I don't know. Fifty miles maybe. We're right in the middle."

"Right in the middle of fuckin' nowhere," Ellen clarified. "Is there even anywhere to pull off?"

At that moment, the answer was no. There weren't even any signs suggesting what 'the middle of nowhere' was called. The Jeep plowed on, the amber-colored fuel light on its dashboard serving only to torque their anxiety a few notches higher. Finally, a billboard appeared on the horizon. They saw it before they could read it, keeping their eyes trained on the vast white canvas with plain black lettering as it approached.

'Traveler's Truck Stop,' it read. 'Exit 51, Purvis, 2 miles.'

"That'll work." Traci said optimistically, grateful for any solution.

"Traveler's?" Ellen asked randomly. "Just one traveler?"

"What?"

"Their sign. It's wrong. The apostrophe is in the wrong place. It should be 'Travelers,' with the apostrophe *after* the s, not before it."

Traci gave her a ridiculous look.

"What?" Ellen replied. "It's something I picked up from Andy. Word Boy loves pointing out misspellings and fucked up punctuation on signs. Sometimes it's annoying, but a lot of the time it's pretty funny. Once you start noticing the mistakes, you see them everywhere. Andy used to say he could get rich just fixing other peoples' incorrect billboards."

"Well, he still needs a job, right?" Traci joked, purposely moving the language back to the present tense.

"Yeah. He does."

"I don't care what it's called, as long as they have gas."

"And a bathroom," groaned Ellen. "I've been waiting all morning to take a dump."

Traci wrinkled her nose in disgust as she pulled the Jeep into the exit lane.

88

A thin black woman in screaming yellow Capri pants and a white, neatly tailored blazer held the door for Jeff. His arms were full as he scooted at full speed into the church's side entrance.

The choir and the other players in the weekly production of Sunday mass at St. Timothy's had already assembled. The curtain would go up in mere minutes, and the sanctuary was filling fast.

* * *

The first snap unfastened inconspicuously, as if by simple accident or happenstance. A second later, a full quarter of the black vinyl tarp was violently displaced by some great, unseen force. That force was Andy's fist. Two more punches and a kick for good measure from underneath, and he'd dislodged the cover entirely.

Andy sat up. The tarp lay in his lap, covering him like a blanket in the bed of Jeff's truck. He tossed it aside and inhaled dramatically as if he'd been holding his breath the entire time he was trapped in the lightless box. His eyes were blurry from the long, dark ride. He rubbed them vigorously with his palms as he rested his head against the truck's back window. An older couple, rightly startled by his sudden appearance, went out of their way to distance themselves as they approached the church.

He didn't move, partly because he physically couldn't. He was exhausted. The big fleece blanket Crand the pillow helped, but the back of a Toyota pickup truck was no place to spend a night. Throw in being tumbled like clothes in a dryer, mercilessly absorbing every bump and pothole in the road for an hour, and it was no wonder his body was sore in more places than he could even process.

Even in his disoriented state, Andy knew precisely where he was. This was the other reason he found it impossible to move. There he sat, propped up against the back wall of a muddy black pickup truck, shoeless and disheveled, no doubt stinking to Hell of cigarettes, spilled beer, and the general earthiness of camping. He sat still, wishing for invisibility, as a flock of Bradford's civilized faithful marched past. Not all of them noticed him. Those of the many who did tried their best to ignore him, keeping their eyes forward and down as they shuffled toward the doors.

Andy was equally uncomfortable. Given a choice, as he had been so many times, he would not be there. He could sense the silent disdain of the passing churchgoers. Andy waited, trying so hard to stay quiet that he was almost holding his breath. For a moment, he was alone in the parking lot. But he knew it wouldn't last. Now was his chance to escape or at least make less of a spectacle of himself.

He pushed aside the tarp and kicked off the green fleece still covering his legs. Andy scanned the truck bed and quickly found one of his shoes; the other was still hiding. Spreading his hands wide, he rummaged around, more feeling than looking for the missing mate. Among several empty beer cans, a fishing tackle box, and some assorted clothing, Andy found his target buried in the folds of the blanket.

Dangling his legs over the edge of the tailgate, Andy had worked one foot into a muddy shoe when he sensed someone approaching from his left. The woman walked briskly and seemed to be coming right at him. Andy bent down and focused on tying his shoes. He wanted very much to ignore her, but basic human instinct took over, causing him to lift his head in anticipation of her arrival. An average-looking older woman in an anything-but-average fuchsia pantsuit came steadily toward him. Unlike the others, she did not look away. At six feet, Andy made eye contact. A pleasant smile unfolded across the lady's face. She carried no trepidation or judgment about him at all. Given her silvery-white hair, he figured she must be in her late fifties or early sixties. Her smile surprised and disarmed him. He again fell prey to human nature, as the involuntary instinct to speak overcame his desire not to.

"Good morning," he uttered with a thick smoker's rasp.

"Oh, it's a *blessed* morning," she suggested, smiling even wider and patting the leather-bound Bible she cradled like a baby. She never stopped or waited for a reply. She simply kept moving toward her morning Glory.

Less adamant now but still motivated, Andy tied the second shoe and hopped off the tailgate. Then he realized he had no idea what to do next. He began by patting himself down. A quick frisk confirmed that even through the travails of last night and this morning, he had managed to hold onto Quenton's former money clip and a pack of crushed and damp cigarettes. Unsurprisingly, he'd lost his lighter. Declaring the smokes unsalvageable, he tossed the damaged box into the truck bed and closed the tailgate. He limped to the driver's side door and found it unlocked.

Jeff had taken the keys, which sealed Andy's fate for the next hour or so. It was at least a two-mile walk from St. Timothy's to their house. Even in his best condition, Andy would never really have considered it. He sat behind the wheel, placed his head against the padded rest, closed his eyes, and exhaled. What now?

His next thought was about food. A quick audit of the area surrounding St. Timothy's produced no real options within walking distance. There was a gas station a couple blocks up, full of cold drinks and nutritionally bankrupt snacks. That was a possibility.

Scanning the truck's cab, Andy noticed Jeff had not left him entirely without rations. A pack of Marlboro Lights sat on the passenger seat, and there was an open can of Coke in the cup holder. He grabbed the cigarettes first. They weren't his brand, but in this situation, he was willing to accept a flavor he found less satisfying. Andy opened the flip-top box, pleased to discover a few still inside. He tucked a cigarette behind his left ear and scooped up a small blue lighter from the center console.

Next, he reached for the soda. To his surprise, at least a third of a can was left. Ordinarily, Andy would pass on sharing whatever ick Jeff had left in the backwash, but he was parched. Dehydration trumped germaphobia, and he took a hefty swig. It was lukewarm but wet and sugary, both big plusses in his current condition.

Andy could have sat in Jeff's truck for the next hour, windows rolled down, smoking those cigarettes. He also briefly considered getting high right there in the parking lot of St. Timothy's. Probably not even the most sacrilegious thing he'd done *that week*, but somehow, it didn't feel right. He knew he wasn't walking back to Cornwall Street, but he needed to stretch his legs, and a change of scenery couldn't hurt either.

89

The smell of diesel fuel hung thick in the air as the Jeep chugged to the top of the off-ramp and turned right. Fifty yards on was the entrance to Traveler's Truck Stop. Gnarly, dilapidated, and massive, it appeared to have Exit 51 all to itself. There were no other buildings as far as the girls could see.

The parking lot was surprisingly full at ten o'clock on a Sunday morning. Rows of eighteen-wheel big rigs stretched on for half a mile. A few were being refueled at stations along the perimeter, but most sat resting where they'd been parked the night before.

"Jesus," said Traci, "that's a lot of fuckin' trucks."

"Do they even sell regular gas, you know, for regular cars, here?" Ellen asked.

"Of course," Traci guessed confidently. "They have to."

"Why? Is there a law or something?"

"Oh. No," Traci corrected. "I meant they *have* to have gas for us, 'cause we're coasting on fumes, and we're not getting back on the highway. It's this place, or we're fucked."

"They also *have* to have a bathroom," Ellen added. "I'm about to 'splode over here."

"Please don't."

Traci swung left, away from the rows of trucks. Now closer, she could see a couple of gas pumps near the front of the main building. She pulled in, relieved to see good, old 87-octane unleaded gasoline on the menu. "Thank God," she sighed, killing the engine.

"Amen!" cried Ellen as she tore off her seat belt. She shot from the car, leaving the door ajar. "I gotta go!"

"I know."

Ellen walked awkwardly toward the building but stopped at the double front doors. "Dammit!"

"What?"

"Fucking diner's closed."

A sign on the wall read 'bathrooms' with an arrow pointing around the corner. Traci chuckled, trying to conceal her amusement from her suffering friend.

"Great. An outside shitter at a dank-ass truck stop in the middle of fuckin' nowhere," she complained, rounding the corner. "There better be paper in there."

"You better hope that one's not locked, too."

"Shut up. I'll be back."

"Take your time." Traci laughed as Ellen disappeared.

90

Andy passed through the gap in the brick wall surrounding the cemetery behind St. Timothy's Cathedral. Roughly four feet tall, the wall obscured all but the loftiest of grave markers beyond it. Several massive live oak trees formed a canopy thwarting the mid-morning sun. It blanketed the plots in a cool, dark shadow Andy found instantly pleasing.

The beginning of the service was only moments away, and no doors led directly from the cemetery into the church. Andy felt himself relax and even smiled, realizing he might go undisturbed here–at least until the congregation was released.

He slowed even further, pacing the time-beaten bricks through the boneyard with uncommon ease. The cemetery was small, less than an acre, but absurdly packed. The spaces between grave markers were tight and uneven. From certain angles, the headstones appeared to be stacked on top of each other. The combination of low light and the antiquity of the stones made some of them impossible to read, but others were easy enough to make out. None were particularly modern. In fact, Andy remembered Jeff saying the most recent internment had been over fifty years ago, and there would be no more; there simply wasn't room.

Andy stepped from the path into the yard, a patchwork of soft red clay and shoddy grass interwoven amongst the stones. He moved gingerly, trying not to disturb the souls sleeping beneath his feet. Winding through the narrow paths, he stopped near the center of the plot. There, he found a crude bench chiseled from unpolished marble. Andy glanced from side to side to confirm he was alone and then sat.

The marker directly in front of the bench was among the largest and most prominent in the whole cemetery. Carved upon it was the name T. Bullit Dancy. Just below, and smaller, were notations identifying Dancy as a lieutenant colonel whose proud service to the

Confederate States of America ended with his death on September 20, 1863. To his left, he found a cluster of sun-bleached stones, each no bigger than a loaf of bread. The inscriptions, which were faded but still legible, signaled the loss of three children–siblings within the Bartow family. There were two sisters and a brother, all of whom lived and died in the brief span between 1881 and 1887. Andy felt a sudden, deep sadness. Thoughts of Tristan and their parents invaded, reminders of the unspeakable pain of parents who lose children. Then, he considered the compound misery of enduring that same tragedy thrice and in such a short span.

He forced himself to look elsewhere, anywhere but at those three stone loaves. Turning his head in search of less morbid scenery, the cigarette tucked behind his left ear grazed his neck. Instinct, boredom, and the need for new stimuli converged. Andy placed the Marlboro Light between his lips and lit it. He filled his lungs with smoke, looked up at the thick oak branches above, and exhaled.

Andy sat in cemetery silence for several minutes. With another exhale of smoke came the undeniable bombast of a pipe organ roaring through the wall of stained glass behind him. The opening processional was beginning. *'Good'*, he thought. *'The sooner it starts, the sooner it's over.'*

Andy sat in the shadow of Colonel Dancy's grave, smoking his cigarette and listening to that organ. He closed his eyes and focused on the majestic tone pouring through the cathedral walls. It was a joyful noise, urgently calling the faithful to worship. The sound itself wasn't calling Andy to do anything. But then it stopped abruptly, as if the organist had just up and died. The sound's end startled him as much or more than its appearance, and the silence brought an instant and unwelcome thought.

Jeff had invited Andy to visit the church, if only to hear him sing, on numerous occasions. Each time, Andy found a reason, an excuse, really, not to go. But now he sat in the backyard of that very church. Whether by divine ordinance or some grand irony, he had been delivered straight to God's house.

The curtain was rising. The show was about to begin. And here Andy was, sitting in a graveyard, smoking a cigarette he honestly didn't even want anymore. The more he thought about it, and regardless of how much he hated it, the truth was clear. Not only was he supposed to be here, he was supposed to be inside. His stomach clenched at the thought. His brain screamed at him to stay put, or even better, to just start walking home. But a smaller voice inside him grew stronger, rising from nowhere with an aim at calling the shots now. By the time he realized he was no longer sitting on the bench, he had already taken several steps back toward the break in the wall. For better or worse, he was now headed straight for the vast Episcopalian fortress. For better or worse, Andy Maxwell was going to church.

91

As far as Traci knew, her late-80s model Jeep Wrangler was supposed to get 15 miles to the gallon, though she suspected it averaged less. The gas light had burst to life twelve miles outside of Purvis. As she watched the outdated rotary dials on the gas pump roll onward, a wave of relief washed over her. She knew they'd come dangerously close to being stranded on the side of the road.

Traci topped off the tank and wrestled the fuel nozzle back into its bent, beaten holster. It took only a few minutes to fuel up, and there was still no sign of Ellen. Traci assumed her absence meant she'd successfully gained access to the bathrooms around the corner.

She walked toward the building, aiming for the set of doors to the left of the ones her friend had found shuttered. Ellen was correct. Lickety's Diner was closed for renovations–and, by the looks of it, had been for some time. The tiny convenience store beside it was open for business, though.

Traci entered and casually browsed the store's two aisles. The middle-aged, overweight Hispanic woman behind the counter never even moved.

She opened the fridge case and pulled out a cold Cheerwine soda. In the racks behind her, Traci found two rows of Hostess Fruit Pies– one apple, one cherry–begging to be bought. Forgetting whatever breakfast items might be in the back of the Jeep, she scooped up one of each. Like Pavlov's dog, her mouth began to water at the mere sight of the treats.

The convenience store's minimal charm wore thin quickly. Traci walked to the cashier, hoping her friend would reappear in time to help cover the thirty dollars she'd put in the Jeep. Ellen was nowhere in sight.

The counter clerk barely looked up from her Hollywood gossip rag as she rang up the drinks and snacks.

"I've got gas out there for the Jeep, too," Traci divulged, thinking it entirely possible the attendant hadn't noticed.

The woman said nothing, choosing instead to repay Traci's honesty with a snide look, which suggested maybe Traci thought she was stupid.

"Thirty-four, sixty-five," she said, addressing the cash register instead of her customer.

Traci pulled her last forty dollars from the pocket of her jeans and slid it into the tray under the glass pane separating them. The cashier took the money, made change, and returned to her magazine. No 'thank you.' No 'have a nice day.' Nothing.

Traci was surprised to find the Jeep still unoccupied. Ellen may have been in worse shape than even her bemoaning had implied. She considered moving the vehicle, but no one was waiting for the pump. Suddenly, she became hyper-aware of how alone she was in the massive expanse of the Traveler's Truck Stop. Traci was small but tough and could mostly take care of herself when push came to shove. Still, she was more than ready to find Ellen and move on.

Around the corner, Traci encountered three nondescript cream-colored metal doors. The first said 'Men.' The second had a small sign reading 'Authorized Personnel Only' and a giant padlock the other two doors lacked. The third door, the one farthest back, was for 'Women.' *Typical*, Traci thought.

The door to the women's room was closed. Traci approached, expecting it to also be locked. She considered busting in but instantly thought better of it. What if there were no stalls? The last thing she needed to see was Ellen glued to some disgusting truck stop toilet amid severe gastrointestinal distress.

What she saw was far more disturbing.

92

The front doors of St. Timothy's Episcopal Church were impractically huge and heavy. Fashioned from dense, dark wood and accented with steel banding and rivets, the medieval-looking portals stood ten feet tall. When shuttered, they offered anything but a welcoming façade.

On Sundays and Wednesdays, or any time the faithful were expected en masse, the doors were left wide open, exactly how Andy found them. He stopped briefly at the bottom of the small flight of stairs leading to the entrance. Compared to the bright sun beating down on Gault Street, the foyer beyond the boundary of those doors seemed as dark as a cave and just as foreboding. Andy stood at the precipice; still not sure he was going inside. He had extinguished the Marlboro but was suddenly aware that he must smell awful. Another reason to turn and walk away, but he didn't.

Andy took a deep breath, let it go, and advanced methodically up the steps. He imagined something terrible and tangible happening the instant he crossed the threshold—a buzzer, alarm, or some other loud, scrutinizing exclamation of his arrival. Of course, there was nothing.

Just inside the front doors was a highly decorative portico—a transitional space no bigger than a jail cell. On either side, ornate tables sat under gilded frames holding paintings of Saints Andy could not identify. Straight ahead, another smaller set of doors was closed. To his right stood a baptismal font. Andy recognized this from his painful childhood trips to weekday masses with his Catholic grandmother. His brain flashed back to the portion of holy water Jeff had 'borrowed' from the church a few days earlier. Stationed to the left of the doors, an old grey lady in a hideous green floral dress sat motionless until she noticed Andy.

The moment he stepped toward those inner doors, the geriatric sentry sprang to life with surprising speed and agility. The organ pipes were muted, and no other sounds escaped the chamber she guarded. He could have easily heard anything she chose to say, yet she operated in silence. Standing between Andy and the doors, not menacing but still authoritative, the Grey Lady raised a bony index finger to her lips. She extended her other hand, offering him a small white booklet, which Andy took. The Grey Lady swept that hand across her body, pointing dismissively toward a flight of steps to her left. In one simple, silent gesture, she'd ushered, shushed, and shepherded him. Andy wasn't sure if he was being denied access to the main sanctuary based on the time or his appearance. It didn't matter; he wasn't getting past her. He turned and headed for the stairs that led to the cheap seats.

Andy passed through the portico and looked up. The stairway was narrower and steeper than seemed necessary, and he couldn't imagine the Grey Lady or many of her elderly compatriots navigating them. A heavy wrought iron rail ran along the wall. He pulled himself up the steps, legs still tight and aching from the poor night's sleep and even worse transport in the back of Jeff's truck. Halfway up, he heard many voices rumble in unison, and more of the organ's bombast.

Holy shit, Andy thought, quickening his pace up the stairs. *I'm missing Jeff's thing.* In truth, it was only the opening hymn.

Andy reached the top and braced himself in another doorway. This one led out to the ample balcony of the cathedral. The contrast between the plain, claustrophobic chute he'd just ascended and the spacious cavern of opulence into which he arrived was immediate and dramatic. He took a huge breath and exhaled.

The sanctuary of St. Timothy's sprawled before him. Twenty feet below were rows of pews hewn from dark, rich wood—most of these held parishioners, a couple hundred in total. The ceiling vaulted another forty feet overhead and was bolstered by a series of enormous wooden arches. Viewed as a whole, the supports resembled the inverted hull of a giant ark. Plastered columns rose from the floor along both sides of the vast room, creating more arches that echoed the shape of a bishop's miter down the center aisle. Each of the sanctuary's long side walls featured ornate stained-glass windows, with more behind the altar. A sea of colored glass glowed brightly as the sun shone through.

For all the rebuffed invitations he had received, Andy had never been inside the building. He had to admit, the room was breathtaking, especially from this elevated perspective. A moment later, he realized he was standing in the doorway, gazing out at the glorious scenery in a daze. He snapped back, suddenly dreading the prospect of a balcony full of people staring at him. To his relief, it was nearly empty. The only other person there was a young woman who looked to be in her mid-twenties. She stood a few rows from the front railing of the balcony in the dead center. Cradled in her arms was a white and blue blanket, which Andy assumed held a baby he could not see. His entrance was less than quiet. She turned and smiled at him, then looked back at the altar. Andy returned an embarrassed grin as he shuffled past her on his way to the front row. Standing with the rest of the congregation, he scanned the rows of choir robes behind the rectory table for a familiar face.

Almost as soon as he'd settled, the choir ceased as the last gasps of the organ echoed up to the ceiling. Andy was still looking for Jeff when the next voice came.

"Blessed be God: Father, Son, and Holy Spirit."

The voice was high-pitched but still solemn. Andy looked for its owner. Before he could find it, another surprise.

"And blessed be his Kingdom, now and forever. Amen." Several hundred voices responded in unison. The unexpected response startled him.

Looking for a cue, he turned to the young mother behind him. She smiled again and raised her non-baby-holding hand to show him the small white pamphlet–the same one the Grey Lady had given him. It contained the order of the service and would prove helpful if he wanted to understand what was happening around him.

He opened the bulletin and read the first few lines. Assuming they'd just completed the Processional Hymn and Opening Acclamation, he correctly guessed the next item on the docket was something called 'the Collect for Purity.'

"Almighty God," the nasal voice continued, "to You, all hearts are open, all desires known, and from You, no secrets are hidden. Cleanse the thoughts of our hearts, by the inspiration of Your Holy

Spirit, that we may perfectly love You, and worthily magnify Your Holy Name, through Christ our Lord. Amen."

"Amen," the congregation affirmed.

Andy focused on the man slowly making his way to the altar. The priest wore a flowing black robe with gold piping from shoulders to hem. Dual crosses were emblazoned across his chest in the same gold thread.

Andy referred again to the bulletin. If the program was accurate, he was about to hear from The Very Reverend Dr. Jarvis Frost. Frost wore glasses with thick black frames, which looked absurd enough. But the man's noticeably bulbous head further magnified the full effect. Frost's disproportionate cranium was bald, save for a ring of black tuft that ran along the back of his skull from below his ears to the middle of his neck. Andy thought the man resembled a cartoon character come to life.

"A reading from the Word of the Lord," Reverend Frost announced.

"Thanks be to God," came the congregational response. Andy had no desire to participate in the dialogue but was intrigued enough to follow along. He suspected it might be like this for the remainder of the service.

"From the Old Testament, the Book of Joshua, chapter 1, verse 9," said Frost, 'Have I not commanded you? Be strong and courageous. Do not be frightened, and do not be dismayed, for the Lord your God is with you wherever you go."

"And Psalm 27:1," Frost continued. "The Lord is my light and my salvation; whom shall I fear?"

"Praise be to God for the Word of the Lord. Amen."

"Praise be to God," the faithful repeated in unison.

"You may be seated."

The flock accepted Frost's invitation, folding themselves back into the pews. Andy did likewise and returned to the printed program in his hand. He looked forward to seeing Jeff showcase his brilliance, but wondered what else he had to sit through to get there.

93

Traci pushed down on the door handle and was surprised to find it moved at all. It didn't appear to be locked, but the door was slightly stuck in its frame. Traci jiggled the handle and was about to exert full pressure when a voice barked from inside.

"Occupied!" she heard Ellen scream with a strange urgency.

Too late. The extra force shot Traci into the women's bathroom. She felt a rush of sickly humidity as warm, damp air assaulted her face.

"Get out!" Ellen yelled from inside the larger of two sea-foam-green stalls.

"It's me!" Traci blurted back. She'd instinctively averted her eyes toward the ceiling, which was severely stained by water damage, cigarette smoke, and God knows what else.

"Traci?"

"Yeah." The clear distress in her friend's voice drew her attention downward.

The second stall extended beyond the door of the first and had a wide entrance for handicapped access. Without stooping, Traci could see the empty floor of the nearest stall underneath its paneled wall, but not to the one behind it. Panning left, she saw something she couldn't even process. She stopped breathing and stared.

Jutting out from behind the cross-piece between the two stalls was a limp, bare foot. From its angle and position, Traci assumed the rest of the body was lying on the disgusting bathroom floor. The slender bare foot was cocked right at her, offering a perfect view of the glossy pink polish on the toes. Just above the ankle was the tattered cuff of a pair of black denim jeans.

"Traci!" Ellen shouted as she swung open the stall door and shot out, "Get the fucking car! Now!"

94

"These words come to us from the Old Testament," Dr. Frost asserted, launching into his sermon. The mild timber of his voice matched his rail-thin stature, and Andy struggled to reconcile both against his notions of what a priest should look and sound like. He considered closing his eyes to see if losing the visual reference made a difference, but he decided it didn't matter. He was only there to see Jeff. The sermon, he supposed, was superfluous.

"But they're part of a larger message," the Reverend continued. "One as old as time, and at the very heart of our relationship with our God, and our Savior."

Oh, Hell, Andy thought. *Here comes all the righteous bullshit that makes me hate the thought of even being here.*

"It's probably the one thing Jesus wanted us to know above all else."

Let me guess, Andy mocked silently. *It's gonna be something about love.* There was a sad irony in that guess, as it came from a heart hardened over recent years and conditioned to reject just such a message.

"It's an idea whose seeds are sown deep throughout the Old Testament; words sent straight from God's mouth to the hearts of the prophets. But it's really in the New Testament, in the teachings of Jesus, that the message I share with you today springs to life."

Andy used the first minute or so of Frost's message to determine that Jeff's solo would likely be during the Offertory and Holy Communion, directly following the sermon. It was the only choral presentation on the program that did not seem to involve congregational participation—a hymn entitled *Sicut Cervus*. Andy figured the title was in Latin, of which he knew none. He chuckled at its phonetic similarity to 'secret service' and was hardly even listening to the Reverend's words until Frost got to the next part of his sermon.

"It's the most repeated command in all the New Testament–by a lot. And it's as crucial today as it was two thousand years ago. And it may just be the simple wisdom we need to find peace in this difficult world. That command, my friends, is 'do not fear'."

It didn't strike any immediate chord in Andy. But it did at least register, because it was not the path he expected the priest to take. He allowed himself to invest a bit of attention, to see where Dr. Frost was headed.

"Ask yourself…" the Reverend invited the audience, "how often are you afraid?"

Andy's first thought was *not all that often.*

"And I don't mean like 'scared of monsters' afraid," the Reverend clarified. "Real fear comes in many forms. Anxiety. Uncertainty. Concern. Desperation. And so forth."

Well, shit. Andy thought. *In that case, the answer is more like 'all the time.'*

"But the Word of God tells us to reject that fear and offers us peace instead. Jesus wanted us to know that despite our worldly troubles, there is truly nothing for us to fear—that with Him in our hearts, there is nothing that could overtake us because there is nothing He cannot help us overcome."

Andy's skepticism flared. The Reverend's assertion was a concept with which he struggled mightily—the idea that belief in God, or Jesus, or a higher being of any kind had the power to soothe one's soul or lessen our daily burdens.

"But that is not to say there will not be hardship or even tragedy. To think as much would be unrealistic," Frost continued. "There are no guarantees life will be carefree or that things will happen just as we want. Of course not. God wants us to live our lives to the fullest. And to be honest, that requires some degree of risk on our part–a willingness to accept there are things beyond our control. Indeed, it requires faith."

Now, Andy was even more irritated, but for different reasons. Now, it wasn't just that this tiny, bald priest with the squeaky voice was countering his desired beliefs. It was as if the other two hundred people in the room weren't even there. Somehow, Frost had colluded with Jeff to craft a sermon aimed directly at him, explicitly designed to conflict and convict him. The message picked up right where Jeff had left off yesterday, hitting Andy uncomfortably close to home.

"But rejoice," Frost carried on, "God did not create us to carry fear in our hearts. He created us in His image, to live in His Glory. 1 John 4:18 says, 'Perfect love casts out all fear.' God *is* that perfect love. He invites us to hand over our burdens, worries, and fears to him so that we can live in the peace of His perfect love."

"So, how does this comfort come to us?" Frost asked.

Great fucking question! Andy thought, still doubtful any answer was coming.

"Listen to the Apostle Paul. In Philippians 4:6-7, Paul writes: 'Do not be anxious about anything, but in everything, by prayer and petition, with thanksgiving, present your requests to God. And the peace of God, which transcends all understanding, will guard your hearts and minds."

"And Paul goes on. In Romans 8:26-28. He writes: 'We do not know what we ought to pray for, but the Spirit himself intercedes for us, with groans that words cannot express. And he who searches our hearts knows the mind of the Spirit, because the Spirit intercedes for the Saints, in accordance with God's will. And we know that in all things God works for the good of those who love him, those who have been called according to his purpose."

"There are many among us today who hear that calling loudly, daily; those who know the love of the Lord deeply and truly in their hearts. And for you, God is abundantly happy. But He yearns to share His love with all of us. God wants us all to be happy. And it was for this happiness that He sent His Son, our Savior, Jesus Christ, to be with us. Because the true miracle is this—through Jesus, through a real relationship with Jesus—there are no barriers between us and God. That happiness is here for us all."

The well of conflict grew deeper in Andy. Here was a man, a meek-looking, bony man, whom Andy had never met and who had no stake whatsoever in his happiness, serving up to him on a silver platter answers to questions that had plagued him for as long as he could recall. Why? And more curiously, why could Andy not bring himself to believe, to accept that gift of happiness?

He began to process the possibilities. The reasons had shifted and snowballed over the years. It wasn't just a single obstacle that stood between him and God. Like every other person at one time or another, he'd been let down, disappointed by prayers that seemed to fall on deaf ears. But unlike some, he held onto ALL of them, stacking them up until they created a giant wall of grudge. On top of that foundation of frustration, he piled his impressions of too many self-proclaimed Christians. Many claimed to bear the mantle of God's love with their words, but showed nothing but intolerance, hatred, and judgment in their deeds. Andy couldn't reconcile, or stand, that hypocrisy. In fact, it made proclaiming allegiance to such a tribe the last thing he wanted to do. And speaking of judgment, how could Andy live as he had for so long, surrounded by law-bending degenerates, and walk with God at the same time? It was the same hypocrisy he questioned in Jeff. And if his supposed God-loving roommate couldn't pass that test, what hope was there for Andy himself?

Andy saw it as a crossroads, a choice between his current lifestyle and embracing a relationship with God. In his mind, they were mutually exclusive camps. One would celebrate his decision to be counted amongst them. As a result, the other would surely spurn and condemn him. His need for approval from the people he'd chosen, those who had accepted him in return, weighed heavily. Andy's need to feed the fleshy desires of the material world drove the wedge between him and the fruits of the Spirit much deeper.

"Rest assured. God wants that happiness for you," the Reverend rolled on. "In Luke 12:32, we're reminded once again: 'Fear not! For it is your Father's good pleasure to give you the Kingdom."

"And here's the best part."

Dr. Jarvis Frost had spent most of the sermon standing placidly near the lectern, moving little and speaking with an even, straightforward tone. But now, a tangible excitement grew from inside him. He moved to the front of the altar, closer to the congregation, and spoke with vigor. It was joy he projected, an abundant joy that might at any second exceed the physical limitations of his slight frame. Frost raised his arms skyward, perhaps inviting more of that Spirit to envelope him. Andy followed the lines of the Reverend's short limbs upward, all the way to the cathedral's resplendent ceiling.

As if he needed more conflict, he now found those rich wooden rafters transfixed. No longer an inverted ark hull, the golden rays of the sun gave just enough backlight to reveal the outstretched limbs of a massive bat-shaped creature perched overhead. Andy was sober, especially by his own standards, and this revelation absolutely required a double-take. On second glance, things got worse. Now, in the shifting light, Andy found two distinct eyes–ominous, squinty, demonic eyes, to be exact–staring back.

If there was a giant Imp of Doom clutching the ceiling of his church, Frost certainly didn't see or sense it. Apparently, this was Andy's demon.

He focused again on Frost, hoping this mind-fuck was imaginary and very temporary.

"All we have to do is ask Him," the orator continued. "Ask Him to share His love, His comfort, His Spirit, and His Glory with us. To do what Paul urged of the Philippians–'present our requests to God, with thanksgiving'."

Andy had been playing mental chess with the Good Doctor almost from the jump, meeting each point with a defensive counter. He'd blocked every parry thus far, deflecting what he perceived as threats to his very identity.

Andy was a pro at grinding out a debate, always ready with an argument or snarky response. But facing demons wasn't part of any bargain he'd made by setting foot on Holy ground this morning. As the Reverend hit the home stretch of his sermon and found yet another, higher gear, his 'opponent', Andy, was disarmed.

Andy dug into his well of discontent, a font that historically overflowed, and suddenly found it empty.

"When we come to Him and thank Him for the many blessings He has already bestowed upon us, and we ask Him to fulfill our hearts' desire, He can, and He will. All we have to do is ask because *He* wants for us what *we* want for us: happiness and the absence of fear."

Distracted and divided, Andy got caught in the current of Frost's suggestion and allowed himself to be carried further downstream. What if he considered the possibility of acting on that suggestion? What if he let himself ask God for what he wanted? What could happen? If the Reverend were wrong, he'd get nothing, the same outcome as if Andy did nothing at all.

"Let us take the advice that David gave to his son Solomon. As 1 Chronicles 28:20 tells us: 'Be strong and courageous and do it! Do not be afraid, and do not be dismayed, for the Lord God is with you. He will not leave or forsake you, until all the work for the service of the house of the Lord is finished.'"

And that was the final truth. Andy *was* afraid. Afraid to change. Afraid to believe. Afraid to ask. Afraid to be let down. Afraid to be wrong. Even more afraid, somehow, of being right. But now, he was also afraid to stay put. Afraid to be alone, especially if something else was possible.

"And when we do—when we ask God to grant us the desires of our heart—we know we can expect blessings in return. Just as God told Abram, 'Fear not! I am your shield. Your reward shall be very great'."

"So, let us go now to the Lord in prayer. Let us lift our desires to Him, knowing that through Him, all things are possible. All needs are met. With Him, we need to fear nothing and no one. Trust that when we commit our work to the Lord, our plans will succeed."

You gotta be fucking kidding me. Andy thought, so incredulously he almost said it out loud.

Any doubt that Reverend Frost had been speaking to him and him alone that morning was shattered. He supposed it was possible that the last line just sounded familiar. But in his heart, Andy knew it wasn't so. He knew exactly what he'd heard. And he knew that if he pulled that small leather rectangle out of his back pocket, it would echo the Reverend's parting words verbatim. He started to reach for the money clip but stopped. He already knew, and nothing would be gained by confirming it. The weathered inscription was all he could see in his mind as he closed his eyes.

"Let us pray."

95

"Oh, God! What the hell happened?"

"I know. It's bad. Did you get the fucking car? Is the car here?"

"It's right outside! It's running!"

"Good. We gotta get the fuck outta here!"

"Can she even move? Hey! Can you move?"

The young woman piled limply on the floor of the truck stop bathroom lifted her head enough for Traci to see the collage of cuts and bruises covering what was an otherwise beautiful face. Tears streamed from the one bloodied eye of hers that was not swollen shut. It was all she could do to nod slightly as she fought back the sobs.

"Fuck it! We'll carry her. Let's go!"

96

Reverend Frost led the congregation in a moment of silent reflection, extending the invitation for the faithful and the not-so-faithful to lay their burdens at the feet of God. Andy knew the priest was speaking, but he couldn't focus on the words. Only a low mumble hummed through his ears as he sat in the balcony, stunned, like a prize fighter stung by a nose-breaking sucker punch. A tightness grew in his chest, and a warm tingle spread through the back of his skull. He knew all too well what panic attacks felt like. This was not that—not exactly—although his body was definitely responding involuntarily to the surrounding stimuli. He wasn't high or drunk, nor had he been sober long enough to be suffering legitimate withdrawal. Still, real chemical reactions were happening within him.

Frost concluded the prayer and began the transition to the Offertory. Ordinarily, the plate-passing hymn would not warrant additional commentary. But this morning, the Reverend felt compelled to connect all the dots. The minister's words were still not fully breaching Andy's brain, and he missed the added context:

"… from Psalm 42:1, in the original Latin, *Sicut cervus desiderat ad fontes aquarum, ita desiderat anima mea ad te, Deus.* As the deer longs for running water, so longs my soul for you, O God."

"Fear not. Let your soul long for the love of God, and may He bless you."

Andy's head dropped into his hands, propped upon his knees. He kept his eyes closed, hoping it would calm the sea of sensations. It only amplified what happened next.

A single voice cut through the silence, not speaking or singing in any manner Andy recognized. It was more of a chant, a rich tenor bellow that seemed small and distant in the vast cathedral. It played alone for just a moment before being joined by others. A soprano soared high over the top, and a deep baritone grounded the exquisite sound. It came as if from nothing, leaping up to fill Andy's ears and mind. It startled him, and he opened his eyes.

His hands bracketed his head, and Andy saw his forearms and the dark wood of the pews on either side. He kept his eyes open but did not move. Eventually, he would see what was making this glorious noise, but for now, he wanted just to *hear* it without distraction.

The chorus continued to grow as more voices entered the fray. The sound swirled to the very top of the cathedral, bouncing back off the ceiling and filling the room with a tone that could be felt as much as heard. There was no organ blasting away or any musical accompaniment at all. There was nothing to diminish the purity of those voices weaving together in a call to God that was somehow lachrymose and joyful.

Andy closed his eyes again and allowed the sound to fill his head. His breathing was shallow, but the tone rushed into his chest as he inhaled, filling him. He held that breath, clinging to and relishing it. He released it slowly and opened his eyes.

As he peered over the railing, Andy saw nearly all the parishioners on the floor below standing. Another wave of heat passed through him. This he recognized as embarrassment. Thankful again for being almost entirely alone in the balcony, Andy turned to the young lady behind him. She stood, blanket-obscured babe in arms, swaying to the hypnotic chorus that filled the room. Again, she offered a pleasant smile.

Andy froze, unsure what, if anything, he should do. He didn't know why they were all standing and what it would mean if he joined them or didn't. It occurred to him that only the girl, and possibly her infant child, would ever notice what he did at that moment. Andy remained seated and turned around. At least thirty seconds had passed since the hymn began. With some horror, Andy realized he was missing the one thing he came to see in this entire production. He widened his eyes and narrowed his focus.

Just to the left of the lectern, near "center stage," Andy found his roommate. Partially obscured behind a knee-high white wall, Jeff was still a focal point. He stood alone. A small cluster of his choir mates, three women and two men, were gathered on the opposite side of the altar. Behind them stood the rest of St. Timothy's choir, perhaps forty voices in all. Andy trained his eyes on Jeff, excited to watch his friend shine at last.

Jeff was a few hundred feet away. From that distance and in this lighting, Andy doubted his roommate could recognize him. And Jeff had no reason to believe Andy was even there. Still, he could have sworn Jeff was looking straight at him.

Watching his friend like this was surreal. He had seen Jeff perform plays on stage and sing songs in bars, but never like this. Andy tried to concentrate on the whole scene and his friend individually, but it was too much. The effort disconnected him from the pure beauty of the sound these artists were creating. Focusing on Jeff, Andy let everything else slide into the background.

The ebb and flow of the music was visceral and otherworldly, a literal epiphany for Andy. The voices rose and fell dramatically. Jeff stood, head tilted high, singing straight into the balcony. Andy couldn't see detailed expressions from that far away, but he assumed there was a quiet, confident joy on his friend's face.

Andy *also* couldn't see the struggle Jeff faced. It was oddly like his own, a battle for composure against a tide of emotions, but one born of very different circumstances. The forces Andy viewed as invaders attacking the thick-walled fortress of his heart, Jeff saw as liberators.

Affected by those forces or not, Jeff was a true showman. He soldiered on, beating back the emotions that threatened to undermine his performance. To an ignorant ear, their impact was imperceptible. But Jeff struggled, nonetheless. Dr. Frost's message hadn't been lost on him either. The invitation to let go of his own fears, to revel once again in the practice of praise, was one he relished. And then, the immediate opportunity to reciprocate, to offer his gifts back to God in the form of melodic worship, filled his heart nearly to bursting.

A similar swell began within Andy, although, for him, it felt foreign and very uncomfortable. His breathing shortened. A rash of heat ran across his face. Beads of sweat bloomed on his forehead. His pulse raced along with the voices, climbing ever higher until he could feel his heart beating in his chest and temples. He pulled for air but failed. A tangible ache announced itself at the center of his sternum. His throat felt tight and dry, and the skin around his sinuses began to burn.

Andy labored to control the sensory overload in his gut and head. Again, his brain was sending signals to his extremities without his awareness or consent. Before he knew how or why, Andy stretched his aching legs to stand. The last congregant to rise had finally acknowledged the celebration happening around him.

Feeling like a passenger in the vessel of his own body, Andy grabbed the railing for support. He clenched the hard, polished wood, still trying to catch his breath. Led by his dear friend, the choir approached a crescendo that seemed to grasp and pull at him. In desperation, Andy lifted his head, extending his neck fully to open his parched and constricted throat. Again, he found himself staring at the ceiling.

The dark underbelly of that massive ark was illuminated on all sides by sunlight pressing through the stained-glass windows. The light revealed the Demon once more. Its two "eyes" funneled orbs of blinding white through tiny slits in the hulking black frame. Andy stared with resolve into the eyes of the Demon, compelled at once to both fight and flee.

And then, he could fight no longer. In one final gasp, one gloriously deep exhale, the dam burst. As Jeff and the choir climaxed, Andy closed his eyes. His chest heaved as a flood of tears rolled down his face. Alternating waves of joy and shame converged, wrapping him in an intense electric heat. By the force of an uninvited yet undeniable Spirit, his heart was summarily crushed. It wasn't so much shattered as melted, as if a piece of cold, bloated steel had been pierced, releasing intense internal pressure as it was reforged.

Andy felt helpless, completely devastated, hollowed out, but somehow lighter. He couldn't move but didn't want to, either.

There were no words. There was no sound at all. The last gorgeous notes of *Sicut Cervus* had floated to the rafters a few seconds ago. Andy stood in the balcony, beautifully broken, as tears of confusion streamed down his blood-flushed cheeks. He wiped his face with a grimy sleeve and blinked. The room was bathed in a new light. The once-dark arches held no shadows. The Demon had flown or perhaps simply ceased to be.

The hymn was finished. Oblivious to Andy's experience, and likely even his presence, the priest led the congregation through the ritual of the Nicene Creed, affirming their shared belief in the sanctity of the Holy Church and the divinity of their Savior Jesus Christ. At its conclusion, in reflex en masse, the congregation knelt for a final prayer of confession.

Andy joined them. He bent, not quite kneeling, but lowering himself against the balcony rail, and bowed his head. He was aware of the Reverend's words but focused instead on the ones trying to form in his own mind.

God? Andy offered silently, as much questioning as addressing him. *I don't know what I'm doing here. I know I've been mad–at You, at everyone, at myself–just angry, for a long time. I wanted to get away from You. And I was sure You felt the same. I felt You leave me. I don't know why You came back for me, and I have no idea what you're saying. But I can't deny I hear You. I'm scared. I'm afraid to try again.*

I'm scared... but I will try; I'll try, Andy confessed. *I will.*

When he was done, so were the tears. He lifted his head and looked out again over the railing. The congregation had been released but still milled around on the floor below. The faithful greeted one another, shaking hands and conversing as they waited to exit the sanctuary.

Andy watched the proceedings with strange fascination until he felt the lightest touch across his left shoulder. He turned slowly, figuring an usher was about to ask him to leave. Instead, it was the young mother who'd been sitting behind him during the service. Now, only inches away, he could see the very pink face of the bundle of joy she'd been cradling. Her tiny infant son was sleeping peacefully; a slight smile curled on his lips. She, too, smiled as she extended her arm.

"May God be with you," she said.

"You too," Andy answered awkwardly.

She shook his hand, never releasing her smile, and walked away.

Andy turned again, hoping to spot Jeff in the thinning crowd. He saw several robed choir members, but his roommate was not among them. It took a couple of seconds before the panic set in.

"Dammit!" he said, with at least enough restraint to do so quietly. It wouldn't have mattered, as he now had the balcony all to himself. Knowing he might only have a few minutes to catch his ride home, Andy wiped his still-damp face and made a break for the stairs.

97

The girl sat huddled in the Jeep's passenger seat, curled in a ball, knees pulled tight to her chest. It was hard to tell if she was rocking gently or just shaking. Ellen climbed in the back and gently cupped her shoulder from behind as Traci manned the wheel. She'd let the two of them carry her from the bathroom to the car without a word, waiting until she was safely inside to speak for the first time.

"Get me out of here!" she pleaded. Her voice was raspy and hoarse as if she'd been screaming. She made the demand several times, growing more adamant with each refrain. It was all she could say until the Jeep was moving safely down the interstate on-ramp and away from the truck stop. Neither Ellen nor Traci pressed her, and it took another minute or so before she spoke again.

"I want to go home!" she cried, still balled up and sobbing into her hands.

"Where's home?" Ellen asked.

"I don't know," she bawled with a stunning, matter-of-fact blankness that was terrifying.

"I'm Traci. That's Ellen. What's your name?"

"I don't know!" she repeated, the sobs growing more hysterical with each exchange.

Traci looked back at Ellen. Their faces were mirror images of shock and distraught.

"Who did this to you?" Traci followed up as delicately as possible.

The girl hesitated, her tongue locked down by shock and shame.

"A man," she stammered. "A man in a truck."

"Is that how you got here?"

"Yes..." she started but then reconsidered. "I don't know."

Sensing she might finally be safe, the girl started taking slow, deep breaths and attempted to calm herself.

The girl stared blankly at the Jeep's floor for nearly a minute. Traci and Ellen waited with patience and nervous energy as their passenger began to unwind.

"We've been driving for days. He had me blindfolded and tied up in the back of his cab. I don't know where we've been or where we are. I don't know."

"How'd you get in the bathroom?"

"He had me tied up the whole time. Kept me gagged with a blanket over me when he'd stop. The only time he'd untie me is when he..."

She didn't want to say the next words, nor did her audience want or need to hear them.

"So, how...?" Ellen attempted to fast-forward.

"He untied me. He wanted me to use my hands..." She was still tearful, but now the fear in her voice gave way to rage. "He held a knife on me 'til he got off, then he'd tie me back up. Last night or this morning, he came at me again. He untied me and did his thing. But I guess he tired himself out. Tied the knots for shit."

Her words came faster now, loaded with anger and adrenaline.

"Afterward, he'd smoke weed. Then he'd just sit there and babble about shit. But he must have scored something stronger. The last time, after he got done, he went back to the pipe. He got crazy high. He was all jacked up for a few minutes and then just passed out. I waited, pretending to be asleep, to see if he was going to move. He didn't. It was easy to slip those shitty knots. I crawled out of the truck as quiet as I could, and left the door cracked. It was already light outside. The parking lot was full of trucks. I'm sure somebody must have seen me get out. And I'm sure they saw me run into the bathroom. But I didn't know where else to go. I wasn't gonna hitchhike. Probably get picked up by another fucking psycho just as bad, or worse, than that other piece of shit." She was seething.

"I don't know how long I was in there before you came in. It seemed like forever. I knew he was gonna find me. And then, he would kill me."

"We gotta get you to a hospital," Traci urged. She was destroying the speed limit, hoping like Hell to get pulled over by a cop.

"I wanna go home!" she repeated.

"Do you know of a hospital between here and Bradford?" Ellen asked.

"No," Traci admitted. "But I'm sure as shit looking for one."

"Fuck." Ellen blurted.

"What?"

"We still gotta find Andy. One of us has to get back to Jeff and tell him we don't have Andy. We can't just leave him. We have to go home."

98

Andy had flown down the stairs and out of the church, desperate to beat Jeff back to the truck. After all this, the idea of walking home was unimaginable.

He rounded the corner in a near sprint and slowed only when he spied the muddy black truck. Shockingly, Andy had won the race. He walked the rest of the way, lungs burning from the burst of impromptu exercise. Lowering the truck's tailgate, he collapsed upon it. The bed behind him was an absolute mess. The vinyl tarp hung loose, partially covering an assortment of their supplies. Andy considered tidying it, but thought Jeff might appreciate his experience more if it was left as-is.

Andy exhaled, feeling strangely relaxed. Scores of churchgoers filed past him. Somehow, their reaction seemed different from the few he'd encountered on the way in. Maybe they were already thinking about brunches, family visits, yard work, or who knows what else, and just weren't bothered by his presence. But, for some reason, the tangible repulsion he'd felt from the faithful just an hour ago seemed to be gone. He reclined against the side panel, watching people walk through the parking lot. There was no telling how long he might be waiting.

Andy figured Jeff would appear from around the same corner he had turned near the church's front entrance. Instead, the side doors opened, and a small horde of people emerged. A few had robes draped on their arms. The choir had been released. Shockingly, Jeff was not the first person he recognized.

The first familiar thing Andy saw in the pack headed toward him was that unmistakable fuchsia pantsuit. He smiled and then laughed. The hot pink lady with the sleek silver hair approached, walking right beside his roommate.

Andy's instinct was to hide, to crouch down in the truck and surprise the living shit out of Jeff. But he fought that. Instead, he just sat there, watching as the group came nearer. Jeff was talking with Mrs. Fuchsia and got almost to the front of the truck before he even looked up.

"Andy? Why the…? How…?" Jeff was confounded to see his friend. He quickened, leaving his choirmate a half-step behind as he approached.

Jeff walked right up to Andy and hugged him, but not sweetly or gently. It was more of a stern squeezing that said *Hey, this is my place of work. Why the Hell are you here, especially looking like that?*

"How the fuck did you get here?" he whispered, low enough that the ladies behind couldn't hear the swear.

"Oh, that's a pretty funny story," Andy scoffed, throwing his thumb over his shoulder and pointing at the disheveled truck bed.

Mrs. Fuchsia had caught up and now stood next to Jeff. The awkward moment when two strangers were waiting to be introduced by their familiar acquaintance had arrived. Jeff stalled, clearly uncomfortable.

"Umm… Andy…" he stammered, extending one hand at him and the other toward the older black lady, "this is Dr. Valerie Cobb. She sings with us in the choir." She offered Andy a big, friendly smile, recognizing him instantly.

"Dr. Val, this is my friend, Andy Maxwell." Andy noticed he'd chosen 'friend' instead of 'roommate' and wondered how intentional the extra distance was.

"Believe it or not, we've met," Mrs. Cobb said, cheerfully shaking Andy's hand.

"You what?" said Jeff.

"I passed Andy on the way in this morning," she grinned, now speaking more directly to him than to Jeff. "You didn't look so good earlier. You look much better now. I *told* you it was a blessed day."

"It's nice to meet you," Andy offered.

"Well, I'll let y'all get to the rest of your day," Valerie said, giving Jeff a quick hug. "You did great today, son," she praised. "Will you be here on Wednesday?"

"Of course."

"Well, good. I'll see you then. Bye, y'all."

Jeff turned to Andy, who stood there wearing a strange smile that his roommate could not decipher.

"I don't know what to say. I don't even understand how you're here."

"I was supposed to be here," Andy said, grinning wider still. "I'd have preferred a smoother ride, but I guess we don't always get to choose the path or the driver, right?"

Jeff was even more confused. If he understood correctly, Andy had ridden nearly a hundred miles in the back of a covered pickup truck. If he knew his roommate at all, that kind of inconvenience usually earned a nuclear reaction. And yet, Andy was calm, cheerful even.

"I don't understand," Jeff repeated.

"I'll tell you all about it," Andy suggested, stepping toward his friend and pulling him in for a hug. His was a genuine embrace, warm, hearty, and relaxed. This might have been the only reaction that could have further befuddled Jeff.

"Thank you," Andy said kindly, giving him another tight squeeze before releasing him.

"For what? Rolling your ass around in the truck for an hour?"

"No," laughed Andy. "That part sucked balls. Thanks for this," Andy spread his arms outward, encompassing the entirety of the massive church.

"You gave me something I didn't even know I wanted."

Jeff had no response, but he somehow understood. Apparently, they had both received gifts at St. Timothy's this morning.

"C'mon," Andy summoned, closing the tailgate and heading for the passenger side. "It's story time."

"Andy?" Jeff asked. "Where are the girls?"

"I dunno," he replied. He hadn't thought about them at all yet today. "But I'm hungry. Let's go home."

99

Andy was right. St. Timothy's was located just over two miles from their house. The drive took a few short minutes. It was long enough for them both to finish a cigarette, but nowhere near enough for Andy to share his whole journey.

The truck chugged up the hill on Cornwall Street. Ellen's Chevette and Andy's SUV sat where they'd been left the day before. Andy hopped from the truck and headed for the front door. He was desperate to pee, wash his face, and get a cold drink of water. Jeff was content to linger. He sat propped against the porch, considering another smoke when Traci's Jeep came charging down the hill.

Traci plowed into the driveway and stopped just behind his truck. Jeff watched curiously as she jumped out and released Ellen from the back seat. The giant oak tree in their front yard cast a shadow over the windshield, obscuring Jeff's view of its passengers.

Ellen broke into a run, sprinting from the car towards the porch.

"Jeff!" she shouted. "Andy's gone. He's lost!"

His cavalier smile was the last thing she expected.

"Actually," he said calmly, "I think he's been found. He's inside. He's been with me this morning."

"What?" she gasped, glad and mad at the same time.

"Yeah. And the most unbelievable thing happened."

"Whatever it is, we've got it beat," Ellen replied with certainty.

"Is Traci coming in?"

"No. We have to go!" Ellen urged, already turning back to the Jeep.

The front door opened, and Andy walked back outside.

"Hey, El!" he shouted.

Ellen wheeled around and stared, ecstatic to see him safely on their porch. Traci blasted the horn, disturbing Ellen's moment of relief and the general tranquility of the neighborhood.

"Geez! Relax!" said Andy, walking into the front yard. Ellen met him halfway and hugged him hard.

"You scared me, you fucker," she chastised, giving him a small kiss on the cheek. "We'll talk later. Right now, we gotta go!"

"Go? Where?"

"C'mere." She ushered both boys toward the idling Jeep.

Jeff, Andy, and Ellen walked to the driver's side door together. Traci was leaning out the window.

"Hey," she said to Andy, "look who it is." She was clearly less concerned about his safety than Ellen, and apparently, she was in the middle of something more important.

Jeff and Andy leaned in and saw the lump of a girl in the passenger seat. Her shoulder-length sandy blonde hair hid her face, which was mostly turned away. Her black jeans were caked in red clay dust, and her shirt was badly ripped at the neck.

"Where are you going?" Jeff asked Traci.

Just as he asked the question, the girl turned her bruised and swollen face to look at them. They'd seen her face enough times in the last week to know exactly who she was.

"Margo?" Andy said in disbelief.

The girl's rescue was cause for celebration. Still, as Ellen looked at her roommates, both boys beamed in a way that seemed out of place.

"I don't know what you guys have been into this morning," she said, climbing back in behind Traci. "And we've gotta go. But this has been one helluva week. When we get home, I want some of what you've got."

"Sure." Andy smiled. "You can get it any time. You just have to know where to look."

# # #

Your talent is God's gift to you.
What you do with it is your gift back to God.
— Leo Buscaglia

AUTHOR'S NOTE

There's a reason people say, "I'm glad I didn't know then what I know now." It's true in spades for me when it comes to this book. When I first began imagining and coalescing the thoughts that would become *Staring at the Ceiling*, I was 21 years old. I was entering my junior year at the University of South Carolina and simultaneously living the best and worst year of my life.

My sister and first best friend in life, Kim, had passed away from cancer just a few months prior, and rather than return home, my parents agreed I should stay and finish school in Columbia, SC. There, I was surrounded by a legion of new best friends and some of the greatest characters I'll ever know in this life. I still have misgivings about not being with my parents during that terrible time for us all, but it's possible it was ultimately the right decision.

Among the many things I love about Columbia is its simplicity. It's not that big. It's built on a beautiful square grid that caters to the part of my brain that struggles with spatial relations and navigation. And in 1993, it was home to some of the most incredibly talented and wonderfully weird people God has ever gathered in one spot. Oh, and it was cheap, too. At the time, I shared a four-bedroom house in a shady neighborhood on Cypress Street with three roommates (and often our girlfriends). My rent to live like a relative king was $136.25 a month, which was easily covered by a few hours a week working the front desk at the local Howard Johnson's – and honestly, by the more-than-generous monthly stipend from my parents. In short, I could afford more free time than is healthy for an angry 21-year-old with flexible morals and no supervision. Idle hands and all that.

Aside from work and school, I filled that time bouncing between our friends' houses, playing spades, (the original) *Mortal Kombat* (on the super-high-tech PlayStation 1), and music. Well, I didn't really *play* music. I tried guitar for a while, but was objectively awful, and very few people were ever subjected to my attempts to be a rock star. But it seemed like everyone else I knew was either in a band, lived with someone in a band, or dated someone in a band. In our little circle, there were real, legit rock stars, and most nights, someone was playing live, in one of Columbia's dive bars or in the warehouse district down by the river that housed practice spaces for countless aspiring bands.

While my friends wielded guitars, drumsticks, and microphones, I chose a camera–an actual film camera–and proceeded with annoying gusto to document our little scene. I have thousands of printed pictures from that era in a big box under a bed. I could throw them away, which I suspect would make my wife happy, if only to chip away at the mountain of sentimental souvenirs I have hoarded over the decades. But the truth is, I don't even need them. Because while I was burning those images to film, they were also being permanently burned into my brain.

Entering my third year in college, I'd had enough of those experiences to start seeing a larger narrative playing out–a story was forming in my head. It helped that I was pursuing a degree in Journalism and taking several writing classes where the constant encouragement was to "write what you know," "write about your passion," and "write about what you see every day." What I saw every day was debauchery and shenanigans. I saw some people caught in the riptide and slowly getting swept away. I saw others furiously treading water, neither succumbing nor progressing. And I saw a precious few rising above the tumult, wading on the shoreline of dark waters and knowing better than to take the deep dives.

I guess I'm glad I didn't know then how dumb I was. I'll be the first to admit I'm VERY lucky to have escaped the '90s without significant injuries or a criminal record–Lord knows I kind of tried. Many of you will join me in thankfulness that the Internet was a mere infant when we were trying to navigate early adulthood.

The people surrounding me in Columbia during those days were equally daring and/or dismissive in the face of authority. They were also unpredictable, wildly creative, hilarious, and endlessly entertaining. I really owe this book to the entirety of the underground music scene in Columbia, SC, in the 1990s. In a very real sense, I didn't have to *write* the book as much as I just had to *live* it and take notes–a few scribblings in a notebook I still have, and all those images burned into my brain.

That sounds oversimplified, and it is. I don't mean to suggest it was easy. But I'm glad I didn't know then that it wouldn't be easy. I'm glad I was naïve about how hard it is to create something. And I'm glad I had no idea how much harder it is to push that creation in front of enough people for it even to get noticed, let alone gain some traction. Movies like *Reservoir Dogs* and *Clerks* came out in 1992 and 1994, respectively. I'm glad I was young and dumb and naïve enough to see gritty, character-driven stories with R-rated dialog and shoestring budgets and think: 'That's awesome,' AND 'I could probably do that. Hell, I know a LOT of people who curse while doing dangerous yet amusing things. I'm gonna write a book, sell it as a screenplay, and make a MILLION dollars! How hard can it be?'

And now, we've reached the apologies portion of the message. First, apologies to both Quentin Tarantino and Kevin Smith. Turns out, what you guys do is incredibly hard and takes a shit-ton of talent and work. And while I'm at it, apologies to ANYONE who read the original first edition of *Staring at the Ceiling*. Parents often struggle to see any imperfections in their newborns. But by the time they're ten years old, you're painfully familiar with the big and little things about them that drive you nuts. *Staring at the Ceiling* was my *baby*–my firstborn at that. It was *perfect*, and I wasn't open to hearing much to the contrary. Except, it wasn't. With ten years of hindsight, I can say it was a decent story, but *terribly* written. I subjected a handful of beta readers to an even rougher draft and begrudgingly took most of their edits. I can only imagine how much worse it could have been without their help.

I also owe a few friends a legitimate apology. *Staring at the Ceiling* is inspired by actual events, which are, in most cases, exaggerated for dramatic purposes. The same is true for the characters. Very few of the people in the story are direct characterizations of real people. Some are completely made up. Others are amalgams, based in part on one or more people, often with characteristics of several individuals blended. The results are fictionalized caricatures which, in some cases, were unflattering–some even more so than I initially realized. I'd like to think that the worst thing that could happen from me writing a book is *nothing*, that it would be inconsequential and not matter, a wasted effort if you will. Unfortunately, there's a (much) worse possibility. A while after the book's release, I spoke with a dear friend who was less than flattered by some characterizations they rightly recognized. In trying to be "cool", I was unkind, which was a little heartbreaking. I was so busy trying to get the whole story out that I lost some of the plot. *Staring at the Ceiling* was, is, and will always be a love letter to the place and people who made me who I was at the time of its writing. Causing anyone's grief is the last thing I'd ever want a creation of mine to do. To my dear friend and anyone else who felt slighted in any way upon reading the first edition of this book, I'm genuinely sorry. Please know that among my primary goals in releasing a second edition was to smooth those rough edges that inflicted unnecessary jabs.

On a related note, I'm glad I didn't know my future wife, Carie, or her family when I first conceived and started writing this book. To be clear, I couldn't have finished it (a feat that happened only after a twenty-year hiatus) without Carie's love, support, wisdom, patience, and encouragement. Shortly after meeting Carie's wonderful parents, I had a dreadful epiphany. I was NEVER going to finish writing this book, because I simply couldn't imagine a world in which those two awesome(ly conservative) people would allow a person who wrote such a book to marry their daughter. And so, I waited. This book sat in its box for a couple more years. Only after we were married and had our first child did I dare revisit it. By then, I had already given them a grandchild, and another was on his way. Could they really cut me loose for writing a silly, raunchy book? I was willing to bet they wouldn't, and the process of writing my characters out of a room they'd languished in for nearly two decades began. Except now, the challenge was completely different. Now, I had to wrestle with and reconcile the TWENTY years of distance between the first 200 pages of the handwritten draft in that box under my bed and the remainder of the story. I checked that original notebook against the plot in my head and found they weren't quite aligned. I'd lived twenty more years and had new problems and perspectives. For starters, and primarily, the original ending I had envisioned had (thankfully) been revealed to be misguided in the extreme. Only with decades of growth (and more influence from Carie and her family than I would have ever imagined) did the ultimate trajectory of most of the characters reveal itself.

I'm also glad I didn't know the impact this story would have on others in general. I've already spoken about some of the unfortunate negative consequences. Thankfully, it went the other way as well, which was equally unexpected.

In the ten years this book has existed, several people have said kind words to me about it. Some friends and family members even put their reputations on the line to be among the NINETEEN people willing to write a public review of that work. I did, and still do, appreciate those who were overenthusiastically kind in their reviews. But I'm also REALLY grateful for the few folks who gave it an *honest* review and didn't shy away from its glaring flaws.

Reviews and sales completely aside, there were some real wins from the effort of writing this book. A person I knew only as an acquaintance in those earlier years discovered this story and credited it with re-igniting their passion for playing music. Today, I'm blessed to count him as a much closer friend who is STILL creating and sharing music live, creating joy for himself and countless others. And he's not the only one.

I already told you about the 20-year-old version of me, the guy who was sure he'd make a million dollars from this story. The 53-year-old version of me doesn't resemble that guy much at all, but we still have a few things in common. I've always had an appreciation for "the big idea." Maybe that's because I was raised by a dad who thought the same way. As I finished writing this story, in my early 40s, I started seeing something else emerge. So much of what I wrote was inspired by the joy and wild abandon of those days watching our friends play music in Columbia. "What if", I thought, "I had a party to celebrate the release of this book? And what if I asked a couple of the people in those bands from the 90s, many of whom were still living in Columbia in 2015, if they'd play a show as the release party?"

I started dreaming of a night where all our friends would descend back upon Columbia from far-flung places like New York, Chicago, Los Angeles, Washington, D.C., Portland, and Atlanta. I started fantasizing about reliving those glory days of drinking cheap beer in a dark club, rocking out in front of too-loud amplifiers, and ending the evening in a sweaty, unsober mess surrounded by scores of my favorite people.

I'm glad nobody told me I shouldn't do that. I tiptoed toward that big idea with no real expectations. What happened was shocking and humbling, in the extreme. Putting together a concert featuring six or seven bands can be complicated, especially for someone with zero prior experience in that arena. Such an event requires the participation of a LOT of people, all of whom need to be willing and available to contribute. I started with friends who were used to hearing my crazy ideas, hoping they'd think such a venture was less crazy than it sounded in my head. They didn't say "yes". They said, "Oh, HELL, yes!" That was followed by more yesses, a couple of "sures," and a "Dude, just tell me what you need, and we'll make it happen." Literally, in the span of a few hours, my crazy little dream of a rock concert release party became a reality.

On Saturday, December 12, 2015, seven bands and a couple of hundred people converged at the Art Bar in Columbia, SC. Bands played music. I read a few passages from this book. There were toasts, cheers, high-fives, and hugs—so many hugs. Ten years later, it's still squarely among the best nights of my life because it was more than a rock show; it was a reunion.

Fast forward a decade–almost. In 2024, I had two separate significant surgeries. I expected this to be disruptive, but had no idea just how much downtime I was about to have. Turns out, it was enough to revisit this book. I spent most of 2021 writing my second book, a memoir of gratitude titled *I Can Appreciate That*. Among the many blessings that came out of that experience was being introduced, by a close friend whose expertise and advice I value, to some new writing and editing tools. Writing the first edition of *Staring at the Ceiling* taught me that I COULD write a book–that I could endure the years-long process of creating characters and a narrative and following it through to its conclusion. Writing *I Can Appreciate That* was much more of an education on HOW to write a book, including proper editing for grammar, tone, style, and story.

In 2015, just "finishing" a project that had lived in my brain for 20 years was enough of an accomplishment. A decade later, though, to my relative horror, I realized what I had "accomplished" was writing a fairly terrible book. Armed with worthy tools and the clearer vision ten years of distance provides, it was easy to see how much help this book needed. And now, I'd been given the time and space to do it–to fix the busted grammar, the broken construction, and the unkind treatments that were the products of laziness and ignorance.

One of my writing tools, Grammarly, assures me this second edition is at least 8-12% "better" than its predecessor. But I feel 100% better about releasing this story back into the wild today. The story remains the same, but hopefully, it's a leaner, less mean, and easier, more enjoyable read.

As of this writing, my children are 20 and 18 years old–one a sophomore in college, the other a senior in high school. Both are almost the same age I was when I first met the people who inspired this story, and who have been among my best friends ever since. To my knowledge, neither of my children has read this story yet, and I'm glad for that, too. However, I now think that would be fine. To be clear, I don't want either of them to be like Andy Maxwell–now, or ever; he's no role model. But I do want them to (safely) have as much fun as I did living the life that made this story possible.

Go, boys. Find your people. Do relatively benign dumb shit. Dream way too big. Ask people for help and accept it. You'll be amazed at what's possible.

To Carie: Thank you, as ALWAYS, for being my rock. Your love, partnership, and support mean more than you could ever know.

To the city of Columbia and specifically its music community, including, but not limited to: Art Bar, The Jam Room, Danielle Howle & The Tantrums, The Soul Mites, Margo, The Ectomorphs, Speed Kitty, Imp, Felonious Swank, Splendid, Skankus, Isabelle's Gift, 49 Reasons, Tarwater, Ken Dubard, Cullen Nolan, Kris Plus, Josh Green, Rob McCue, David Lee, and Jennifer Moore – Thank You! I'm forever blessed to have been dropped into your universe.

In the immortal words of our Angel Boy, Jay Carson:

"WE BELONG TOGETHER."

Marietta, GA

4/20/2025